# Turnabout

A change of opinion, or loyalty…

*A Novel Written by*

# *April Alisa Marquette*

Books by *April Alisa Marquette*.

## Fiction

~The Cohort Trilogy
*Absolution*
*Progression*
*Iniquities*

~The Cohorts, Generation Next
*Improbable*

~The Sea Isles Series - A Trilogy
*Exodus*
*Affinity*
*To Be Announced*

*Turnabout*

~A Tranquility Tale
*Rebuke*

——————————————— * ———————————————

## Non-Fiction

Co-Authored with Jessica Janna

~The Relinquish & Reap Series
*Seedling*
*Sowing*
*Yielding*

**Ask for them … at your local bookstore!**

**April Rain Publications**

Books that captivate

**Turnabout**
© Copyright 2010 by April Alisa Marquette
Cover Design by April A. Marquette

ISBN 978-1-61539-573-6

Printed in the United States of America

Visit the author at www.aprilalisamarquette.net
Library of Congress Catalog Card No.: On File

To Guen Norris Lopez, R.N. BSN - thank you for umpteen years of unwavering friendship, and for sharing hard-won knowledge.

To Biju K. Jose, P.A. – a special thank you for clinical input.

We are divinely chosen to bring good into the world

*Yoruba Proverb*

# 1

OPENING his front door, Joseph ushered Abigail into his den.

She looked around and took in the enormity of the room. Again, Abigail saw the blond wood, the contemporary décor, and the wall of un-obscured floor-to-ceiling windows. Through those windows, she saw the wet and dismal night. On Joseph's cocktail table, Abigail saw pencil-marked music scores. On his sleek, black, baby grand piano, other scores were fanned out. Seeing Joseph's work, Abigail felt like she just might be intruding.

Glancing away, her gaze fell on the computer screen. There, the program that Joseph used to compose and edit music glared. Then it seemed as though nearly everything in the producer's den intimated that Abigail was interrupting. Even the muted basketball game on his large flat-screen TV seemed to shout 'Bad timing! Go away.' Abigail bit her lower lip because just *maybe*...turning up in Long Island, unannounced, this one time, had not been a good idea.

Stepping before her, Joseph offered aid. He did so because he had seen Abigail's eyes dart around. He'd also noticed the haunted look. It let him know something had happened. That something was the reason Abigail wasn't her usual together self. Whatever happened was probably why, too, on this dark and blustery evening, his baby had gotten chilled and wet. Joseph only hoped she hadn't done so while outside his Tudor home. Hopefully, he hadn't been so caught up in his music—as was his way—that he hadn't heard the initial chimes of his doorbell.

When her coat was removed, Abigail shivered and Joseph wondered aloud, "Just how long were you out there? In all that rain..."

Abigail didn't reply because how could she sound sane saying she'd stood before Joseph's home for fifteen minutes? Instead of staring at the lovely facade, she could have escaped to the portico. There, her clothing and her hair would not have become flattened and wet.

5

Again, Abigail felt a chill but remembered she was inside. Oh. She recalled the real reason she couldn't reply; it was the crux of the matter. Plain and simply; she had *had* to come. She'd *had* to seek Joseph because there was no one else, and there hadn't been—come to think of it—for a while now. Sure, Abigail had been involved with that other man, the one whose name she didn't want to remember. However, that man had been involved with others.

Allowing Abigail's soggy all-weather coat to slip to the floor, Joseph gathered her close. Rubbing her back through her sodden blouse, he just *knew*. Her silent tears had something to do with *the clown*. And for the life of him, Joseph couldn't understand why Abigail allowed that buffoon to hurt her, repeatedly. Just because Darré Clankston's monkey-ass said he loved her –when Darré's actions always proved otherwise? Joseph nearly scoffed. Then he dismissed thoughts of the clown because Abigail needed *him*. She needed the consolation that *he* could provide, after whatever had happened.

Heck, Joseph thought, lil precious probably needed what his mother called a hot toddy. In a minute, he would get Abigail something warm or liquor-filled to drink. After he told her that she was in *his* arms, now.

"I've got you, baby," Joseph murmured.

His tenderness became Abigail's undoing. All evening, she'd tried to stifle the sobs that suddenly erupted. "Baybeee... it's alright," Joseph crooned as Abigail wet his hooded shirtfront with her tears. "It's alright, Star," the pop music producer repeated. Although he said it, over and over again, he knew one thing. If his baby was this hurt, things were definitely not all right. Therefore, holding Abigail, Joseph guessed he was going to kick somebody's ass.

When Abigail no longer cried, Joseph eyed her, slumped on his camel-colored sofa. Torn between leaving and staying, he felt she might need him. Then again, he would only take a few moments, so he promised to be right back. Carrying the coat that dripped on his raffia runner, Joseph strode down his wide, butter-colored hallway.

"Upsy daisy."

Abigail blinked because tall, brown Joseph, who looked a lot like the actor Laz Alonso, was back. Towering over Abigail, Joseph had a bath sheet in one hand and a fleece throw in the other. Pulling Abigail up, Joseph rubbed her sodden blouse. Upon drying Abigail's face and neck, Joseph ordered her to turn.

In her hair, Abigail felt Joseph's hands through the towel. She felt her throat sting, but she remembered, Joseph didn't need to see more tears.

However, hearing muffled sobs, again Joseph folded Abigail close.

Her heart was so obviously broken until it broke his, and Joseph wondered, for the umpteenth time, *why*? It was all so stupid. He would tend her wounds, only for her to wind up destroyed *again*. It was their never-ending cycle, and Joseph was sick of it, even if Abigail wasn't.

"Gaye," Joseph used her nickname. "Why do you allow this?"

Touching a crumpled tissue to her swollen eyes, Abigail wanted to answer. She wanted to admit that she had finally hissed, "Enough!" It was why she no longer had a man.

"Sit," Joseph ordered and knelt before her. Reaching for the fleece he'd brought back with the towel, he snugly tucked the softness around Abigail. Through the throw blanket, he clasped her hands. "So you gonna keep letting him hurt you."

Shoot! He hadn't meant for it to sound so like –a pronouncement of doom, but oh well. It was out now and couldn't be helped. Looking away, Joseph swallowed. He also wondered. Was his throat aching? It only did that on two occasions. One, if he had strep, or two, if he became emotional, and he had neither.

Oh no. He remembered being tall and manly-looking, at nineteen. However, seated front-'n-center at his grandmother's funeral, he'd felt small and so like a crying baby. Wait, why was he thinking miserable thoughts? Shoot. Whenever he pictured Nana's remains or Mama sobbing, Joseph's throat ached as though it were on furious fire.

Yeah, just like the night he'd stood over Hal. Now, why was *that* image coming up? At twenty-something, with tears streaming, Joseph had eked at his stepfather, who lay in a hospital bed. "Dad, man, you can't leave me..."

Hey! Joseph yelled inside, get a grip. Banish hurtful thoughts. Joseph told himself to do so because Halloway was the best, the only father he had ever known. That cool old dude was still kicking, too. Thank God.

Joseph forced himself to recall sweet Nana. She was up in Heaven. Now she no longer ached, and she probably had the most beautiful wings. Yep, and one day, soon, Joseph predicted, *Abigail* would be pain-free too. She would know how much she was loved. Then she would avoid all the hurt that came from being involved with the wrong man.

Yet kneeling, Joseph swallowed. His throat felt marginally better until he realized that facing him, his baby held to the back of his hoodie. She whispered, and Joseph leaned lean in. Still, he had to strain to hear what sounded like… She'd driven around, with no idea that she'd wind up there –in his home.

All Joseph could think was darn! His throat ached for real. Momentarily closing his eyes, he forgot that Abigail hadn't wanted him to see her tears. Yet, with his thumbs, he'd brushed her glistening cheeks. He spoke too, to shift both their focus. "Star, this blouse is wet."

Abigail looked down, and Joseph suggested it come off. "That is if you don't wanna catch a cold." She had better not think he was trying it, either, because the truth was if she remained damp, she'd wind up ill.

Therefore, with drawn lips, Joseph undid Abigail's first button. He pushed her breasts, her nipples, and his own suckling mouth from mind on button two. No need to think about any of that tonight. "Yo, since we're at it," Joseph also said, "your lil' skirt has to go too, and the pantyhose." The way sexy, seam-up-the-back sheers that turned him on.

Abigail watched as her clothing was laid aside. Feeling wan, she asked, "Joe, why do you do it?"

"What?"

"Care," she noted his averted eyes. Why did he care any time anything happened to her? He could have said, 'Another sob story, Gaye? Please.'

To silence Abigail's nonsense, Joseph lodged a finger against her lush lips—the lips that were great for kissing, he remembered. Unaware that she suddenly felt foolish, he watched Abigail's lashes flutter downward.

Here Joseph was, Abigail thought, on his knees before her, and she'd started moaning. Oh well, guess it was a good thing that Joe hadn't let her finish, or he too would doubt her. Lord knew she doubted her*self* lately.

Joseph noted Abigail's sheepish look, so he tipped her face up. He touched his lips to hers. "I just *care*, Star, so come to me," always.

Abigail fought tears, and her voice sounded croaky when she asked, "How'd I wind up with you," the caliber of man he was, "in my life?"

Joseph swallowed. Now his throat all-out ached. It caused him to wonder just *when* he would get a handle on his love for her.

Forgetting his throat and pain, Joseph took Abigail in his arms. While stroking her back, he murmured, "My baby, I'm nobody's prize. You deserve better than me. And way better than the mess you've gotten, from that Clankston clown."

Abigail chuckled, and Joseph's heart galloped as he thought, dag-blame-it! He couldn't even rub Gaye's back without getting a woody. Joseph guessed it was her incredibly soft breasts pressed to the hard wall of his chest. Nixing thoughts of being inside her, he got up. He reminded himself, this evening, Gaye needed comfort, not seduction.

Glancing at her drying hair, Joseph spoke. "I'm not really in your life, Star." Not like he needed to be, "I'm old 'n broken down, besides."

Joe needed to stop, Abigail thought, because he and those other words didn't even go together. Not when the man was thirty-nine, healthy, wealthy, and way too sexy for his—or anybody's—good.

Unaware that he was thought so highly of, Joseph wanted to say he truly loved Gaye... but the timing. It was all wrong, so Joseph simply reassured Abigail that he was there for her, even as annoying images of copulation fogged his mind.

Missing the man's body heat, Abigail repositioned herself on the sofa. Slowly, she scanned Joseph's den and again appreciated the room. She liked its size, the wheat-colored walls, and the vaulted ceiling. Abigail liked that the molding-to-floor windows were bare, allowing one an unobstructed view of the lush landscape beyond. She also liked the smooth lines of the only adornment for Joseph's wall of windows, his beautiful, black baby grand.

He said he'd courted Curvaceous—the Dark Lady—his beloved piano, at her downtown home. Back in the day, he had often gone to see her. Even before he'd had a home of his own to move her to, he'd visited, just to run his fingers over her. Now Joseph adored Lady, standing in the arc that his wall of windows created. She was sleek and exposed for all to see. The composer said that no matter what time it was, the Dark Lady welcomed him. She received the outpouring of his soul. Together they made beautiful music. Their shared melodies had built this

9

home and others. Funds from J & Dark Lady Productions had also paid for his parents' Harlem home and the older couple's little hideaway. J & Dark Lady's music was what millions the world over partied to, cried with, and made love to.

Allowing her gaze to leave Joseph's muse, Abigail's eyes roamed the room that was enigmatically inviting. Eyeing the den's highly polished blond natural wood, Abigail nearly smiled. For her friend, there would be none of that lacquered, plasticky fake flooring now all the rage. With a pillow beneath her breasts, Abigail cogitated on the fact that visiting Joseph's home felt like a return to a lover's arms. And being with *him* felt the same. "Joe," she called, opting to think different thoughts. "A few minutes ago, you sounded like an old man."

"What'd I say?"

"You didn't say; you groaned, when you got off your knees. Pulling at them cute lil' drawstring shorts, I might add."

"Yeah?" Behind his marble-top bar, Joseph eyed flowing cognac. "Well bae, the big dawg's not as young as he used to be, and neither are the knees." Joseph grabbed a napkin. "And you, pretty Lady, aren't as young as *you* used to be either. So, you think you'll stop running, at some point?"

Abigail nearly sighed because Joseph could always mention it. He could say, with just a few words, that she was obstruction personified when it came to them having a relationship. They were friends, though. Why muck it up by getting involved? If they broke up, things could become acrimonious. Then she and Joseph would no longer be friends. That, Abigail did not want.

Barefoot and crossing polished maple, Joseph pressed a brandy snifter into Abigail's hand. Then he sat and inconspicuously watched. He imagined the distilled liquid as it passed over Abigail's lush lips. He imagined it seeping down her throat. Joseph silently envisioned the liquor's heat expanding, to fill Abigail inside, the way *he* longed to.

Argggh! Joseph knew he had to stop tormenting himself, but heck, if he couldn't 'see' himself part Abigail's curvy thighs. He could all but taste her, as he used his big hands to open her and...

Resting his head atop the sofa back, Joseph told himself to stop thinking about Gaye that way, tonight. She needed to recuperate, from Heaven only knew what. Him picturing his virile naked body between her nude thighs was inappropriate. It was appealing but not appropriate.

Unaware of the stir she'd caused, Abigail set her glass down. She remarked that her toes and fingertips felt aflame.

Oh, the drink, Joseph vaguely recalled. He thought of how easy Abigail was to please. When she was not in one of her turbulent moods.

Hey, he and she could have a daughter whom they could name *Stormy* because she was sure to be her mother in miniature, a spitfire.

Shaking his head, Joseph knew he had to get a grip because here he was, 'having a baby with the woman,' when he couldn't even touch her.

Still unaware of the havoc she wreaked in Joseph's thoughts, with an elegant hand, Abigail fanned herself. Through slatted eyes, Joseph watched and liked her clean, neat-length nails. He liked that she wore subtle fragrances and natural, earthy colors. She spiced it up too, in the sultrier months. Then she wore blinding white or curve-hugging silver.

Hey, he and sexy could have a second daughter, Summer...because baby two could wind up all sunshine and fun, like her Mama's alter ego.

Joseph closed his eyes and knew he was losing it. He had to be nuts because he really didn't want to stop 'seeing' himself with Gaye and their daughters. Joseph even imagined his girls' lovely laughter as he told himself that a brotha had to have dreams. Still, he forgot dreams because in time, like his mother said, all would come. Joseph hoped, and prayed.

Opening his eyes, he saw that Abigail had shrugged off his fleece throw. Have mercy! He thought it as his gaze fell to her silky camisole and cleavage. Dragging his eyes away, Joseph told himself to just be glad she was no longer all shivery and crying.

However, Joseph's thoughts ran amok. Therefore, he caught his bottom lip between his teeth, Abigail's habit. Then he forced himself to look elsewhere. If he didn't, she would know he was nuts when he leaned over and fastened his lips to hers, or over a nipple, or at the little— Joseph re-focused. He placed his feet on the lovely Olefin yarn rug beneath his cocktail table. His interior decorator had insisted he couldn't live without the table or the rug. Shit, for what they'd cost, he could have.

Movement on the flat-screen that hung like artwork on a wall caused Joseph to reach for the remote. His basketball team's boy wonder was about to make free throws.

Joseph rolled his shoulders to ward off the waiting jitters. Knowing 'Kid Soar' could make both shots, Joseph still held his breath.

The ball was released, and...all net, two times!

"Buckets! Yesss!" Joseph cheered and glanced over at Abigail.

She smiled and opened her mouth. However, an inner voice scolded her because *what if Joe wanted to watch the fourth quarter –in peace?*

Oh. She hadn't thought about that.

Joseph tore his eyes from his New York Knicks on a favorable run. He noticed Abigail was quiet when moments ago she'd looked like she would speak. Now she looked sad. Joseph hoped she didn't regret giving the clown the boot. That news was priceless. Still, with lil honey's face appearing crinkly, Joseph wasn't so sure bozo would *stay* booted.

Suddenly Joseph felt uneasy because Abigail kept looking at him...as though she expected something.

Oh no. Joseph's eyes widened because she wanted him to *say* something! But what? He had nothing. He'd said it all before.

Moments later, Joseph forced himself to grudgingly speak. "Star, you're upset..." Uh, where to? "Oh, and things seem messed up right now, but maybe...um, this'll wind up a blessing –in disguise." He sure hoped so, for *his* sake. He hoped the sheer stupidity would finally turn her to *him*. Whoa! Joseph looked from the game back to Abigail. Why was she griping, in heated patois? Why'd she say he had offended her? He had hurt her feelings? Oh brother. How? She could not have thought his stupid little speech meant he'd taken the clown's side.

"Yo, hol' up, Star. Wait a minute." Joseph affirmed that he too was offended, now. "The very notion that I could have betrayed you is unfair. Hell, you know I care. You know I'd never side with—" Joseph couldn't even say that jackal's name, "What's-his-face, because he hurt you."

Ignoring him, Abigail spat, "Answer me one question, Joezeff."

"Only one," Joseph allowed. He recalled that when upset, baby girl sounded a lot like her Jamaican father.

"Is dis a man ting?"

Bewildered, Joseph nearly sputtered. "A *what* kind of thing?"

"You know," Abigail huffed. "Is this a thing where you, a man, will stick up for another man simply because y'all both have penises?"

Joseph palmed his forehead. Gaye had gotten ridiculous, and Heaven knew he didn't want to fight. He just wanted simple stuff, like for his team to stop making stupid turnovers. Joseph wanted to check his rhythm section revisions and drink his cold wet. Since Gaye was present and oh so enticing, Joseph wanted her too, but that wouldn't happen, tonight.

"Maybe mi [me] shouldn't run to yu when I tumble down," Abigail huffed. "Mi gotta quit leanin' on Jack, and learn to lean on Jill, alone."

Joseph frowned. So now he and she were nursery rhyme characters?

Abigail rose and looked around. "Where mi few piece of clothe?"

Now she contemplated leaving? Well, no, Joseph cogitated. Sista girl was in no shape to drive. Therefore, Joseph leaned, and pulled. He hoped Abigail wouldn't fight either, as firmly he pressed her head to his chest. "Shut up," he ordered before he spoke softly. "Stop, girl. Just let me hold you. Okay, baby? Ms. 'Jill' who can stand on her own two feet..."

Joseph got it! Tears sprang to Abigail's eyes, because he got *her*. He always had. Therefore, surprising him, she did not resist but lay meekly on his chest. And miraculously, in time, most of her anger subsided.

In the stillness, Abigail felt her heart creak open. It opened further when Joseph murmured that he knew she was hurting.

As a tear trickled from Abigail's eye, Joseph swallowed and focused on the television. He forgot that he, too, was hurting. Joseph refused to contemplate that the woman in his arms might never know how much.

"Look, Star," he said, with his throat all-out aching. "Since there's all this pain, we should both remain quiet for a while. Okay?"

As Abigail nodded, Joseph gently stroked her back and her semi-dry cloud of hair. Half-lying beneath her, Joseph recalled that all he had ever wanted was for his baby to be happy —with him. Since that hadn't happened, yet, he was dealing with it. He didn't press the issue every chance he got. Sure, he could have used these silly 'restorative' sessions—when she ran to him—to jumpstart his own cause, but no, that wasn't his way. Joseph wanted Abigail free and clear. So again, he prayed and placed all in the Master's hands.

Then Joseph reiterated because he needed Abigail to understand. "Sweetness, I would never take that guy's side because he hurt you."

13

In fact, the clown was always hurting her, Joseph recalled. Suddenly, he wanted to ask a few questions. Joseph really wanted to know why couldn't Abigail forget silly boy. Couldn't she see that *he*, Joseph, waited to love and lavish her with everything that she'd ever dreamed of, and he had waited *so* long...

"Look," Joseph sighed, "let's get you past upset."

He felt Abigail nod. Joseph also felt peeved because, again, he had not spoken his piece! He should have told Abigail to denounce Darré's clown-ass because he, Joseph, was the man for her. He should have made Abigail think too, by asking her questions. –Because truthfully, where had the clown been when her father had that stroke? The one that had nearly killed him. Where had bozo been when Abigail's older sister had gone into the eating disorder hospital? Where was the ridiculous court jester back when Abigail's younger sister had nearly died in childbirth? And the real question was: *why* had that joker been missing every single time that he—her so-called man—had been needed?

However, every time, Joseph Forrester had been there, for Abigail.

Pursing his lips, Joseph realized. He couldn't force those questions. If he did, he'd be doing what Mama called taking his burdens to the Lord but not leaving them there. Therefore, since he'd prayed, Joseph had to believe God would work. If he couldn't believe, then he should just worry instead.

With Abigail lying on his chest, Joseph blindly felt around for the remote. He needed to re-focus and forget the one question that ever plagued him. What was he going to do? He wanted to forget the other question that always followed. Then again, really, what *could* he do?

With a sigh, Joseph allowed his brown eyes to stray back to the game that was over. Sure, a few seconds remained, but his team had managed to lose, again. The dispersing crowd knew it too. Pressing mute, Joseph felt like he wanted to cuss a blue streak. Heck, this losing, on all fronts, really sucked. Still, Joseph would not allow depression a doorway. Too many people, at J & Dark Lady Productions and at Midnight Music, two of his companies, depended on him for their livelihood.

Unaware of Joseph's turmoil regarding her, Abigail spoke. She acknowledged that her little explosion had been uncalled for. "So Joe, mi apologizing." With her head on Joseph's chest, her voice reverberated through him as she added he was good for her, just what she needed.

A ragged breath caught in Joseph's throat, but he remained silent.

"Joe, did you hear me?"

"I did." Abruptly, he sat up, dislodging Abigail. "Star," Joseph's voice was rough with emotion, and his eyes darted between hers. "You've got me," lock, stock, 'n barrel, and wasn't a thing either of them could do about it.

However, Abigail felt shame because to her, Joseph's tone had implied that she was foolish and needy. Well, after tonight, she would no longer bother him. *Go, Jill.* She would do as his mother often said. She would take her burdens to the Lord and leave them there. Yes, because worry only grayed the hairline and added inches to the waistline.

Noticing the range of emotions that crossed Abigail's face, Joseph again found himself besotted. The woman's downcast lashes, so like dark feathers, lay against her unblemished cheeks. Her luscious lips, the bronze tops of her breasts; just every part of her called to him.

But wait. A moment ago, Abigail said something. He'd needed to hear it, for Heaven only knew how long. Abigail said she needed him.

However, something wasn't right. Therefore, Joseph mentally backtracked to opening his front door. He fast-forwarded past closing it and walking Abigail to his den, and it hit him!

She didn't need *him*, per se. She needed his *arms* around her. Abigail needed sweet words, from him, to dislodge the harsher ones hurled by the clown. Abigail needed Joseph's lips, on her thigh insides, along with his honed *skillz*. She needed Dr. Feel Good's big kahuna. As his ego inflated, Joseph stroked his chin because he *could* lay it down. Then again, he realized, he could do more than stroke it. He was more than just a toned body and a thick stick.

Suddenly, Joseph felt weary and old. This going about things bass ackward had become loathsome. Heck, he actually wanted to do right! Joseph wanted to *commit* before God and family and friends, but Gaye held things up. Sure, other women wanted marriage with him. However, Joseph wanted Abigail. Thus, he'd have to try new tactics.

Joseph glanced over. With a sigh, he said—as he had in the past—that he cared, deeply, "But the other stuff, Star?" The open-mouth kissing 'n sucking, the pushing and pumping? "It's not gonna happen, not tonight."

Purposefully then he ignored Abigail's stunned look. Leaning back, Joseph nearly hated himself. Heck, he *wanted* a fast and furious romp! He wanted to be all up in Gaye, especially since he hadn't had any since... she'd last given him some.

Oh, his bad; he'd gotten a piece recently, from a curvy brown actress. Still, Actress wasn't Abigail, the woman with whom Joseph wanted to get things right. Actress had even called him Laz, when he'd told her, several times, "No, I'm Joe." Actress was an effin' fraud too because she'd come on to him, whispering what she'd do and let him do. Then during the do, she laid there—like some dead thing. With a sigh, Joseph forgot Actress, because Gaye would never have done that.

Joseph's thoughts returned to Abigail. She'd have climbed all over him. She'd have made him lose his mind. Sure, if she rode him, right now, that would ease the ache in his groin. He would hold her hips, lick her tits and—

Joseph reminded himself. He needed *more*. At nearly forty, he needed to be said woman's *man*. He needed to build and have *a life* with that woman. With her, he needed to share his hopes, dreams, and fears—not just his bed and his Jacuzzi.

"Gaye," Joseph swallowed, "I'm here for you." His home was hers; he said it again, "But till your head's clear, let's not complicate things."

Abigail allowed her lashes to flutter downward to obscure the luminous pools that her eyes had become. Inwardly, she told herself to be strong. Maybe then she would stop feeling strange, and sad, like she was unworthy of love and fidelity. Perhaps she might even forget her and Darré's break-up. If she could clear her mind, she might also forget that Joseph had just refused her too –like she had swine flu or something.

Abigail wondered, why hadn't she gone home half an hour ago? Back then she'd feebly asked about her clothes. Now her strength was gone. With a sigh, she attempted to assemble her jumbled thoughts. And one question stood out.

Why had Darré's leaving taken a bite out of her? She should be thanking him for freedom. He was a goal-less grown man, one to whom she could have wound up unhappily married.

Maybe it wasn't Darré, or the break-up... Maybe she just felt old. At thirty-six, sometimes now, Abigail felt 'on the shelf,' especially when people tried to hook her up. Everybody 'knew the perfect guy.' And her relatives, sweet people, they were the worst. They always had questions. 'Why no marriage? Why no beautiful babies? What's de mattuh, gurl?'

The older white admins on her job had questions, too. The Jewish matrons where she lived, and the blue-black, high yella, and pecan brown women at Sinai Baptist also vexed Abigail. Sure, they all meant well, but their words cut. Regardless of ethnicity, each older woman would pat or touch Abigail's hand, like they pitied her. They'd all say the equivalent of, 'You just wait, honey...' Shoot. She *had been* waiting—on God! And Abigail could admit it; her life wasn't bad. She had two degrees, a beautiful condo, a fast car, a cute financial portfolio, and a modicum of health, but she had no man! She wanted a man—all her own.

She wanted a husband, her own husband.

Seated wearily on Joseph's sofa, Abigail worried her lip with her teeth as she cogitated. Perhaps men saw her as a liability. Once they learned her age, they probably figured she wouldn't want to just kick it. Likely, they realized, she wanted to be boo'd up. Hey, maybe that was the real reason her ex had gone frolicking. Maybe it was why Joseph didn't want any of her, either. Then again, maybe she was experiencing the wages of sin. Abigail had indulged in a bunch of pre-marital sex.

Her churchy Grandmother, Gram, often said fornicating was sin.

Watching Abigail, who was so obviously in turmoil, Joseph felt like he'd stabbed her and turned the knife, although he knew he'd done right. Abigail was hurting, and she didn't deserve to be used—any more than she already had been, by the clown. Therefore, Joseph quietly promised, "Things will get better, Star."

Abigail allowed Joseph to pull her close as he also said, "You'll see."

Yeah, right, she thought and again laid her head on his chest.

Darn it! Joseph suddenly wished he didn't need to be Abigail's *only* desire. If it wasn't necessary for him to do right by her, he could have been savoring sweet punanny right then! Heck, she'd offered him some, just moments ago. No, Joseph reminded himself, Abigail needed to get over her lost clown. And *he* needed to face that she might never reciprocate his love.

17

As Abigail quietly half-laid on Joseph, she *knew* he wanted her, even though he had said otherwise. She had seen his singular, jagged vein.

Telltale, it pulsed in Joseph's forehead whenever he wanted.

But since he'd refused, for whatever reason, Abigail forgot the remembered feel of Joseph's lips on her erect nipples. Oop, he tore the little that she still wore from her yearning body, and—

*Get real,* the little voice in her head mocked.

Okay, but nowhere was it written in stone that she couldn't slip a hand up the leg of his shorts and play along his powerful thigh.

Joseph's eyes widened as he wondered, what the Sam Hain? Clamping his lip between his teeth, he realized. The vixen on him intended to torture him! He knew it when he felt her warm hand vise around his gearshift. Well, he wouldn't respond. He wanted all or nothing. Thus, Joseph pictured himself raking leaves, a chubby-killer.

Abigail moved her warm hand, up, then down, pumping Joseph.

Got-durn! He thought, she intended to make it hard. Well, he would just conjure more leaves —or snow. Imagining himself out there shoveling was a control tactic that rarely failed. Yet Abigail's warm hand explored uncharted territory. And still, Joseph rose. He hollered inside, too, because now the minx had him seriously pondering waving his wand! Enlarged and stiff, it was ready. Joseph quickly turned to Abigail, needing to get his stick wet. Until he recalled, all or nothing.

After a few moments that yielded nada, Abigail lifted her head. Since Joseph wanted to remain stoic, and since she wouldn't get to sink sensually down on his engorged member, maybe he would engage her in conversation. But damn did she want to feel him inside her!

Perhaps, she sighed, Joe might even explain a few things. Like, how had her fiancé married another, after saying 'insurance purposes and appraisal.' "The sorry ex," Abigail moaned, "didn't even lay out a dime for that ring." The pretty piece had been handed down by his mother.

Abigail further apprised Joseph that the slickster hadn't even *said* the relationship was over. He'd simply re-gifted her ring., "Now, that girl—who probably didn't even finish high school—is wearing my jewelry." Abigail's bare left hand went to her heart as her eyes filled. "Joe, even if

I overlook that, I still have a hard time with him getting that girl pregnant while he was with me! And the bum drove her around in my car."

Swallowing against rising bile, Joseph remained silent; but hadn't he just known the clown was the cause of Abigail's angst? Now it looked like the court jester had approached Abigail earlier in the evening.

"As I left work, Joe, he was in the lobby, following me. He said me 'n him ting don't have to be ova." Impulsively, Abigail screamed. "We got no ting! Not since he stuck it in that young girl."

Joseph felt riled up, too, as he watched Abigail dab her swollen eyes.

However, she attempted to compose herself. "Since the baby, the break-up, and 'that marriage' happened a while ago, I was getting over it. But tonight, with him saying hurtful things, I wondered, *what about me?*"

Joseph's heart broke as Abigail said no one considered her. Joseph felt hurt, as with seeping tears, Abigail closed her eyes and laid on his chest. Feeling her brokenness, Joseph only wanted to love Abigail that much more. He wanted to kiss away all her tears. He wanted to show her how much he cared. But he couldn't. To blurt all his feelings amid her suffering? To attempt to make love to her, tonight? That would be using her disadvantage to his advantage. And that wasn't Joseph's way. Therefore, he prayed, so quietly that Abigail couldn't hear. "Father, my baby needs comfort, the kind that only you can provide. And after tonight, please help her choose wisely—a choice that would be me. Thank you. Amen."

Later, as he half lay beneath Abigail, Joseph realized. He should have also prayed for strength because he felt the need to take a little ride. Over in Hollis, Queens, he would kick the clown's trifling ass. A few times. However, after what seemed like forever, Abigail fell asleep. Joseph knew it when her breathing deepened and became rhythmic.

Holding still, Joseph thought good, because maybe in sleep, sweetness would find a semblance of peace. And just maybe, one day, *he* would get *his* chance. When he did, Joseph promised, he would never intentionally hurt Abigail Denise Wallace. Never would he willfully disrespect her, or make her cry, either. Well, not anything other than tears of joy, because she would be –no, she already was…his queen.

## 2

"GAYE?"

"Mona," Abigail was surprised her friend was back. "Nice trip?"

"It was tired, like the man I went with, but forget that. How are you?"

"I'm fine," Abigail revealed, "and you?"

"I am fiiine, too!"

Abigail's grin emitted through the phone "So says your mirror, right?"

Mona Lisa chuckled. "Laugh it up, girl, but this sista gotzta keep it together. Oh, speaking of together, G, you sound like yourself again."

"I feel like it." Abigail switched it up, "You got plans for tonight, Mo?"

"Yes, girl, Momma's gonna par-tay— and I'm wearing your jumpsuit."

Six months prior, Abigail returned from a business trip bearing a beautifully wrapped box. Mona Lisa had nearly cried, seeing it was from an exclusive Chi-town boutique. She'd felt teary too, because no one else did 'just because' things for her. Hastily, she'd torn the shiny paper. Lifting out the fire engine red jumpsuit, Mona Lisa knew. She had never owned anything more beautiful.

Nervous, Mona Lisa checked the tag; she hadn't been offended either that Abigail had left it on. Mona Lisa knew her friend had done so in case the garment needed to be returned. Mona Lisa Reid peeked. The piece had cost a small fortune! She'd noticed too, that unlike others, Abigail let her be. Others often tried to fit super-curvy Mona Lisa into their stifling molds. However, in allowing her friend to be, Abigail had purchased the jumpsuit a size too small. She'd recalled that her friend liked her clothing 'to fit.' Therefore, Mona Lisa knew the precious piece would look perfect!

The overly made-up woman quickly stripped, eager to feel the spandex hug her dangerous curves. She fingered the beaded bustier top and the attached crepe pant. She couldn't forget the cost. Gaye had paid more than Mona made in a month! That caused Mona Lisa to ask, "Why, G?"

Seated on Mona Lisa's futon, her sofa in the daytime, and her bed at night, Abigail shrugged and laid a magazine aside. "It looked like you."

In her thong and no bra, Mona Lisa clutched the piece and tried to stifle emotion. Before Abigail, Mona Lisa had known very little kindness.

In the quiet, Abigail looked up. Seeing tears, she embraced Mona Lisa.

Dashing away the water, Mona Lisa replied to Abigail's question. Mona Lisa told her executive friend that she had done nothing wrong...

Standing in the drab rear office of the carpet showroom where she worked, Mona Lisa forgot gift day. She'd recently made up her face in that pissy bathroom and couldn't afford to become puffy-eyed. She had to look grand, later. So again wishing that she, a carpet salesperson, could have her own desk and phone, she asked, "You partying tonight too, G?"

"No," Abigail replied, sounding preoccupied, "but..."

She was probably looking at business documents, Mona Lisa mused.

Retrieving the conversation, Abigail admitted she would meet Joseph.

Shaking her head, Mona Lisa knew Abigail's 'after nine' business meant she would work late. When she should have been living a little. "For crying out loud, Gaye, it's Halloween, a holiday. Get your swerve on. Heck, you work late all the time. Tonight you should live a little."

Abigail mock-whined. "But this sista's got to keep it together."

"Cute." Mona Lisa wanted to get into her friend's business. "G, what *do* you and Forrester have planned for when you get off?"

Mona Lisa only hoped she hadn't sounded too interested, although Forrester was most interesting. The man was tall, sexy, and rich.

Wearing a dove-gray, wool skirt-suit, Abigail revealed that she and Joseph Forrester hadn't made plans. "I hope we eat, though," she admitted while eyeing her ankle-wrap pumps. "I'm starving, but I haven't got time to get or order anything."

"Well, eating ain't all y'all gonna do," Mona Lisa voiced. Mentally, she conjured a picture of the man whose money made him twice as attractive. However, silly Abigail didn't seem to notice. Probably because of all her trying-to-be-a-good-Christian mess. Abigail treated Forrester like a friend —when the man had the potential to be so much more. If she and Abigail could trade places, Mona Lisa figured, she'd skip the friend shit. She would make Forrester, his fame, and his riches, all her own.

Mrs. Mona Lisa Forrester. Now that sounded nice. Yep, Mona Lisa thought, and if Abigail was thinking, she'd notice. Abigail Forrester also sounded cool. Mona Lisa further cogitated, as a husband, Forrester would be obligated to pay, whether his woman stayed with him or left him. That was the best part, sweet security.

"G, why not step to Forrester?" Mona Lisa asked. "Since he wants you 'n all."

Abigail sounded irritated. "Why think of every man as a conquest?"

The heavier woman, who believed she was more free-spirited, rolled her eyes. She supposed attitude was what she got for voicing her opinion. Remaining undaunted, she sighed. "Look, Forrester's fine, and he wants you. Simple as that, like a man in the Sahara would want water." However, Mona Lisa recalled, Abigail knew all that. Therefore Mona Lisa just had to say, "Gaye, I'm a tell you something. If Forrester was interested in *moi*, I wouldn't play your game. I'd be all over him –like tar on asphalt."

Well, Miss Ass Fault, Abigail wanted to say, "Joe and I don't have that kind of relationship. Our thing is more…emotional. It's mature."

Yeah, Abigail wryly though, because on a recent dark and stormy night, the man had refused her.

Mockingly, Mona Lisa made her voice nasal. "Well, since you 'n Forrester are so mature, why not get emotional and physical?"

Abigail actually felt irritated when she asked, "Can we drop this?"

Mona Lisa grudgingly acquiesced, but not before she said, "G, I don't get how you, who could care less about a man's possessions, keep meeting men that are extra." Yeah, Abigail should have dated Mr. Good Heart, Mr. Little Dick, or Mr. Hooptie—Mr. Raggedy Ride, with whom Mona Lisa had ridden that morning. She'd torn her tights exiting his lemon. If Miss Gaye, who got everything, experienced some of those men, then she would see how she liked it. "Talk about unfair."

"I've explained it all before, Mo," Abigail advised.

With a scoff, Mona Lisa eyed the bizarrely painted fingernails that matched her outlandish outfit. She forgot her squat, florid-faced boss; the man had asked her to tone things down, during the day. He'd whispered that what she wore in the evenings, when he paid her, off the books, would be their business, alone.

"Gaye, please," Mona Lisa jeered, wanting to forget the man she detested, the one she slept with for cash. She didn't want to face the truth, she didn't hate her boss. He could eat out like no man before him. She forgot how Boss made her feel when he put his mouth on her. Loudly she scoffed, "G nobody believes 'what they give, they get.' You just lucky."

"Okay." Abigail shrugged, aware that her girlfriend had not yet tired of attracting self-serving, sexist men, men who were her mirror image.

"Gaye, I'm feeling you," Mona Lisa blurted. "And your negative vibes make me ask: if you're so perfect, why'd you wind up with Darré?"

"One, I'm not perfect," Abigail pontificated. "Two, I wondered the same thing. Then I realized, fooling with Darré showed me what I will never again tolerate in a relationship."

"Oh, turn everything into a learning experience, will you."

"Picture Girl, you asked, so I'm telling you. I'm am also learning to forgive —myself, first, for getting involved. And I'm attempting to forgive the ex, for lots of things."

"Look, all I was saying –before you started preaching," Mona Lisa yowled, "is that Forrester's fine. Just th'ow ya leg up for big daddy."

Abigail spoke softly, "I'm not you, Mo."

That had not worked for her either, but Mona Lisa would never tell. Abigail did not need to know that her friend had informed Joseph that he had to lick it to stick it. Abigail really didn't need to know that the man had been most uninterested.

Breaking into Mona Lisa's thoughts, Abigail said, "I want you to have fun tonight, Mo. Oh, and stay out of trouble. Love you. Bye."

Disengaged, Abigail pressed the intercom. "Sunshine?"

"Abigail?"

"Would you put our client through, and—" Abigail did a double-take as a tall man sauntered into her office. As the dark-skinned tasty snack took a seat opposite her cherry wood desk, Abigail gaped.

Now, what did his narrow behind want? Abigail wondered before realizing she didn't care. She only wanted Darré Clankston to disappear, forever. Therefore, she said, "I have business," and hoped he'd leave.

Dang! Now the client's office had her on hold. Oh well, Abigail would remember to mention a specific stipulation in the contract before her.

Minutes later, Abigail calmly returned her client's greeting, as though Darré were not present, or wearing the super-sensuous cologne she'd once bought for him. "Mr. Nakamura, I perused the delivered documents—"

Smooth-shaven, The Ex appeared as inviting as he had on the day that he'd roughhoused his way into Abigail's life and heart. Seeing it caused her thoughts to jumble. Abigail wondered if she babbled incoherently.

Then her door latch clicked. Quickly, she regained her train of thought.

When her call successfully ended, in burgundy leather, Abigail swiveled. Viewing the russet and gold of autumn, she screeched, "Whoo-hoo!" because her deal was right as rain. "Yesss!" And bozo was gone.

Suddenly an idea struck.

*His* sexy baritone caused her heart to trip as she said, "Hey, it's me." After pleasantries, she explained. She had all but wrapped up her doozy of a deal. "The one I've been moaning about for weeks."

Joseph chuckled. "You persevered, Star, and I'm proud of you."

Touched, Abigail predicted that following the John Hancock, she would break out the bubbly and pick up her fat bonus check!

Joseph smiled, liking Abigail's elation after her recent sadness. "Hard work rewards," he encouraged, "despite what your 'girlfriend' says."

Ever refereeing the two, Abigail cooed, "Joe, Mona's not serious. She just thinks I should live a little. She wants me to get out, have more fun."

Yeah, be an effin' floozy, like her, Joseph thought. He offered a terse, "Aiight," because he and Gaye could easily wind up 'debating.' "So," he changed the subject. "Does this mean Cuvée and caviar tonight?"

Abigail recalled. That champagne was deep golden with very fine bubbles. And caviar, ick, but Joseph was wishing her well, so she said, "Suga Man, tonight, maybe mi ah go 'long with anyting yu desire…"

Joseph wondered if she'd meant to get a rise out of him. She knew using that sexy JaMerican voice always did it for him.

Amid the teasing, a shadow fell across Abigail's desk. Glancing up, she frowned. Who was Darré—to be saying, "Yo, put that call on hold."

Abigail quickly covered the telephone mouthpiece because who the devil did the man think he was, trying to order her about, in her office?

Joseph heard a muffled male voice. "That your VP? You gotta go?"

Shaken, Abigail skipped the first inquiry to agree with the second.

On his end of the line, Joseph's eyes narrowed, and he recalled the critics. They didn't say he had a perfect ear for no reason. He had heard the slight timbre change in Abigail's voice. Joseph knew, too, as the hackles on his neck rose, that something was up. "Yo, you okay, bae?"

Abigail mumbled that she was. Yet Joseph felt wary because never – before… had sweet thang hung up on him, not even during one of their overly loud 'debates.' Staring a moment at his cell, intuition struck.

Joseph would just bet *the clown* had forced his way into Abigail's office! Joseph would call back! Feeling anger's slow burn, he decided not to. That decision, however, did not negate the two questions that ever plagued him. What was he going to do? Now. Then, what *could* he do?

In her office, Abigail fumbled the receiver into its cradle. Oh, shoot! She hadn't bid Joseph adieu. Well, she would apologize, later. Now, she had to stop her fingers from trembling and rid herself of a pest.

Placing both hands beneath her desk, Abigail looked up at the odious male who had the audacity to stand over her. With him gone, she'd been putting her life back to rights. Now, he was here to what, undo her?

Abigail's lips twisted wryly because she thought not. She would simply be strong, like she'd had to be when this clown, as Joe called him, crept 'n left. People had asked, 'Why'd you call off your wedding?' It had been embarrassing. Yet, she'd kept it together, despite a non-relenting ache, and despite her co-workers discussing her. Abigail would never forget approaching and watching each gossipmonger eerily freeze.

*Forgiveness, remember*? It seemed her conscience was always at it, but she could forgive. And she could face the demon of her past. Therefore, Abigail rose. With her hands behind her, she brusquely spoke.

"Dar-RAY, you want what?"

Sensing his presence still riled the attractive brown-skinned woman, Darré nearly laughed because doggonit! Chickie, with the gorgeous mane, was still hot-blooded, like he liked his women. Today she seemed even more volcanic, and for Darré, that notion churned up desire.

Abigail ignored the man who longingly leered.

Watching Abigail, Darré felt himself swell, while recalling that at times he, like her little skirt, had strained at her hips.

"Look," Abigail began, forced but mildly. "If you want nothing specific, then forget waltzing in and out of here. The party's over."

Purposely, Darré toyed with Abigail's words. "I didn't come to waltz today, baby." He looked around, again impressed. Indeed the place with its ornate frosted glass, fresh flowers, oiled wood, and quiet aura of money and influence would do nicely. That was if he needed to party in style.

Sensing folly, Abigail made it clear. She had no time for games. "Whatever you're here for, Darré, spit it out," or get out.

With a devious grin, the cocoa-colored man spoke. "The frosty ice-princess act is so not you, love." Gesturing at concealed paperwork, he also inquired. "You overwhelmed, by work, maybe?"

Angered, Abigail knew he hadn't been sarcastic! Not when she'd been to Hades and back on account of him! "Look," she said through clenched teeth. "Don't use that word –overwhelmed– with me. Why're you here?"

Darré clapped because Abigail had added that he would never understand that word. Man, was she something! And how he wanted her, although she was way too bourgeoisie, he felt, for any man.

Abigail closed folders while fuming because odious would never know how overwhelmed she had been. Paying for raised-letter, foil-stamped wedding invitations – and then cancellation notices!

Overwhelmed? That she had been, sorting through caterers, florists, limo services, and lakefront reception halls. Over-friggin'-whelmed? That had included Jacques Jorge, the fustiest East Coast wedding coordinator, and a costly dress. All after she'd spent a hellified two years with a fake-ass Rico Suavé. Abigail remembered having spent her ducats, but the worst was that she had lost irretrievable time!

*Breathe.* Abigail's conscience soothed. *That's it, honey, and forgive.*

Abigail silently prayed, knowing she was powerless to change, but with heavenly help… Abigail opened her eyes. At her office door, she palmed the knob stating, "Darré, you've got two options. Talk, or walk, fast."

The Ex grinned. "What if I choose door number three?"

Abigail's voice became sickeningly sweet. "This ain't no game show, mess around in here, and security will th'ow you out a window. *Capiche?*"

Darré hated it when she used Italian, but he shrugged because he had to go soon. "Look, Abbie, I would'na come up here, were it not necessary..."

So why take a seat, unasked? Abigail mentally inquired.

"But I came," Darré said, "Because… Mama died."

Abigail had heard Darré's vocal tremor as the news stole her breath.

*Just don't get all caught up*, her conscience advised.

Abigail could only imagine Darré's feelings. Sure, his family knew that Mrs. Dottie-Mae had cancer. Unlike Abigail's family, who'd suffered a sudden loss, the Clankstons had been prepared. But still, the pain...

*Okay*, Abigail's conscience was at it with a question, *but what's his mama's death got to do with you?*

"Abbie, Mama loved you. So will you attend the funeral, and—"

Abigail did not hear another thing because it seemed the man's only goal was to keep her in turmoil. Then, she remembered. She was no longer in a relationship with him. She didn't have to do a thing for Darré. She could refuse and not worry that he'd disappear, or not call, because now she no longer cared.

"So you'll do it?" Darré inquired, his eyes bright.

Blinking, Abigail queried, "Do? What?"

"I asked," Darré articulated, rising from the mauve and cherry wood guest chair. "If you'd do the reading that Mama wrote for the fam."

Why was he speaking like she was a dim-wit? Oh, it didn't matter. Her answer was, "No." He and she had not married; she was not family.

"What d'you mean no?" Darré squawked, nearly flying at Abigail.

"I mean just that," the executive responded, remembering that her ex hit, spit, cussed, and kicked when enraged. Yet, she felt no fear as the 91st Psalm came to mind. *He shall give His angels charge over thee...*

When the man's eyes narrowed, Abigail nearly laughed, especially when Darré barely managed not to holler. "Why 'no' Abbie?"

"Why me?" she retorted. Slowly she strolled toward her desk as her conscience asked, *Why not one'a your big, greasy, biscuit-eating cousins*?

"Just say you'll do it," Darré begged. "Please, Abbie..."

"Look Dar-RAY, I've told you a hundred times, don't call me that, and even though I loved your mother, I refuse to bail you out," anymore.

Darré's features screwed up because the witch before him had always been a stick-in-the-mud. "Yo A, this ain't bailing me out!"

"Hey! This is my place of business," Abigail cautioned. "Lower your voice, and I said no." Abigail winked. "Oh, why not ask your *wife*?" Watching Darré's attitude worsen she recalled. He'd never managed well when things went awry, so boldly Abigail pushed. "Can't wifey read?"

The Ex nearly lunged as Abigail side-stepped suggesting, "Surely, you can coerce your nineteen-year-old baby mama to do this—reading."

Darré spoke sulkily, "We're not talking 'bout her."

Just aside of her desk, Abigail pretended to cringe. "Oh, I guess I'd betta hush then, talking 'bowt your little princess." Noting that Darré's

27

eyes had become mere slits, Abigail glimpsed the mean-spiritedness that often drove the man.

"You're being heartless, Abbie. You know that, right? And—"

"Heartless?" Taken aback, Abigail hissed, "You prick! If mi was so heartless, you'd not have t'ought bowt coming here, asking mi favors!"

"No favors, Abbie—and quit that coconut shit! You know I hate it."

Although she backed up, Abigail felt compelled to taunt the man who had not despised her patois when she'd said what he wanted to hear. It was why she spat, "Mention 'coconut' again, mon 'n mi peel off your skin!"

Clenching his fists, Darré could not understand. The defiant witch knew he could knock her into next week, so why did she challenge him?

Again, Abigail walked to her office door. "Look, Darré, get out. Mi cyan't do anyting for yu. You need to go."

Grudgingly then, Darré realized; to get Abigail to do his mother's bidding, he couldn't use the scare tactic. For some reason, it wasn't working. "Baby," he called, "I ain't asking you to go out your way, but—"

"Save the sweet talk." Abigail didn't need it, *or* the nosey folk along the corridor pealing their ears to hear what went on in her office. Therefore, she pushed her door to, and crossed the new pearl gray carpet. She crossed the mauve border that matched her guest chairs, and wearily she sat. She realized. She was so tired of this man and his mess! Abigail simply wanted to move on. Therefore, she softly inquired, "Why won't you go away, and stay away? You do remember you left me, right?"

Watching a frustrated tear race down Abigail's cheek, Darré became astounded. He also felt like a door inside him creaked open. Now he actually heard his ex's plea. She wanted him to take all the old hurts that seeing him dredged up, and she wanted him to disappear, for good.

Abigail covered her face while Darré stood there, stirred nearly to tears himself. "Hey, don't cry, Abbie." The Ex couldn't believe he felt so bad. "You hate me, and you should, but don't cry, ack! I just need to know—"

No longer hearing Darré, Abigail slowly swiveled to face her window. She really wasn't happy about his loss. This Abigail realized while noting Darré's reflection in her window. However, it was interesting to know that pain could find anyone. Indeed, it had found the man who had seemingly gotten away Scott-free, while she'd cried a river.

Behind Abigail, Darré felt enigmatically bare and trapped when he usually managed to flee any type of emotion. Uncomfortable, he groaned. "Dammit, Gail—I mean Gaye, this is not for me."

Abigail nearly smiled because The Ex was no longer smooth or smug.

His loss of composure Darré blamed on the woman behind the big desk. If she was decent, she'd have faced him, and she'd have said yes.

Not quite hearing all the blubbering about 'Mama's love,' Abigail strove to remember something... Yes! In the Clankston's kitchen, Ms. Dottie-Mae had spoken.

"You know honey pie," the frail, light-skinned older woman had said while handing over a coffee mug. "I'd sho 'preciate it if you," her youngest son's girlfriend, "would honor me by reading something I'm working on." The recitation, Dottie-Mae had explained, would be for Mr. Raymond Sr. and the whole Clankston clan.

Easing into a kitchen chair, Dottie-Mae continued, her drawl South Carolinian. She desired to express a few loving things, firstly to her husband, Ray. She wanted other precious things said to her adult children, then her grandchildren. "I didn't forget my sister Rubenstein, or my brother William, my Rubie and Willie, but I gets choked up," the woman admitted. "So, honey pie... that's why Mother needs you."

Abigail wondered why, and Mrs. Dottie-Mae chuckled, like life was right and fair. "Why Ab-bu-gay-ul, you supposed to be my daught'-in-law. In my heart, you are." The woman's voice hardened then. "If only my dumb son would move quickly and use the sense he was born with."

Dottie-Mae did not say that she had also chosen the polished, professional younger woman because she was not apt to be as grieved as the Clankstons. "So sweet girl, in time, jest do like Mother asked..."

The memory faded, but Abigail wondered. Did she smell lemon verbena? It was the scent Mrs. Dorothy Mae Ella had favored all her life.

In her office, Abigail swiveled to face The Ex. While she spoke, she ignored gooseflesh on her arms. "I made your mother a promise."

Abigail realized her vow had nothing to do with the deceased's son, his betrayals, or his broken promises. Therefore Abigail stated, "I'll be there. Have your sister call me. Now you," Abigail pointed, "leave. And don't ever come back, either."

## 3

SHE took her belongings from her car. Inside, she rode to twenty-seven. She noticed the tension, too, courtesy of the Darré 'n his Mama drama. Abigail rolled her shoulders, as Joseph often did. She also reminded herself how much she loved living at Branford Court, the twin set of high-rise buildings. Between buildings Alpha and Omega, there was a magnificently manicured flagstone courtyard and a fountain. There was an indoor pool, a state-of-the-art fitness center, and a resident business center. However, what had sold her on the place was its cosmopolitan New York location. Not her baby sister's ceaseless chatter about how now Abigail would be one of the 'in' people.

Abigail loved exchanging pleasantries with building Alpha's door attendant. Upon exiting glass and brass, she would find herself in mini Manhattan. With artsy residents—filmmakers, authors, and modistes—her little town was trafficky but perfect. It was located on the border of Queens and Manhattan. After midnight, Abigail could see a movie or patronize sidewalk cafés. If she wanted fresh brioche, aromatherapy, a massage, or dance lessons, she could step from one door to another. Or she could hop a train. In minutes, she would be in Manhattan, at work.

However, while jangling her keys, Abigail realized none of those things negated the feeling that she'd been in a cat-scratching fight.

In her condominium apartment, Abigail relished the silence. Dropping her designer purse and matching attaché, she was grateful for having safely arrived home. Then in a rush, she pushed her shoes off, one foot with the other, before she made a beeline for the half bath.

When back in her living room, Abigail started her audio system. As strains of jazz diva, Sarah Vaughn's 'Black Coffee' wafted around her, Abigail lit scented candles. Then in the flame light, Abigail sat and viewed buttercream walls and her plush off-white furniture. She eyed splashes of color in the form of throw pillows and gilt-framed artwork. Abigail saw regal colors, too, in blown glass vases of fresh flowers.

Visitors often mentioned her décor, Abigail remembered. They spoke of the peace in her home. That serenity, Abigail knew, was a gift from above. And on this evening, she imitated her ever-praying Jamaican grandmother by thanking God for that peace.

In the flickering light, Abigail noticed the best-seller. On her sumptuous cream-colored carpet, it was 'Exodus' by her favorite author, *April Alisa Marquette*. Beside Exodus was an ivory leather bible. Books, Abigail's passion, happened to be another thing garnered from Gram. In fact, books were everywhere in Abigail's home. Cookbooks were even in the kitchen, where she headed to pour a glass of Chardonnay.

Minutes later, Abigail stood before a large darkened window. Following a sip, she decided. She would fill her claw-foot tub with hot water and bath beads. Then she would luxuriate and soak.

As she lounged, surrounded by scent and music, Abigail asked for forgiveness. She knew she'd dropped the ball, again. She'd done so earlier with Darré. She really had to stop allowing that man to rile her.

When she finally eased from the tub, Abigail was glad she hadn't acted on impulse. Begging off with Joseph would have been impulse, and a mistake. In her bedroom, while applying fragrant body butter, Abigail figured. A night out in Joe's company was what she needed. Sure, he'd recently refused to sex her, but he genuinely cared for her.

Forgetting the man who would one day make some woman a great husband, Abigail glanced at the clock. Quickly, she donned a little black dress and stilettos. Teetering to her dressing table, she checked her face, subtly highlighted. Merrily, Abigail also chirped along with Ms. Vaughn on the wonderfully accusatory 'You're Mean To Me.' Then, grabbing her coat and purse, Abigail breezed down to the monitored and lit parking lot. Minutes later, she zoomed up the ramp.

Soon the New York City skyline appeared, lit against the night sky.

Abigail made her way to 54th between 9th & 10th while hoping she wasn't overdressed for this simple Halloween outing with an old friend.

Inside, she said, "Hey Rory," and wondered at her full bladder, again.

In the rose-veined marble foyer, big burly in uniform gave her a chin-jut while murmuring into his cell phone. Abigail stifled laughter because some security he was, kicked back with his size thirteens up.

Exiting the elevator on the lavishly appointed tenth floor, Abigail narrowly avoided a collision. "Kilo—hi," she breathed before hurrying to the loo.

31

Tan and honey-haired, the engineer with gold-flecked green eyes grinned. Beachboy good-looking, Connor Ostrowsky still carried the name given him in juvie. The California native had worked with Abigail's friend Joseph on numerous projects. Believing her unaware, Kilo ogled Abigail from the rear as she dipped into the ladies' room.

Moments later, when she stood at the studio door, Abigail peered at Joseph through the glass. Seated at the audio production console, he spoke to a young man opposite the window that separated them.

Yet outside, Abigail scanned the room; not a studio rat present. Not one greedy hang-about who didn't consider herself a groupie... go Joe!

Abigail felt nervous. That was absurd given all the years she'd known Joseph. And she'd visited the studio times too numerous to count.

Abigail eyed the caramel-colored 'yummy,' her sister's word for the young man in the booth. As he absorbed instructions given by the movie soundtrack's producer, Joseph D. Forrester, Abigail slipped inside.

Facing away, Joseph startled Abigail by admonishing her to stay put.

How had he known she was there? Abigail wondered as Joseph's sweet baritone rose. He informed everyone they had fifteen minutes.

"And," they all chorused with him, "don't leave the building," yeah, yeah. Someone chuckled as Mr. Broad-Shoulders approached.

Placing a cellophane-wrapped gift in Abigail's arms, Joseph said, "Congratulations, Star, on your deal." He watched her part clear paper.

Abigail touched a variegated pink and white antique rose on the cusp of bloom. She sniffed soon-to-flower tea roses as well.

Aware that her mother had been an avid gardener and that Abigail knew the rarity of both varieties, Joseph was pleased when she spoke.

"Joe, the 'Rosa Mundi'?" Abigail touched the latter, "And scarlet 'Christian Diors?' Where did you find these—this time of year?"

The producer shrugged, pleased that his efforts had not gone unnoticed. He then produced a tower of treats, hand-held boxes that varied in size, from the smallest to the largest. All were beautifully wrapped and beribboned.

Opening a box, Abigail learned that she could sample imported truffles and bing cherry chocolates. "Joe, you know I love—"

He pulled her close, "I know. So just a few sweets for my sweet."

Suddenly Abigail winced, and Joseph stepped back. He looked down. "Baybeee..." he crooned remembering the thorns; through the fabric of Abigail's dress, they'd pricked her girlz. "Star, I do apologize."

"No need," Abigail waved. "I should have held these aside."

Joseph's eyes twinkled, "I can kiss 'n make it better..."

Feelings of warmth and desire blossomed inside Abigail as Joseph's large hands slipped beneath her suede maxi coat. *Ohhh.*

Pleasure crossed his face as he dipped his head to taste Abigail's lips. Content, Joseph sighed, and glad she'd made the trip, Abigail exhaled.

Joseph felt he never got to hold baby cakes long enough, and Abigail relished the feel of Joseph's strong arms around her. She inhaled his clean, masculine scent, and both their thoughts veered to the erotic.

With Abigail moaning, Joseph's libido leaped, and his lips sped like quiet fire over her closed eyelids, her face, her exposed shoulders, and her breast tops. Pressing closer, Abigail met Joseph's erection.

Suddenly he wondered—because he wanted Abigail right then—why were others around? Why weren't he and she some place quiet, like his Long Island Tudor home. He spent weekends there, if he had off. Or why weren't they at his Harlem duplex, or in a deluxe suite? High above a dazzling Connecticut Casino, there they had once stayed.

"Gaye," Joseph softly called, "Baby... I'm gonna let you go."

"Okay," Abigail murmured, "because yu 'n me 'bowt to find trouble."

How Joseph *wished* as he stepped back, inhaling the subtle fragrance that unbeknownst had signaled her arrival. Wanting, Joseph explained. "Star, a lil' trouble I can handle. It's just you that I have problems with."

Abigail laughed and wondered if Joseph's voice always sounded like a midnight invitation. She noticed the telltale vein too. It currently pulsed the length of Joseph's forehead, and she loved it!

Joseph pressed his face to Abigail's. "Star, I'm gonna catch my breath. Then I'll let you go. I promise."

"Don't." Ever, Abigail thought. "Can you promise me that?"

"Got to, Star," Joseph said, squeezing her derriere while fusing his supple lips with hers. Then he said, argumentatively, "Look, girl, I'm trying to get back to work." Again, he snagged her luscious lower lip. "If I don't, now, I can't be responsible for what might happen next."

Abigail wondered, had *she* asked who wanted to be responsible? If so, she was fast becoming a cheap act, as her sister Patria would say.

With a sigh, Abigail stepped back, but sexy Joseph moved with her. She laughed. "Lemme go," she moaned, realizing 'this' was crazy.

Joseph refused, as mentally, he acknowledged that things were nuts between them —the desperate desire, the groaning and grinding...

Abigail placed a hand on Joseph's chest, and beneath her palm, his pectorals jumped. "Ohhh," she murmured because that, right there, was entirely too good. Raising wantonly glazed eyes, Abigail near-whined. "No fair," because Joseph shocked her system with open-mouth kisses.

"Ooh. Okay. Mi seeerious," Abigail insincerely stated, while yet offering Joseph the column of her neck. "No more." Please.

She shivered as forcefully Joseph turned her to press kisses to her sensitive nape. With hands at Abigail's hips, he brought her backside to his pelvis, and grinding against her, he closed his eyes. "If I don't look at you, Star," Joseph whispered, bent and wrapped around her. "Maybe I'll get hold of myself. Then maybe I can let you go," for a second.

Untethered, Abigail tossed her head to clear it. With her burnished hair again covering her neck, she felt more in control...until Joseph reached for her. He did so just after she removed her suede maxi coat.

In his arms, she moaned, "Yu want to see how far yu cyan push."

"Don't mention pushing," Joseph murmured as someone approached.

Both people watched the studio door open. Abigail welcomed the reprieve, while at the same time she felt disappointment. No more playing. Joseph only experienced annoyance, especially when Kilo stalked quickly and angrily past.

Green-eyes did so after assessing the situation. Clattering down a laden tray from the first-floor deli, Kilo fumed. Hell, he'd thought he would finally holler at Abigail. Since she and 'Mr. Hugging Her Up' were supposed to be just friends. Well, so much for that.

Joseph pulled Abigail close, dismissing Connor Ostrowsky. If lil honey hadn't come 'round to see him, Kilo would never have met her.

"Sugar, baby," Joseph breathed, "this man's gotta earn his keep, so..." Stepping back, Joseph's eyes roamed Abigail. She looked like she'd been poured into that black —and have mercy! Joseph thought it as words fled, and the cloakroom, not five feet away, clouded his mind.

Feeling deliciously nude while caught in Joseph's amorous gaze, Abigail attempted to forget desire and the coatroom that beckoned.

Joseph forgot plunging into the dark and warmth.

Abigail forgot the tension rod and slipping inside.

Instead, she forced herself to follow Joseph. Behind the console, she sat on the small sofa. She watched as he jammed fists into his pockets.

This way, he thought, maybe the urge to run his hands over Gaye's exposed knees would quell. But what if he traipsed his long musician's fingers up her beautiful thighs until cupping her buttocks he could—

Yo, get a grip! The ordinarily soft voice in Joseph's head thundered it. Seamlessly, he transitioned back into producer mode. In a voice different from the one that had Abigail's heart tripping, he spoke. He said the session wouldn't drag on. He claimed it might last only another hour.

An hour? Abigail felt sunk. Please. She knew Joseph and his crew. When they worked and the music pumped, when they collaborated, trying to get the right sound and feel, time meant nothing to them. And she wanted fun this evening, since she'd put forth the effort.

At the board, Joseph nodded. At the channel assignment matrix, the engineer's silver-ringed fingers sent output to the desired tracks.

Abigail listened as a string introduction began. Reminiscent of a living creature's heartbeat, the chords pulsated and rose to fill the air. Amazed, Abigail held her breath. She noticed Joseph too. Over the music, seemingly unaffected by it, he mentioned a schmooze affair.

"You know," he dryly stated, "just another mode of networking."

Abigail's eyebrow arched because he said, "We're all going down, to hide behind masks on sticks, and you should be my guest."

"It's a masquerade ball, of sorts?" Abigail inquired, amused.

"I guess," Joseph winked, liking that she'd chuckled. He never forgot being long 'n lean and cruising around with his smooth stepfather Halloway. In Hal's shiny pewter gray Riviera, the music of Sassy or Ella had played. Over the song-stylists, Hal had said, "Son, if you can't get a gal to laugh, likely then, you've got no chance with that lil cookie."

Therefore, Joseph guessed, he might have a chance with Gaye because lil cookie had laughed. She also wanted to attend the shindig.

"Aiight Star," Joseph remarked, his mind mostly on getting her naked. "But I only mentioned the club to give you options. Really, I'd rather celebrate you closing that deal elsewhere, and alone."

Abigail remembered. Joseph had given her celebratory gifts. So now, she wanted to go to the club. There, she could wind up in his arms. While dancing, she could feel him, so she suggested, "Let's go, hang out."

"If you're sure..." Joseph returned his attention to the console and the slim young man who patiently waited with half-on headphones.

Abigail glanced at Kilo. He eyed Joseph, who touched her knee.

Yeah and they were just friends, right? Kilo appeared disgusted.

Not caring, Joseph rasped, "Commeere." He clasped Abigail's nape. Pulled forward, she involuntarily gave the man a generous view of soft bronze cleavage as sensuously he massaged the back of her neck.

Man! Joseph could all but see himself holding Abigail at the sentient small of her back as he— Return to reality, he told himself. Then briskly, he advised, "I'm gonna need to be alone with you when we leave here."

"Well..." Abigail willed herself to breathe. "Maybe, after the club."

"I'll hold you to it," Joseph said, and open-mouth kissed her.

Noisy SOB, Kilo thought with a scowl.

Back in producer mode, Joseph spoke to yummy in the booth. "Take it from the bridge. Ah, and chief, let's not be flat on the crescendo."

Joseph sat back as again Kilo started the fluttering stringed heartbeat.

Tears stung Abigail's eyes because softly and melodically 'Yummy' moaned about devastating loss. In seconds, however, the chords progressed from minor to major. Then adjusting her off-the-shoulder collar, Abigail moved to the funky beat. She liked the catchy hook, and then she really heard Yummy. Abigail's hand went to her chest because what an angelic voice! Wow. Joseph's young protégé would go places, and fast too, Abigail mentally predicted.

Yummy sang on, and as she had known, it became stop and go. Do another take; pan right; now stack that. Joseph spoke to his engineer. "Lo, we'll need to cut 'n paste." Then back to Yummy, Joseph said, "That was a li-i-ttle sharp; do it over. That's it, big breath first. Staccato; now siiing it—melodiously. This is the top note. Show me whatcha workin' wit' –come on, man. Okay, you got it. Breathe, from your diaphragm. Work it. Go, kid. Ahhh yeah. Take us to church, baby!"

Joseph and the crew were excited, and Yummy enjoyed good-natured ribbing. He smiled as the playback was listened to, its signals fed to monitor. "Lil' playa!" the men chorused. "Yo, you were in da zone, kid!"

Finally, the session ended, and Abigail was able to stretch her cramped limbs. Shoeless and carrying her purse, she padded alongside the long-legged Joseph. He carted her coat, gifts, and her shoes. At his spacious suite, he unlocked the door, and Abigail entered the quiet.

For the umpteenth time, she noted the thick beige carpet. Through the huge window, she viewed sparkling Manhattan, and the George Washington Bridge. It was suspended against an indigo sky. Abigail admired a watercolor ocean scene that spanned a whole wall.

In Joseph's private space, Abigail thought the same thing she had on prior visits. Everything was so like him, unpretentious yet elegant.

"Star," the man stowed her coat. "I mentioned Club whatever, right?"

Turning, Abigail watched as Joseph pulled his Henley up and over his head. When his toned midsection was exposed, she managed, "You did."

Removing boots, Joseph asked, "What *is* that club's name?"

Abigail did not know. She only knew she yearned to run her hands over the taut skin covering Joseph's strong arms and muscular chest. When his hands dropped to his belt, she tore her eyes away. At the same time, she thought, legendary steel-driving man, Paul Bunyan, got nothing on you, baby. Abigail even attempted to sound unfazed when she teased, "You know Joe, not remembering is a sign of just one thing. Old age."

Joseph appeared confrontational, "Well, you name that club."

Caught in his penetrating stare, Abigail stammered. "I c-can't, not now." Not with you looking like a bronzed Adonis, "But I do know it."

Joseph's laughter carried through French doors. "Now who's old?"

Abigail scoffed, "You're three years my senior."

Wearing a lopsided grin, Joseph poked his head back out. "Granted, but we both know one thing, girl. This 'senior' is young where it counts."

She would have laughed or retorted, but suddenly Joseph was back, bare-chested, and too close, pulling her up and into a sensual embrace.

With lips on Abigail's, he wondered if her head, like his, was spinning. Joseph wondered too if her intoxicating fragrance coaxed out the beast in him. Pressing Abigail along his length, he was aware that their kissing changed. Initially playful, it became intensely demanding.

Removing her hand from Joseph's nape, Abigail eased her leg down. Wow. She couldn't remember when she'd last been that out of herself.

Joseph watched her step back. Predatorily, he stepped forward. Abigail laughed when caught. He pressed her face to his chest, and beneath his silken skin, she felt his heartbeat. So he was excited too. It was good to know.

Using a fingertip, Joseph tilted Abigail's face up. With lips nearly touching hers, he admitted he hated to tear himself away. Yet he had to, and he gave her a choice, again. "You still wanna attend this shindig?"

Electricity crackled between them as Abigail ran her tongue over her lips. She tasted Joseph and recalled the *other* taste of him. Closing her mind to carnal desires, Abigail forced out that she still wanted to go.

Joseph stood a moment, reading the collage of expressions passing over her face. He also hid a lopsided grin, although inside, he crowed with the knowledge that lil' honey was as shaken as he. Okay, Joseph nodded; he wasn't in this by himself. Although it would take a minute before Abigail would reveal that her feelings were more than platonic.

Quickly he bent. Holding Abigail's arms, Joseph repeatedly kissed the swell of breast just above her portrait collar. However, when his greedy tongue sought her nipples, Joseph backed away. "Gimme ten," he said, although he needed a lifetime, really, to love her.

When she was alone, Abigail hugged herself. She bit her lip while trying to forget all that had just transpired—especially the intense heat. Abigail told herself to focus on the displayed measures of Joseph's success. Then she would think straight.

Abigail gazed at platinum albums and plaques, but her thoughts returned to the man in the adjacent room. She ran a finger over an Essence Award and 'saw' Joseph's brown skin. Abigail touched the Black Achiever's Association award and was 'touching' Joseph. She eyed numerous AMA's and Grammy awards and recalled sexy saying each next award brought more demands for his services.

How *she* needed his services. Abigail sighed and told herself no more thinking about slipping out of her dress and tiptoeing through those doors. No more 'seeing' herself nude and stepping into Joseph's shower. His mouth would be on hers as water sluiced over them. With his big hands at her sides, he would slide down her body, and his mouth would trail heat over her breasts. Oh, Abigail looked up, and her eyes widened because she was not supposed to have actually entered his cozily lit mosaic-tiled lavatory!

Joseph saw her, as glistening, he exited the doorless shower. He watched her eyes travel from his parted lips to his sparse haired muscular chest. Joseph watched Abigail's eyes round when they traveled downward, past his taut belly to his formidable male member.

Abigail licked her lips, as forgetting his towel, Joseph crossed to her. Her hands rose and her palms rested on his chest as he pulled her close. She got stuck again, this time not by thorns, but by Joseph's throbbing male staff. Wanton, Abigail moved against him as he took her mouth. With his, he forced hers wide as he gave her his tongue. Joseph kissed Abigail as though he was hungry and hadn't eaten since who knew when.

Then before she knew it, with skilled musician's fingers, Joseph had her dress at her waist, her thighs parted, and the crotch of her teddy aside. Sucking a nipple through her dress's fabric, Joseph also slipped a middle finger into... Abigail's heat.

Deliciously, she moaned, as within her mouth, Joseph's tongue moved, like his finger below. He caressed Abigail's clit and slicked it with her juices until she just had to have him or collapse.

Clasping the silken skin that encased his rock-hard rod, she breathed into his mouth. "Let me feel you..." please.

Glad to oblige, Joseph bent his knees and positioned himself where Abigail could feel him, pressed to her core. He thought of hefting her up.

She shivered. He moaned, but suddenly she wrenched free. With wide eyes, she stared up at him. How had she so utterly lost her mind?

Instinctively, Joseph knew she wasn't ready, so battling, then winning, he leashed the beast. He also bit out, "Go. Now," he croaked, yet glistening from his shower, "or I'll have you on this floor."

Hurriedly, Abigail turned. She yanked her dress down while her body screamed with unfulfilled longing. Then in Joseph's office proper, she couldn't think! Abigail didn't know how long she stood there, willing her body to yield to disappointment. However, finally, she remembered. Joe was her friend. She wanted him to remain so because friends always outlasted lovers. In Abigail's peripheral, something moved. With butterflies in her belly, she turned, with her arms around herself.

The epitome of sexy, in black, approached. For the second time that evening, Abigail chided herself because she had known Joseph for years. She had seen him in custom-tailored finery many times. Tonight, a different shirt and slacks should not have had her libido leaping.

Shrugging into lengthy leather, Joseph eyed Abigail. "You ready?"

With a nod, she licked her lips and said she was. Abigail tried to make her voice sound convincing too when she said she felt like dancing.

Transfixed, Joseph stood with eyes riveted to the flare of Abigail's hip, outlined by her clingy dress. "I guess," he hoarsely managed, "We should get you to the club then."

Good idea, she thought, because there, in the near-dark, they could engage in the next best thing to what she really wanted.

"Put your arms in." Joseph ordered while holding Abigail's coat. Damn, did they have to leave, he thought, and fast too, because he felt like a horse chomping at the bit.

"Thanks, I've got it," Abigail stated when Joseph's fingertips sensuously singed her shoulders. Still, he buttoned her up and slipped his large hands around her neck. "Wait," he murmured. "Lemme hold you a minute." Abigail nearly liquefied. "Okay," Joseph breathed and grabbed the woman's things. Practically dragging her from his office then, he forgot his desk, ripping off her clothing and laying her out.

ABIGAIL'S roses lay in the rear of Joseph's car. The cellophane was parted like a woman's beautiful gown at an evening's end. With their soft petals, the flowers reminded Joseph of a lover—one who looked significantly like the woman beside him.

Driving, he glanced over. Seated aside and opening a treat box, Abigail slipped a delicacy between her lips just before she sang out, off-key. Joseph laughed outright because poor baby, for all her great qualities, she really was tone-deaf. Howling, like the wind on a lonely winter night, Joseph nearly thanked Abigail for the distraction. Now, maybe, he could get his body to calm down.

Now, he could also see that he should not have inched Big Boy into her soft heat because that was nearly all he could think about.

The song changed to 'Trading Places.' Joseph knew a moment's peace before the images Usher set Joseph's lustful thoughts afire, again.

Joseph glanced over and wondered if Gaye was aware. He'd called her office twice after his abrupt 'dismissal.' He wondered if she'd checked her home and cellular voicemail. He sighed because sometimes she worried him. Not because Abigail was given to mood swings, but because she allowed people to hurt her. Sure, she could get tough, but really, she was such a softie inside until it was detrimental.

Joseph shook his head imperceptibly because his baby, who mentored teenaged girls, cared too much –and often for the worst offenders. Abigail did so because she believed there was good in everybody. She said it simply had to be found and cultivated —like people were plants.

Joseph exhaled and realized something else. The clown had not been fully ejected from Abigail's life. Joseph knew because that had been Clankston's muffled voice that he'd heard earlier. That wishy-washy mother-effer, Joseph thought as his eyes narrowed. Clankston had made his choice—and it had not been Abigail, so why was he coming around?

Joseph involuntarily jerked as Abigail screeched like an old tire. Again, he forgot her 'singing' if it could be called that. He ignored the growl inside that said she was his. The growl said it was now his turn. Heck, for nearly seven years, he'd possessed patience and cool. However, at present, both had almost ebbed clean away.

On the steering wheel, Joseph's hand tightened. Palming the gearshift with his right, he forgot holding his member the same way, just before he nudged it into Abigail. It was what she wanted, Joseph knew. Moreover, he was aware that he could actually use his stick and sexuality to bind Abigail to him. Joseph could easily make her forget that corny-assed Court Jester. The one he would flay alive if Jester again touched her.

Joseph thought it because he would be the next man in Abigail's life—until they had a son, perhaps. Funny, Joseph had never thought about children, not before her. But he could 'see' his boy moments after birth. Baby would lie on Abigail's chest because she was *the one*.

Yep, it was clear, Joseph thought while driving; Abigail Denise Wallace was *it* for him. Outside of Nana and Miz Maddie, Abigail was the only other woman with whom he had ever gone to church.

Joseph just needed to make sure Abigail's ex—that debaucher of young, almost-women—was not trying to weasel his way back.

# 4

INSIDE Club La-Laa! Joseph watched Abigail. She hid behind a purple-feathered mask. Dang, was he worn, partly from the infernal turmoil she kept him in and partly because a project was running behind schedule. He knew it was the way things sometimes went; still, it sucked.

Inconspicuously, Joseph eyed Abigail and nineteen-year-old Wonder Voice. Many in the music industry called the kid Won for short. Forgetting Won, Joseph knew he had to speak with Abigail about becoming his woman. But how, he wondered, when the time was never right? There was always somebody vying for a moment with her, like Wonder Voice at present. Won played peek-a-boo with a Batman mask.

Well, when he got the chance, Joseph vowed he would be cool, despite lately feeling like a cat on a hot tin roof. Yes, now that he'd acknowledged he loved Abigail, although he hadn't said it to her. Big deal, he'd said it to the man in the mirror, in his lavatory, while she'd inspected awards in his adjacent office. Minutes later, he'd also wound up fighting a mighty battle to get Big Boy away from her Kitty-Kat. But he couldn't approach Abigail yet, Joseph thought, because of the ongoing Darré fiasco. The one she thought he didn't know about.

Joseph pondered crashing the clown. That was one way to get rid of him, but that could backfire. Bozo didn't need the advantage of having Abigail feel sorry for him. So no, Joseph wouldn't bash Clankston, just yet. Joseph would just outmaneuver Bozo with positive thoughts. He would also speak his desires into existence. Hadn't Joseph done it with other things? Wasn't his life and his so-called 'charmed career' proof that the universe would yield whatever a man could conceive?

Yeah, but Ms. Pot-Stubborn had to conceive too for it to work. Lord, please, Joseph nearly growled, let Ms. Obstinate give in. If she did, he could get laid. More importantly, though, she would love him. Abigail could even suggest taking things slow. Heck, they'd been doing so for years anyway. Although he hadn't been pining while waiting. For crying out loud, a man had needs; but Joseph had found out. Other women definitely could not take Abigail's place.

Joseph eyed Won. Standing beside Abigail, the kid mirrored an infatuated pup. Boy did the kid aim high. Joseph couldn't blame him, not when he too had been ga-ga upon first encountering Abigail...

There she had been, a sista with incredible lips, sitting in his favorite restaurant. He often frequented it during the dark wee morning hours. Usually, after leaving the studio, he and Raul sat and conversed in the softly lit eatery. Nuria, Raul's wife, would pour Joseph's drink and Viognier for her restaurateur husband. All the while, Raul's employees would clomp back and forth over the scrubbed to nearly nude wooden floors. Wearing white aprons, some stacked chairs, while others who handled glassware would cause a steady clink-clink in the background. That delicate sound Joseph loved. To him, it was musical.

But back to meeting his baby... Back then, she had been in his haunt, waiting for a different clown, a cad who hadn't bothered to show up. For a while, Joseph had watched the woman, then he'd offered a drink.

Gorgeous accepted, and Joseph's eyes twinkled as he asked, "What if your date turns up? What if he's beaten badly, with a story to match?"

Abigail had sipped. "That would be a problem, for him, wouldn't it?"

Joseph laughed and had immediately liked her. And to think, if he hadn't sauntered in at seven that summer evening, he'd never have met Abigail. Thank Heaven his artists had missed their flight. Abigail had worn open-back shoes, and she had lethal legs. Joseph had tried to concentrate on her joke about someone being stood up, but she'd been such a honey! She hadn't moaned that all men were dawgs n playas either, just because one had jilted her. Abigail had actually said the male genus were like buses; another would trundle up soon, and Joseph had.

Seated in Club La-Laa! he would never forget that a month later, Abigail had winked and said she'd let him place both their orders on meeting night. She had done it so she could check him out.

When they'd met, Joseph had mentioned being a pop music producer. It was something he didn't often tell women. He'd noticed Abigail's flicker of surprise. Later, she admitted she'd heard of him. "You were nominated for producer of something, on some show."

Joseph stifled a laugh because she was too much. Abigail said she'd seen his Harlem duplex in magazines, People and Ebony. "Not bad," she'd revealed. That was after he'd had her on her back. Her raised brown knees had touched her buoyant tits, while perspiring he'd glided in and out of her. Lying spooned together after that first time, Joseph had kissed Abigail's nape and thanked all the saints. Heck, the woman had finally broken down enough to give him some. She'd been so open, even though she'd said, her Gram had taught her and her sisters that 'engaging' was sin. Well, to Joseph, engaging with Abigail was Heaven.

As he sat in the smoke-filled club, Joseph remembered. Abigail had briefly mentioned her career. "It's not interesting." She was a commercial property account executive. Her office, they'd realized, was located not far from his second home, a historic brownstone. During the workweek, Joseph lived on a tree-lined lantern-lit street in the invigorating Mount Morris Park section of uptown New York. In good ol' Harlem, USA, where there was a bevy of culture and vitality.

Joseph recalled thinking Abigail was gorgeous, and she'd dubbed him charming and ruggedly attractive. "But then again," she had coyly stated while stripping for him. "You could be acting, to get your face' n stick near my...Kitty-Kat." She'd gestured to her neither region. Lopsidedly Joseph had grinned. Then Abigail sat on him. She'd faced away as he'd buried himself in her. He'd also thought, so that's what she calls it, huh?

In the club, Joseph tipped his chair back and realized. He had been further attracted to Ms. Abigail because she hadn't tried to impress him, like so many wannabes. In this nouveau age of overly self-conscious individuals, Abigail had been nearly unaffected for seven years. It was the same length of time that Joseph had been in love with her.

A female admirer of his had once asked. What was special about the woman who'd captured his heart? Joseph hadn't divulged that Abigail was caring and authentic. It wasn't the other woman's business. Besides, boy, was Abigail interesting when she got upset! Then her fiery JaMerican temper—because she was Jamaican and American— would flare. Abigail would cuss, like a demon, and throw things.

"You forget your religion?" Joseph had once asked her, after being treated to an obscene gesture. However, later, in quieter moments, she had apologized. That Joseph liked. Abigail wasn't con-artist-y or fake, and she truly desired to walk with God. However, sometimes, she was just plain ornery, as his Nana used to say.

"At least with Missy, you'll never wonder where you stand." Snazzy older Maddie had nodded one evening as Joseph sat in her cozy boudoir. Enveloped in a comfy wingback chair, he'd lamented the 'fit' he and 'Missy' had. Then he'd noticed Duke Ellington's 'Perfume Suite.' It seemed like Vintage jazz was forever playing in Madeline's charming but creaky old house.

Back then, Joseph had watched the woman float past, while outside her cozy bedroom, rain fell. Pounding a fist into a palm, he'd moaned. "Maybe you don't understand. 'Missy' as you call her, won't talk to me."

Madeline was consoling. "Y'all had a fight, or a 'fit' as your Nana used to say. Abigail's upset right now SweePea, but she'll come around." Knotting a silk scarf, Madeline muttered, "Lord only knows when."

Joseph sounded stern as he spoke to the woman attired for their evening out. "I heard that." Joseph said he liked her white satin and black velvet. "And I hope you're right, Miz Maddie."

"Tell me something, Joseph Desmond." Madeline re-capped a glass perfume bottle. "When you ever known yo' Mama to be wrong?"

Actually, while seated in the smoke-filled club, Joseph could not recall a time. That helped him to feel marginally better. While watching curvaceous, Joseph realized his mom was most likely right. 'Missy' was taking her time. With her fine self, Joseph thought as his eyes caressed Abigail's soft brown breasts, a bit bigger than a mouth full. Above her portrait collar, the exposed swell jiggled when she laughed.

Joseph's eyes traveled downward to her expanse of hip. Then she turned, and he noted her 'onion.' He was nearly sure it had been the timeless scribe Maya Angelou who'd said a woman's onion could bring tears to a man's eyes. Yep, if said man watched Abigail swang that thang. But beyond the outward, Joseph thought, Abigail was truly selfless and giving. Therefore, he prayed that Pot-Stubborn would give in. Heck, an impressive financial portfolio, extravagant trips, and houses that weren't yet homes would continue to mean nothing. That is if he couldn't share them with her.

Joseph noticed a new man—a photographer, this time—up in Abigail's face, like there weren't other women present. See? Joseph cogitated if men tried to holla, and Abigail was his, he wouldn't feel lousy. He'd feel proud, but now, with shit up in the air, he only feel agitated. Running a hand over his freshly shaved jaw, Joseph called for a couple of cold golds. Maybe they'd still the insidious nagging that said no woman should have the kind of power over him that Abigail had.

"Joe..."

He raised his eyes. "Hey, pretty lady."

Abigail's heart tripped as Joseph's large hands eased up to cup her buttocks through her dress. Joseph squeezed, and Abigail linked her hands back of his head. Wow. She couldn't remember what she'd come over to ask, but no wonder, with Joseph's face pressed to her abdomen and his warm hands molding her waist. "Oh," she remembered. "Wanna dance?"

Reluctantly, Joseph released her. "I've got a couple of chilled wets coming, so I'm a decline, but I'll catch you on the rebound. I promise."

Standing between Joseph's knees, Abigail shrugged. Turning, she headed for the dance floor. There, uninhibited, she began to move to the beat. Again she looked away from blue-eyes who lustfully eyed her.

"Hey, brown baby," someone said. "Need some company?"

Kilo. Abigail realized she had known somebody would approach her. Too bad it wasn't sexy Joseph.

"Girrrl, moving like that," Kilo said while eyeing her gyrating hips; "you'll put a hurtin' on every man in here."

Gently, Abigail pushed him. "Lemme apologize. You, back up."

Kilo obliged as, over the music, Abigail asked about his girlfriend. Hunching his shoulders in time with the music, the man appeared puzzled. Grinning, he asked, "What's that word—girlfriend—mean?"

Suddenly Kilo's grin faded. He indicated blue-eyes who attempted to cut in. "Yo, what's up, Mr. Clairol?"

A while later, green-eyed Kilo again groaned. "Look, pal, take your tight-assed pleather pants and move along. Hey, blondie—" Kilo jumped back. "Watch that drink! You're getting sloppy!"

Abigail stifled a laugh, then winced. "Oh—ouch!" She limped toward Joseph and safety, while Kilo backed drunken blue-eyes down.

Frustrated, Kilo thought, there went his chance to kick it.

Away from the packed and hot dance floor, Abigail detoured and hit the bar for club soda with a twist. From the buffet, she also took a plate and noticed Joseph. Coolly he beckoned from his candlelit table.

When she approached, one of the studio heads prepared to depart.

"Big guy," the salt-n-pepper haired man said, "see ya on the green." With a fading tan and a waning cigar, fifty-something, Joseph's comrade chivalrously pulled Abigail's chair. "The fifteenth, Bay Hill."

Yet seated, Joseph's eyes flicked upward. "Travel with money, Stan, and bring Nora's gift…because you will lose, to me."

At the mention of his wife, the portly man adjusted his trés expensive watch. "She'd kill me." Then with a beefy hand, the man touched Abigail. "Beware of this gent and your jewelry." The portly man turned, but his voice carried. "If you two can stand much more of this—noise, then enjoy yourselves."

Abigail scooted closer to the sexy brown man who remained. His voice sounded pensive as he trailed fingertips over her exposed shoulder. "I saw you, Mommy. You know, you can give a man a heart attack."

Abigail's pulse raced as inconspicuously, Joseph fondled one of her girlz. He watched as she stabbed things on her plate. Why had her hunger fled? Abigail nervously wondered before inwardly she acknowledged. She felt like prey. Therefore, she raised her utensil. "Want an olive?"

Joseph stared. Slowly, he spoke. "You – know – what – I –want – is *not* – on the tip – of anybody's – *fork*."

Speechless, Abigail hunched a shoulder in an attempt to deter Joseph's rousing fingertips. He enjoyed seeing the nearly indiscernible pulse at the base of her neck. It jumped as she beseeched him to quit.

Joseph blew smoke opposite her. "You don't want me to stop."

Joseph was right, but forgetting that, Abigail asked if he was upset.

He watched her lick the lips that he wanted to lick. "Should I be?"

"I don't know," Abigail replied and licked again because her mouth felt dry and so like the glowing embers of Joseph's cigarette. "But I do know one thing. You don't smoke, until you've really had it."

Joseph shrugged because she was right. He had nearly reached his limit. He wanted Abigail, and she played games – almost. So purposely, he stubbed out his cigarette because he'd just decided. He would take action. Now. Leaning over, he licked Abigail's exposed shoulder; but she sat unmoved, through sheer force of will. Therefore, Joseph placed a hand beneath her breast. He sensuously kneaded the underside. At the same time, he erotically skulked, open-mouthed, up Abigail's neck. Yep,

47

he wickedly mused while nibbling on her chin; in a moment, baby girl would know. He had ways to move her.

Abigail involuntarily shivered and begged Joseph to stop.

He did not, knowing the hunger and the need lurked just beneath her calm façade. With a hand at Abigail's back, slowly, Joseph rubbed, up, and down. The constant movement was both soothing and arousing. Then he squeezed a bountiful bun. "When I lay you down... tonight, Star," Joseph predicted, his voice mesmerizing, "not only will I fill up your body. I will fill your mind as well."

Then Abigail would think of, and desire, only him.

Abigail couldn't look at Joseph, not with that wicked vein pulsing. However, in a shaky voice, she managed, "Lea' me alone."

Joseph guffawed because she'd sounded quirkily juvenile.

When Abigail's eyes flicked back to his, Joseph winked. Oh yeah, he was going to have her, for keeps. Therefore, he decided she would need him so badly she would ache. To get the party started, Joseph leaned over and pulled Abigail closer. With his lips lingering just at her earlobe, he felt her try not to shiver. So he put more into it, and angling his head, he feasted on her neck. Then in the dimness, on the side where no one could see, he eased Abigail's knit dress further down her shoulder. Staring at a pretty breast peeking from beneath black lace, Joseph licked his lips. Adroitly, he ran practiced fingertips under the thin material; to scintillating five-finger suck Abigail's nipple. Pinching it up, he lowered his head and laved it. Then looking up into Abigail's glazed eyes as he held the lovely orb tilted upward, Joseph whispered, "Give in, Star."

With his mouth on her, inciting her, it seemed so simple, to Joseph, but to Abigail, it was not. And over Joseph's head, she noted a collage of haters. Unaware of other women, Joseph heard Abigail sigh. He also liked that her voice sounded dreamy when she murmured, "Dat feels so good." Therefore, with magic fingers and tongue, Joseph continued his ministrations until Abigail forgot the haters.

Joseph lifted his head and winked. Abigail drew herself away. This was game! She tugged at her garment. Game she did not need.

Joseph attempted to pull Abigail back, but she became firm. "Look, this has gone too far, already. So mi need yu to stop. Okay?"

Joseph nodded, not in favor of abeyance, but because Abigail had said the magic words, 'she needed,' and in that sultry JaMerican voice.

"Gaye, Baybeee," he moaned and bit his lip, her habit. "You need me, already, like I need you. So face it, and let's get on with this love, life, thingy we should have started years ago."

With a sigh, Abigail's eyes drifted shut as Joseph's lips covered hers, and his tongue simulated sex. *Wow*, she thought. Then she thought, no! That was not what she'd meant, at all. The man was insufferable, even though his lips and hands, roaming her body, were lethal.

Engaged in kiss, Joseph felt Abigail's resolve all but melt. He knew she didn't want him re-awakening desire, but she was passionate. She was a delectable woman, one he was not about to let go to waste, just because she'd had a bad experience. With a clown.

Although she kissed Joseph back; Abigail really didn't want her libido leaping, or conversation and music drowned out.

Triumphant, Joseph knew he had her—until Abigail changed tactics. Wanting up and air, she floundered and quickly rose. "Excuse me."

Leaning forward, Joseph playfully grabbed for and nipped at her backside with his teeth. Noticing a woman watching, he shrugged because, at last, *he* was having fun. Joseph laughed out loud, too, because Abigail's hasty retreat had been priceless! Now lil honey knew.

She could run, but she could not hide.

In the winsome ladies' room, Abigail breathlessly reminded herself. She and Joseph had come *that* close! Had she not had the presence of mind, she'd have pulled her dress up and straddled that man's powerful thighs. She'd have sunk down on the thick rod that she couldn't stop thinking about, and it would have been on!

Forget that, Abigail told herself. She wanted the woman in the other stall to leave so she could be alone, with her thoughts.

Finally, the next door creaked, water ran, paper was pulled, and the outer door opened. Abigail heard music before all became quiet.

Alone, she faced the tiled wall. With a hand splayed across her heaving bosoms—as Gram called them—Abigail half-smiled because Joseph had her revved up. However, she could not be stupid. He was a man. He was having fun. *She* couldn't let things get out of hand. It would only be at her expense. Her vulnerable heart would become involved.

49

When Abigail exited the ladies' room, she found Joseph's belongings at the table, but he was gone. Feeling dejected, she realized that like her, he, too, had probably vowed to let things dissipate. Maybe he'd recalled that lovers came and went, but friends were forever. If they were smart.

Pushing her plate aside, Abigail suddenly detested the raucous, bass-thumping party atmosphere. Why had she wanted to attend anyway? And why couldn't she stop thinking of letting Joseph get it?

Abigail recalled something. Repeatedly, in the past, Joseph had proclaimed love for her. As cognition dawned, Abigail realized. She'd continuously hidden from her feelings, unlike Joseph. She had done so by remaining involved with clowns.

Abigail bit her lip and told herself to remember one thing. Joseph was bigtime. He had been deemed one of People's Most Beautiful, along with powerhouse actors and musicians who were household names. That type of print/media coverage guaranteed a man a veritable feast of women. So how could she be the one? She could only wind up hurt, again. So Abigail told herself; Joseph saying he was in love with her was enough.

*You liar.* Her annoying conscience. Okay, so Joseph was all she had ever dreamed of and more. He was caring, spiritual, and he liked children. He had even helped her understand the importance of investing, planning for the future, instead of living day-to-day, paycheck-to-paycheck. In addition, Joseph's 'middle aged' body, as he teasingly called it, was toned. Moreover, talk about honed sexual skillz…

Abigail closed her eyes because she needed to keep in mind that her friend only thought he loved her. After all, she hadn't fallen for him, like 'the others.' They were women who fawned impossibly over 'the Producer.' Abigail forced herself to watch. See? Joseph was schmoozing. He was also being introduced to yet 'others.' Surrounding him, some had bought boobs. Others had food-deprived and corseted waists. A few people had barely concealed surgically-enhanced behinds. There were a few men in the midst, too, hoping for Joe's cast-off women, while some hoped for him.

Abigail watched the parody of sorts and told herself she didn't want Joseph or his kind of life. And all of this, she surmised, looking around, was part of his life. Shoot—Abigail scoffed inside—Joe could take photos with the whole heap of hussies' n hustlers. She was fine, alone.

*You're being catty.* Abigail realized it when the man caught her eye and winked. Abigail looked away and tried to forget that he'd kissed her and called her precious before telling her not to be afraid.

"I love you, girl," he'd murmured, those times that she'd let him remove her clothes. Sometimes he'd been on his knees, worshipping her while allowing his mouth to pleasure her. Other times Joseph had proclaimed his love while helping her do mundane things like laundry and dishes. Once, he'd even pleaded, "Love me a little—can't you?"

Abigail's eyes misted as she remembered Jazzy Miz Maddie with the gold rings bought by her son. While poring over a blazer in an upscale department store, older, elegant Madeline Forrester had opined that a person had to allow another to love them. While checking for imperfections, Madeline said she well knew. "I was young once and tossed aside by a man who promised me the moon—until I turned up pregnant. Not my intention." Madeline batted her eyelashes. "Back then, Missy, with no husband, pregnancy was a scourge." Madeline appeared thoughtful. "Still, the deed was done, and I was stuck, literally. So I prayed and decided to do what I had to do."

Madeline's voice changed and became unmistakably reverence-filled. "When my lil SweePea was born, girl! It hurt like the dickens, all that pushing, but I loved that baby from my first lay-eyes."

The woman smiled, peering at Abigail over half glasses. "Why do I do this?" She held up the price tag. "SweePea says I should stop inspecting and get what I want." Madeline's big fine son was so generous, yet she would never be a spendthrift. She would never be one of them mamas who thought her son owed her, just because. "Miss Abigail," Madeline picked up the threads of the previous topic. "Through SweePea, I learned to love." Holding her blazer, retired school teacher Madeline also said, "Eighteen months later, Hal came along. Took me a while, but again I had to pray. Then I had to decide because God doesn't do that; He doesn't decide for us.

"Therefore, I decided to allow Halloway to love me. Sure, I had been hurt, and some days had been dark, but I wanted to live in the light. I wanted my boy to know the love of a good man too, so he could grow up to be one." Madeline explained that when she gave in, to love, and to

Hal, she and her son received a new last name. "I blossomed and so did my boy. You see what he turned into. You'll never meet a finer man."

Madeline turned. "Now where'd I see that register?" Her eloquent voice carried. "Missy," the elegant woman threw a look over her shoulder. "One day, you'll have to decide. Can you allow someone to love you? You'll have to decide too, Missy, if you can love him back…"

Seated in the noisy, smoke-filled club, Abigail crossed her legs. She contemplated the differences between her and the man who had been called SweePea all his life. He had always known love. She, too, had known love, but for her, tragedy had overshadowed it. So, unlike her, Joseph had never questioned whether or not he was loved. He had always known that people felt the sun rose and set on him. Back in the day, he had been encouraged to go to New York's High School of Performing Arts, then to the all-male, historically black, Morehouse College in Georgia. It was one of the HBCUs that produced Rhodes Scholars. There, Joseph received a B.A. for majoring in music with a concentration in performance. Then he attended New York's famed Julliard School of Music. There he became a classically trained pianist.

However, after the murder of her mother, Abigail attended college on loans. She also worked in the office of the Registrar. Then tragedy had again struck, during her studies. Young Abigail had felt so alone, especially during the trial. However, she'd received occasional encouragement from Gram, whom Abigail had called in the West Indies.

So, of course, Joseph could believe he was in love, Abigail mused. Like every person's love pattern, his positive love pattern had been set during his young years. Hers probably needed to be re-set.

Seated in the noisy club, Abigail swung her top leg and tried not to watch the new hottie. This shameless heifer sauntered up to stand beside Joseph, where she removed her mask for notice. Abigail watched as the twit brazenly held her mask aside, to icily stare at her! With narrowed eyes, the occasionally hot-tempered Abigail forced herself not to go whup the water out that child. Instead, she refocused inward. If only she could be sure, she wouldn't wind up hurt…

*No guarantees in love, or life, girlie.* Abigail bit her lip and told herself that she was fine then, alone.

*Liar. You're lovesick, but you just don't want to face it.* Perhaps, but she would squash the feeling. She would begin by scrutinizing big boobs. This one had intercepted Joseph at mere feet from his table. Disgusted, Abigail looked away. However, sometime later, when she meant to look back, her eyes were drawn up.

How long had sexy Joseph stood there, Abigail wondered, just waiting, to run a hand down her cheek? And why did his eyes say that he'd had to come back, to her, despite the others?

Abigail blinked away tears as gently he pulled her up and out of her seat. Ignoring scornful stares and the derisive mumbling of the hating others, Abigail allowed Joseph to guide her from behind, toward the crowded dance floor. When she stepped into the booty-shaking throng, Joseph leaned forward. "I promised you a song, Star."

Wait. Why was the momentum slowing? Disoriented, Abigail half-turned and found herself enveloped in strong arms. Her face was pressed to a male wall of chest. She'd meant to head back to the table, to wait out the round of slow jams, but Joseph drew her closer. She could smell his skin beneath the smoke that clung to his garments. She also smelled the crisp of his cologne. He had drawn her so close until she felt his maleness pressed to her. It caused her to recall being in his office when he'd stepped from the shower.

On the dance floor, Joseph softly crooned with the Maestro. He had been really attempting...to keep his feelings back. He'd done so, for way too long, but if she felt like he did, then they needed to... 'Get It On.'

Wrapping himself around Abigail, Joseph imperceptibly nodded. He was wordlessly thanking Swerv for not playing one slow jam. Not until Joseph had reached the floor with the woman in his arms. For that, the producer was grateful, as slowly Abigail's body conformed to his. Warmly, he palmed the back of her head.

Joseph felt Abigail slip, but he could not know that it was due to legs that had grown weak at his touch. Yet, he gathered Abigail close, and held her tightly. Slowly then, he and she floated in place on the crowded dance floor.

"You know I love you..." the man murmured with a big warm hand on her neck.

With her arms around Joseph, Abigail closed her eyes. She told herself that the swaying couples all around were the reason why she felt dizzy.

However, Abigail knew. She had to stop lying to herself. What she felt was so much more. Therefore, shuddering with a sigh, Abigail allowed herself to relax, even when Joseph pressed her head to his chest.

Why, she wondered, was his heartbeat steady while hers was erratic? Why was he calm while she felt overcome? Abigail felt as though warm Caribbean waves cascaded over her, head and all.

Inhaling, Abigail guessed…she had slipped, and was now drowning, in Joseph.

## 5

HE adjusted his Bambi-brown leather and took Abigail's hand. With long, lean strides, he led her from the decorous and smoke-filled room.

Out of doors, the wind whipped and stung; and to think, while inside, Abigail had nearly forgotten the cold. With her hand in Joseph's and her suede maxi coat flying out behind, she trod double time to keep up.

In Joseph's car that had yet to warm, again, Abigail noted the wee-morning chill. Stealthily it crept between her skin and clothing as she watched Joseph press a button. Lovely, an alto sax's melodic wail filled the car as vigorously Abigail rubbed her cold hands.

Noticing, Joseph took them in his own to warm them. Then all too quickly, he pulled Abigail close. It was silly, but she felt self-conscious, although she had known Joe for years. They had even been intimate on occasion. Still, she stammered when she said she needed to get her car.

Had she bumbled idiotically, Abigail wondered, because she sat in Joseph's sporty coupe, watching him palm the gearshift—a phallic image if she'd ever seen one? Or was it because she throbbed with need? Abigail did not know, but before she could ponder it, Joseph recaptured her attention. Deftly, he unbuttoned her suede coat. Touching his lips to Abigail's, Joseph mumbled about never being able to get enough of her.

Lord, were his hands magic, Abigail thought when Joseph fingered a taught nipple. Still, she reminded herself, she was not to get used to this. Actually, she should not allow any of it. Shenanigans led to...sin.

Not Gram again, Abigail groaned, while Joseph fanned desire's flame. Sensing that Abigail had slowly come to life in his arms, Joseph was reluctant to release her. Following a searing kiss, he put his magnificent machine in gear.

Riding along, Abigail stared from her window. She hoped Joseph could only hear the sexiness of Walter Beasley's sax and not the hammering of her heart. Um, why did it seem too soon for him to be nosing his car behind hers? Why had he taken her keys before he disappeared?

Sliding back into his warm vehicle, Joseph snaked an arm around Abigail. "Figured I'd start it," he divulged, not wanting her to go cold.

Desire-ridden, Abigail averted her eyes. "Joe..." She felt school-girl shy, "If you want, I—I can follow you."

Joseph hoped Abigail didn't feel self-conscious because they were adults, both consenting, so he replied. "I'll trail you, Star." Joseph said so because Abigail was changeable. Should she renege, she would be at home and not out driving around at all hours.

Abigail nodded. "Joezeff, my mind is made up."

"So is mine," he revealed, gathering her close. Pressing his lips to hers, he tapped her hip. "Scoot," he said, "so we can get to it," perhaps.

She reached for her roses and her treats as again Joseph opened his car door, ready to help. "Don't," she told him. "I've got it, this time." About to walk away, she looked back. "You'll keep up, right?"

Lopsidedly, Joseph grinned. His reply was a double entendre as well. "I ain't had problems before, Star..."

OUTSIDE Branford Court, Joseph parked in the visitor's above-ground lot. He eased his long frame into Abigail's passenger seat. "You know, bae," he remarked as they rode the ramp. "This is musical chairs."

"Yep, the only thing is the seats are in different cars."

Abigail stepped on the elevator at P1, the lowest parking level. An older gent inside nodded and attempted to ignore the simmering looks between the young woman and her man. Instead, the gent focused on the woman's spray of flowers. For those hybrid teas, someone had paid handsomely. Glancing at the male wall, the gent thought; indeed, the wall warranted a second look—if he'd purchased those flowers. With Pocketed hands, the older gent wondered how much longer? Then *ping*, the elevator opened. Exiting, the older man felt like a voyeur no more.

When she stood in the attractive paisley-carpeted hallway outside her condominium apartment, Abigail groaned. "Joe with you behind me—"

"Pressing on you and feeling you up," he interjected.

"You're making it hard for me to get my key in the lock."

Joseph nibbled her neck. "If it wasn't hard, Star, it wouldn't go in."

Amused, Abigail inadvertently dropped her keys. "You're so nasty."

"And you, my sweet," Joseph retrieved Abigail's property, "are butterfingers." Nimbly, he inserted Abigail's key and her lock clicked.

"Hey, you're alright at that stick-it business."

"I got a few tricks," Joseph winked. "Some I'll even show you." Following Abigail into the dark, Joseph allowed his sight to adjust. When she reappeared in moon glow, Joseph caught her. "No lights."

Content to relax within the confines of Joseph's strong arms, Abigail sighed. Then she reminded herself, none of this could last.

Having no idea why she went rigid, Joseph peered down. In the moonlight, he saw the shine of tears and asked, "I do something, Star?"

"No," Abigail replied. How could she say that Joseph had caused her to feel again? When previously she'd felt her heart would never thaw.

Concerned, he cupped her face. "Then why the tears?"

Why was he so sweet? Abigail wondered and thought, uh-oh. If she could again feel, wouldn't she also experience pain?

Joseph's voice was barely audible, "Talk to me, Mommy." For once, he wanted to understand what kept her from him all the time.

Abigail tossed her head because never could she say, 'Oh, I realized, tonight, that I want you for my man.' How ridiculous! Joseph might then run off for good. Therefore, Abigail lifted her moonlit face for a kiss.

"Gaye..." Joseph's mouth was against hers, beseeching. "Talk to me," please. He needed to know how to fully win her heart.

Since she truly could not, Abigail vowed to simply enjoy the moment. She started by admonishing Joseph to make love to her.

His heart leaped, and his eyes darted between hers. They narrowed too because why couldn't he read her? Usually, he could, and so easily.

Sensing hesitation, Abigail's heart thudded. What if Joseph turned her down again? With a sigh, Abigail dared ask, "Something wrong?"

"No." Joseph was firm, "I just want this to be what you really want."

Abigail licked lush lips. "You have no idea how much...I want." You, all of you, your heart, and more, she thought but did not say.

Joseph chuckled as his fingertips tripped lightly over Abigail. Her fingers followed Joseph's, playing over him as well.

"There's no zip?" he asked of her dress when he turned her.

With her back to him, Abigail raised both her arms. "It comes up."

"It certainly does," Joseph intoned, pressing his erection to her. With hands on Abigail's hips, he again turned her. Lifting her hem, he revealed curvaceous hips. Joseph ran his hands over them. Reaching Abigail's waist, languorously, he walked his fingers higher, the backs of them keeping her garment off her skin. However, just beneath her breasts, he stopped, and Abigail's breath caught.

Slowly, Joseph's fingers began another sensual creep; and Abigail, who had not been cognizant that she'd inhaled, exhaled as Joseph's fingers crept higher. His warm hands covered her breasts.

Weighing the beautiful bronze globes, Joseph's fingertips traced her nipples. Then filling both hands, Joseph allowed his lips to close over one peak and then the other.

Abigail's breath caught, as cradling Joseph's head, she pushed further into his mouth. Suckling, he squeezed a breast. Aware that he felt ravenous, Joseph slid his hands to Abigail's sides. Pushing her orbs together, he laved first one and then the other. Raising his head, Joseph's mouth met Abigail's. With his tongue, he told her what he intended to do to her. Breathless, Abigail felt she couldn't take another minute of them standing up, the two of their bodies touching but not fitting together as they should. So she told Joseph, "I need you."

"Then undress me," Joseph simply stated while pulling Abigail's garment up and away. Slowly, Abigail removed Joseph's clothing.

"Dang, woman," he moaned because he didn't appreciate her taking her time. He didn't want her walking her fingers down over the sparse hair on his belly. He didn't want Abigail slowly letting her hands descend to his heavy Johnson. However, Joseph wasn't a Neanderthal, so he remained silent until she took him in hand and massaged him.

She dropped to her knees and kissed his throbbing head and the glistening slit. With moistened lips, she teased him with her tongue. Running it around him and kissing a trail downward, she fondled silken skin. When she took his rigidity into her mouth, Joseph lost his breath.

Again licking his tip, Abigail kissed the broad head, then she stood. On tiptoe, she placed her mouth on Joseph's. However, she gave a small startled cry when his long fingers splayed against and opened her. Then one, and two, slipped inside.

Slick, he used them to scintillatingly caress her sensitive, swollen nub. Then Joseph probed, and slid fingers up and into her inviting cavern. His tongue too, in Abigail's mouth, mimicked his fingers below, as sensually, within her he built momentum.

Audibly, Joseph breathed because Abigail was so warm and wet, moving steadily against the hand that pleasured her. All too quickly though, ache and need roared relentless. Therefore, with what little sanity that prevailed, Abigail reached aside. She grasped a small foil packet. As Joseph's hands slid over the half-moons of her bottom, she tore the pack with her teeth. When his fingers scintillatingly raced down her cleft to find her yearning hollow, this time from the rear, Abigail moaned.

"Inside Joe... Now."

Pulling her down to lie on clothing and carpet, Joseph kneed Abigail's thighs apart. Then raising her legs, he lowered his head. Aware that she wanted him to fill her with his staff, he simply had to taste her. How could he not when she lay open, beautiful, and beckoning.

Beneath Joseph's mouth and the hands that pushed the backs of her thighs higher to open her wider, Abigail writhed. Her body arched to more firmly meet Joseph's mouth. And aware that she was as ready as she would ever be, Joseph chuckled and his breath feathered over her.

Then Joseph raised himself. Beneath Abigail, a large hand cupped her bottom as he positioned his throbbing staff. Then he drove deep.

Inside, Joseph took up all the room, filling Abigail, as he had promised. Experiencing the sensation of overflowing, she uttered a choked cry, even as she clutched and desperately desired more.

"You okay, babe?" Joseph asked, stilling the heavy rod within her.

"Ooh," Abigail moved, meeting him. "Yes. Yes —now go!"

Joseph chuckled. Then in, and out, he thrust, making Abigail gasp. Oh! she had nearly forgotten it could be so intense. As Joseph moved, each stroke was different from the last. Dragging fingernails over his flesh, Abigail pulled Joseph closer, needing him to sink totally into her. Greedily, against his neck, she breathed, "Need...more."

"Then take all of it," he told her as, tilting her bottom upward, he drove deeper, slicking and sheathing his thickness to the hilt. With pleasure, Joseph groaned. With every thrust, against his muscular thighs Joseph felt Abigail's buns and her moist warmth that saturated his balls.

Within the confines of Abigail's body, Joseph felt her meet his every move. Ever thinking in musical terms, the producer realized. With her, there was such rhythm, even as she nipped at his shoulder with her teeth.

Finding that she was opening more and again for Joseph, somehow, Abigail's eyes slowly filled, as did her mind. Then she could think of nothing but him, just like he'd predicted.

Subsequently, within Abigail, Joseph felt the change. He felt like he'd been sucked deeper. Attuned to Abigail and cradled within the warm apex of her body, Joseph sensed the metaphysical.

Abigail felt it too. She knew then that her and Joseph's extraordinary copulation had become spiritual. It was no longer just him open-mouth kissing her lush breasts, or her cushiony body absorbing the shock of his thrusts. It wasn't just fingertips and tongues probing heated orifices.

The conjugal had become new and different. It had taken on a life of its own. For both people, inexplicable feelings sprang to life. These were accompanied by a yearning to please. Both experienced the absence of anxiety, replaced by a sweet splendor, a special savoring that caused them to slow things down.

Enveloped in the newness that was as tender as it was intense, Joseph swallowed against his throat's constricting. Then through a bevy of emotions, he ordered, "Look at me, Star." Joseph said it because he needed to see himself in her eyes. He needed to know that *he* was the man, *her* man.

As with his rod, he pushed her higher; Abigail teetered on the precipice of ecstasy, and something she could not name. "Joe, I—"

"Don't fade, bae," he panted. "Stay – with me. A little – further."

Abigail nearly screamed as everything within her began to pull taut. Clutching Joseph, she didn't fight the involuntary shaking of her limbs.

Panting and sensuously stroking Abigail, Joseph was determined. He would edge them closer. "Come," he breathed, "with—me."

"This," Abigail wheezed while locking her legs and arching up, "is madness." Joseph felt the breath leave his lungs, as around his member, Abigail's inner muscles began to cyclically contract. Amidst, she felt like crying for sheer joy, and Joseph, molten and liquid, poured out.

In the ensuing silence, both people were spent. Beneath Joseph, Abigail laid as he attempted to breathe normally. In the stillness, they felt reality creep back. Joseph realized he had tried to reach Abigail's soul, not just on this night but on numerous occasions. He only hoped she wouldn't do her norm and retreat. She had a mental place where she often hid. If Abigail again did that, she wouldn't acknowledge what Joseph knew, that she loved and was loved. It was why Joseph spoke into the darkness. "You're mine, Gaye, and you know I'm yours."

It didn't matter that he received no reply. This Joseph told himself as he rolled off Abigail. Beside her, he relaxed on the plush cream-colored carpet. Then smooth ol' Hal's words from years ago floated back. A man knew his wife. Long before that man stood before God and others, long before the vow or the rings, in his heart, a man knew his woman.

Did a woman know her man, though? Joseph wondered as Abigail stirred beside him. Did a woman know when a man was hers, alone? Because during the thick 'n the hot, it sure seemed like Gaye knew.

Joseph's eyes...Abigail recalled, as she breathed near right again, his eyes, ever expressive, had appeared shockingly more so just before climax. Closing her own eyes, Abigail told herself it was the moonlight. It made everything seem surreal. However, she had seen that same look in Joe's eyes earlier, at the club.

*It's obvious...the man loves you. You love him, too.* Her pesky conscience. Abigail nearly shook her head because love was not an option anymore. For her, trying to get to it hurt too much.

Nevertheless, love, for her, is what Joseph had proclaimed all along. Although she had chosen not to believe, Joseph's eyes had never lied.

Oh God, that was why he'd appeared strange while standing over her at the club. Running a hand down her cheek, Joseph's eyes had spoken volumes. Abigail realized Joseph's eyes had eloquently stated what his mouth had—for nearly seven years. Suddenly, she wanted to weep, because poor man. He had been holding on for so long, for her—and why? She wasn't one of the 'beautiful people.' Neither was she nouveau riche or from old money, as were some in Joseph's social circle. Abigail was a woman born of humble parents. She was a good person, though, one who had done semi-well for herself, but she was not celebrated.

Still, looking back, she could see that Joseph had loved her for so long. He had been with her through her many triumphs and sorrows. Joseph had been solid, Abigail's rock. Sometimes he'd upheld her with quiet strength. Other times he and she engaged in loud, heated debates.

In the moonlight, Abigail shifted to look at the man who had shown her such love.

"Gaye," Joseph called, having noticed her glistening lashes.

"I'm not sad," Abigail quickly announced and reached for Joseph. Dashing away tears, she didn't want him to think he'd hurt her or that she regretted what they had just shared. "I'm fine, Joe. Really."

However, Joseph didn't feel so sure as he took Abigail in his arms.

Placing her arms around him, she laid on his chest. Then resting her arms on Joseph, Abigail spoke. "It was different this time, right?"

"Yes, love." Knowing she could so quickly retreat, Joseph quietly asked, "You okay with that?"

Abigail pressed her face to her splayed fingers. Through them, Joseph felt her breath on his chest as she said, "I am."

As she lay on him, he rubbed her back. "You don't sound like it."

"I am." She was, sort of, despite her quick heartbeat and fresh fear. It sang that now Joseph would leave, for good, when the novelty of sticking her wore off.

"Star?" Joseph called because he could feel her thinking, retreating.

"Joe, I'm scared." The truth tumbled out. "I'm happy too," Abigail added. "I want you to know that, but I'm terrified. Of us, you know?"

"I know." The big man sighed and hugged his little star tighter. Really, he didn't want her feeling like he often felt concerning her. However, Joseph told himself to be grateful that they'd made progress. Lil honey hadn't curled into a ball after realizing they'd shattered some barrier together. She had even said some of what was in her heart. Still, she was afraid. That was okay, Joseph guessed because when it came to Abigail, sometimes he felt fear too. He felt the fear of not being good enough and the fear of her never actually wanting him enough. None of it was pleasant or induced calm. Regardless, Joseph said, "Everything will be okay, Star." He had to believe that. And silently Joseph prayed that his baby would believe, too...

SOME time later, Joseph woke and wondered if he was a pig for wanting Abigail again. As he caressed her apple-round behind, she stretched and said she had something to tell him.

Could it be? Nah, Joseph shook his head because it was too soon. Gaye would not have the words for him yet. Although they had skirted a few hurdles in the lunar-lit dark, but her saying she loved him was one hurdle more than Abigail could manage right now. Although, Joseph recalled, his honed skillz had caused others to say all sorts of things.

Forgetting others, Joseph stretched. "Tell me your something, Gaye."

"Look at my hip." She turned so he could see it.

Joseph reached out, concerned. "Looks like a bruise is forming."

"It's from being down here on the floor."

Joseph admitted he hoped he hadn't banged her up that badly.

Abigail pushed at him. "Hush, with your play on words."

Joseph kissed her. "I'm serious, Star."

Nestled between his thighs, Abigail took Joseph's face in her hands. With her mouth sweet on his, she felt him press his raging hard-on to her.

Moments later, Joseph called out, "Hey—where you going?"

Abigail turned back. She looked down at him while rubbing an ample hip. "I've had enough of this on-the-floor stuff."

"Come back, sweetness," he cajoled. "We're not finished."

Abigail turned and saw the telltale vein as Joseph lay amid their rumpled clothing. Yep, he was sexy as all get out, but her bed called too.

Joseph attempted to sound suave. "Big dawg got something fuh ya..."

Pitching forward, Abigail burst out laughing, and for Joseph, smooth elderly Hal's words rang out. 'If you can't get a gal to laugh...'

Chuckling, Abigail headed away, and Joseph scrambled up after her.

In her barely moonlit boudoir, everything hid in shadow as she crawled onto her comfortable bed. Nestled beneath the covers, she thought, boy, would she rest well tonight! Abigail also hoped Joseph would hurry, so she could give him some before she drifted off. He could snuggle up behind her, and she would raise her thigh, thus allowing him to slip into her warmth. Then with his wand, he could 'rock' her to sleep.

Unaware of Abigail's sensual desire, Joseph's voice rumbled like barely controlled thunder. "Babe, what's up?"

"I need sleep," that's what was up. "Come," she murmured, lazily brushing aside a book on art. Sleepily, Abigail flung back the comforter. She crooked a finger, needing Joseph behind her. She'd love it when he nudged his thick rod past her engorged walls. She wanted his arms and body heat surrounding her while his hands splayed over her breasts.

Joseph's eyes caressed what he thought of as Abigail's beckoning bottom. Again, he was reminded that a woman's 'onion' could bring a man to tears. When, of course, it seemed there would be no partaking.

Abigail's eyelids drifted shut, and Joseph could only wonder, was she kidding? She had seen Big Boy, so he called out, "Star."

"Hmmm?" Sleepily, Abigail patted where Joseph should have been.

Liking the new turn of events, stealthily, he crept forward.

Abigail screamed when playfully Joseph picked her up. It was cold without the cover.

"Don't fight," he murmured and turned to hold her against the wall.

Abigail woke up altogether. She pushed at Joseph. Frantically, she shoved his head and torso. Abigail hit Joseph in the face and screamed as though she didn't know him. "No, no," she grunted as doggedly she fought. "No...not like this," she whimpered. "Please."

Oh, shit! Quickly, Joseph allowed Abigail to slide downward and into his cradling arms. "Gaye, Baybeee..." He tried, unsuccessfully, to calm her. Dumbfounded, Joseph noted Abigail's stricken look. She was literally frightened, and it hit him. She had been *forced*, before!

Oh, no. The knowledge stole Joseph's breath. "Gaye, I'm sorry."

For her, it was vivid all over again. The merciless backhand slap that had split her lip just before she'd been called dirty and a whore.

Lord, what had he done? Joseph wondered as his heart beat too fast while tears spilled from Abigail's eyes. Again, he whispered an apology. "Star, you gotta believe me," Joseph pled, filled with anguish, "I'm sorry." Hesitantly, he offered a large hand, hoping she wouldn't take the gesture the wrong way, and begin to fight again.

Trembling, Abigail allowed Joseph to rub her back. As he did, she hunched into a fetal ball with her eyes closed.

"Gaye, precious," Joseph whispered with his throat all-out aching. "I would never hurt you. You gotta believe that." He smoothed Abigail's hair. "I wouldn't hurt you for all the world." And never again, if he could help it, would anyone else do so.

Abigail's breathing slowed somewhat, and Joseph realized it must have been awful, whatever she had been through. Therefore, he apologized for what had been done to her.

Abigail's voice was small when she spoke. She said she knew who Joseph was. Although to him it probably sounded strange, Abigail had to remind herself that he was Joseph. He wasn't the monster that had angrily raised fists to her face. Abigail told Joseph he was not the man who had repeatedly punched her in the stomach.

As he listened, horrified, Abigail told Joseph he wasn't the man who had bruised her ribs and tilted her spleen. He wasn't the fellow college student who'd forced himself on her while she'd struggled and fought while saying she actually meant no. Joseph wasn't the scornful, foreign, pompous, oil-rich ass that she'd had to face in court, after pressing charges, despite her so-called friends, Asian, black, white, Pakistani, and Latina, who had refused to come forth with truths of their own.

Aloud, Abigail recited the tragedy for Joseph's benefit. She had been young, without anyone to tell really, no one other than Gram. Abigail had sometimes called the West Indies. At first, Abigail had been alone, but she'd had to let her attacker know. It was not okay to take what had not been given. Neither was it okay to overpower, just because it was possible. Abigail had just had to say, emphatically, that it had not been her fault. She didn't care that her assailant's attorney had tried to make that the case. Abigail said she hadn't asked to be assaulted or defiled! She had said no, which was a woman's right. It was any person's right.

Abigail mentioned the rape kit – the forensic exam for preserving DNA/physical evidence. She'd learned it was standard procedure in a sexual assault allegation. She spoke of trained medical personnel, a sympathetic woman who'd lessened the humiliation of it all, including the photos that had to be taken for legal documentation. Despite all of it, Abigail stated, sounding hollow, she'd pressed on and stated her case.

A violet-eyed fellow student had responded to counsel. "She's not lying, you know." Violet had been followed by another, and another...

Forgetting all those who had finally found the strength to speak their truth, Abigail recalled that she was safe, now. In a detached voice, she told Joseph that she would again forget the harrowing trial, even though for her the outcome had been favorable. Instead, Abigail said, she would choose to see the man offering comfort. He was her friend, her lover, and not a different man. Abigail divulged that Joseph wasn't The Ex. Darré had attempted to shake and slap her whenever he didn't get his way.

As Abigail remembered that Joseph was strong yet protective, she could almost stop shaking. Through chattering teeth, she told Joseph the rest. She would again close the door on the monster that stalked her in her dreams. And, Abigail revealed, she would again pray for peaceful sleep—without pharmaceutical aid.

Asking to pull Abigail on his lap, Joseph sat on the side of her bed. Feeling anguish and anger, he wondered aloud, "Why didn't I know?"

Abigail battled tears, as she admitted, "I kept quiet because it all happened before we met, back when I was in college. I found out, too late, that that's the time when many young women are assaulted, but a lot don't speak up, for various reasons."

For that very reason, Abigail had started a mentorship for girls and young women. She wanted them to know they had options –in every area of life.

Staring at the wall, she whispered. "I almost thought I was over it..."

"Oh, little Star," Joseph knowingly winced, "some things we never truly get over." Gingerly, he kissed Abigail's forehead. Joseph's lips lingered lovingly then, protectively, like her father's had when she'd been a small girl.

Abigail felt enveloped in love and no longer as afraid.

With his massive arms around her, Joseph admonished Abigail to lie back. He said they would sleep, nothing more, and nothing less. Tenderly, he pulled the cover up and around them.

Joseph held Abigail close while hoping her trembling would soon subside. He hoped too that after this, neither of them would want to part, ever again.

# 6

THE gray light of dawn filtered through the sheer ecru panels. It caressed Abigail's eyelids. With lashes fluttering, she sighed. It was bliss to wake in Joseph's arms. However, she did not disturb him.

Still, he opened an eye. "Morning, Star."

"Morning, yu." She held his chin. "You workin' today?"

Wearily, Joseph sighed, and his eyes roamed the room that he thought of as cozy. It was like a page ripped from a designer magazine. The mango accent wall, the subdued Gamboa and Earl Jackson paintings, the extravagant down comforter that had slipped off the queen size bed; Joseph relished it all. Again, his gaze fell on Abigail because she awaited his reply. "Gaye, I work every day," well nearly. "You know that."

"Mi know money haffie mek," Abigail stated, aware that Joseph had to make money. Yet her voice was wistful, "But yu not wurkin' every day because you have to…"

She was right, and Nancy Wilson's voice sang in his head. You'd be so nice by the fire … all that I would desire… "But, Star," Joseph paraphrased the song's title, "I don't have you 'To Come Home To.'"

The phone rang while Abigail marveled at the man's ability to speed her heart rate. On that side of the bed, Joseph lifted the ringing phone.

Accepting the receiver, Abigail mouthed, 'Thanks.' "Hello?" She said and listened. Then she announced, "It's early, Saturday," the only day she slept in. "Okay," she acquiesced, "accepted." She opened her mouth and closed it. She cut in, "My whereabouts are no longer your concern." She sighed and asked, "What?" Then she said, "Listen, will you?"

*Why you being upset early in the frigging morning?* Abigail ignored her conscience and stared at her knees, outlined beneath the super-soft sheet. "Don't shout mi down! I agreed. Why yu eatin' mi head off?" She folded her arms. "It's not joyous." Abigail sucked her teeth. "I hafta go."

She slammed the receiver down and called for Joseph.

His response was muffled, coming through the bathroom door. He was angry. Manically drying his hands had forced him to take notice.

He wondered, what was he going to do? Heck, what could he do?

Wearily, he went to sit at the foot of Abigail's bed. He stared away, knowing she watched him. With arms folded across the sheet wrapped around her torso, Abigail knew. Joseph went out of his way to calibrate the muscles in his back. She wondered if he was okay but didn't ask.

"Well," Joseph sighed, "looks like I'd better bounce."

Abigail watched him stand. Moments ago, they'd been lying skin to skin, about to discuss the day, or so she'd thought. Now Joe was leaving.

"Where are you going?" Abigail near-whined.

"Gotta work." Joseph slipped on a hardcover. "Your books need to be on shelves!" he scolded.

Ohhh-kay. Abigail bit her lip. So she and he were on that page, huh? Joseph was leaving because he was angry. About what? Abigail didn't know. She did know though, that Joe didn't have to work until evening. And he knew she attempted to keep books off the floor because she'd told him. Abigail watched Joseph shrug into his clothing. She knew his nonchalance was feigned even as he said he'd shower at home.

Abigail gnawed her lower lip. She really hated the fake eff-it attitude Joseph displayed when he tried to hide anger. Within Abigail, emotion wildly churned, but she refused to give vent. She wouldn't invite trouble.

Joseph looked over a shoulder. "Yo, I might shout-out, later."

Abigail's eyes narrowed. He'd said it like she was one of his boyz. Look at me! She wanted to yell. I am not a brotha that you give dap, at The Garden, minutes before a game –so don't treat me like one.

Breathing deeply, however, Abigail vowed not to let Joseph get to her. She would simply play his game. Outwardly, she would remain calm while inside; that was another story. Oh, forget it. She'd ask her question, after all. "Joe, what's this shout-out stuff, and what does 'might' mean?"

His voice became uncharacteristically soft. "What do you want me to say? I said I might call." Joseph sounded angry, "If time permits."

Abigail's eyes narrowed, and she wondered, why had she opened herself to him last night? Heck, the moment a woman felt something for a man, then he had—and used—that propensity to hurt her.

Joseph glanced back, and Abigail loathed the sting of their silly exchange. "Yo, I'm not pushin' up on you," he gruffly reminded her. "And I've said it before. I ain't that brotha who'll sweat you." Yet Joseph felt he had been doing just that, for far too long. Oh well, now she would have to advance on him, because he was done. No more chasing her.

Again, Joseph turned, this time to button his shirt, and Abigail could have slapped him. *Acting stupid, over a friggin' phone call.*

"Yo, you got your life, Gaye," Joseph reminded her while adjusting his shirt cuffs. "You're doing you, and I'm doing me." As a matter of fact, sometimes he had too much going on. However, he recalled, it was all nothing. If he couldn't share it with this one woman.

Forgetting that, Joseph focused on his anger because Gaye had no right to keep him in turmoil. Heck, he was an eligible bachelor for crying out loud! Ebony Magazine had dubbed him so. He was one of The Most Beautiful, so said another magazine.

Better forget the hype, his conscience scoffed, because if the glossy prose were true, why did he have the devil's time with this one woman?

Other willing women came to mind. However, adjusting his slacks, Joseph forgot others because he wanted stubborn Abigail, exclusively.

Seated, she worried her lip. She recalled that she had simply wanted to spend more time with Joseph. Perhaps they could have even wound up making love. That had been before all of this, and after what?

The stupid ringing phone! That was it —*Darré, again.*

"We really need to talk," Joseph said and sounded worn. He pulled his jacket from the back of a frou-frou fabric-covered chair. "I need something from you Star, but not like this." Then more to himself, Joseph muttered, "I don't need anything, from anybody, if it's like this."

Abigail's eyes widened as he stalked from her bedroom. Tossing the covers back, she clamored after him, but her foot got tangled in the sheet.

"Joe!" Darn it, he couldn't leave before she got to him. "Don't go!"

On bare feet, quickly, she sprinted down the hall while wondering. Why did she feel let down? She had done nothing wrong.

At her kitchen door, Abigail blurted, "I wanted us to do a few things."

Joseph faced her, his fire-angry eyes roaming her body before he caught himself. He gazed from Abigail's breasts to a place beyond her.

She noted her nudity and mentally shrugged. She hadn't had time to grab a robe. Joseph had seen it all before anyway, so she wasn't about to start worrying. Abigail stepped into her kitchen. "Joe, let's not be upset."

Swiftly, she was drawn against his hard male body, and lovingly she wrapped him in her arms. Abigail rubbed Joseph's back. Internally, she acknowledged that the phone call had changed both their demeanor.

"That was Clankston," Joseph spewed, clasping her tightly. "Right?"

Barely able to breathe, Abigail couldn't recall the last time she'd seen Joseph as upset or as intriguing. It made her want, right then.

Unaware, all Joseph could think was Gay's stupid clown really had radar. That jackal's extrasensory perception had him calling or turning up every time somebody else made headway—and Joseph was sick of it!

Abigail sensually ran her tongue along the edge of Joseph's ear, but he didn't allow himself to shiver. Therefore, she pressed her lips to the stubble on his jaw. Her voice was sand-papery and sultry. "Know what?"

"What?"

"Big bwoy kinda sexy when 'im upset."

"Yeah? Well..." Joseph groped for words as he cupped Abigail's conniving bottom. "You're too damn sexy, all the time." And using that titillating JaMerican voice? She knew he couldn't resist it.

Feeling the cold, Abigail looked down and saw that Joseph had set her on her granite countertop. Well, she thought, she might as well encircle him with her legs, as slowly she unzipped his pants.

When his rod sprang free, her nipples pearled. Anticipating becoming the recipient of Joseph's engorged member, Abigail scooted forward. With widened thighs and an open sheath, she arched her back. Pressing forward to receive the thick inserted stick, she recalled. This, the sweetness, the sensual give, and take, she had almost let her ex ruin.

Frantically, Abigail and Joseph tangoed, their mouths fusing, their bodies meeting. With hands holding her head, Joseph kissed Abigail. Their lips were noisy, as their pelvises made sounds as well. Joseph dipped to devour a bronze breast before he slammed into Abigail, his weight jolting her. She received him. Grasping Joseph's buttocks, she squeezed, refusing to let go or to let him back too far out of her. She yearned and squirmed. He thrust and sucked, and the sheer sensation of not being able to get enough coursed through both people. Joseph bit at Abigail's plump perspiring breast, and loving the fine mist, the sheen on him, she ran a hand over him while opening more and again for him, body and soul.

With probing fingers and firm hands, Joseph held Abigail steady while he pumped her to delirium. Clasping him, she pressed her breasts to him, for just a moment. Oh, it was good! She thought, eliciting a gasp from him. Locking her legs at Joseph's nude waist, Abigail stifled a scream as avariciously; she pressed forward for more of his stiff rod.

Moments later, Joseph stiffened. He rested his perspiring forehead against Abigail's as yet her breasts trembled from all of the delectable bumping about. When he could again think, Joseph told himself he could not keep allowing Gaye to reduce him to all hormones, and never again when he was displeased.

Although the truth was… he wasn't upset with her, but more so with the situation—and her clown. Therefore, Joseph vowed to mention it, when he caught his breath.

Abigail took Joseph's face in her hands. Gently, she kissed him, his lips, his eyelids, his cheeks, and his nose –but she was not falling in love.

*Call it what you want, coward. It's all the same thing.*

"Star, look," Joseph just had to say before she sidetracked him with her sweet assault. "If bozo is out of the picture, make sure he knows it."

Abigail's hands fell to Joseph's broad chest. Why did he want to ruin the good time they were having by mentioning Darré, who was no more?

"I know I ain't your man and all..." Joseph hid a sardonic grin because he'd had to throw that in, "but, as your 'friend' with fringe benefits, I'm telling you, with that clown, let bygones be bygones."

"Look," Abigail began as Joseph helped her off the now slippery countertop. "He called, period. He means nothing to me."

Yeah, right. Wryly, Joseph's mouth twisted, and suddenly everything he had not previously said tumbled from him. Afterward, he grumbled.

"Look at this shit. You got me up in here whining like a little girl."

Abigail chuckled. Then she spoke. "In defense of young sisters, I have to remind you. All little girls are not whiners."

Joseph agreed. "Then let's just say you've got me carping, like Lo."

Abigail sputtered with mirth. "No poking fun at Kilo, either."

"Later for him," Joseph growled. His engineer didn't need anyone's sympathy. Connor Ostrowsky didn't have the misfortune of being locked in a dead-end relationship with a woman who remained emotionally beyond reach. Kilo didn't belong, body and soul, to said woman.

Resuming the previous topic, Joseph said sometimes it seemed as though Abigail and Darré still had ties. "—Even though you say no."

Joseph's palpable aggravation had Abigail gnawing her lip. She wished, once more, that she had never met Darré or his now-deceased mother. He'd claimed he was calling for her when he'd caused trouble.

*Focus on the man in front of you.*

Quickly, Abigail looked up and into Joseph's eyes. She registered the torment and the longing. Even before he sincerely asked, "Gaye, when will all that you and I have been through, together, stand for something?"

Shushing Joseph, Abigail took him in her arms. Rubbing his back, she told him she loved him because, really, it was about time.

Joseph's body went rigid, and she wondered what was wrong, now. The man backed up. "You said that like I should get over you."

Feeling doused with ice water, Abigail argued, "I did not." Perhaps though, she thought, hurt, that had not been the best way to tell him.

Joseph turned and pulled his shirt from the kitchen table where it had been tossed. He wondered if he looked like he needed placating. He felt that had been low, the way Gaye had casually tossed out the very words that he'd longed to hear, just to shut him up, about the clown.

Well, he would hurriedly get out of her home, and he would...what? Joseph did not know. Angst lodged in his throat, and he couldn't think, so he would leave, but his heart would remain, damn it!

Joseph snatched up his pants. He'd think later, when the pain subsided. But could the clown be whom she really wanted? Joseph wondered. Then he mused, perhaps he'd been wrong about Gaye. Maybe she wasn't different from others. Some stayed with men who treated them unkindly. Perhaps she was the same, or maybe he'd been misled. He had previously believed she didn't need drama, but that was what kept cropping up with her, but truthfully, from one source. The clown.

Zipping his pants, Joseph grabbed leather. With crazily spiraling, emotions he realized Gaye knew she had him open. Thus, the problem. With her beckoning booty, glossy hair, beautiful skin, and high cheekbones, her sexy behind could have nearly any man she wanted. She was intelligent. She made caboodles of money, so maybe she just wasn't into the old-fashioned thing, like he was. Joseph couldn't recall her ever mentioning the desire to be married or have kids, come to think of it. Shit! Joseph thought, he had to get unwrapped from around her little finger! Then maybe, Abigail might want him like he wanted her.

Tear-filled, Abigail's eyes roamed Joseph's back as she wondered how to fix things. Oh! She should have kept to herself that she loved him. Now she was doomed. He would soon realize he wasn't in love with her, then he would move on. But she couldn't let that happen!

For Joseph, Abigail's silence was unbearable, and it spoke volumes. He completed dressing as he cogitated that perhaps she really didn't care.

Watching Joseph, Abigail searched the recesses of her mind for just the right words. A great speech might turn all this wrong around.

Perfunctorily, Joseph kissed the tip of Abigail's nose.

To both people, it felt like good-bye.

Abigail grabbed Joseph's hand with the innate female knowledge that she could make him stay for a while longer.

Gently, Joseph extricated his hand under the pretense of moving a chair to make sure he forgot nothing.

So what, he didn't feel great; he glanced down at sweet-sweet; still, he could be proud of one thing. He had finally said his piece. For the first time since knowing her and loving her, Joseph had not thought about the needs of someone else versus his own. The one thing he should have told Ms. Elusive, though, was that she needed to decide, and soon. Or he would have to bounce, for sho, because he couldn't go on this way, loving her, but not being loved.

Joseph didn't say anything because he guessed it was pretty obvious now. Therefore, he hoped lil precious would come to her senses. Then if he could forgive, they could forget and become a couple. If not...

Abigail blinked back tears while feeling strange. She was sick and sad. She probably felt like many other women with whom Joseph had carelessly frolicked. She wondered if they, too, had lost their hearts to him. Closing her eyes as he quietly left her home, Abigail became cognizant of one thing. Joseph was the man she had been born to love.

Abigail involuntarily shivered. Now she understood what her yet living grandmother had meant all those times. On occasion, Gram had said she felt as though someone had tiptoed over... her grave.

## 7

NEARLY two weeks later, Abigail sat in her office. She was astonished that she hadn't heard from Joseph. She'd called his cell, his Long Island home, his historic Harlem duplex, and the studio, to no avail. She'd even dialed his friend Lyon's home, but when a woman answered, unable to tell a total stranger her dilemma, Abigail hung up.

For the same reason, she fell short of calling Miz Maddie. Abigail didn't need to announce—to Joe's mother—that things had gone awry.

Although as her son's confidant, Miz Maddie probably already knew.

However, what if Joseph was hurt? Or left for dead somewhere?

*Quit being pessimistic.* Well, even if he wasn't, Abigail wanted to know. Didn't all that she and he had been through, together, afford her that much, at least?

She downloaded a file. Abigail bit her lip too and prayed again for the man. The one she actually acknowledged that she loved.

Unwrapping a ream of paper, Abigail also vowed when she finally heard from Joe, she would rip him a new one! He deserved it, worrying her. Sure, he might tell her to piss off, but she would know he was okay.

*Please, girl, you would be devastated.* Abigail dismissed her conscience. If Joe spurned her, she would deal with it. It was what she did. She dealt with things –like that little fiasco on the cold day that Mrs. Dottie-Mae Clankston had been eulogized...

ABIGAIL had only wanted Darré to quit hounding her. Outside the church, she had been headed for her car.

"You should stop by, after the interim," The Ex had said, again, about some dinner thingy to be held at his mother's house.

Please, Abigail thought. She was going home. She had only shown up to keep her promise, and to pay her last respects. Subsequently, she'd found the church stifling hot, and the scent of all those flowers had sickened her: that and the mix' n mash of too many perfumes, colognes, and hair gels.

Outside, Abigail had breathed deeply. She hadn't cared that the chill fall wind had stung her nostrils as pebbles crunched underfoot.

Oh no, another Clankston stepped in her path. Where'd they keep coming from? Regarding her and Darré, why didn't they keep their tiresome inquiries/suggestions to themselves? The man was *married* to someone else!

'You know Miss Abigail,' one Clankston had nervily said, 'I hear oysters will put the magic back in a dying relationship.'

Hello-oh! Abigail had smiled sweetly as her inner lady sang out, *you people are in serious denial*. Forgetting that, Abigail hurried on, with her car in sight. However, she nearly screamed when the next cousin attempted to draw her aside. Then Darré's Uncle Willie appeared, saying, "Thank you for reading my sister's words with such feeling. Rubenstein and I know Dot was there, in spirit, as you read them."

The smooth-shaven man mentioned his nephew's new wife, and Abigail smiled, despite the desire to be out. When Darré's Uncle leaned closer, the clean scent of Bay Rum rose. "Really, Miss Gaye," Uncle Willie sadly smiled. "That girl is nothing like you." The older man shrugged, defeated, "but then, she's not you."

Abigail had always thought the man, her father's age, was sweet. However, she was mortified when others were drawn toward them.

These Clankstons said things like, "This'n here new wife of Darré's is kind of silly." "Oh you noticed too?" "Yes, honey, she is brash."

A blue-haired woman nodded. "The child is truly...unpolished."

A spinster in gold lamé waved. "That one is too damn loud." "You know," a woman squinting at smoke from her slim brown cigarette offered, "Dottie did not approve."

"Maybe," Darré's Aunt Rubie sighed, "this, coupled with the cancer, is what sent my dear sister on."

People also said Darré's 'girl' "Does not take care of that baby." "Not willing to work, she just lays up." "Yeah, but I bet she'll cash them county checks," someone harrumphed. "Like Dottie-Mae's boy is Rockefeller." Then a ghastly thin, windblown man raised a skeletal hand. "All I wanna know is where in tarnation did Darré get this one?"

This one? Raising an eyebrow, Abigail knew. The Clankstons had likely had fried her the same way while she'd been involved with Darré. They had probably dubbed her uppity, bougie, and all else.

*But they're talking about the skank wearing your ring.* Abigail did not care. She had never liked hearing people malign others, so she turned, telling Darré's Aunt Rubie she was leaving.

The woman clutched her long-dead shoulder wrap. "So soon, baby?"

Abigail nodded and informed Uncle Willie.

"Well, lambkin..." Aunt Rubie clucked while her lifeless furry wrap stared unseeing at Abigail, "Don't be a stranger."

At last! Abigail forced herself not to gallop away, but she heard footsteps. Glancing back, she said, again, "No, Dar-RAY." She avoided his touch. "I'm not stopping by your mother's house."

Opening her car door, Abigail threw her purse to the passenger seat. From her peripheral, she noticed the infamous child bride. Hopefully, Abigail thought, the little Mrs. would cart her pesky husband away, so Abigail could vamoose.

The eighteen-year-old stepped past her husband. Placing hands on non-hips, she addressed Abigail, beginning a litany of 'thangs' that bothered her. "Numba one," wifey pontificated, "Darré is my man," so Abigail "ha' betta reca-nize. And numba two..." Intending to pique the curiosity of those about to drive to the cemetery, NaPammitha raised her brittle streety voice. "You gotta face shit, my boo chose me over you."

Feeling harsh autumn winds, despite the glaring sun, Abigail stared, amazed. Had she really been ordered not to call 'that house' again? And when had the skanky child-bride heard Abigail's voice on the phone?

"Oh, a-nuva thang," NaPammitha cautioned, "If Pammi catch you on her property, which includes her huzzbin, she'll beat yo' old ass down."

Abigail's eyebrow rose. First of all, why was the child speaking of herself in the third person? And old? "Oh, you hardcore, thinking you want some of me." Abigail told the street urchin, "Don't let this healthy hair 'n these designer shoes fool you. I'll beat your raggedy lil behind."

Smacking on neon green gum, NaPammitha cockily dismissed the threat simply because she had youth on her side.

Shedding her coat, Abigail told herself that she should have walked with petroleum jelly. Then she could have greased up before lighting into the little loudmouth before her... In the posh Manhattan office building where she worked, Abigail barely recalled what happened next. She believed Darré had said something stupid, as usual.

Abigail retrieved her stack of printed sheets. That had been the last straw, Darré's attempt to keep Pammi believing a lie.

Heck, when would she, busy Abigail, have time to harass Darré's new wife? And breathing into a phone? Abigail would never, not outside of phone sex. With her schedule and her nice nails? Abigail would never personally slash tires or brick a windshield. She wouldn't tack up notes in the hood either, about a soon-to-be dismembered wife and a cooked kid —all that ol' Fatal Attraction mess. Abigail worked! And she had experienced the very same foolishness—at the hands of Darré's other woman, Crazy Sheila. Therefore, it was safe to assume he was still romping with that nut.

Walking the hallway back to her office, Abigail chuckled upon remembering Uncle Willie's call. On the evening following that of his sister's funeral, the male gem had unwittingly helped Abigail piece things together, namely why her hand was so sore. Older Willie said there'd been a collision involving Abigail's fist and his nephew's mouth.

"Yo, you hit me!" Darré managed, stunned, as searching fingertips sought the red that oozed from his lip.

During the phone call, Uncle Willie had also mimicked NaPammitha who'd squealed when caught off guard. "Gittt offa me-ee."

"I don't know what you said when you snatched her up," Uncle Willie soberly stated. "I only know you were in that gal's face and she was fearfully wide-eyed. Now, I'll guarantee one thing, she 'n my nephew will think, before they jump bad with the next person. Oh, and," the elder gent added with admiration, "your letting things go was nice."

"I don't think I meant to," Abigail admitted. Vaguely she recalled Darré's child bride staggering away. "Maybe my soft spot for wayward girls kicked in." In her office, Abigail bound her downloaded guide sheets and remembered. Outside the church, Aunt Rubie had fussed over Darré's cut lip and his bruised pride. Abigail recalled seeing the pair when she made that broken u-turn. Snidely, Abigail had waved while thinking. Had the Clankstons all been where they belonged, seated in the limousine behind the hearse, there would have been no ruckus.

What a fiasco! Abigail sighed and realized again that Darré—and now Pammi—were her tests. In life, everybody had them. The only thing was where The Ex was concerned, Abigail was failing.

"Father, I need your help," she prayed. She recalled something more. People often said life was one thing after another. Really though, it was the same thing, repeatedly, until a person got it right.

Therefore, Abigail wanted to get this right, so she would never again suffer an achy bruised hand because she'd The Ex in the mouth.

Abigail filed a document that Sunny would have filed had Sunny not been away due to a family emergency. Sure, Abigail had temporary help.

However, the young woman did not follow instructions. Forgetting her new non-assistant, Abigail recalled that she would suffer through unbearable heat later in the evening. At home, maintenance had ordered a part that had not yet arrived. And in her car, there was clicking each time she turned. Her CV boots or joints most likely needed replacing, but who had time? The deadline for Abigail's latest proposal loomed, too. Oh, and she'd nearly forgotten. Her younger sister and baby sis's toddler were coming. Abigail knew she was crazy for having agreed to let that pair stay with her. Still, she'd handle all things with the help of the Lord.

Nevertheless, the Joseph situation loomed! Argggh. Abigail just wanted to know he was okay!

In her quiet office, now in disarray, Abigail's private line shrilled. Reaching for it, she hoped it was Joe—or Sunshine. Maybe he would be jovial, or her assistant would say, 'Gaye, I'm back and on my way in.'

"Mona." Abigail frowned. "I don't know what time I can leave." Abigail had no desire to look at lingerie, "I'm not feeling well."

"Well, who would?" Mona Lisa scoffed. "You're doing two jobs; yours and Sunshine's. Really, you should lose that temp; get you another one, but remember, incompetence is a pre-requisite for all of 'em."

Following a chuckle, Abigail said it wasn't so.

Actually, to Mona Lisa, Abigail did not sound like her usual chipper self. Therefore, Mona Lisa exhibited concern the only way she knew how, by using sarcasm. Mona Lisa asked if her friend was sick, for real.

Although she had never voiced it, Mona Lisa truly cared for Abigail, who never complained of illness. Abigail often boasted about her dual heritage, citing her parentage as the reason she 'neva got sick.' Her speech was old and tired, about the Jamaican Papa who'd taught his girls to eat 'soil stuff' –fruit and vegetables. And who could forget Abigail's 'Mama Nightingale,' the nurse from the Lord? Woo-wee.

Dismissing Abigail's fam, Mona Lisa badgered her friend. "Gaye, you just need soup, then you'll be okay. You know, there'll probably be some at Cassanka's gran'muhva's house. She's catering tonight."

That settled it. Abigail would not opt for ptomaine poisoning. "Look, Mo," Abigail advised, "call me tomorrow. Tell me all about it."

"No," Mona Lisa persisted. "You're going, G! I'm the fun coordinator, and you need fun 'fore your sister gets here with that baby."

Abigail wondered aloud how she'd let herself get talked into the visit.

Mona Lisa gave herself an A for being astutely conniving. "Look," she huffed, intent on getting her way. "Just tell Pat," the forty-one-year-old, "To take lil sis-n-the brat in. That's the big sister's job."

"I can't do that, Mo."

"It's the only way they'll quit bothering you," Mona Lisa huffed. She also wondered, why were they discussing Gaye's fam? They really needed to decide where to meet before the lingerie party in a few hours.

"I gave my sisters my word, Mo."

"Your word? Please." Mona Lisa scoffed. "That means nothing—to most people nowadays. Besides, 'family' will always use 'n abuse you."

Oh no, Abigail ruminated. She had work to do and a misguided temp to instruct; she had no time for Mona's bone of contention. Her family.

"Bless her, Lord," Abigail breathed because Mona Lisa could constantly moan about her nearly non-existent family. It was sad. Her mother had been a drug addict who'd 'lent out' her daughters' bodies to supply her habit, before her dealer killed her. Then the father, a drunk, had repeatedly raped Mona and her sister Carla. Younger, Carla had attempted an abortion with a wire hanger. Afterward, Mona's sister had never again been quite right. Sadly, Abigail recalled, the saga had not ended there. Mona Lisa's brother, Montego, had taken his own life...

With vacant eyes, the heavier woman had dropped onto Abigail's cream-colored sofa. "Why should I feel bad?" Mona Lisa had asked as betraying tears fell from her eyes. "Monte was a sick fag. He ate his gun. Now, he don't have to suffer no more or desperately look for love."

"Mo," Abigail called amid angry words. "I'll speak to my sisters."

"Yeah, do that," Mona Lisa huffed, aware that those two witches felt disdain for her, although she didn't care. Suddenly, Mona Lisa remembered being little and rag-tag. Kids had called her dirty. Then in high school, she'd been called fast, a ho, and a trick, but she had only wanted someone to care. Not finding that, Mona Lisa had dropped out. Subsequently, she'd realized that sweeping up sawdust or flattening meatpacker boxes would never do, so she'd gotten her GED.

Then Mona Lisa had happened upon the one person that she had been searching for, her whole life. Abigail. As a clerk in the office of records, Mona Lisa had known it from moment one. The knowledge was cemented when before leaving that office, Abigail had suggested meeting for lunch. Amazingly, the two women had, and to Mona Lisa it was clear, Abigail understood. No one chose the parents or the circumstances to which they were born. That was when Mona Lisa fell in love.

However, Abigail had two sisters, Beavis' n Butthead, who thought they were better than Mona Lisa...

"Look Mo," Abigail sighed, attempting to find neutral water. "I'm super-busy today. Besides, for me, tonight is not a looking-at-lingerie kind of night. So go without me. Have fun, and call me tomorrow."

"G, you promised." Mona Lisa sounded let-down. "Look," she proposed, "go with me for just half an hour, okay? That's all."

"No, picture girl," Abigail remained firm, "I cannot."

"I'm pissed, and quit calling me that," Mona Lisa griped, "because if I had been Da Vinci's model, I'd be paid! Then I wouldn't have to beg for company—although you've known about this for weeks."

"Yu' bowt to get mi heat up," Abigail voiced, despising pushiness.

"Yo, I'm not the one you're really mad at," Mona Lisa snidely sing-sang because Gaye had used her JaMerican voice. "Tell the truth, G. Your problem is Forrester. He hasn't called." Ha.

Abigail hated that Mona Lisa was right. "You could be sympathetic."

"Why?" Mona Lisa quipped, "Plenty of other fish in the sea."

Abigail ignored the jibe because she needed to express, to someone, how unlike Joseph it was, to not call.

"Personally, I think you should relax, come out with me and—"

Was that all Mona thought about, partying and herself? Abigail wondered, shutting her door on the temp who openly listened to private conversations. Forgetting that, Abigail mentioned having toyed with Joseph. "I didn't do it on purpose Mo," Abigail stated, reecalling the stroke that felled her father. Abigail nodded, "Joe just may hate me now, and I deserve it," because, supportive, he'd flown with her to the West Indies. Joseph had remained while Abigail tended her ailing father.

When she'd changed careers, Joseph had generously helped Abigail with her bills while she'd worked through the initial pay cut. "So you won't have to dip into your 'growing' stash," he'd said of her savings.

"Even when mi raises came in, I had to force payback on him." How had she been so blind? Abigail wondered because she had been searching for the very thing that had been before her all the time. "Mo, that man neva asked mi for one ting." And Why me? Abigail wondered, when Joseph could have nearly any woman he desired.

Abigail knocked at her head because she had been stupid, praying for a husband, a good, God-fearing man, with whom she would not wind up neglecting her spirituality. She had asked for someone gentle and caring. Then when the man was sent, she'd acted a fool, for seven years.

Really, she'd behaved like the people in her new translation bible that read like a beautiful novel... In Acts, the 12th chapter, there had been a teacher of the gospel, Peter. He had been thrown in jail. However, Peter's friends knew he didn't belong there, so they prayed for his release. Nevertheless, when Peter was released, like the friends had requested in prayer, they were surprised to see him!

Abigail knew she had been like Peter's friends, a bit simple.

On the phone, Mona Lisa felt jealous because although Gaye hadn't said it, it was now apparent. Abigail had finally faced her love for Forrester. It was about time, too, Mona Lisa grudgingly acknowledged because Forrester's love for Abigail was written all over him. It was a fact that Mona Lisa had tried to ignore, a time or two. Now, why couldn't a man like that love her like that? Mona Lisa wondered. She forgot Forrester and love. She contemplated how to rewind the talk back around to the lingerie show that evening. She also felt strange when Abigail blurted out her desire to simply talk to Joseph. "He could say he doesn't love me, just long as I get to hear his voice."

Mona Lisa closed her eyes. She wanted her friend happy, but she wondered. Would anyone other than Gaye ever love her? The truth was Gaye was all Mona had; however, Mona Lisa knew she needed to listen.

Abigail said she'd prayed for more than just a warm body in a bed. "Then I missed my blessing because I didn't recognize him." Again, Abigail knocked at her forehead. "Stupid."

Imagine that, Mona Lisa thought, praying for a man. Well, it must have worked because Gaye was always turning some man away. Nice ones too, some good-looking, some with manners, and lots with loot.

"Mo, did you hear me?"

"I did." Ms. Overly Made-Up surprised Abigail by saying sometimes men needed tenderness. "Most will never say it. You just gotta know."

"Why don't they say things, Mo? We're women, not mind readers."

Mona Lisa sounded exasperated, although she was elated. At last, she got to teach Gaye something! "G, they don't say things because they'd feel less like men. Usually, it's women who voice their needs. Men keep their feelings in, until they explode or whup up on somebody—during a mean game of street ball up on 155," in Harlem, "at Rucker," [the park].

Wow. Inwardly, Abigail acknowledged that her girlfriend had been called brainless, a man-eater, and a barracuda. Still, she'd just made fine points, thus proving Abigail's theory. Mona had a heart and a keen mind. Again, Abigail's thoughts veered to Joseph. "Real love," she softly stated, more to herself. "That's what Joe showed me."

"Well, at least you know love." Mona Lisa sounded pinched and somber. "Other people spend their lives fighting and never get any."

Abigail shook her head. Now, both she and her friend seemed a sorry pair. However, Abigail reminded herself and the heavier woman that real love came from one source only. "True love may be found in people, Mo, but actually, it begins with God."

"Yeah? Well, buck all that." Mona Lisa bounced back, as was her way, "because come hell or high water, I'm gonna survive. And you, Honeydew? You need to get yo' behind in gear. Find that man and work this mess out. "Oh," Mona Lisa added as an afterthought. "Then I just might ask your God, your Jesus, Ali Baba, or whoever he is, to hook a sista up!"

Abigail chuckled, then sounded sober, "Uh, Mo, about tonight..."

Relenting, Mona Lisa chose to sound sardonic. "Look, G, I don't need you crying that you let love slip away, so get you some rest. Then go get your man."

## 8

SABRINA Dudley sat in Terminal B. Glancing at her watch, she knew her sister would soon appear. Peering past someone in her line of sight, Sabrina saw Abigail and wildly waved. "Gaye Denise!"

Abigail turned toward that voice, so familiar.

"Hey, Ma-Ma—over here!"

"Binky!" Abigail rushed forward. Feeling slightly dizzy, she shrugged the feeling away because it was probably just the after-effects of racing. Hurriedly, she'd left her office. Then to reach the Queens New York airport, she'd plowed through mad Manhattan rush hour traffic.

Abigail's nephew sat up as she approached. She laughed while exclaiming, "Sabrina!" Bent, Abigail kissed the child's mother. She also admitted she'd wondered at the bundle across her sister's knees. "Now I know it's you." Abigail beamed at the sleepy toddler. Lovingly, she caressed the round face and honey-hued eyes stared back at her.

"Say 'hi Auntie,'" the child's mother prompted.

The toddler raised a chubby hand. Both his mother and aunt laughed.

Abigail touched her sister's coat, a fabulous faux fur.

"Mi like."

"It's fake crystal fox." Sabrina mimicked an accent, "Frys-stal," as Abigail noticed sable brown, high-heeled boots. "Looks real, right, Gaye Denise?" Sabrina forgot her coat to slip her son's hood onto his head.

Abigail watched as, with evident maternal pride, small Jamaal Dudley, Jr. was set on his feet. Abigail recalled the day he'd been born. There had been endless hours of labor, profuse sweating, and crying, during which Sabrina had tightly held onto her older sister's hand.

As Sabrina gathered her things, Abigail attempted to dislodge a bag from beneath a nearby seat. "Binky," Abigail huffed, "why din yu say you were coming today?" They'd spoken twice earlier that week, but with no mention of flight. "If I had known, I could've been here sooner."

At the touch on her elbow, Abigail straightened up to watch. Uniformed, a young man effortlessly slung her sister's bag onto his cart.

Cheerily, Sabrina shrugged. "I didn't wait long." The younger had called her sister just before the elder was due to leave her office. And—

Sabrina mentally congratulated herself—things had worked out. "All set," Sabrina said and looked down. Her son leaned against her. Raised arms were his signal that she should pick him up.

Well, Sabrina would not. "No 'up' Jamaal. Big boys walk."

Disconcerted, the toddler screamed. When his mother didn't flinch, he let loose a high-pitched wail. Abigail noticed disparaging glances.

Calmly, Sabrina walked away as her child watched. Realizing he hadn't gotten through, the toddler took a deep breath and screamed again. This time louder, and he held his high note for longer.

Abigail rolled her eyes at miniature Pavarotti. She also trotted up to nudge her sister. "Make him stop –unless he's gonna break into song."

Sabrina turned, took a few steps, and grabbed her noisy baby. "He'll stop on his own, Gaye Denise." With one hand, Sabrina pulled her yet screaming son toward the automatic exit. "Cut it out," she commanded while also carrying his cumbersome car seat. Half-turning, she spoke over the boy's near conniption. "Listen, Ma-Ma, you cannot let a child think he's fazing you –if you want to maintain control."

Control? Abigail's eyes widened as she belted her coat. She saw her sister's, a mass of natural-looking fur, blow out behind her. Stepping into the drawing dusk and whipping wind, Abigail again thought, control? Heck, the meaning of that word, her sister did not know.

Stylishly dressed, with her knotted silk scarf billowing and her brown leather purse strap over a shoulder, Sabrina pulled her son along as she glanced back at the young airport aide. Hunched over to block ferocious howling wind, he addressed Abigail. Yeah, yeah, she was parked illegally, under a light, for all to see.

With a frown, Abigail opened her trunk as she thought, oh, hush up. She didn't need to be told that at least she didn't get a ticket. It had nothing to do with luck, in which she didn't believe. She also didn't believe in getting sly lectures from a near-kid with ashy hands.

As her sister's luggage was stowed, Abigail realized. The young airport aid's hands were chapped due to hard work and cold, poor thing.

"Will you throw that last bag on the back seat?" Abigail asked as she noticed that her young helper shivered. Pulling a twenty from her billfold, she knew it wouldn't buy him thermal undies, but she did suggest a few cups of hot chocolate. "Tell them to put whipped cream on top, okay?" Opening her driver's door, Abigail advised, "Keep warm."

"I will," the youngster beamed, pocketing the tip. "Thank you!"

Maneuvering his cart and dodging traffic, he hugged his thin uniform closer. Looking after the youngster, Abigail asked God to bless him. The truth was he was somebody's child. He was, quite possibly, some small child's father too, just out trying to make an honest living.

Abigail closed her car door. In her head, she heard Glenda's voice. Hadn't Mama always said everybody belonged to somebody? That Abigail tried to remember. While waiting a minute for her car to warm, Abigail turned to hug her sister and said she was glad Sabrina had come.

"Me too," the younger stated. Sabrina wriggled out of the coat that had her name scrawled in calligraphy all over its mocha satin lining.

Again, Abigail ran a hand over that fantastic, expensive-looking 'fur.'

"Mon, have we got to talk!" Sabrina gushed, "But weere to begin?"

"We'll start with dinner –of course," Abigail nodded. Pulling into traffic, she said, "Hey, what yu laughing 'bowt?"

"You would want to start with food," Sabrina smirked. "But that's because your stomach is growling mad loudly."

"Well, I haven't eaten, not since this morning," the elder pouted. She glanced aside, "Yu feel like seafood?"

Sabrina clapped. "Mi feel... like The Scarlet Shellfish!"

Abigail nodded, although she had actually pondered a seafood specialty restaurant. She'd have chosen one exuding elegance, not crude nets and fiberglass swordfish tacked up on dusty walls. However, since Sabrina was her guest, "The Scarlet Shellfish it is."

The elder noticed that in the rear, small Jamaal dramatically whimpered. "Why's he carrying on?" the toddler's aunt inquired, peering at him through her mirror. "I know he can't still be pouting. Can he?"

"He can," Sabrina replied while gazing out of the window. She forgot her son. It had been a little while since Sabrina had been in NYC proper. Again, she would have to get used to the noise, lights and the vitality. She'd again adjust to the pace and the streets that teemed with people. Not tonight though, Sabrina thought. Turning from the city she loved, Sabrina faced her son whom she took in with greedy eyes. When she spoke to him, her tone was doting. "Hey, lil' boy blue," she called out, maternally in love. "Momma's gotta wuv you, right?"

Sparked by the sweetness in his mother's voice, the child quickly stood. He attempted to fit his snowsuited body between the front seats.

"He's loose?" Abigail asked, seeing the kid in her peripheral. Maybe, she thought a moment later, she should not have said it like the baby was a tiny feral animal.

Not offended, the child's mother laughed. Awkwardly twisting in her seat, she sounded strained, "Ma-Ma, dis bwoy is smart." To the child, Sabrina spoke softly. "Jamaal, Momma needs you in your seat. Help me get you back up there."

The toddler refused. Instead, he grunted with determination as he continued the attempt to force his bundled body between the front seats.

Abigail burst out laughing, and her sister speared her with a look. "Don't become his audience." To her son, Sabrina spoke in patois, telling him to help her. She bobbed her head, hoping he'd agree by association.

The child had other ideas, including screaming and throwing himself madly about in the rear of his aunt's car.

Abigail, who'd thought things were funny, became annoyed. When the wailing continued, she felt frazzled. How, Abigail wondered, did her sister stand it every day? Abigail glanced at the child's mother, who faced forward: did she not hear that slap-awful racket? Over the toddler's ragged angry screams, Abigail ordered, "Binky make him stop. Now."

After moments of seemingly ignoring both her toddler and his aunt, Sabrina caved in. She struggled to get the boy on her lap.

Abigail nearly lost it. "Bee-na! I can't see in my side mirror –over him!" Lil sis knew the law; her husband was a lawyer. And everyone knew, small children belonged in the rear, in a child seat, for safety!

Protectively, Sabrina folded her hands across her son's midsection.

Abigail's lips thinned because her sister said, in a snippy little voice that nobody used side mirrors. "They're only good for parallel parking," Sabrina chirped, "and we're still moving, Gaye Denise."

Abigail rolled her eyes because *how* would she survive even a week of this madness? Also, how unbelievable was it for her self-centered younger sister to skip over her discomfort? Sis blabbered on about how 'this' would be her and big Jamaal's permanent separation.

"Hallelujah," lil' sis whooped, and her kid joined in. Sabrina said she felt so free. Yeah, Abigail nearly groaned, probably because now *she* felt sandbagged, sunk; *and* the kid was kicking her dashboard!

Abigail was ready to slap somebody. "Stop it, Jamaal," she growled. Boomp. Boomp. More kicking.

"Bina, he has got to stop that," Abigail coolly managed.

Boomp. Again. Edging toward infuriated, Abigail wondered if she would be wrong to pull over—and whup both the kid and his mother. "Hey," Abigail called, her voice firm. "Jamaal, Auntie will spank you," and your momma, "if you don't put your feet down, and keep them down." Scuffing up her dashboard. *Too much foolishness today*, her conscience offered as she thumbed behind her. "He goes in the back."

Moments later, Abigail guided her sleek automobile into the Scarlet Shellfish parking lot. Removing her key, she fervently prayed for a pleasant visit with her family, despite their seemingly bleak start.

In the chilly evening air, Abigail looked up at the dark, starry sky. The moon was bright, her family was safe, and she was grateful. As briskly she grasped her nephew's hand, Abigail gulped chill night air. Then the trio began to gallop. Between the adults, the baby ran, and Abigail grinned. "Wee! Wasn't that fun, Poo?" This Sabrina asked her son, who had repeatedly lifted his feet high off the pavement.

Yet holding the little hand, Abigail inwardly marveled that youth was wonderful. At a point, it was full of trust. Evidenced by the way her nephew had just known, beyond doubt, that his adults would uphold him each time he raised his booted feet and small bundled body. Abigail realized. She was working on trusting God the same way.

The toddler lifted both his feet again. "Wait, baby," Abigail advised, pulling on the heavy door with her free hand. "No more right now. We'll do it again when we come out," if he wasn't asleep.

Inside, again Sabrina monopolized the conversation. At the same time, she absentmindedly fed broken appetizer bits to her son.

Ravenous on the drive over, Abigail found that she was no longer hungry when her meal arrived. Actually, she hadn't even touched her appetizer. The spicy smell had turned her stomach. Sipping water, she watched baby Jamaal turn his head each time his mother put food to his lips. Obviously, he didn't feel like eating either. Still, the boy's mother, chattering away, didn't seem to notice or care.

When the child began to cry and twist himself as best he could, away from the mean fork lady, Abigail admonished Sabrina to stop.

Yet the younger woman persisted and wagged her utensil, telling her son that he would be hungry later. Frustrated, the toddler threw himself backward in his booster seat and stridently wailed. Again.

Oh, for crying out loud! Abigail became annoyed. The boy was howling, and their table and the floor around it was strewn with appetizer bits. People glanced their way, yet Sabrina kept talking.

Leaning over, Abigail pulled and got her nephew into her arms. "Hush honey," she cooed as gratefully almost, the baby snuggled against her. His cries diminished to mere whimpers as sweetly she spoke. "Auntie knows." The toddler had to be tired, "So sleep now, baby."

Sabrina stared, and Abigail noticed the silence, although the subdued buzz of other patrons' conversations continued. No more wailing baby. Ahhh, it was bliss, Abigail felt, as she smiled down at her nephew.

Again, she noticed. He looked infinitely like his mother, with her unblemished fawn brown skin, pouting lower lip, and sandy brown hair. With her eyes on the little cherub face, Abigail spoke. "You know Bina, dis chile looks just like yu."

His mother sounded indignant. "Why yu take 'im down?"

Abigail glanced up, her smile frozen. "Did you hear what I said?"

"I heard, and mi still asking why you took mi baby outta his cheere."

Abigail settled her nephew more comfortably against her. She knew her sister was angry because Sabrina had spoken in hushed patois. So Abigail spoke the same way. "Dis baby was loud. Mi lost my appetite."

"You'd have an appetite—if you stopped being everybody mama!"

Abigail's eyebrow rose. She forced herself to take a deep breath. And she told her sister to let it go.

Ignoring the advice, Sabrina leaned forward. With fingertips on her son's arm, she ordered, "Gi' me chilc." Curtly, she nodded.

Abigail's eyes narrowed. Self-centered Sabrina hadn't thought about holding her son until someone else paid him attention. Well, too bad, Abigail mused.

Heartsick, Sabrina realized. Her toddler felt comforted and secure in his aunt's arms and not her own. Crestfallen, she watched as her toddler profusely sucked on a pudgy thumb.

"Why don't we order dessert or coffee," Abigail suggested.

"Mi don't want dessert, nor coffee." Sabrina hissed, "I want mi chile. Look, Gaye Denise," the younger almost yelled. "I want—"

"Watch it…" Abigail cautioned with her eyebrow winging up.

"Or what?" The twenty-five-year-old taunted. "Yu smack me up?" As Abigail had when the youngster had been a too-grand teenager.

"I just may," Abigail warned, reiterating, "you will be respectful."

Sabrina looked down, aware that she had been impudent. "Well," she began, somewhat penitent, although she mainly felt defiant. "I'm telling yu: I am Bina, BEE-na. I don't want you callin' me Binky anymore, because I am a woman, now. I no longer want you, or the fam, treating me any other way. Yu got that?" While she was at it, Sabrina figured she would go on and mention other things she found perturbing.

After the litany, Abigail shook her head, and Sabrina felt rising ire. "I know yu not pitying me," Sabrina said, itching for a fight. "If you are—"

"If I am," the older sister struggled to calmly reply, "that fight would be well deserved. Oh, and pity might keep me from kicking your butt."

"What's that supposed to mean?"

Abigail exhaled. "It means yu pushing me. But I can look past that… to see what yu saying. And I can abide by your wishes."

Subsequently, though, Abigail revealed that she saw the baby that she'd bathed whenever she looked in Sabrina's face. "I see the little Miss Poo that I kissed. The one I loved through things like bullies, chickenpox, runny noses, and sprained ankles." There had been bike scrapes, nose bleeds, "And I loved you BEE-na, through losing Mama…"

Sabrina folded her hands because she had known Gaye Denise would go there—saying she saw the two of them, growing. All that sappy stuff.

"And since I happen to be more a mother to you…than your own mother," Abigail offered, "You will never speak disrespectfully to me." Their mother had been deceased since Sabrina was a toddler. "Mi don't care how old you get or how many babies you have. You understand?"

Dutifully, Sabrina bobbed her glossy head. "I'm sorry."

Abigail waved. "Keep your apology. And know it'll be hard for me to stop calling you Binky." Abigail cut her eyes. "Shoo, mi been callin' yu dat all your life, but I will try calling you Bina. It is more grown-up."

The younger sister fought a smile because Gaye Denise really was silly, making that last sound so much like a chore.

"Oh, and another ting." Abigail smoothed her nephew's hair. "I would think you'd be glad to let this baby's Auntie help. The truth is you must feel overworked—what, with your job, your husband, and your house that needs running. Then you got charities, church, finance classes, whew! Gurl, Mi don't know how you do it. How do you and working moms manage? When I can barely keep up lil' ol' me together, just one."

Sabrina lowered her eyes. She didn't want Gaye Denise to see pooling tears. However, it really was good, finally, to have someone acknowledge her. This Sabrina thought while recalling the yelling match she'd had with her husband before she'd decided to leave him.

Although she'd not mentioned it; lately, Sabrina felt as though her life was in overdrive and like there wasn't time for her. Sabrina hadn't revealed that recently too, her son pushed her buttons. At two-years-old, now he challenged her, exerting his new, non-passive little personality.

Sure, Sabrina knew her job. As Jamaal's mom, she was not supposed to break his spirit. She needed to simply teach and guide her son, but doing so, lovingly, was sometimes hard. Therefore, Sabrina thought with closed eyes; it was good to know that someone understood. Even though, Sabrina recalled, that someone should have been her husband.

Huh? Sabrina heard Abigail ask why she'd run off from Jamaal Dudley, Sr. Then Sabrina wanted to punch her sister, forget floating on feel-good, because how did Abigail know 'that man' loved his wife? Who said his wife loved him? Sabrina was angry with Jamaal, right now.

Abigail didn't care that her sister's eyes were closed. As the mother-sister, Abigail compelled Sabrina to wake up. "Bina, honey, say you're on holiday –or anything but that 'separated' stuff."

Sabrina wanted to scream because she hated preaching, but she controlled herself and tried to block out Gaye Denise's words.

"Bina..." Abigail spoke on, despite the younger woman squinching closed eyes. However, Sabrina's honey-colored orbs flew open when she heard the jarring words, "Too late." Sabrina yowled, "What'd yu mean?"

Abigail sighed because she would have to spell it out. Her sister had a good man, one she could lose. Men didn't wait around forever. Then Sabrina would be crying when it was too late. She needed to realize that Jamaal was a loving husband, father, and provider. Big chocolate was even thoughtful on occasion. "So quit your whining," Abigail advised. "You don't have lots of time—what mother does? Count your blessings, anyway. Maybe start a journal of things you can be thankful for."

Please. Sabrina would just bet Gaye Denise had seen that on *Oprah*, although the list could wind up endless once a woman started it... Grudgingly then, Sabrina recalled that Jamaal Dudley, Sr. really was a good father. Abigail had indeed spoken the truth. The big burly man made sure everyone knew his son was a priority, his pride, and his joy.

"I got me a boy, a son," Jamaal had proudly nodded. Seconds after their infant's birth, he'd kissed his wife's perspiring forehead.

Tuning back in, Sabrina heard that women—even some that Sabrina knew—would gladly take up with her husband if given half a chance.

What?! And why did Gaye Denise also say that Sabrina needed to forgive and forget? What law said that in good working marriages, partners should not keep score?

Abigail fell silent. For a while, she simply sat, rocking her sleeping nephew, as Sabrina mentally journeyed back. That disturbing scenario of Jamaal and other women had her eyeing her dazzling wedding set.

Suddenly, Sabrina felt possessive because big sexy was hers, alone. Vaguely, Sabrina heard her sister say it was time she grew up, mentally. Unable to retort, in her head, Sabrina saw a parade of women. Hazily familiar, they marched around the law firm where her husband had recently made partner. Lord! Had she really left him—to the she-wolves?

"I tell you these things, Bina, so you won't travel my lonely path."

What did Ma-Ma mean; Sabrina wondered aloud, her interest piqued.

After a few moments, Abigail admitted she'd once had her own thing going on. Unwisely though, she had taken all for granted. Now she could wind up an old maid.

Sabrina waved. "Joe would never let that happen."

Abigail sighed and mumbled, "Joezeff gone."

"What?" Sabrina blinked, confused because Joe had always been there—so who else was Gaye Denise talking about? She sure couldn't mean that dusty Darré. He wasn't worth squat, and good riddance.

Sabrina leaned forward, needing to know. "Gaye, who's gone?"

Abigail could not raise her eyes. "Joe. He and I are ova."

"What?!" Sabrina's voice rose because now she needed to administer a lecture. Heck, they had known Joe so long until he was family. When Abigail kicked Darré to the curb, Sabrina had felt like; finally, big sis had wised up. Now Sabrina wasn't sure as she asked, "What happened?"

Abigail reached for her nephew's outerwear. "We're just going our separate ways. It was nice though, while it lasted."

"Why didn't I know?" Sabrina queried. "Yu and mi speak— sometimes two, three times a week." Sabrina attracted the passing server. "Check, please." Again she faced Abigail, "You never said a word."

Truthfully, Abigail pointed out, each time they'd spoken, it had been about Sabrina. "Since you arrived, it's still been about you. I couldn't get a word in edgewise—until I upset you with this baby."

Sabrina pulled a platinum card. "I'm quiet now."

Abigail stopped zippering. "B, I didn't bring you here for you to pay."

"Well, I didn't come here for you to pay. Relax Ma-Ma. I got this. No more treating me like a child, remember?"

Abigail acquiesced, but she felt funny having to thank her adult baby for dinner. She wondered too if Sabrina would leave a nice tip.

Folding her receipt and donning her faux fur, Sabrina rose. Instinctively, she reached for her boy.

Needing to hold him a little longer, Abigail made a suggestion.

Sabrina agreed to drive Abigail's car. Still, to the twenty-five-year-old, one nice vehicle was just like another. However, with her driving, they'd hurriedly arrive at Gaye Denise's home. There, Sabrina would seclude herself. On the phone with the family queen she would say, 'Patria,' Pa-TREE-uh, 'mi thought you needed to know, our middle sister has it—the mommy bug!' Abigail just didn't yet know it.

Walking beneath the light of the moon, Sabrina jangled her sister's keys and wondered. How would the mommy thing work out? Sabrina frowned as she started Abigail's car; if Joe was out of the picture...

AS they stood in Branford Court's paisley-carpeted hallway, Abigail pointed, "That key." Nauseous, she leaned against the wall.

Unaware, Sabrina swung wide the condominium apartment door. Stepping inside, she breathed deeply. Barely noticeable were the scents of potpourri and culinary spices. However, because the fragrances were so familiar, so homey, to her, Sabrina reveled in them.

In the dark, she walked, and her voice was wistful. "Gaye Denise, there are some things a person never forgets."

"Like what?" Abigail inquired, gently pushing the door to with a foot.

"Scents, from another life." Sabrina never forgot the spices, the golden crunchiness of Abigail's fried chicken, her tuneless humming, or the fragrance that lingered on her pillow after she rose. As a girl, Sabrina had often crawled into Mother-sister's spot at the start of a day.

Feeling for the light switch, Sabrina allowed the memory to fade. In the warm glow, she added, "You know Ma-Ma, there are a bunch of things a girl misses when she gets married and moves away."

"Mmm." Abigail laid her nephew down. She thought about things a woman missed when she lost her man.

Sabrina plopped onto the plush, cream-colored sofa and stretched. Taking a look around, she felt as though she saw the place for the first time. Come to think of it, Gaye Denise always had exquisite taste. Although Sabrina realized, back in the day, she, the younger, hadn't known it. Sabrina thought aloud, "Got this place looking trés elegant."

"Don't poke fun," Abigail advised because her sister lived upstate. In Buffalo, New York, her home was in an affluent gated community.

"Mi serious," Sabrina protested, sounding like their West Indian father. "De place lookin' good. It's tonal, with shades of white on white, and I like the range of textures used."

"Now you sound like John, the interior decorator at Joe's Tudor."

"Collab with designers and you pick up phrases. Oh, and his name was *Johann*. Mispronounce eet darling, and receive fire 'n breemstone."

"That phony," Abigail waved. "That was just how he said it, too."

Sabrina pointed, "That has got to go."

"Your middle school sewing attempt? Never." A doting mother figure, Abigail took Jamaal Dudley, Jr. down the hall. Her voice carried. "B, come see your room."

"In a minute," Sabrina called. On the phone, she currently spoke with their elder sister. "Patria, mi got news..."

Abigail lay the baby on the queen-sized guest bed. She crawled up beside him. "Beee-na, de chile so heavy! What yu feeding 'im?"

His mother appeared, shrugging. "He doesn't eat much, but you've seen his huge Nana, Ms. BigStuff a.k.a. mama-bear."

Abigail sputtered, laughing. "Quit talking 'bowt your mother-in-law."

"It's true. That family is big; I think their genes passed to my baby."

Abigail watched as small bear-cub-covered pajamas were produced. She spoke while feeling envy. "Bina, you've always been that size."

The child's mother laughed, "These are Jamaal's!"

Abigail dismissed the pjs. "B, how do yu stay so trim?"

Sabrina patted her son's back when fretfully, although asleep, he turned. "Not so trim anymore, Ma-Ma. I may wear the same size but in women's. Misses no longer fit my booty and hips —my lady lumps."

Abigail, who worked out, chuckled and closed her arms around her bent knees. "Well, lately, if I look at food, it adds to my lumps."

Sabrina grinned. "Now that's a problem."

On impulse, Abigail unwound herself. She pressed a kiss to the fold on her nephew's chubby neck. "Maybe I've got his Nana's big bones."

Both sisters chuckled before the elder asked, "Yu want coffee?"

"No instant," Sabrina replied, "But yes if you brew it, and dash in three fingers of Jack. I know you got a fifth 'round here somewhere."

"Sounds like somebody is a lush," Abigail remarked.

"Yep, I'm falling-down drunk," Sabrina teased, "and you love me."

"I do." Amused, Abigail pirouetted to her kitchen.

Sometime later, she was roused from a light sleep by a knock. In her bubble-filled tub, she cleared her throat. "Come in."

Sabrina entered, sniffing. "What's that luxurious scent?"

"The foam you sent this past Mother's day."

"Wow. I did like it—I still do. Here. Take this."

Abigail accepted the china cup and saucer that her sister bore.

"I thought this might be nice." Sabrina sat at Abigail's vanity.

"It is, and thanks. Mi fell asleep. It seems I'm so tired lately."

Holding the liquor bottle so as not to tip it, Sabrina leaned forward.

Sipping coffee, Abigail sputtered, "Bina—stop! No splashing."

The younger smiled and shook water from her fingertips. "I had to," redolent of sun-kissed childhood days. "For old times' sake."

Guessing some things would never change, Abigail cut her eyes.

Sabrina smirked. "I'll hook your hair up tomorrow. Hey—do you remember the pool you bought me years ago?"

"That clear, purple-ish thingy with fish along the sides?   How could I not?" In it, Abigail's chubby baby had sloshed for hours.

Sabrina recalled the sunshine and her sister's comforting presence.

Actually, Sabrina could not remember a time when Abigail had not been there for her. Back when baby Sabrina had splashed about in her little pool, Abigail had sat on the grass just beyond, often reading a book.

With closed eyes, Abigail sipped and realized. In a way, now, her and her sister's roles were turned about. Yet the elder felt strangely content as she divulged, "I'm glad you're here, Bina."

"Me too, Ma-Ma," the younger nodded. "Me too."

## 9

HURRIEDLY, Abigail stepped indoors and out of the rain. Greeted by the scent of spices, onions, and garlic, she saw Joseph, at last. Folding her wet umbrella, her heart hammered. It did so because he sat at the very candlelit table at which they'd met nearly seven years prior.

When she approached, Joseph helped with her coat. "How are you?"

"Fine," Abigail nodded. "And you?"

"I'm well." Re-taking his seat, Joseph informed her that he'd ordered for them. "Hope you don't mind."

Abigail didn't, Joseph knew what she liked. Anyway, she really wanted to know if he'd suggested they meet simply because of Miz Maddie. Abigail had finally broken down and called. Then Madeline had assured Abigail that SweePea was okay and that he would get back to her. Now, hopefully, Miz Maddie's prompting had not been Joseph's only reason for getting in touch. Hopefully, he'd missed Abigail like she'd missed him.

Nervously she fiddled with her napkin. Suddenly, she wished she hadn't called Joe's mother, although, at the time, it had seemed feasible.

Abigail thanked the waiter for her steaming platter. She stared at it because how could she eat? Her stomach volcanically churned. Abigail glanced up at Joseph, who was silent and so unlike himself. She told herself not to be a pessimist; the evening would go fine.

"Abigail," Joseph began, "I asked you to meet me tonight—"

Joe only used her given name, she recalled, when he had a problem.

Yet he spoke, "—To speak with you face to face. Phones are so impersonal." Joseph shrugged and hoped he appeared nonchalant like he'd practiced. "Anyhow, I was away and got the chance to think."

Abigail clenched her bottom lip between her teeth. She tried to forget that Joseph had picked up his merlot glass twice. He'd put it to his lips but had not drunk. That wasn't a good sign, and his spiel sounded rehearsed, primarily since she hadn't known he'd been away.

Yet Abigail told herself not to anticipate drama, just as Joseph discontinued speaking. He sensed he didn't have Abigail's full attention.

His eyes flicked upward to encompass the approaching server. "Everything's fine," Joseph curtly offered before the man could ask. Wide-eyed, Abigail stared. She knew she mirrored a deer caught in headlights, but suddenly everything seemed wrong. Although she'd wanted to see Joseph, now she just wanted the evening to end. She'd seen that Joe was okay, so now she wanted to go home.

Unaware, Joseph attempted indifference. "I love the music here."

It aggravated Abigail, as did Joseph's search for words. "It's—"

Sickening, she thought for the first time since they'd been frequenting Raul's. Pressing her wineglass to her lips, Abigail willed herself not to scream. However, if Joseph kept eating... Hey, she could make use of the time. She could truthfully say, again, that she loved Joseph. She could even— Wait. That was all she could do.

Chewing, he glanced over. "You haven't touched your plate."

Like you really care, Abigail thought and quickly turned her head. Perhaps Joe really did despise her, after his sojourn to wherever.

Making elaborate work of placing his napkin on the table, the tall man got around to saying he'd received Abigail's messages. "I was out of town. I took off that Saturday that I left you." Joseph forced a chuckle. "When I left, though, I didn't know where I was headed."

Abigail looked down. She had been there, done that, and had wound up in the refuge of Joseph's arms, many times.

"Found myself on Martha's Vineyard," he admitted and failed at another casual chuckle. "There, near the water," Joseph sighed, "I got the chance to sit and think, clearly, about things, mostly us."

Is there an us, Abigail wondered as his name escaped her lips. "Joe?"

Raising a hand, he said, "Lemme finish. Now Star, you know I've loved you for years, but," Joseph rushed words together. "I didn't ask you here to strum that same ol' song again." He appeared disgusted, saying she could be sick of it. "So," he picked up his napkin, "I just needed you to know something. I'll love you for the rest of my life."

Abigail's heart leaped, and she so wanted to respond. She wanted to kiss Joseph repeatedly while saying she loved him too, but she knew he hated to be interrupted. Therefore, she would wait.

He sighed. "But Abigail..."

*Given name, again.*

"It seems I've loved you so long until I can't remember not loving you." Joseph looked away and shrugged, "But life goes on."

Abigail's eyes widened and her mind whirred. Joe had said it in such a level voice, she had almost missed the underlying indifference.

"I've told you, Star; I've got a place inside me only for you."

Abigail bit her lip and guessed where this was going. She willed herself not to cry before wildly she looked around. She knew. Anything else Joseph might say would not be good. And that muzak! Why didn't somebody shut it off? It was supposed to be background, a conversation cushion, but instead, it was distracting. It magnified the heinous words that fragmented her heart. This Abigail thought as Joseph spoke.

"Gaye, I've often said—"

She looked down because she could no longer listen.

Yet the man reminded her that he had always tried to be there, for her. He'd wanted to give her everything. However, lately, he'd realized—

Abigail no longer heard a thing. So what? She still mirrored Bambi in a phalanx of headlights as frantically she gazed around. The truth was she couldn't breathe! Oooh, Jeeziz—she couldn't hear a thing anymore either, not even that plug-awful music. Abigail no longer listened to the clinking of glasses or the conversation of other happy patrons. She needed cool air! Now. Perhaps if she got up and ran outside…

*No, just sit, and breathe*, her conscience advised. *Hear Joe out.* Abigail tried, but she could only hear the wail inside her head. It asked why they couldn't go back a few weeks or years even. There, Joseph would ask her to love him. He would say, 'girl, stop running.' He would ask her to be his woman, as he often had, and she would!

*Listen!* Forcing herself to tune back in, Abigail heard Joseph mention no longer giving her him. "No," she managed to squawk.

With incredulity etched on his face, Joseph said, "No 'no,' this is how it is. I'm through. I'm not so stupid, you know, that I can't see when something's not working. So I'm giving up."

Abigail knew she was going to suffocate, right at that table. Or she would shatter the glass clasped too tightly in both her hands.

*No*, the fighter in her resolved, *you – will – get hold of yourself.*

Abigail did. While looking at Joseph, her eyes shimmered, tear-filled, in the soft light. Inconspicuously, she gulped air. Then with her voice raspy, she asked why couldn't he look at her, "When you're saying all these things, Joezeff, that, to me, don't make sense."

"Star—I mean Abigail—Gaye," Joseph shrugged. "Our thing, or what I'd wanted to think of as our thing, is hopeless." He added that it had been, for years, but he hadn't seen, despite her saying so, many times.

Abigail wailed that she'd been wrong. She attempted to keep her voice from spiraling shrilly. "I can see clearly now." She knew she sounded like an advertisement for window cleaner, but she didn't care. "Joe, I love you. And I told you that last day at my house. You chose not to believe me." Abigail quickly added that she had been thinking about 'them' too while he'd been gone. "Joe, don't look at me like that."

Joseph immediately looked elsewhere because Abigail's stricken face tore him up. Still, he had more to tell her. It was the rest of what he'd practiced. "Gaye," Joseph called with averted eyes, "we'll be friends."

Friends? What was that? She wanted all of him! "Mi was foolisssh," Abigail admitted, as her mind matriculated. She had to make him see and understand because once Joseph made up his mind, stubborn man, he was immovable. Oh! Abigail eagerly leaned forward. She said, "Joe, something this big, we have to decide…together. One of us can't just up 'n do so."

*But you've been doing it for years...* She wanted her pesky conscience to stifle! Abigail very nearly felt triumphant when Joseph appeared to ponder her words. "If two people are in something," she continued, grasping at straws, "Then both have to agree. And I disagree."

Joseph appeared confused, as with widened eyes, Abigail further proposed to do something, anything to make things better or right.

Then reason flooded back. Joseph's voice became deadly low. "Stop it, Abigail," he commanded. "What we had—rather—what we could have had is over. Face it." He revealed that he hadn't said anything to make her put him on. "I voiced those things because we need to be happy, for a change. We need to go on without each other."

Abigail blinked. She knew Joseph didn't mean to sound cold and calculating, so she reached for his hand. Artfully, he slid it from beneath hers as she moaned that she didn't want to be without him.

With a sigh, Joseph felt utterly exasperated. Heck, none of this was turning out as he had envisioned. In his musings, it hadn't been this hard or harrowing. "Look, Gaye," he groaned. "What we have has changed."

Then because she appeared stunned, Joseph asked, "How come you never saw me breaking up inside when I watched you with all them clowns? The ones that mistreated you? Shit," Joseph bitterly spat. "At least I wouldn'a felt so bad if you'd gotten with somebody who would not have kept hurting you."

Spurned, Abigail's eyes filled. "So things done turnabout now Joezeff, is that it? You want to hurt me now too?"

"Don't take us there," Joseph cryptically advised. He also said it was simple. "We need to get on, with our separate lives."

"Okay." Abigail nodded. She knew when to acquiesce. "However, I've got one thing to say, to you Joseph Desmond Forrester. You said you hadn't heard me all those times when I said—whatever. Well, on that score, you were right. You really don't listen."

Defiantly, the man's chin shot up. "I hear everything you say."

"That may be," Abigail wearily acknowledged, "but I said listen. You don't do that well. Not with me, but you do it with music." Ignoring the look of incredulity on Joseph's face, Abigail continued. "Joe, you imbibe every nuance, every timbre in music, but when I speak, you only hear discombobulated words, dissonant chords. You don't grasp the meaning. It's how you could believe I'd ever agree to let you walk out of my life."

Joseph sighed because never would he understand the woman who gathered her things. Then again, he told himself, he knew her all too well. Ms. Abigail was changeable. Tonight she said she loved him. He knew she did, in her way, but that love, such as it was, was not enough. The following day, if given half a chance, she would say so. Therefore, he would remain resolute. Joseph felt he needed to shut Abigail down because, for whatever reason, she wouldn't honestly give her heart.

Wryly, Joseph looked away as Abigail rose from her seat. She could cry, he told himself, but her tears and soft words would no longer beguile him. He'd had enough! He had finally realized. Show always beat tell. It had been doing so for the past seven years.

With slumped shoulders, Abigail realized she had known. She wasn't good enough for Joseph Forrester, 'one of the fifty most beautiful.' So she would go and leave the big-time producer to his glamorous life.

Seated, Joseph couldn't manage to look at Abigail, who pushed in her chair. In the soft light, he'd noticed her eyes shimmering with tears. Doggonit! Things weren't supposed to have turned out this way!

"I can wait for you, Joe," Abigail whispered. She knew she had just given him what some would say was entirely too much power.

She turned to go as he stared beyond her. Abigail could not know Joseph wondered why he felt angry. Why the fuck did he need a cigarette? The smoke would only aggravate his throat that all-out ached.

Abigail, who had begun to walk away, stopped and turned back. She realized that her life if lived without love, would mean nothing. So bravely, she faced the man with whom she had come through many things. "Joe," she called, looking directly at him. "I've always heard people say that turnabout is fair play. In our case, it would have to be."

She continued, although he had yet to look at her. "Joe, you waited for me. So, for you," *my love*... The words hung in the air. "I will wait."

Abigail forced herself not to rush out of Raul's Place. Slowly, she stepped onto damp Eighth Avenue. Light, sad and yellow, pooled beneath street lamps, and darkened stores appeared mournful. Abigail forced herself to take measured steps, despite the urge inside that screamed for her to run back to Joseph. Stiffly, she clomped on. If she went back, she would throw herself down before him to plead for them.

As she trod on, Abigail realized. Perhaps Joseph needed to leave. Hadn't Mama said that people sometimes needed to clear their heads?

Therefore, Abigail sighed, Joseph could run. She would grant him that, but without her ever giving chase, he could not hide. This she knew. It was as he had once said. They were inevitable, like Jack and Jill.

*Uh, sweetie...* Abigail blinked past salty tears. She wondered how she could have walked so far. When she was back at her car, she had her key out. She refused to look in that window as she slid onto her leather seat.

*Oh, sweetie, don't cry. Be strong.* Abigail swiped at her eyes because although she'd been strong in the past, now she was dying inside. In times gone by, she hadn't really loved. Darré, she realized, had just been a diversion. He'd been something, and someone, to do. However, Joseph was Abigail's heart.

*You just have to face this.* Again, Abigail touched at falling tears because she didn't want to miss her turn onto the 59th Street Bridge. She steered into also-turning traffic. She sighed too because somehow, she would get through this, standing. *On your own two feet. Right, Jill?*

HOURS and hours later, Joseph sat, staring. Around him, Raul's employees clomped back and forth over the scrubbed-to-nearly bare wooden floor. Some stacked chairs.

Joseph heard the clink of glassware in the background. Somehow, on this night, it was neither soothing nor unobtrusive. What a turnaround. Actually, to him, it no longer sounded musical.

Joseph wondered, was it because Abigail had gone, after so acrid an exchange? Was it because of all that she and he had said and not said?

Woodenly, the music man rolled his shoulders, tense that they were. He was also plagued by the incessant question.

What was he to going do? Now.

Then the other hateful question arose. Really, what could he do? After all that had transpired earlier that evening.

## 10

WEARING a haze blue unitard, Sabrina slung a hand towel over a shoulder. Thirstily, she ingested a bottle of water. Abigail's baby sister also wound her hips to the sultry sounds of Maxi Priest. Having heard something, she turned. Palming the remote, she watched her sister's condominium apartment door open.

Seeing it was Abigail, Sabrina relaxed. After a greeting, she made the name sound dirty, "*Mona* rang." Sabrina re-upped the sounds of twilight for lovers. Over it, she said, "Jamaal and I were headed to Gymboree, so I told your girl to ring back."

Abigail turned, and Sabrina noticed the hollows beneath her eyes. "Gaye Denise," the younger woman ventured. "I wasn't gonna mention this, but lately, you haven't looked well. And tonight..."

Sabrina took the borrowed 'fur' that was dejectedly shrugged off. She watched Abigail sigh and slump down beside the cream-colored sofa. Sabrina knelt too and reached out. "Awww hohneee..." Seated on the sumptuous carpet, Sabrina took Abigail in her arms. "Don't cry."

Gently Sabrina rocked, as Abigail pressed her tear-stained face to Sabrina's chest. Forgetting how tightly she was clutched, the younger surmised, "Yu saw Joe."

Abigail's face crumpled, and her voice was small. "He and I had a long speak. Then 'im stay, while mi left, walkin' and cry."

Embracing her sister, Sabrina asked, "You want to talk about it?"

Abigail shook her head no, as she said, "Him thieve mi love."

Closing her eyes, Sabrina wished hurt hadn't found Gaye, and so soon after that costly and heinous Darré no wedding fiasco. It just wasn't right. Gaye Denise didn't deserve heartbreak. She loved everybody; she cooked good stuff for anyone. Abigail gave large sums of money to charities and colleges. She bought beautiful presents for people, often for no reason. She mentored teenaged girls, healed hurts, bandaged scrapes, and looked after everybody, even those undeserving. The woman was so sweet until their elderly Jamaican aunties often said she wouldn't mash ant. It meant Abigail wouldn't harm a fly. Now, this.

Rivulets raced downward as Abigail wheezed, "Mi can't breathe."

On her haunches, Sabrina quickly placed her hands behind her sister. "Head down. Now. Deep breath, Ma-Ma. That's it."

When Abigail lifted her tear-streaked face, she was asked, "Yu feel betta? Some?" To which the elder affirmatively nodded.

"So," Sabrina sighed. "I'm assuming Mister said it's over."

How did Bina know? Abigail wondered, fighting the breath-stealing ache that again threatened to double her over.

"He'll come around, Ma-Ma."

"Yu didn't see him," Abigail blurted, tears flowing again. "Yu didn't hear what Joezeff said—Oh, Jah!"

"Hohneee…" the younger rubbed the elder's heaving back. "Listen. Then mi need you to imagine something." Sabrina told Abigail to picture herself loving someone forever. "Now, see that love never blossoming, never fully coming back to you."

"I don't want to," Abigail groaned, not wanting rationalization. Either she wanted Joseph, or she wanted to dissolve in sorrow. However, Sabrina, it seemed, was determined to break up the pity party. And Abigail wanted to run, but Sabrina held her fast. "Why are you tormenting me?" the elder cried. "You know I've been traumatized."

Sabrina nearly laughed. "Honey, I know, but this is *turnabout*. You simply have to wait my good brotha out. He did it for you in the past."

It made sense, Abigail thought as tears slipped down her cheeks. Yet it didn't ease her pain, nor would the knowledge make waiting less hard.

As though she'd read her sister's mind, Sabrina spoke. "Big Joe needs space, just like I needed space. I now see that my Jamaal isn't bad…"

Abigail's eyes popped open. She forgot her pain. "He called?"

Sabrina was truthful. "No. I called him. We had a good long speak. Then my sweet man said he misses mi cold feet. So I'm going home."

Abigail felt like someone had punched her twice. First, Joe had seemingly belted her. Now Sabrina had, too.

"I won't leave before Thanksgiving," Sabrina announced. When her sister sighed, she smiled. "But I won't be foolish anymore, Gaye Denise. I'm going to try to quickly learn all our mother would have taught us about men, had she lived." Sabrina winked. "I'm also gonna do what you told me at the Shellfish. I'm going to grow up, mentally."

Hesitantly, Sabrina said, "Ma-Ma, I suggest you do the same… Life can be a lemon, sometimes, but get some sugar and make lemonade."

"I don't like lemonade," Abigail moaned.

Sabrina chuckled. "You know what I mean. Make the best of this."

Sabrina's eyes widened as again Abigail burst into tears. Clutching the younger, the elder sobbed hard because the remembered agony of losing their mother, coupled with losing Joseph, was too much.

Abigail shook with the grief that never entirely dissipated but crept up at any moment of weakness. She also thought, through salty tears, that she had been robbed. It should have been her mother comforting her, not her baby sister.

"Hohneee, honey," Sabrina crooned, pulling her sister close. "Lean on me, okay? Shhh, just let me rock you like I rock mi chile."

Abigail let herself sink deeper against Sabrina's oh, so comforting chest. Actually, Abigail thought, beginning to regain equilibrium, her sister's arms felt like those of another. They felt like the arms that Abigail had sought every single day for twenty-some years. All the years that their mother had been gone.

Feeling consoled, Abigail sighed, as somehow she also re-lived Glenda's presence. Abigail did so in the arms of Glenda's last baby. The baby, who was now a beautiful woman –one Glenda would never know.

Sabrina rocked and exhorted her sister to remember one thing. "If you ever need me, Gaye Denise, even if I'm not here, just pick up de phone. Call me, and mi ah come runnin' with mi bells on."

Abigail smiled. With her sister rubbing her back, Abigail realized she had been so wrong. Before this visit, she had unwittingly thought think of Sabrina as a child. Abigail had attempted to encapsulate Sabrina in a time long past.

"Bina?" Abigail called, snuggling in. "Mi can't believe something."

"What's that, Ma-Ma?"

"You. You turned out to be real momma, after all."

Sabrina felt herself swell with pride, and goofily she grinned. "Well, Gaye Denise," the younger sagely stated, "I did have the best teacher."

## 11

WITH the phone wedged between her ear and shoulder, Sabrina advised her father to spend the upcoming holiday with his daughters. "Then Gram won't have any excuse for not coming as well. Yu two can ride de plane together. Then we'll make soursop ice cream."

Radcliff chuckled because his youngest could make anything sound reasonable if it meant getting her way. However, perhaps he would leave the lovely isle of Jamaica to partake in family festivities.

Sabrina heard her grandmother, Inez, in the background. Raising her fist, Sabrina knew she'd won! Gram had said they would visit. Smiling, Sabrina also knew that had Gram not spoken, her father would have done as she'd asked, just because she looked like her mother. Everybody said Glenda had been beautiful. Sabrina never stopped hearing it or that a hit-n-run driver had torn Glenda from her doting husband and family. The same accident had also taken the life of a wealthy elderly woman. Glenda had been that woman's private nurse.

Hastily, however, Sabrina pushed the incident from mind. "Look, Papa, today's Saturday, so hurry. Soon call and give us your airline info, okay? Oh sh—" Sabrina hissed, noticing her busy brown boy.

He wreaked havoc on Abigail's beautiful enamel on steel cookery.

"Dis bwoy got de bright idea," Sabrina told her father while waving the child away, "To beat on A'ntie pots wit' a spoon."

"Well, go," The child's grandfather laughed. "Gram said kiss him."

Motioning for her baby to scram, Sabrina spoke into the phone. "Love yu Papa." She made kissing noises, "Gram, too. Bye!" As she shooed Jamaal from amongst the cookery that he'd assembled on the floor, Sabrina heard a door open.

Having heard also, the toddler ran tearing and screaming toward it. Into his aunt's outstretched arms, he jumped.

With a smile, Abigail pressed noisy kisses to her nephew's cherub face. She did the same to his pudgy neck while he squealed.

"Look what Auntie bought for de little sweet one." She produced a book of pop-up felt shapes. Carting her nephew, Abigail entered her kitchen. She laughed as her sister hurriedly closed a lower cupboard. "Bina, gurl, yu look like yu been fighting."

"You would too, Ma-Ma, if you had to chase him all day."

Abigail poked her nephew. "You're no trouble, are you, man?"

The child's mother took the bag handed her. She shook her head too because her sister had shopped, again, for her nephew. "You gotta stop this," Sabrina said. Then she asked, "Why yu back so soon?"

Abigail shrugged, bending to put Jamaal down. "It was time." She burst out laughing and gestured at the two-year-old. He'd wrapped his legs about her and clung. "He's keepin' me from dislodging him."

His mother shook her head. "Yah, because yu spoil him."

As though she hadn't heard, Abigail re-settled the toddler on her hip. "Yu know, mi got to thinking; yu two will be gone in less than a week."

"Dat why yu rushed back here?"

"Mi guess," Abigail shrugged. She didn't say she'd told her friend Kismet Staar that she needed to spend more time with her family.

Sabrina knew, though, and advised Abigail to keep a life. "Betta not brush off all your friends on account of little him and me."

Abigail squeezed her nephew. "What mi gon do when you gone?"

Sabrina waved. "Jump for joy."

Abigail left her kitchen as she called out, "Be right back."

After a moment, Sabrina poked her head into the hallway. "I spoke wit' Papa." With folded arms, she waited and counted the seconds.

Her sister reappeared, with Jamaal at her heels. Holding his new book, the child watched Abigail step from her jeans. "What 'im say?" the Auntie asked, scratching the groove they'd etched in her waist.

Adoringly, Jamaal rubbed her bare legs.

Both Abigail and the child's mother laughed. Appearing sheepish, the toddler wrapped his arms around Abigail's knees and hid his face.

Tousling his hair, she grinned. "Well, he likes girls... "

Sabrina winked. "About Papa; he was hedgy, but Gram said yes."

"That sounds like them."

Immediately, Sabrina clapped a hand to her cheek.

"What, Bina?" Abigail asked because with her mouth ajar, the younger woman appeared bewildered.

"Gaye Denise, where dem gonna stay?"

"Who?"

"Everybody. Gram, Papa –the family."

"Oh." Abigail breathed easier. "They'll stay here, of course."

"We can't sleep everybody here."

Abigail shrugged because sleeping people was the least of her worries. "Quit scaring me," she ordered. "Mi got more important stuff to worry 'bowt—like what mi gon cook, and buy, and if I need days off."

"You wouldn't have to worry," Sabrina moaned, "if I was at home."

Abigail was careful not to let her jeans swing into her nephew's face. "I'd think you'd want somebody else to host once in a while." The younger woman had hosted for three years. Didn't she need a break?

"That would be nice," Sabrina admitted, "but when Papa, Gram — when dem all ah get up in here, complaining, you gonna wish…"

Abigail waved because she thought it would be fun, "Everybody over to my place, for a change." Granted, it wasn't her sister's 'mansion' in upstate New York, but it would be cozy. "I like the idea."

Sabrina appeared dubious.

"Come on," Abigail cajoled, "work with me. We'll do this; you and the counselor stay in your room. Gram will go in my room with me, and Papa can have the den, or the living room, his choice."

"You're forgetting Pa-TREE-ah."

"No," Abigail spoke of their elder sister. "Peaches will go to a hotel for privacy, long showers, and her spa experience; so see? All settled."

Sabrina picked up the phone. "Still sounds too easy."

Abigail appeared puzzled. "Who're you calling?"

"Will Wong. Let's order Chinese. I'm hungry. What do you want?"

"The diner up the street." Abigail poured club soda and added lime. She laughed when allowing her nephew a sip; he made a face. "I want a Greek salad with anchovies and olives."

Sabrina frowned. Only someone who was expecting would come up with that combination.

"Hang up, Bina," Abigail ordered, "and call my diner."

Sabrina covered the mouthpiece. "It's Chinese. Wong's on the line. Hi Will. It's Sabrina at Branford, building Alpha. I'm good. You?" She asked Abigail, "What?" Sabrina spoke to Will. "This is for delivery—"

When Sabrina hung up, Abigail sounded pensive. "This'll be the first holiday in a decade that I won't see Joezeff. Wonder what he'll be doing?"

"Missing you." The younger took silverware from a drawer. "Didn't you say that loud-assed Mona is coming for Thanksgiving too?"

"I did."

Sabrina sucked her teeth, "I don't like her."

Abigail chuckled, although she partially understood. Yet she said, "Mona Lisa is just Mona Lisa."

"That's why yu shouldn't fool wit' her."

Abigail sighed. "B, we accept others for themselves, so why not her?" At Sabrina's frown, Abigail said, "Bina, I'm not asking you to like her."

Sabrina sucked her teeth. "Good, because I never will. I won't go out of my way to be mean, but you know she's gonna be obnoxious."

Abigail opened her mouth, but Sabrina raised a hand. "Hold up, I'm aware that we've all got our faults, so…if she don't start nothing—"

"Won't be nothing," Abigail finished the famous phrase.

Sabrina forgot 'that woman' to say, "MaMa, I've said it before; you're not yourself, lately. Maybe you should see a doctor."

Abigail admitted she felt sick sometimes, "But it's not major. And," she stated, with gleaming eyes, "you can help. Cook our holiday bird."

"Oh, you ain't slick," Sabrina moaned.

Abigail acknowledged, "I know the one hosting should cook, but—"

"My turkey is the best," Sabrina cockily stated. "So I'll do the honors. Now, a question."

Abigail sighed, relieved. "Wait—mi got to tinkle," again.

Gaye Denise sure went to the bathroom a lot, Sabrina mused. When Abigail returned, Sabrina said, "Okay, I've got a question. Gaye, do you want children soon?"

Taken aback, the elder asked why the younger inquired.

"Just curious," Sabrina stated. She said Abigail wasn't getting younger, and she was great with her nephew. "You were excellent with me, too."

Abigail recalled being thirteen. Their mother had recently passed. Therefore, the two-year-old, Sabrina, had needed her.

Seeing the faraway look, Sabrina knew thoughts of Glenda had surfaced. "Actually," Sabrina murmured, "I don't remember her."

"I'm to blame," Abigail cogitated aloud. She had so wanted their mother, gazing from heaven, to be proud of her. Abigail had wanted Glenda to see her, the older sister, loving and caring for Glenda's baby.

"None of that means you made me forget," Sabrina argued.

To tell the truth, Abigail averted her eyes and said she had tried to make it so Glenda's baby would never long for her mother, "The way I did." Abigail explained. She had been trying to live up to what her name sounded like when said by their father, Radcliff. 'A-big-gurl.'

"Gram also drew the simile between Papa and me. And I liked it, too much." Gram had said Abigail was the second sister, just as Radcliff had been the second brother. Moreover, when Radcliff's father had passed, Radcliff had become the dependable second son.

"So you became the dependable second daughter," Sabrina surmised, "When Glenda died. But you were really still a child, yourself."

"I was, but I didn't think about it. Caring for you was probably my way of coping with grief." To cope, their elder sister Patria ate.

"But you toted me," Sabrina recalled. "Patria was seventeen, to your thirteen. Why didn't she keep me?"

"She needed to be a queen," Abigail offered without malice. "She was always stocky," like their mother's family, "so she was fastidious. Everything had to appear just so. Toting you might have changed that."

"Well, I still say it's not your fault I thought of you as my mother."

"Okay, if you thought that," Abigail inquired, "then who was Gram?"

Sabrina shrugged. "She was Gram. I knew. However, since Glenda died when I was two, and my friends had mothers, you were the only mother I could have. Since you bathed me and fed me, the baby, naturally, you were the momma. You taught me jump rope and checkers. Papa bought my bike, but you taught me to ride, running alongside it."

Sabrina's eyes filled. "You taught me to tie laces and to do my hair."

"I remember," Abigail wistfully smiled. "And oh the knots, in both."

Sabrina sighed. She acknowledged what her sisters felt; she didn't rightly reverence their deceased mother. "But Glenda was your mother, not mine. You had thirteen years with her, Gaye D. Patria had seventeen. Somebody took Glenda when I was two. Therefore, you were my mom.

"You," Sabrina whispered, assailed by tears, "sang," off-key, "the hymn 'Rock of Ages' while you held me and chased the boogeyman."

111

Abigail had also read the 91$^{st}$ Psalm. *He that dwelleth in the secret place...* "You read it so much until at five, I could recite every line."

The passage tumbled from Sabrina's lips whenever she felt fearful.

Abigail watched her adult baby close her eyes. "Gaye, I teach J those verses. To him, I've become the mother that you were to me." A bevy tears fell from Sabrina's eyes because Abigail had given her so much. Abigail had paid and sought grants so Sabrina could attend college. "Gaye D," Sabrina eked, "You dressed me for prom. Long before that, you bought my first bra. I was eleven. You were twenty-two."

Softly, Abigail spoke. "Your first bra was lacy and pink. You didn't want the plain white one. We went to Werther's on Jamaica Avenue."

Sabrina chuckled, despite tears. "I wanted a bra like yours, even if I could only fill it with the tissue that I molded with my hand."

As mirth dissipated mirth, Sabrina whispered because she felt more than ever like she was about to become irreverent, "Gaye Denise, I would like it to be otherwise, but for me...you are momma."

Abigail's eyes filled, and it dawned on her. That was why Sabrina had always called their mother 'Glenda.' Sabrina actually felt no connection with the woman. It was why Sabrina often called her sister Ma-Ma. Afresh, the hurt of losing Glenda sprang forth. Again, Abigail felt accompanying fury. It was directed at the drunk driver who had run two unsuspecting women down. In his death machine, he'd jumped the curb. Afterward, he drove a few more yards. Then on foot, he attempted to stagger away. If not for angry bystanders...

Finding herself as shaken and as upset as she had been in the past, Abigail patted her startled nephew's back, and Sabrina jumped. Oh, the door. Returning with delivered food, Sabrina was told that although she had heard it forever, it was true. She was the mirror image of Glenda.

Yeah, yeah, Sabrina thought, removing wax containers from the food bag. Everybody said she was like Glenda. Frankly, she was sick of it!

"You should feel proud," Abigail stated, unaware of her sister's true feelings, "because everybody loved Mama. She was one of those rare beauties –inside and out. And get this, our Jamaican Gram," Abigail chuckled, "wasn't supposed to have fallen in love with 'Yankee' Mama.

Still, she did. At the funeral, Gram admitted she'd felt her son should have married a West Indian woman."

That was, Inez had divulged, before she'd gotten to know sweet African-American Glenda. Kissing two arthritic fingers, Glenda's mother-in-law had touched them to the casket. Then Inez watched as pallbearers walked Glenda's remains away.

"Over in Jamaica," the West Indies, "there was the ritual nine nights of mourning. Really," Abigail smiled, though her heart ached and tears rolled down her cheeks, "it was a celebration of Mama's life. I know hearing this is hard, Bina." Abigail dabbed her eyes, "but sometimes, mi feel like she's been given back to me, through you."

Abigail mentioned that sometimes Sabrina did things that were so much like what their mother would have done until it was amazing.

Sabrina spooned Dim Sum into her son's mouth as she admitted her wish. Sabrina wanted to know Glenda, whom she could not recall. "It's probably why I've never felt comfortable calling her Mama." To Sabrina, it felt fabricated, and so she said.

Recovering from surprise, Abigail bit her lip. Then softly, she divulged, "Bina, you have a right to feel that way. Still, let me say something..." Abigail asked Sabrina to recall the night at the Scarlet Shellfish. "You exploded," the elder stated, "when you said you weren't a child and that you have adult interests. You mentioned gardening."

Sabrina looked away from her virtually untouched plate. "So?"

Abigail swallowed emotion. "Mama was an avid gardener."

Sabrina looked up, and noting her surprise, Abigail revealed that often Glenda would pick up her baby, Sabrina, from the sitter. "In the spring and summer, when she got home though, there wasn't much time left for her to get out among her flowers." However, sometimes Glenda had been able to when her second eldest volunteered to watch the baby.

"I would jounce you around," Abigail admitted, "while Mama got her things together. Things like: her gloves—"

"And her straw hat with the scarf attached," Sabrina interjected.

"Yes!" Unaware of her sister's attempt at sarcasm, Abigail beamed with pleasure and pride. "That's just what Mama wore," Abigail said and was amazed that Sabrina knew.

"I didn't...know," the younger insisted. Sabrina rubbed chilled arms. "But I do know that I have that same hat, for when I tend my jasmine, my roses, my moonflowers, and my gladiolas."

"Oh!" Abigail gasped, "Moonflowers were Mama's favorite! She loved roses, and she even toyed with naming you after her jasmine."

Mentally transported back, Abigail could smell the subtle scents wafting on an evening breeze...

Sabrina stared. So she really was like her mother, after all.

"You could not have known," Abigail stated. "But that's why everyone says that out of Mama's three girls, you're the most like her."

Unaware if she felt better or worse, Sabrina held her son tightly. "I only wish I could have known her like you and Peaches did. —Not that you weren't good to me, Gaye D, but I needed time with her."

Abigail twisted her fingers, wanting to console her baby, her sister. "Bina, maybe Peaches and I can help. You know, by telling you stories about Mama..."

"Yeah, Ma-Ma." Sabrina swiped at angry tears. "That will really work." Not in this lifetime, the younger woman thought but wisely did not say.

## 12

TUESDAY morning, Abigail answered her office phone.

"Papa, dem call," Sabrina began, aware that sister would know her voice. Sabrina said the older Wallace family members would arrive the following day, "So mi need to give you their flight info."

Abigail loaded her electronic calendar. Momentarily, she forgot her father to mention something different. "Bina, a day or so ago, you asked whether I want children. I do."

Quickly, Sabrina followed. "What made you think of it?"

"My wanting Joezeff back." The elder acknowledged, "I know I sound like a scratched CD, saying it all the time, but it's how I feel."

"Well, call him," Sabrina suggested.

Shock shimmied up Abigail's spine. "Mi can't do that!"

"Gaye Denise," Sabrina huffed, "Adults, dem ah play stupid games. Yu wanna talk to de man. Sure he wants to talk to yu. Call 'im already."

"What if he acts funny?"

"What if he doesn't? Either way, you will have tried."

It sounded reasonable, Abigail thought as she said, "Okay…"

"Call me soon, Gaye D. Tell me if we need extra stuffing."

Nervous, Abigail stared at her phone. Her heart hammered because what would she say? How would Joseph react? Would he feel she'd called out of the blue?

Breathing deeply, Abigail realized she didn't care. Therefore, she buzzed her ever-capable Asian-American assistant. "Sunshine?"

"Yes?"

"I need to speak with Joseph." Abigail bit her lip, "But… "

"You've got butterflies," Sunny Deng sympathized. "Say no more."

Abigail exhaled and felt relieved. "Thanks, Sunshine."

The incurable romantic laughed. "You know I'm all for luuuv."

Abigail smiled, recalling that Sunny had once said that Abigail and Joseph should hurriedly get married. Clutching her chest, Sunny had moaned that her heart couldn't take much more worry. "You and Joseph probably even get on Cupid's nerves." Sunny blurted, "With your managing to stay apart when everybody knows you belong together!"

Sabrina had said something similar, Abigail recalled, immersing herself in work. Half an hour later, she was startled when Sunny buzzed. Sunny's jubilantvoice emitted through the intercom. "Joseph, line three!"

Attempting to steady her trembling hands, Abigail grabbed the phone. "Joezeff," she called and held the receiver tightly. "How are you?"

He loved the way she said his name, yet he sounded strained. "I'm aiight. And you?"

Abigail's conscience admonished her to tell the truth.

"I'm missing you," she candidly stated.

Audibly, Joseph struggled because Abigail had caught him off guard. However, he managed, "It's nice to be missed—I guess." He hoped he'd sounded unfazed, as he admitted that he'd wanted to call, "But—"

Abigail forgot that fateful evening at Raul's. "You should have," she stated, "because when has a fight ever stopped us from speaking?"

She wondered if she had sounded desperate.

*To him, you probably did.* Oh, stifle, because she didn't care! Abigail wanted her man back. She forced the big booty Bama with the pendulous breasts from her mind. That brazen hussy who'd worn the Cleopatra mask had been all over Joseph at the club. Hopefully, Abigail mused, he hadn't spent their time apart with Bama. Oh-oh, Joseph was speaking.

"We never had that kind of fight before, Star, so I didn't know I could still call. Not when for all intents and purposes, we were done," before we'd even really begun, Joseph sourly thought.

Abigail sounded surer than she was, "We don't have to be ova..."

"Yo, you say that—now." Joseph sounded agitated as he rounded a corner nearly on two wheels, "But with you, I never know. You know?"

Why not just tell her you love her? The small voice inside Joseph, most likely his conscience, nudged. Yeah, tell her you'd like to try again.

Stubbornly instead, the man adjusted his audio's volume. He spoke over songstress Teena Marie's Can't Last A Day. "Gaye, it's not like you and I can agree on anything, not for long." But that's the fun of it, so quit bellyaching, the little voice inside Joseph snapped. Just tell brown sugar you've got a hard-on, one that would rock Venus and Mars.

"Then again, Gaye, we can do whatever you want." Joseph blinked because from where had those words come? He further thought, what the heck? Might as well get it all out since he had nothing left to lose. Yeah, now that he had all but lost her. "Gaye, I've spent every waking hour with you on my mind."

Suffused with love for the man who would be as good to her as her father had been to her mother, Abigail felt giddy.

"Gaye?" Joseph hoped he'd been well received. "Did you hear me?"

"Oh, I did!" Abigail blurted, then tried to sound less elated. "I mean, I've thought about you, too." Oh, the sexy thoughts she'd had.

With a smile, Joseph suddenly felt happy. They were again on speaking terms. Since they were, maybe he should tell Gaye that he was more confused now than ever. Perhaps she needed to know that he had heard her proclamation of love at Raul's, but in safeguarding his heart, Joseph had dismissed Abigail. He'd told himself the woman was a changeling. Therefore, he'd believed he had to stay his course so he wouldn't incur more heartbreak.

Joseph also recalled the visions. Those he couldn't mention or that his mind had involuntarily conjured 'Abigail' at the most inopportune times. The woman would think he was a loon, especially if he revealed that once while driving, she had appeared before his car with open arms!

There had been other times. One afternoon in an eatery, she'd appeared, opposite a plate glass window. Then at his Harlem duplex, Joseph had been in the shower, feeling eerie, when in his peripheral, a naked apparition appeared. Outside his steam-fogged door, Abigail's nipples had pearled as 'she' begged for another chance at love.

Driving, Joseph shook his head because he couldn't say any of that! Still, he had to say something because they couldn't continue in silence.

"Star, listen," Joseph earnestly began. "I think stuff happened the way it did because, for years, I'd received the brush-off from you. Then when you up-'n-decided you needed me, I honestly didn't know how to react."

Abigail beseeched Joseph to forget all the negativity. "Let's start fresh," she proffered, "by spending Thanksgiving together, at my place."

Feeling trepidation, Joseph admitted he didn't know if they should.

"Come on," Abigail cajoled. "Please? Mr. Sexy, please..."

Knowing he would wind up doing whatever it took to see her again, still Joseph felt unsure. "Gaye, your peops opt for the close-knit thing..."

"You're one of us," Abigail stated. "You and I belong together, and my family loves you, especially Papa." Radcliff Wallace nearly worshipped the younger man. "In his eyes, yu, Yankee, are de greatest ting since ackee and saltfish, which, by the way, I'll fix for breakfast."

Throwing his head back, Joseph heartily laughed.

Lord, did Abigail love that sound! Suddenly she decided to build a stronger case. Therefore, she mentioned her sister. The younger Sabrina would be sorely disappointed if Joseph didn't show up to have some of her stuffed bird. "Oh, you know big Jamaal doesn't take kindly to people upsetting his wife. So..." Abigail held her breath. "What d'you say?"

"Well, I haven't seen the Dudleys, or their little guy, in a while... " Joseph sounded like he considered it. "Yeah, the last time I saw the kid, his head fit in my hand, and his body was no longer than my arm."

Abigail wanted to push, and Joseph wanted to agree, but neither did. She gnawed her lip. "Joezeff, please? Everybody will miss you..."

"But will you?" He asked, realizing he needed to know.

A bevy of things to say barreled in, but Abigail remained silent.

"Gaye?" Joseph called. "You there?"

"I am," she replied, "and I miss you now, like crazy." Abigail admitted that Heaven knew she wanted to be in Joseph's arms, to feel him pressing kisses to her nape, her temples, and her forehead. She also needed to know...if he yet loved her, as he had said in the past. "If you do," Abigail unabashedly divulged, "then I can live and breathe again."

"Star," Joseph called, exhilarated. "I'm gonna tell you something. You scare me sometimes, but I love it. And I love you, bae. Always."

Oh Gosh! Abigail wanted to shout. Grasping a burst of courage, she suggested that Joseph meet her, "For a late lunch."

"I – ah—I've got a three o'clock, Star...sorry."

The man had sounded genuinely disappointed because he did so want to see her. However, refusing to become disillusioned, Abigail demurely told Joseph she had something for him. "So you must come."

Securely baited, he asked, "What if we meet later?"

"No. You'll wind up tied up." Abigail knew how Joseph's days went. "Joe, cancel or postpone, so you can meet me. Three o'clock, okay?"

Maneuvering through Manhattan traffic, he sounded preoccupied.

"Why mi gotta beg, Joe? Meet me at Mr. L's, off Broadway." Then without allowing Joseph time to refuse, biting her lip, Abigail hung up.

It took a second for Joseph to register that she was gone. Then heartily, he guffawed. That woman! Gaye was something. While driving, Joseph shut off the music and simply hummed. The tune was one his dad had always played while splashing on aftershave. Whenever Lou Rawls' baritone floated off spinning vinyl as he sang 'See You When I Get There,' thirteen-year-old Joseph felt excited. He would attempt not to bounce on the guest bed while Halloway, who owned several dry cleaners, fastened his cuff links. Hal had always gotten dressed in the guestroom when he wanted to surprise Miz Maddie.

Joseph left his silver coupe with the valet. Crossing a busy Manhattan street, he entered the rose-veined marble foyer. In his office building, he remembered that smooth ol' Hal and his mom had often gone on dates, although by then, they had been married for most of Joseph's young life.

Well, Joseph thought, perhaps he and Gaye could go on a date too. Hey, he could take her dancing! Not a bad idea. Entering the opulent elevator, Joseph didn't see the woman who suggestively licked her lips. He only saw himself holding Abigail as they moved slow and syncopated to the strains of a live quartet while in a lavish and candle-lit hall.

Yeah, Joseph mused, Gaye would wear something sexy, daringly low cut, to display her beautiful tits. It would hug her onion and show some leg. He would hold her at the sentient small of her back.

Joseph exited the elevator, imagining his hand locked just above the swell of Gaye's posterior. From his assistant, he accepted hot coffee as his 'hand' slid down to feel the curve of Abigail's rear against his palm.

Striding to his private quarters, Joseph realized he would reschedule his 3 p.m. because he needed to get under Gaye as soon as possible.

ACROSS town in her office, Abigail was busy, but she remembered Sunny; and oh, she had to speak with Bina, too.

Standing just aside of Sunny's desk, Abigail's coat was over her arm. "I'll be out." She laughed when a smile lit Sunny's heart-shaped face.

"Wait." Hastily, the raven-haired fashionista moved folders and coffee from her desk. She tugged. "Sit a minute, and briefly tell me."

"There's nothing to tell—yet, Sunshine." Abigail did, however, rest a hip on the desk edge. "Looking like that, yu 'bowt to make me blush."

"Then you should be a blushing bride," Vietnamese Sunny winked.

"You should cut it out," Abigail chuckled.

Sunny wagged a finger. "Face it. You gonna be like me, real soon."

Abigail raised an eyebrow. "How's that, Sunshine?"

"You'll be married," Sunny decreed, tossing back her blunt-cut glossy hair. "He's nice and so sexy, your Joseph. Yes, you two will be happy, as happy as Nguyen [Wen] and I are," Sunny declared. "Girl, it doesn't get much better than where we are right now. But do it on your own terms. Other people don't make the rules; you two should, as you go."

Abigail laughed, receiving the advice and the blessing bestowed upon her. "However, Sunshine, Sexy and I are only going to lunch."

"Well, go to dinner later," Sunny suggested. "Give the man a ring, with diamonds, like I did Nguyen. Propose to him already, and end this madness. Then dance for him. Strip, take him in, and rock his world, girl." Sunny sing-sang, "I could be persuaded to become a bridesmaid, one last time..."

Abigail laughed. "Sunshine, I love you. Oh, and if I'm not coming back—"

"Don't! Just call me if you want, but anyway, enjoy yourself."

Abigail stood and bent her knees in gleeful anticipation. "I'll do that."

"Well, don't stand around." Sunny waved. "Gloss your lips and go!"

"Sunshine, you're a dream," Abigail called, pushing on the glass door.

"Tell that to the honchos upstairs when you put in for my raise."

"I will," Abigail promised as a male executive passed.

Sunny pointed. "Out! Now—and sex him good," she stage-whispered.

On Madison Avenue, Abigail squealed into her cell. "It's on!"

Sabrina laughed, "Extra stuffing coming right up, and thank God."

"Yes, baby girl," Abigail agreed, "for all things."

## 13

ARRIVING before Joseph, Abigail felt strange as she sat in the dim quiet of the near-empty restaurant. She stared at the white tablecloth and the heavy silver cutlery. Abigail refused to think that Joseph might not show. She and he would make things right. It was their destiny.

*That's it...do not entertain negativity.* Heeding her conscience, Abigail took Sunshine's advice. Abigail touched up her lips. Then...she saw Joseph and told herself to breathe. Good Lord was the man beautiful!

Wearing wool and Italian leather, Joseph approached.

With a shaky sigh, Abigail stood and shyly smiled.

Joseph hesitated for just a second before he kissed her cheek.

Then their lips met. For him, it was Heaven, with Abigail, soft and curvaceous against him, while for her, his fresh woodsy scent and hard body tantalized.

Afterward, stepping back, Joseph requested that Abigail not sit just yet. He took in her tailored, self-belted magenta skirt suit and suede heels. Noticing her lethal legs, his grin was lopsided. "You're butter, baby."

He was smooth too, and with hammering heart, Abigail wondered how she had let this man slip through her fingers? Well, not again, she vowed.

They sat, and Joseph raised his glass to hers, sparkling with spirits. "The shoes," her sexy suede slingbacks, "give you that extra."

As she sipped Rivesaltes, Joseph inwardly acknowledged that Abigail was every bit as appealing as ever. She took pride in the way she presented herself. That he had always admired about her. Seated beside her, he inhaled. Then he just had to tell her, "You smell amazing, Star—actually, good enough to eat."

She was enveloped in one of the fragrances that he had given her for no particular reason. Having him notice was thrilling. However, she teased, "Maybe it's not me smelling good. Maybe it's dem food here."

"Nah, bae," Joseph countered, reaching for her glass while feeling akin to a pubescent boy on a first date. "It's definitely all you."

Lowering her lashes, Abigail said she was glad he'd come.

Joseph admitted he was too, and suddenly, Abigail wanted him to cum another way. He strove to forget swiping aside the centerpiece, to stretch sexy out. He forgot her heat, and she forgot wrapping him with the legs he deemed beautiful. Joseph tried reining in his thoughts, as Abigail forgot feasting on him. He reminded her. She had something for him.

"Oh," she had nearly forgotten. Yeesh! What had possessed her to tell that lie? Now, Abigail wondered, what could she give Joseph?

Quickly, it came to her. She raised herself slightly. Pinching, she pulled. She bent too, then straightened. Beneath the table, she took his hand.

Harry Connick softly crooned, 'Baby, I Just Had to See You.'

Joseph felt something soft folded onto his palm. Huskily, he inquired, "When can I look?"

With her heart hammering, Abigail replied. "Anytime."

Plum-colored lace. Discreetly, Joseph raised her thong and inhaled.

Before she knew it, he'd tilted her face up, and his lips were on hers. Their kiss became smoldering and sweet. Abigail moaned as Joseph pulled her closer, wanting her on his lap. He wanted her, and him—them—naked.

Abruptly, he discontinued the kiss; while placing a trembling hand at her throat, Abigail blinked. They needed to converse, but oh, how she wanted to feel. Joseph was rock hard and rigid, as ready as she was, but didn't they need an understanding? They should speak—of what they wanted. That is, they both thought, if they'd make a relationship work.

Nonetheless, both knew how much talking they would do when Joseph murmured with his mouth on Abigail's. "Let me have you."

She closed her eyes as he kissed her neck. "I'm already yours."

Moist for him, she remembered. Things between them were unresolved. He, too, wanted to hammer out dents, but it was so hard. With his lips moving like quiet fire over Abigail, Joseph suggested they go. At his Harlem duplex, he could get at her, away from prying eyes.

Reaching for her purse, Abigail said she wished they could fly.

Pressing his forehead to hers, Joseph smiled and spoke, momentarily halting hedonistic tendencies. "I hate to admit this, Star, but I feel like I've been in the dessert for way too long, and now you're water."

Abigail burbled with laughter because Mona Lisa had once offered that same analogy. With eyes darting toward the door, Abigail clasped Joseph's hand. "Mi can't wait."

As he pulled her away from the linen-clad table, their server approached. Thanking him for nothing really, Joseph tossed down a bill. "That should cover her drink and the tip," he said and hurried his lady out.

In his new coupe, Joseph asked Abigail to remind him of his uptown address. Leaning back, he snaked an arm around her. "That's how hungry I am for you. I can barely think." Clasping her neck at a light, his lips met hers. Then before his lovely terracotta brownstone, he stopped his vehicle.

Abigail eyed the sycamore inside a wrought-iron scrollwork fence as Joseph opened his car door. "Wait," he ordered. He strode around to assist.

With crackling late-autumn leaves underfoot, they hurried up the walk. Rushing up the outside steps, he opened lead-paned double doors.

Finally! They were alone, in shadow. Purposefully, they glided beneath a soaring ceiling and past a currently resting wood-burning fireplace. On parquet, they hastened through plush rooms and eclipsed a marble half bath. Behind Abigail, Joseph steered her up a shadowy, short, and narrow staircase. On a carpeted landing, one boasting a small decorative window, he turned her up and onto more stairs. Then in the stillness of his darkened duplex, Joseph commandeered Abigail into his elegant library.

In the lone shaft of bleak late-autumn sunshine, they stopped.

Joseph traced the planes of Abigail's face. Silhouetted on a patterned wine-colored carpet, mostly shrouded in darkness, he hurriedly undressed her. Fully clothed, Joseph kissed and stroked Abigail. He smoothed her sun-burnished beautiful hair. Watching his fingers, as they tripped downward and over her sepia skin, stunning, supple, and brown, Joseph barely breathed.

Feeling self-conscious, with his eyes roaming her everywhere, Abigail lowered her own; and was commanded to raise them.

"That's it, look at me, Star." Edging fingertips beneath the breasts that he'd longed to touch and taste, Joseph spoke. "Watch me, beautiful baby." Testing the orb's weight, he licked a nipple. "Watch me love you."

Abigail did so as Joseph bent to trail kisses through the fragrant valley created by the parting of her breasts. She watched as he sucked, laboring over, and laving first one nipple, then the other. She watched as his lips ambled lower to meet her navel. Lower still they traveled, a scintillating sight, especially when on his knees before her, Joseph raised his head.

Again, his eyes met hers. Glazed with desire, they spoke volumes; and Abigail's eyes filled with tears.

Quickly, Joseph rose to remove restrictive clothing. When he stood, powerfully nude, he pulled Abigail to him. He ground himself against her. Caressing her silken skin, he recalled imagining it while they had been 'on hiatus.' Tilting her face, he kissed her eyelids, her nose, and just when she thought their lips would meet, he dipped to again devour her breasts.

Then Joseph parted Abigail's lower lips. He slid a finger inside. Feeling wet and warmth, he felt the squeeze. Raising eyes in which desire blazed, he spoke. "I'ma ask you to do that again in a minute, Star."

With elation, Abigail noted the telltale vein as knowingly she murmured. "But you'll want it for a different part of you, right?"

Joseph nodded, as at her core, his tongue began a tantalizing dance.

Abigail staggered. With outstretched arms and fingers fisted, she moaned. Clasping her thighs, Joseph drew her closer, intent to continue his sweet assault. Then away, he lifted his hands and let her sway.

Unsteady, Abigail moved and slowly opened her eyes. Why had Joseph stopped when it had been so good she'd wanted to weep?

He watched Abigail, having decided. He ached to please her and be inside her. Still, he needed her to want him as much as he wanted her.

Abigail, too wanted them to lick, suck, and fervently kiss. She needed them to continue. Therefore, she moaned, "Joezeff, please." She reached for him, but his big hands at her waist backed her away.

Forcing himself not to pull her forward, not to kiss and fondle, he watched her, as slowly he offered the words. "Gaye, I love you."

Her face changed, softened, and she breathed, "I know. I love *you*."

He knew it was true. Now. Rising, he folded her to him and pressed her close. "I've loved you, Star…since soon after we met."

"You say that like it's bad," Abigail alleged and took his member in hand. "Bend your knees." Sliding forward, she rocked on Joseph's rod.

Wow! She'd slicked him, and though it was nirvana, he had to do it now, Joseph thought, or he wouldn't. So leaning over, he reached into an accessory table drawer. "This, made with new technology," he said and tore foil, "Neither of us should feel." He winked, "Supposedly."

Gazing at the rubber on her palm, she remembered. "Gotta call Sunny."

"No," Joseph grasped Abigail's wrist. "She knows you won't be back. Drop your brow, babe. I called and told her —after you hung up on me."

Abigail laughed. "Okay, but what about your three o'clock?"

Joseph watched Abigail slightly unroll the rubber. He moaned when between her fingers, his ignited rod strained toward her. "Star, you're it," he managed. "You're my midnight and morning too if you want to be."

"I'd love that," Abigail breathed, as with a leg, she drew him closer.

"You've got moves," Joseph moaned as in her hands his member jumped. Ravenously, he covered Abigail's mouth with his own, his body tensing in anticipation of entering hers.

Abigail stilled, and only wanting to lay her down, Joseph nearly missed it when she said, "Joe, my loving you is why I need to...talk to you."

His eyes widened. There was no way she wanted conversation now. He had to have her or explode. "We'll get to that, bae," Joseph vowed and eased Abigail to the floor devoid of sunlight. "Just say you want me."

Greedily, her legs and arms enfolded him as her hips undulated, readying her for his sweet invasion. "Joseph Desmond Forrester, I want you," Abigail acknowledged, as, with a knee, he edged hers apart.

Snaking a hand beneath Abigail, Joseph tilted her upward as she spoke. "I want you." In the dimness, their eyes met. "But we need to talk."

If he sank down, Joseph thought, his shaft would nudge and glide into her. Then he could stroke her silent. He could make her forget everything, except how he filled her. Inside, he would slide over her silken spot. He would also turn Abigail; have her on her knees, as from the back, he'd push past her curtain, currently swollen with desire. He would—

"Joe," with balled fists on his chest, she held him off.

Dammit! Something within Joseph thundered it because he could not believe Abigail! Unable to mask aggravation, he let his rod go. On the floor on both sides of her, he braced his hands. With his voice uncharacteristically soft, Joseph asked what was there to discuss? They wanted each other. "Hell, that's enough, right?"

With her hands flat-palmed against his chest, Abigail pushed. She moaned that wanting each other was not enough.

With a disgusted exhale, Joseph rolled onto his back.

Abigail sat upright and hugged her knees to her chest. She rocked for a moment, then thinking better, she hauled herself up. Hurriedly fishing around on Joseph's mahogany velvet sofa, she found her plum-colored bra. Fastening it, she remembered, he had pocketed her thong.

In oncoming dark, Joseph watched Missy, as his mother called her. She'd actually begun to re-dress, and it incensed him! This crap was just like her—lately, and he was sick of it! However, Joseph forced himself to say nothing because he didn't want anything to beg pardon for later. Watching Abigail step into her skirt, Joseph wondered, as usual, what was he going to do? Then he wondered, what could he do with Ms. Obstinate?

"Gaye," Joseph called, unable to remain silent. "What is it—now?" Removing the constricting condom, he needed to know, before she left. "A minute ago, we both wanted, so what happened?"

Abigail looked down at his formidable yet-erect member as hastily she belted her jacket. "This was a mistake, my asking you to leave work to meet me." She bit her lip. "I just kind of thought we…could…talk."

"Talk," Joseph dryly repeated. "What were we going to talk about?"

"Us," Abigail replied, ignoring sarcasm, "About what we want, from a relationship. That is, if you really want one, and not just sex, with me."

He could have sex with almost anyone. Abigail knew that. So could she. Therefore, Joseph stated, "You gave me your panties, a string, and some lace really, so we could talk." He was still stuck on that.

Abigail felt stupid as she fastened a suede shoe. "—About us."

Disbelieving, Joseph could only shake his head before he quickly informed Abigail that there were more ways than one—to talk.

So now he was funny. "Joe, please."

"No, you please," he said because he was no longer willing to allow this woman to run away and hide, as she so often did. In the velvety dark, he decided, as he stood too, that she would face him and this situation.

"Abigail," Joseph called, in her face. "If there aren't more ways to talk than vocally, then tell me that when I'm inside you, you don't know how I feel. Say that my body and actions haven't let you know that I don't want this stupid back-'n-forth. Or tell me, truthfully, that you've never known that I want a relationship with you." Joseph nearly hollered. "Tell me, girl, that yo' wet behind don't want me, right now—like I want you!"

Abigail glanced downward, assured that Joseph wanted something. However, how could she be sure that she, the whole woman, was it?

With the situation looming preposterous, Abigail stamped her foot. "Joezeff, I can't say I don't want yu!" Her yearning had been evident, as he'd mentioned. "But I need all of you, not just a screw!"

Joseph pressed himself to Abigail. "I'm trying to give all of me to you."

"You missed my point." She pushed at him while hiding a smile. The man was too cute, with his trying-to-give-all mess.

"Talk, Star," Joseph coaxed, following a weary sigh. "Tell me what to do, so you and I can get out of this gad-awful maze, for once."

Leaning on the sofa back, Abigail sighed and reminded herself that Joseph wasn't difficult. He would actually listen. Yet she mumbled, "Joe if our thing weren't such a trip, it would be a joke."

His broad shoulder touched hers. "What's that mean?"

She looked up at him. "You and I can't seem to get it together."

"No," Joseph shook his head. "You are not together. I am, and I have repeatedly made my stance—what I want—clear."

Abigail raised an agitated brow.

"Yo, I'm right, princess. You're playing games. You do it," Joseph accused, "because you got me open. No, close your mouth and listen. Thank you. First, you want to be friends—by the way, I hate that word. Then despite your stupid 'friends' speech, I've wound up your lover, and a durn good one, on numerous occasions. Then you decide you want something else." Joseph sighed. "Star, this shit keeps unfolding, like a cheap made-in-China fan, and I'm tired of it."

Stunned, Abigail dared to ask, "So…you're saying?"

"I'm saying you called me, away from my work. You led me to believe one thing and decided on another. Now my question is: when do I get to decide? Because 'our thing' has got to encompass both of us."

"Okay." Abigail began to undo her belt. Softly, she implored Joseph to make love to her because what else could she say? She'd fervently prayed for him to be part of her life, and here he was. So what, he wasn't perfect? He didn't understand what she needed, but he wanted her, with all her issues. Therefore, she wouldn't bicker. She would simply let him have his way because maybe a sista didn't get everything. Perhaps she had to make do, as some older women suggested. Maybe in time, she could get more, though. Abigail really didn't know. She only knew that Joseph had been right on one thing. She did need him. She wanted him to wave his thick hard wand, and make fireworks and magic.

Joseph sounded disgusted, although he didn't feel so, watching Abigail undress. "Don't placate, Star, because I don't need consolation coochie."

She raised her eyes, and Joseph whispered, "Gaye baybeee, if you're picking door number two, tell me why—so we can quit going in circles."

Baffled by his capacity for sweetness, especially when she most likely made things difficult, Abigail shrugged.

Tenderly Joseph stated, "Tell me what you want, Star. I'll do it."

Inhaling, herky-jerkily, Abigail spoke.

"Look at me," Joseph whispered, standing so close that Abigail could smell his decadent cologne and his very own pheromones. "Now talk."

Abigail placed elegant hands on his chest and felt Joseph's pectorals jump. "Joe, you love me. Now, I want you to want me, for good, bad, everything. I want no promises," Abigail articulated. "Mi just want us to make dis ting wurk. I want to know that for the remainder of our years, we'll maintain our commitment to each other, come what may."

Previously unaware that she felt so profoundly, Joseph was taken aback. Gaye wanted to commit like he did. Thank you, Father, in Heaven!

Joseph was especially astounded when the woman mentioned her desire to have children, with him, her lover for life. Breathlessly, she stated, "We should work hard at making babies."

Joseph grinned and between them, his rod jumped. Abigail laughed. Then he could barely swallow the ache in his throat because what a turnabout; Abigail had spoken the very sentiments of his heart.

In the ensuing silence, she bit her lip and awkwardly fumbled with her jacket. With a plethora of emotions swirling, Joseph quickly clasped both her hands. "Look at me," he nearly barked and stepped back. "See me, baby," six feet of virile man. Joseph said, "Forget the image and the hype. Then believe," he told Abigail, "that I'm your man. Believe I'm committed to you." Stepping forward, he enveloped her in a searing kiss and embrace.

"Understand this too," Joseph advised. "There'll be no more retreating. You've gotta talk to me. Then ain't much I won't try for you."

Abigail realized she had gotten the whole kit 'n caboodle! This man, her man, wanted to get inside her head, as well as her body.

"Star," Joseph called with her face in his big hands as he kissed her. "Star, don't cry." On her lips, Abigail felt Joseph's lopsided grin.

"Everything's okay, Mommy. And if you think about it, you'll see that things won't change too much."

"Huh?" Abigail blinked. "Why do you say that?"

Sexy Joseph chuckled. "Although it was never said, I have always been your man—even when yo' lil fast tail ran around on me, with clowns."

Abigail laughed, pressing her pelvis to Joseph. She whispered with such feeling that it took his breath away, "I love you, Joseph Forrester."

Finally! He thought it while deftly undressing his woman; she'd offered and meant the words. Kinky Joseph advised, "Leave them suede heels on."

Abigail noted Big Boy, who insistently nudged her. "He's ready."

"He is." Quickly Joseph maneuvered nude Abigail onto his sofa. With strong hands, he turned her, "Over, baby." He stood her up.

Facing away, she bent while parting her shapely legs. "Oh—yes," she gushed, feeling his thumb and the knob of his rod. "Please."

Upon penetration, she gasped. Inside, Joseph slid, then out. Back in again, he went, slicking himself. He noted his glistening rod. He enjoyed viewing his body joined with Abigail's, his groin pressed to her juicy round buttocks. He kissed her neck, loving that with every stroke, she backed up, striving to meet him. Therefore, with one hand before her, he held her upright against his solid nude body. At her abdomen, his large hand forced her back and onto his thickened staff, while his other found and fondled a sentient teat. Abigail experienced sensation, Joseph's scathing skin, and his greedy erection. She cried out as she felt him glide within her again, and again. She welcomed Joseph, gloried in his strength and his wonderful weight. Insatiable, she begged for more.

Joseph obliged. He held his woman in place while his hands vised at her waist. When her legs grew weak, she leaned forward. Panting and intending to enjoy every mind-blowing tremor, she grasped the sofa cushions and its back. With hands at Abigail's hips, Joseph held her tightly, as he sheathed himself fully. Then draping over her, he fingered a nipple. Raising Abigail's rounded arm, he turned her, just slightly, to trace her areola with his lips and ravenous tongue. He had waited so long for this. To make love to her, not as Gaye and not as his friend, but as *the one*.

Once again behind Abigail, while pumping and stroking, Joseph nibbled her nape and knew he had edged them closer.

However, before they free-fell, he whispered and meant every word. "Always...come back –to me, Star."

**14**

THE day before Thanksgiving, Abigail's family members arrived. In her home, she carried towels and remembered the airport. She'd picked up Radcliff, her father, and Inez, her Gram. Gram's sister, Aunt Agatha, had been present. Without incident, all had arrived from Jamaica. The trio had also brought along a surprise, a woman named Anna-Maria. It seemed she, too, would partake in the Wallace family festivities.

Abigail sighed, grateful that she had nearly gotten each guest cozily settled. Soon, she might even sit down, after she answered her door.

A tall, dark-skinned man stood just across the threshold. Raising a grocery bag, he jovially announced, "Six-pack!"

"Jamaal!" Abigail screamed and was engulfed in a bear hug. With her voice sounding muffled, she said, "Big game's not till tomorrow, bro."

"I know, sis." The clean-shaven man stepped inside, "But I thought my wife 'n her sisters might like to get their drink on, early."

"Baby bwoy," Abigail chuckled. "It sounds like you're gonna need a couple of days off."

"Yo, you tryin'ta call me an ahcaholic?" Jamaal teased and noticed his small son. With abandon, the toddler raced toward him. Aware that he had been missed, the child's excited squeals warmed the father's heart. "Hey, my J!" Jamaal Sr. laughed while scooping up his toddler.

Abigail beamed as the man asked, "You miss your Daddy?"

"Heeey...you," the new voice was softer, female, and wavering on trepidation.

Clasping the toddler in a giant bear paw, Jamaal Sr. turned. He grabbed his wife, and noisily their lips met.

"Here we go," Abigail grinned. She needed her camera because her nephew was too cute, with his tiny arms around his parents. Squeezing past them, Abigail asked, "May we move the mushy stuff to the side?"

In her kitchen, she laughed as she lifted red cans from her brother-in-law's grocery bag. She called out, "Six-pack, huh Maal?" With a hoot, she poked her head into the hallway.

"Cola, girl." With a wink, big strapping also stated, "I didn't forget you, though. Your real treat's in my luggage, wrapped up tight."

Abigail knew that soon she would receive a lovely bottle of spirits. "Ooh—get the door," she advised the two who softly murmured.

Well, now, Patria and Thomas—who looked like the comedian Sinbad—had also arrived. This Abigail surmised upon hearing the commotion. If only Joseph were present, she wistfully mused, the holiday would be complete.

With a sigh, she told herself she could wait, one more day.

FINALLY, the Wallace sisters congregated in Abigail's kitchen. Then it seemed as if no time had passed since they had last been together. Raucously, as was their way, they discussed men, movies, and politics. They talked fashion, shoes in particular, and entertainment.

Drinking her usual rock 'n rye—whiskey, ice, lemon, and a rock candy stirrer—Patria spoke of new perfumes and the latest at work.

Finally, the conversation wound around to Radcliff's guest.

"Who is she?" one of the sisters asked regarding Ms. Fifty-Something.

"I don't know." Sabrina poured ginger beer, "But mi don't like it."

Ever giving good face, Patria Wallace—also called Peaches—batted her adhered eyelashes. Super-sized and forty, she sat at the laden kitchen table. Gladly, she took the bowl handed to her. "Pineapple upside-down cake, yay." She actually glowed as she licked the from-scratch-batter off a dainty polished fingertip. She looked up. "What don't you like, Bina?"

Sabrina eyed the eldest whose skin resembled the color of a peach-inside, thus her nickname. "I don't like papa bringing women here."

Never without her intoxicating, dark, sultry fragrance or her larger-than-life 'I'm every woman' attitude, Patria did not smear her lip color as she sucked another fingertip. "Bina, the word 'women' is plural. Papa, 'im brought one person. Wheere de wrong in dat?"

"No wrong, everybody's got guest," Sabrina informed the Philadelphia-based ethnic hair care, Product Manager. "You've got Thomas, Gram's got A'nt Agatha... " It was just the way the woman had been paraded around, Sabrina voiced, "Like she's some kind of trophy. Ick."

Throwing her head back, Patria laughed. Darn if her youngest sister didn't sound jealous, especially when Sabrina petulantly announced the woman was old, for crying out loud.

Abigail handled a succulent baked ham. Removing her oven mitts, she asked, "Bina, what you got against older people?"

"Gaye, you sho' an old soul—thirty-six, and sound sixty-six."

Sabrina agreed with Patria, as Abigail countered.

"Bina, I'm just saying don't judge the woman. We barely met her."

Patria guffawed, and Abigail knew Sabrina made faces behind her. Abigail shook her head because some things never changed.

Mirth aside, Patria, the eldest, announced she had one thing to say. "Mi just glad de woman's not young and on Papa's arm. Den we all be mad."

Abigail sighed. "Well, I fretting 'bowt something different."

"What?"

"The way Papa did this." Abigail said of Radcliff, "He said nothing."

Patria licked a fingertip, aware that her sisters had not known their great aunt would show up with Gram, but they hadn't moaned about that.

"It would have been out of character for Papa to speak."

"I know, Bina," Abigail groaned. "But it would have been nice to know we had to sleep another," because there went her carefully laid plans.

"I told you I should have gone home," Sabrina mewled. "There, we'd have had room for everybody, including this woman."

Patria pinched a taste from Abigail's ham and nearly burned her fingertips. Glancing at Sabrina, Patria finally said, "You two sound like yu need Prozac. Quit whining, and relax. Everybody, dem all ah be fine."

Abigail and Sabrina spoke simultaneously. "Ms. Brilliant." "Patria Anita Wallace." "She staying in a hotel;" "Wit' her big self;" "She ain't gotta be in this tonight;" "Yah, when yu 'n mi be tired." "She'll be in a Jacuzzi;" "Probably with a book;" "Or wit' her man;" "Then de Queen show up tomorra;" "Pretty as a peach." "Ready to eat," "As always."

"Mi sick'a yu two!" Patria hissed because she had known it would come. Abigail and Sabrina believed they were the only ones who made family affairs happen, and perhaps it was true. They initiated things. They made arrangements and cooked, but they didn't have to lord it over her. And they didn't have to mention her weight during every disagreement!

"Look," Patria huffed. "Mi don't cook, or make beds like you two, because I don't want to, not because mi cyan't. Oh, another thing." She raised a dimpled hand. "Why y'all always gotta bring my size into the picture? Yu two know, well as anybody, that I pull the best of them, sometimes more so than the rest of them." She always had. Men liked Patria, with her bouncy hair, beautiful skin, and bubbly personality. They loved her voluptuous frame, too, of which she was no longer ashamed.

Bordering on upset, Patria pushed her chair back. She huffed that she didn't know why she had to say the same damn thing repeatedly. When would people get it? Full-figured did not mean figure-flawed. She pointed. "Y'all studied history. If a landowner's wife was thin, people felt the landowner couldn't provide. What about art?" Her sisters had seen works by Botticelli, Degas, and Diego Rivera. Even artist Monica Stewart's works displayed curvaceous African-American women! "Furthermore," Patria huffed. "Why I gotta go there with you two, my sisters?"

Quickly and sincerely, Abigail apologized, while Sabrina averted her eyes. Frankly, Sabrina felt Queen Patria read too much.

Pursing her lips, Patria returned to the topic that had started the upset. "Uh, about the bed situation? Gurlies, do not make mountains outta molehills. Things fall in place when we let them."

In silence, Abigail and Sabrina stared at the woman, who then nonchalantly reached for one of her brother-in-law's fizzy cokes.

"Okay, Gaye D," Sabrina dismissed Patria, "You and I will rework arrangements. And it is my hope that Papa's 'guest' won't bed him here."

Abigail shook her head, "Not our business, Bina." Stepping into the hallway, she called, "Watch my potatoes! And check mi white yam."

As she trotted toward the powder room, Abigail noted the squeak of sneakers on hardwood; someone was watching the basketball game. In the background, 'Jingle Bells' softly played. A merry conversation could be heard, and suddenly Abigail knew. The holiday would be glorious.

Behind her, wearing denim and the latest-rage basketball shoes, Jamaal Sr. stepped into the kitchen. He placed a bottle of rum on the laden table. With a sniff, he articulated, "Sis got it smelling good up in here!" Retrieving two glasses, he also sensed he was being watched. Therefore, without turning, he asked, "So, how are you, Queen Patria?"

"You don't care."

Masking a smile, Jamaal asked, "Why you gotta start? Why can't a brotha be nice to you, pretty girl, with you simply returning the favor?"

When Patria did not answer, Jamaal Sr. shrugged and lifted his glasses from the tiny spot previously assigned him on the cookery-laden table. However, when he turned to exit, he did a double-take.

Bent, his wife adjusted the flame beneath Abigail's potatoes and then the callaloo. Strange. Jamaal experienced lust, like a fist to the gut.

Putting his glasses down, he pulled Sabrina close. He suggested that she come with him for a moment. He had something to show her.

Patria looked up. "Yu feelin' Irie, mon?" Sucking her teeth, Patria reminded Jamaal, "Yu said de same mess when y'all made de little monster who is currently tearing up de otha room."

As Sabrina and Jamaal hurriedly exited, Abigail re-entered her kitchen. "What's the grin for?" she asked, knowing that most likely her older sister had been taunting their brother-in-law, who would have it no other way.

"He's too silly," Patria waved, sighting something she hadn't tasted.

"Yeah, but you love him." Abigail forgot the man who often claimed she and Patria were troublemakers. Preparing to make potato salad, Abigail reached for a knife and eyed her sister's palazzo pantsuit. "Yu lookin' good, Peaches."

About to thank her, Patria could only stare as her sister's knife clattered to the floor. Abigail then appeared about to hurl as she covered her mouth.

A prayer escaped as Patria quickly rose. Placing an arm around her sister, Patria moaned, "Gaye D, what de mattuh? Lord, gurl...come now."

The younger slumped onto a chair as the elder ran cold water. "Drink this." Patria lit the kettle. "Mi fix yu ginger tea to calm your insides."

Abigail nearly smiled because Patria never walked without her staples.

"Gaye Denise," Patria clucked, "yu doing too much, like always."

"I am not," the younger argued. Abigail said she'd be fine, momentarily. But she sure didn't look it, Patria thought, remaining silent.

Dutifully Abigail tried to allay Patria's fears by claiming 'this' was minor. It came every so often, lately, but just as quickly, it went.

"Alright," Patria nodded, "still, mi want yu to put your head down."

Abigail protested. "Mi cyan't rest until I finish cook." However, Abigail lay on her arms, grateful for the spot previously carved for Jamaal.

"Maybe it's a paltry stomach," Patria suggested.

A what? Abigail didn't ask. Patria, a bookworm too, had probably read about that somewhere. "I told you, Peaches, mi be fine."

"Maybe," Patria remarked, yet concerned, as she dabbed her sister's forehead with a wetted paper towel, "but still, take it easy."

Abigail nodded. "Peaches, mi not bother with the tea." Abigail wanted club soda, "Wi' lime." Hoping Patria didn't see, Abigail pressed the damp paper to her lips. Combatting nausea, she sucked the water from it.

"Need to eat," the heavier mused. "Got all this food, and still starving."

Abigail thought as she had before; some things never changed.

Patria rolled a lime and huffed. "Yu betta not be on no fad diet." Then she ordered Abigail to go lie down, "Mi take care of dis stuff in here."

Abigail inquired, despite knowing the other woman was capable. "You mean *you'll* make the potato salad?"

"Yah! Quit looking at me. Just go!" Patria barked, "Before I change my mind. Go to bed for a while. I'll bring this lime stuff –in a minute."

Rising, Abigail did not argue with the family queen.

In Abigail's bedroom with the frosted bedside lamp hazily glowing, Inez turned from the closet. With round eyes, the coffee-colored woman told Abigail she wasn't looking well at all.

So everybody's a critic, Abigail thought as she closed the door, muting holiday sounds. Wearily, she turned her comforter down.

Inez watched and felt a stab of pity because her granddaughter really had to feel bad. That was the only reason that she, the consummate host, would ever get into bed while her house was filled with people.

When Abigail lay face-down, Inez sat, and the younger woman became grateful for the comfortable weight that pulled the covers taut. Abigail remembered as Inez made an inquiry that Gram's voice had always been deep and soothing. Precious Gram had been through a lot, yet she had joy.

Gram had lost her mother, husband, firstborn son, and beloved daughter-in-law, Glenda. Decades ago, Gram had even lost a breast to cancer and her insides to a hysterectomy. At present, she had all but lost the mobility in her hands due to debilitating arthritis; but never had she lost the light in her eyes or the little song that she always hummed. How precious Gram must have been to God, Abigail thought, just before she remembered that sweet Gram had asked a question.

"Joezeff supposed to arrive tomorrow." Abigail wondered, why did her heart dance at the thought of the ecstasy so recently shared in his powerful arms? Just remembering made her grow wet with want.

Unaware, Inez tenderly caressed her granddaughter's face. With a gnarled but loving hand, she also stroked the hair at Abigail's temples.

The youngling felt herself drift as she noted the familiar but ages-old hymn that Gram hummed, as usual. Bless her heart.

Moments later, Inez discontinued mentioning a series of dreams that she'd recently had. Due to the dreams, she deduced aloud, change was upon the Wallace family.

Gingerly, Inez leaned over. She peered into her granddaughter's face. Well, Savior...that was why Abigail had offered no response. Lil' Sugar was asleep.

Inez leaned back against the tufted headboard. With closed eyes, she murmured. "Well, what do an old woman's dreams mean, anyway?"

## 15

THANKSGIVING Day began with breakfast, à la Inez. As usual, Gram rose before the sun. Softly humming, the Wallace family matriarch carefully prepared her mouth-watering codfish cakes and cornmeal porridge. She hummed, "Comforter, Bread of Heaven, please bless this day. Bless mi three girls too, so they may bless others."

Abigail companionably sat, sipping coffee in socks and a robe, while Inez browned bacon, turned eggs, and buttered thick, soft home bread.

Family members began to straggle in, and Inez, despite pain, was pleased, especially when her sweet coconut drops were well lauded. Both she and Abigail felt it was great to hear why each person was thankful.

One praised God that another was no longer ill. While eating fruit, one gave thanks for love in life, another for Abigail's open home, and so on, with all being grateful that the Wallace family had again gathered.

Following the sumptuous repast, Patria put away the dishes. "Now that I've pigged out," she whispered, grinning at Abigail, "maybe I'll go bring everything back up. You know, to make room for dinner."

"Ill," Abigail groaned, knowing her sister would not. Abigail smiled too because Peaches hadn't spoken of her disorder in denial or shame.

MID-afternoon, Abigail noticed. Her cheery, warm apartment was overflowing. "Thank you, Lord," she whispered; she'd been wrong to worry. Then she heard a scream. Oh, Lord... Rushing to her front door, Abigail watched as joyfully Patria embraced first cousins with identical smiles. They parted, and Abigail gaped at her mother's mother.

"Gram Mary," Abigail exclaimed as Patria was caught up in a hug. In turn, Patria watched as Abigail was embraced. Standing in a semi-circle, both women marveled at how the matriarch never seemed to age.

"Well, the good book does say the Lawd will beautify the meek..."

"Hold on there," a male piped. "Don't go closing that do' just yet."

"Uncle El!" Abigail clutched her mother's brother.

The brown, stocky man grinned, "Heeey behby."

"Hey, baby you." Embracing him, Abigail inquired about her aunt.

Then a round woman with moles dotting her cheeks trod forward. Carrying an infant, she spoke as she was kissed, "Hey baby."

"Hey, baby you." Abigail touched small rosy cheeks. "It's cold out."

When seated, Mildred caressed her grandchild's head. "Gaye Denise, you 'n Peaches remember me combing your hair?"

Her husband Elroy caught Patria's hand. "Aw, come on, Queen Peaches, you 'n Gaye Denise were tender-headed. Right, Millie?"

Mildred nodded. "Their dos sho' are coiffed today, though! Don't they make you proud, Mama?" Mildred spoke to her mother-in-law, Gram Mary. "They're not strung on drugs either," like Mildred's son had been.

Abigail adjusted a decorative throw pillow. "Okay, Gram Mary?"

"Fine, baby." The older woman acknowledged that she didn't get to see her two oldest granddaughters often, "But y'all always in my prayers."

With open arms, Mary called, "Sabrina Cecile, commere dahlin'."

"Yes, Ma'am." Sabrina stepped over teenaged twin cousins Jenna & Deidre, who sat cross-legged on the floor. Sabrina passed their father, her mother's brother Will, and his wife, Danielle.

Then Sabrina was folded into a lavender-scented embrace. On her knees, with her face pressed to Gram Mary's pillowy bosom, Sabrina wondered. Why had all become blessedly quiet? Then she felt the warm dense body quake. Sadly, she realized, the matriarch noiselessly wept.

"Mama," Will murmured and patted her arm. "Mama, it's okay."

"I know." Gram Mary released Sabrina, who noticed that hurriedly her father Radcliff left the room. Patria followed, intending to console.

Dabbing her eyes, Gram Mary apologized, "But whensonever I look in that child's face..." the older woman blew her nose. "I see her mama."

Back in place on the sofa, unnerved, Sabrina sighed. As the room again came to life, she could not forget stocky Gram Mary's words. Sabrina looked so much like Mary's only daughter who'd been snatched away. Sabrina rubbed chilled arms as Abigail dabbed tears. Why had Gram Mary stated the age that Glenda would have been had she lived? Sabrina wondered. Then she sadly reminded herself. Glenda was dead. Gone.

Abruptly, Mary changed the subject, telling an amusing tale, as Abigail stood alongside and adoringly rubbed her grandmother's back. All exploded with laughter. Afterward, they moved about to chat and chuckle.

Mary indulged anyone who approached her, before she attempted to hoist herself up. "Babies," she nodded, "Gram'ma cain't stay long. No, no," she said, eyeing the cream-colored carpet. "Peaches, rech me my handbag. Gram needs her coat. She got a house full'a folk her own self."

"Then what are you doing here?" Abigail wondered aloud.

"You girls come to see the old lady, so today I came to see you."

"I brought her over," stocky Elroy piped up.

"Thass right." Gram Mary nodded and looked past her son to his wife. "Mildred, you or Willie need to take me on back. El drives too slow."

IN the late afternoon, Joseph stood outside Abigail's condominium apartment. Bearing Stargazer lilies and a beribboned bottle of Cuvée, he waited for someone to let him in. Hearing and smelling the Wallace family festivities, Joseph felt as excited as he had as a boy...

Mother's Day, Easter, any and all holidays had been exceptional in his childhood home. Yes, because, as usual, Hal Forrester rose early to shower, shave, and stroll out for bakery-fresh goods.

Then back at home, while coffee percolated, Hal would 'spiff up' by dashing on a smashing-smelling cologne. In a crisp, button-front shirt, he would approach Miz Maddie who never looked half-bad. Hal would extend a hand while asking, "Ladylove, may I have this dance?"

Placing his holiday reveries on hold, Joseph closed his eyes and listened. The roar of the football game... that had to be Sabrina's Jamaal, watching with Radcliff, his father-in-law. Charlie Wilson crooning; Patria chose that tune. The music changed. The slow grooving wind instrument, the thump-thump of the bass, sexy but subtle... that was Duke Ellington's *Take the A Train*; definitely nostalgic, and all *Abigail*. And the delicious roasted smell? Sabrina's tender, juicy turkey, for sure.

Joseph hoped she'd also made brown stew fish, just as he recalled Maddie Forrester's bird, that had choked the stuffing out of him earlier... "Here, SweePea, drink some cider," Joseph's mother had hurriedly offered. She did so because he coughed. Coughing more, he tried to remove all the jagged bits. Damn! Joseph had thought, his mom's turkey might forever scratch around in his throat.

At the same time, silver-haired Hal grinned. "Son, do this," Joseph's dad's eyes deviously gleamed. "Push what's in there on down. Use you another piece of wood—er, I mean *turkey*." In a dress shirt with the sleeves folded back, Hal laughed. The older man raised his glass too and his onyx ring glittered. "Sawdust-y ain't it?"

"Stop it, Halloway," Madeline mumbled, annoyed at Hal's teasing.

"You mean to kill me, old man," Joseph sputtered, just before Hal shook his silvery head.

"Now, Joey," Hal said leaning over Maddie's delicately dressed table. "Shouldn't we, and your mama's guests, say that to *her*?"

Following Hal's reply, Joseph and his dad, along with Madeline's other guests, all guffawed themselves to tears.

Suddenly Abigail's door swung wide. Joseph forgot goofing with his dad, as on tiptoe, Sabrina kissed him. "Happy Turkey Day, Joe!"

"To you too, Ms. Baby." Again, he noted the striking resemblance that each Wallace sister bore to the others. Following Abigail's baby sister into the understatedly elegant but bustling apartment, Joseph saw sprays of camellias in cut glass vases. He mentioned having smelled Sabrina's turkey out in the hallway. "It made me hungry all over again."

"Oh, you ate earlier, at Miz Maddie's," Sabrina knowingly stated. "How is she—and how's your dad, that silver fox, Mr. Hal?"

"They're fine. Momz asked about you ladies." Joseph nodded at a man carrying a board game and at an older woman who looked familiar. He couldn't recall having ever seen Abigail's home so full. Joseph wondered how she was doing, since Gaye always made everyone comfortable. She was probably exhausted. So he would find her, see what *she* needed. However, his thoughts detoured when he saw a friend.

"Whassup, Joe!" Jamaal Sr. greeted him. "Where's the Luv, man?"

Joseph laughed and grabbed Sabrina's husband's hand. They pounded one another on the back in a shared manbrace. "Whassup, big Maal?"

"So Joe, you hanging out with the mere mortals today, huh?"

Joseph chuckled. "Thought I'd give it a try." He also shook Abigail's father's hand. "Mr. Wallace. Papa, good to see you."

"You too, son," Radcliff nodded, "especially when *someone*," Radcliff grinned and nodded at Jamaal, "went 'round saying you might not show."

"The man that said it," Joseph threatened, "I'll clean his clock."

Laughter rose as Joseph acknowledged others who warranted attention. "Hey Peaches," the producer leaned to kiss her pretty face. "I know that was you playing Uncle Charlie, my good friend."

Patria flashed her megawatt smile before touching an older woman's arm. "Joe, this is Aunt Agatha. You may have met her."

"Yes," Joseph said, "years back, in Jamaica. Nice to see you, ma'am."

Gram's sister softly spoke. "Hello, good night."

"This is Anna-Maria, Papa's guest; and," Patria turned, "this—"

"Is Thomas Boyd," Joseph interjected with something akin to awe in his voice. "The man," who looked like Sinbad, "rules, at poker."

Abigail's sister appeared puzzled. "Joe, you know Thomas?"

"Patria, come on. Last year? Sabrina-n-Maal's backyard boogie?"

"Oh. July fourth," Patria recalled the pool party. There had been decadent dance and drink. There had been grilled kingfish, lobster, *and* Sabrina's excellent chicken salad in scooped-out pineapples.

Forgetting Sabrina's blue Curaçao cocktails, Joseph looked around. Entering the dining room, his baby carried a dish of berry cobbler.

Spotting her rough-hewn honey with fresh-cut hair, Abigail smiled.

Joseph noticed that her sparkling eyes danced, and he licked his lips. Sabrina's bird would wait because now he had another feast in mind.

Noticing all, Patria took the dessert dish from her sister, while Joseph held out a hand. Grasping it, Abigail followed him, leaving the hub of things. In the cooler, dimmer, semi-quiet of the front hallway, she was grateful she'd discarded denim. Now she felt alluring in a clingy cinnamon knit dress, with her hair smoothed to the side.

"How are you?" Joseph asked, content to gaze down at Abigail.

"Fine, *now*," she said as, in his arms, he pressed her along his length.

"Star," Joseph whispered, "you look like heaven."

"Well, Joe, you smell like it."

"Oh, but I look bad," Joseph teased, noticing tiny light prisms thrown by Abigail's aurora borealis earrings. And to think, when he'd bought them, he'd wondered if she would ever wear them.

"You know what I mean," Abigail clarified, squeezing Joseph. Recalling their last time together, she moaned, "Make me wanna holla."

Catching her face in his hands, Joseph repeatedly kissed Abigail. "Star, why are you laughing?"

"Mi just happy."

"Show me how much."

"You forget," Abigail lowered her lashes, "we are not alone."

Joseph nodded and changed the subject. "You know Gaye, for me, as a kid, before I heard disco, salsa, rock, pop, or hip-hop, there was *jazz*."

Expectantly, Abigail prompted Joseph, "And?"

"Well, while waiting for Ms. Baby to open your door, I heard *the Duke* and remembered *my* Harlem and mama's brownstone, years ago."

On starlit Saturday evenings, the beautiful but creaky old house came alive with jazz and interesting people. Some were highly educated, while others, no less, were neighborhood stork clerks. There had been the butcher, office workers, accountants, teachers, transit and social workers, wait staff, and pest-rid people. "Gaye, everybody would stand around, shined up, laughing and conversing. They all had some kind of drink in their hand, probably because my Mama never could cook." Joseph chuckled. There were pink gins, and vodka gimlets, with cherries at cocktail glass bottoms. "There was bourbon and club soda."

Joseph spoke of the windows. "Miz Maddie's lace curtains would be pulled back so anyone, inside or out, could see and be seen."

Inside that Harlem home, in historic Mount Morris Park, red-lipped ladies and men with spit-shined shoes leaned against Madeline and Halloway's mahogany mantle. Smoking, others stood on the Forrester's paisley area rug; all sparkled and socialized.

As a child, Joseph had loved watching everyone, including fashionable Madeline, in her long flowing skirts and high heels. This he'd done from his vantage point, "Behind my door, or at the top of the stairs. I used to mimic the adults dancing, especially Hal," Joseph fondly divulged. Joseph recalled that back then, Hal had seemingly floated across the parquet. "But Star, you want to know what I remember most?"

Seeing all, as Joseph had just described it, Abigail asked, "What?"

"I remember…the music, *jazz*." The tinny whine of the trumpet, the sulky thump of the bass, the nearly indiscernible brush of the drummer's high hat… Music, the razzmatazz, the swing 'n the sway, had ever been part of Joseph's life. Thanks to Miz Maddie. With Abigail, jazz would remain part of Joseph's life because it was intricately woven into hers.

"For that, I'm grateful." Overwhelmed with love for Abigail, Joseph squeezed her waist. "Gaye, baby, I didn't tell you that because it means anything, I just wanted to share." The producer shrugged. "On this day of thanksgiving, I'm grateful for memories, and for *you*."

Abigail smiled because she was most thankful for Joseph. After so saying, she asked if he had eaten.

He replied, clasping her arm, "Not what I really wanted."

Provocatively, Abigail wound her hips, and Joseph inclined his head. "Don't start something, girl—"

"That we can't finish," she laughed and caught her running nephew.

Tousling the toddler's hair, Joseph marveled at his growth. "And you, little Maal, dashed out here to say Auntie and I have to wait, right?"

Abigail's eyes danced. "Joe, you don't *have* to wait."

Taking the small boy from Ms. Suggestive, Joseph motioned for her to about-face. "Go on inside. Open your gifts, and don't tempt me."

Following sexy, Joseph remembered the person staying at his Tudor home. He mentioned it while tickling the small of Abigail's back.

Aware that Joseph's friend from college was in town for a day, Abigail knew more. Joseph and his friend wanted to visit another Morehouse alum. Headed to her kitchen, Abigail motioned for Jenna, a cousin, to relieve Joseph of her nephew. Then in the food-filled room, she saw a family friend. With a nod for another who poured coffee, Abigail pulled the ribbon from Joseph's box. She held up the bottle. "Champagne!" She winked. "Yu and mi get to celebrate. Later, Joezeff. You can drink it off me."

Joseph hardened as Abigail turned, arranging the lovely lilies he'd bought. As she moved on to fix him a plate, Abigail recounted how Jamaal had shown up the day before, "With a coke and a smile." Joseph sampled the sweet potatoes that Abigail spooned up. "Oh, she digressed, "I still have to tell you about a funeral I went to." Joseph would thoroughly enjoy hearing she'd hit 'the clown.' This Abigail knew.

All became quiet, and suddenly, it appeared they were alone...

Abigail audibly breathed, as aware too, Joseph stepped close. Locking her into place between his pelvis and the cupboard behind her, Joseph removed a few pins from Abigail's hair while showering her with kisses.

Enjoying the sweet assault, Abigail moaned they should stop.

Engaged in kiss, Joseph queried, "Now why would we do that?"

"Somebody might come in, or they'll notice my hair's different."

Joseph nibbled Abigail's chin, and his hard body simulated sex. "Good, then they'll know I take care of business; they'll know I was loving you."

Abigail's heart stuttered because she had never known anyone as unafraid to feel as Joseph, and he was feeling *her*!

Noticing the shimmer in her eyes, he caught her face in his hands.

"I'm happy," Abigail stated before Joseph could ask. "Really."

"Show me," he said, cupping her breasts together.

The heat of Joseph's hands penetrated Abigail's dress. Yet she shook away thoughts of whipping off the clingy knit. Nearly nude beneath it, her supple brown flesh, especially her nipples, begged for Joseph's attention, although soon he would need to leave. Suddenly, Abigail gasped because Joseph's nimble musician's fingers found an opening. Stroking her, he coaxed forth liquid heat.

*Ohhh*, she mused, wouldn't it be nice to have her apartment emptied, if just for one blessed hour? Abigail grabbed Joseph's hand. "Come."

Hurriedly the man fell in step behind Abigail, touching her all he could. Dragging her back against him, Joseph's lips met Abigail's neck and her exposed shoulder. Against her skin, he growled. "I'ma tear this dress off you." With a hand molding her breast and her belly, he squeezed while pressing his erection to her derriere. Softly, in Abigail's ear, Joseph promised, "I'm gonna run so hard up in you—"

"Shh-shh," she begged, bending over and taking him, curved around, with her. Grinding against Joseph, Abigail whimpered.

With hands at her waist, in seconds, the man had her dress above her hips. "You're gonna drip for me bae, again," he bit her neck, "and again..." While running greedy fingers along Abigail's thigh insides, Joseph admitted he couldn't *wait* to be out, then back, because heck if he didn't have things to do to her! He'd start by removing her thong.

"Dat why mi gon gi' yu a reason to rush back here."

Bent, Joseph sensuously strained over Abigail. His hands were on her everywhere. Then they heard... fabric—a woman's thighs rubbing together, to be exact. Shit! Someone approached. Aggravated, Joseph turned, as did Abigail, while tugging her dress down.

With *her* coat draped over an arm, Mona Lisa felt elation, power, and frustration because, undoubtedly, she'd stemmed the flow of what indeed would have been hot, quick, and intense. Perhaps, Mona Lisa thought, she should have hung back and watched. Forgetting that, she noticed Joseph's desire glazed-gaze and Abigail's heaving breasts.

About-facing, Abigail stepped possessively before Joseph, who pressed his concealed erection to her. He did not miss Mona Lisa's narrowed eyes.

Hoping to keep the jealous twinge from her voice, Mona Lisa, fairly bursting out of a tight animal print, stated she'd had fun; "But G, I gotta run." Mona Lisa didn't mention the 'overtime' she would put in for her boss that evening. Purportedly then, she struggled with her coat. She pivoted too, headed in the opposite direction. With her grin unseen, Mona Lisa knew her gracious host would follow. Good, Mona cogitated because Gaye had no business riding Forrester with her house full of people. Although Mona Lisa would have let the man lick and stick *her* before everyone. At Abigail's door, Mona Lisa still 'struggled.'

Wanting only to get back to pushing and pumping, Joseph grudgingly accommodated the woman.

At last, Mona Lisa thought and smiled up at him. "For such a sexy man, Forrester," she winked, "you're strong and thoughtful too." Mona made sure her pendulous breasts protruded.

Quickly, Joseph stepped back, but Mona Lisa had made her point. *Her* gurlz were the ones the man would be missing. "Thanks for the help," she breathed, using her young girl voice. Then to Abigail, Mona Lisa said, "Wonder what we'd do without Forrester?"

"*I* don't intend to find out," Abigail stated, opening her door.

Mona Lisa got the message, but so what? Gaye was perturbed. It had only been a little harmless flirting. Heck, it wasn't like Gaye owned the man. Mona Lisa thought it as she made her voice sweet-ish. "Bye Joe— oh and;" Mona recalled the heat and the humping she'd intruded on, "be good—*or*," Mona Lisa's eyes flashed, "be good *at* it."

She attempted to air-kiss Abigail but met the door instead.

'Well eff you too,' Mona Lisa mentally snarled because Gaye hadn't wanted Forrester a little while ago. Now, shit had changed. Oh well. Sashaying provocatively in the exterior corridor, the heavier woman hoped the man noticed the extra sway she exhibited just for him.

Glancing back, however, Mona Lisa saw that slick Abigail's door was closed! Mona Lisa sighed. Whatever. She would meet her boss. When he crawled over her, naked, rotund, hairy, and reeking of liquor, she would fantasize about Joseph. Then she would pocket her pay, for this episode.

That transparent hussy, Abigail thought with narrowed eyes. "Joe, I hope you know that damsel in distress routine was for your benefit."

He eyed the woman he knew so well. Her level voice belied her true feelings. Therefore, Joseph said, "Gaye, I may be a man, but—"

"Oh, you're *all man*," she interrupted, running hands over him. "Hence Mona's act, and my suffering through. I should've punched her."

"I was saying," Joseph smirked, "that since most women think all men are stupid, your friend is the same. But I knew she didn't need help. I just wanted to get her gone. Now, can I lift you? Don't ask why."

Although she agreed, for just a second, Joseph felt Abigail's distrust. However, positioning himself beneath her, where it would do them both the most good, he vowed to ignore it. Then he just had to advise Abigail. "Babe, lose the hater. She's not a good friend. She's somebody you'll always need to check. You'll always be glancing over your shoulder."

Subsequently, Joseph cogitated but did not say it, then Abigail might wind up feeling the need to watch him too, which was unnecessary.

"So you've gone cold on me," she stated when he allowed her to slide to the floor before him. "Guess I can thank my cunning friend for that."

"Cunning-schmunning," Joseph sounded dismissive. "Just watch your back." That said, he caught Abigail's lower lip between his. Again, he hoisted her up, one hand lowering his zipper. "Now, where were we?"

Abigail clung and kissed him. "I try to skirt you around trouble..."

Joseph spoke while maneuvering. "Yeah, but you sound jealous."

"Can't I be, sometimes?" Feeling his hands on her bottom and his probing fingers, Abigail realized they'd never discussed jealousy.

"You can be," Joseph managed, bathing his tip in her honey. "Still, understand," he bit out, "I—don't get down—like that." Joseph then told himself to stop, to remove the swollen head, before he simply couldn't ease back out. Forcing himself to release Abigail, he growled. "Understand, Star, this is *you and me*." He fought to zip his uncooperative rod back in, "Only."

Man, did he want Gaye! Joseph wondered if it was her perfume, now all over him, that slowly drove him insane? Or was it her soft, warm, wet, bootylicious bod? "Star," he hungrily rasped. "No panties later."

"I can lose them *now…*" she suggested, far from satisfied.

Resting his head against a wall, Joseph banged it since he couldn't picture leaves or a rake. "Not now," he groaned, minus control. "Later."

"What then?"

"Kinky shit. Maybe I'll have you upside down…"

"What about now?" Abigail asked, wanting Joseph so badly.

"Now," the man sounded far from firm. "We're going back inside."

She nearly laughed to keep from crying in frustration. With the image of him, hard, hewn, naked, and glistening with sweat and skeet foremost in mind Abigail moaned, "I wish you'd go, so you could hurry back."

Joseph glanced at his watch. "I've got a few minutes –I think. I could break you off. You know, 'practice' for pleasures to come…"

Pondering it, Abigail moaned. Then thinking better, she shot back into her apartment. Grinning over a shoulder, she said –without words– that she wasn't about to get any more hot or bothered. Not just yet anyway, *but* she did mouth 'I'ma wear you out, later. I promise.'

Joseph watched the woman go. He felt akin to the big bad wolf as he ambled through her home. Putting fingers to his face, he inhaled. Smelling her, he told himself to stop, or he'd follow Abigail and—

Joseph forced himself to refocus. Dinner was over, and the dining table had been cleared. Those there debated illegal word use in a mean game of Scrabble. Passing the guest room, he glimpsed Sabrina and a few chattering cousins thrown haggardly across a bed. When laughter and the scent of special smoke floated from Abigail's bedroom, Joseph peered in.

Hunched over the phone, Patria puff-puffed and guffawed. With a sigh, he guessed he really would wait. He went to watch the game.

IN her kitchen, Abigail spoke to Radcliff's guest. "Anna-Maria, you don't have to put things in the dishwasher."

The woman's voice was sweet. "I don't mind."

"In this house," Abigail stated, "I wait on guests, and you're a guest."

Anna-Maria sighed. "Please, I really need to do something."

Carefully, Abigail eyed the woman who said she felt much like an outsider. The Scrabble table was full, and in the comfortable chairs, the older people discussed old times while the younger people stuck together.

Abigail heard the unvoiced plea to be allowed to fit in someplace other than before the TV. The woman added, "I know nothing about football."

Abigail smiled. "Well, maybe this once I could bend the rules."

"Thank you," Anna-Maria breathed, and Abigail's heart thudded. There was something about the woman, Abigail thought. Anna-Maria's smile and her soft voice seemed vaguely familiar, so Abigail leveled with her. "I once spent a holiday with a man. It was miserable because I spent the entire time feeling unknown and unwanted, so I do understand."

Washing a serving dish, Anna-Maria said Abigail was kind.

"Call me Gaye –and you think so because I want a clean kitchen."

Anna-Maria's refreshing chuckle caused Abigail to again analyze her. In just seconds, inconspicuously, Abigail noted the clothing, the shoes, and the jewelry, carefully chosen. The dark skin, so like satin, the sun-streaked hair –a cover for gray– and the unobtrusive fragrance; indeed, Abigail mused, all of that had to linger in Radcliff's ruminations.

Experiencing chest thuds again, Abigail turned away, not ready to face that the woman reminded her of…Glenda. However, wanting Anna-Maria to feel comfortable, Abigail touched the arm adorned with gold bangles. "Ma'am, you may have heard things that were said. I can only apologize and invite you to enjoy your stay here, in my home."

Abigail wondered had that come out right, just as Anna-Maria smiled. The older woman thanked the younger, a moment before Abigail's face froze. Watching Abigail ball a fist before her mouth, alarmed, Anna-Maria hesitantly spoke. "Gaye, are you alright?"

"I'm fine." Abigail waved to create a breeze. "I'm a bit hot. And," she added while taking a seat, "I've probably had too much excitement in too short a time." Artfully, Abigail shifted both their focus.

Aware that someone would ask, Anna-Maria truthfully replied while washing a large bowl. She'd met Radcliff in Jamaica. They'd both been at the home of a friend. "I believe she's your friendship aunt."

"Chunie!" Abigail recalled playing beneath the woman's soursop trees. "Oh, and talk about cook?" Abigail beamed, as Anna-Maria chorused with her, "She!" "Cow foot!" "Stewed tripe—" "Fried dumpling—" "Wi' a smidgen of salting." "And broad bean!"

"I'm sorry, Anna-Maria…" Abigail apologized "for re-directing the conversation. You were speaking of meeting my father."

Unperturbed, Radcliff's guest said, "Call me Anna," before she explained that Chunie had thrown a soiree. Radcliff, who'd also attended, asked Anna-Maria to dance, "Two left foot me. Well, after punishing his feet, mi not bother wi' letting your Papa outta mi sight again. Not that night, and not with the way the other women dem were flirting with him."

Abigail was delighted that the woman felt comfortable enough to candidly speak. Abigail was further impressed to later hear that Anna owned rental units in the states. She had prime property abroad, too, some of it left to her by her late husband. Well, Abigail mused, it did not appear that the woman was after what little Radcliff had put by. Although, Abigail thought, she might still discreetly dig a bit for true peace of mind.

She coaxed Anna-Maria to sit. Then she heard. Radcliff proposed.

Abigail looked down at the sparkling but modest ring as a lump rose in her throat. At long last, her father had found another to love.

Abigail fell silent as Anna-Maria poured a glass of sorrel. Not thirsty, the woman did so to allow the younger woman to absorb the news.

Abigail felt melancholy. She felt happy too. Slowly, the happy rose to overtake the sadness. Then she was left with just a twinge of sorrow.

In silence, Anna-Maria watched Radcliff's daughter, knowing that inside, the younger elegant woman emotionally churned, although calm was her façade. Their eyes met. Then Abigail's became luminous pools.

"Oh dear, Abig—Gaye, I did not mean to hurt you," Anna-Maria truthfully stated. She suddenly felt awful, and like perhaps she should have waited for Radcliff to inform his family, his way.

Abigail shook away tears and said she was happy for the couple. "I just feel for my mother." Abigail knew Glenda could never be replaced. She knew too that her father had to go on. Yet, Abigail felt a little sorrow.

"As a widow myself," Anna-Maria divulged, "I wondered whether my husband's memory would become less poignant over time. So I understand. You might wonder that same thing about your mother –with your father, the devoted husband she left behind."

Abigail felt semi-stunned as Anna-Maria continued. "For me, my Gil never will become less poignant or less loved. For your father, I suspect it will also be the same. He told me he will always love your mother."

Feeling marginally better, Abigail said, "You understand…"

"I do." Anna-Maria patted Abigail's hand. "Certain things need time. It is never easy to get used to there being another in a loved one's life."

Abigail agreed and revealed that indeed she had known. She said her father would not have brought Anna-Maria had she meant little to him. "He knows how critical his daughters can be. Aside from that, I trust Papa. I trust his choices. If I had to, I would trust him with my life."

Anna-Maria's hand went to her chest. The sentiment was beautiful.

Leaning forward, Abigail had to ask. "You know how she died?"

"Yes. Your father explained." Anna-Maria had also seen firsthand. The Wallace family still strove to deal with the after-effects of their loss.

Brightening, Abigail spoke. "Anna, I just realized. Papa can be happy again." She said that for too long, Radcliff had needed someone loving in his life. However, had he become seriously involved, he'd have felt most unfaithful. "He tried so hard not to disappoint my mom."

Abigail revealed that perhaps now she too could release painful memories. Maybe she would no longer remember her father trudging day after day to his church. Maybe she would stop thinking about him lighting candles for his lost love. Perhaps she would no longer feel thirteen again, at times, and so hurt because she had to retrieve him from the sanctuary. Now Radcliff could voluntarily come and go. Now, he might no longer desire to sequester himself away in tomb-like dim quiet.

Now Abigail could tuck away memories of pulling her father's hat down over his ears and buttoning his coat before they left his only solace. Seeing all in the eye of her mind, softly Abigail disclosed, "One day, when mi was grown, Papa and I had a long speak." Abigail said she had taken Radcliff's chilled hand. Softly she'd said, "Papa, yu must let go. Please." Abigail had admitted that memories were fine, "But they won't keep yu warm. Memories won't chase the lonely. Anna, I told Papa that memories cyan't rub a person's back, or kiss dem forehead, or do all de sweet little tings that a living lover would do."

Abigail sighed. "Papa said I was right, but memories were all he had."

Anna-Maria blinked back tears as her heart went out to her betrothed and his daughter. They had loved, and still loved, their special Glenda so. It caused one to wonder, had Glenda known how blessed she was?

"Well, Anna," Abigail sighed and reached for the woman's hand. "Enough of that. I would simply like to welcome you to de family. Oh, but I must warn you…" Abigail smiled. "One day yu may ask, what in blazes mi get myself into?"

Anna-Maria chuckled, and in her heart, Abigail whispered. She's not you, Mama, but you would like her.

Movement caught Abigail's eye, and she glanced up and into her father's smiling face. Gray now peppered his hair and goatee. Ah, what a dashing figure he cut, Abigail thought, just as her doorbell rang. She rose. In passing, she squeezed Radcliff's hand. "I like her."

## 16

ON her way to the door, Abigail got sidetracked. She watched Joseph and Jamaal Sr. chest bump. She laughed as her brother-in-law annoyed others. When Joseph sat, Abigail caressed his face. "Yu just wait," she whispered when he kissed her wrist inside. "Mi got something for yu."

"Gaye Denise..." Sabrina approached, looking strange. "There's a Courtney at the door—for Joe."

Abigail turned toward her kitchen. "You let him in, right?"

Grasping Abigail, Sabrina spoke slowly. "Gurl, this is not a him."

Abigail eyed her baby sister before she bent to Joseph's ear. "Are you expecting a Courtney?"

Absently, he responded. "Uh, yeah. We're 'bout to bounce." Prompted to turn back to the last few moments of the game, Joseph threw over a shoulder, "Say I need another minute, okay, bae?"

Abigail did not move, and sensing her behind him, blindly Joseph asked if she and his friend had met.

Churning with fury, Abigail stepped back while thinking, boy, did this man have nerve—inviting a woman to her home!

Through barely moving lips, Sabrina offered to tell the person to wait in the hallway. Turning, she swore. "Nobody invited this hussy in."

With the game over, Joseph headed after Abigail. Meaning to kiss her and promise to hurry back, he reached for the arm that she madly swung.

In the dining room, she maneuvered so that he missed. Yet he caught her around the waist. Brittle with rage, she rasped, "Shouldn't you go?"

Puzzled by the frost, Joseph wondered why lil cookie looked like she could spit fire. "Yo, where's all this anger coming from?" he asked.

Abigail stared and could not believe Joseph! He actually appeared shocked, like he wasn't the one wrong. "Unhand me," she hissed.

"Un-what you?"

"Get off me," Abigail spat, attempting not to let anger best her. To act out—like Gram Mary called it—would be easy. However, it would make her legitimate guests uncomfortable, when Forrester and his groupie—whom she would kick out—were not worth it.

"Gaye," Joseph pulled at her. "In the kitchen, talk to me a minute."

Talk? How could she even speak when hostility all but choked her? This was her Thanksgiving as host, and Joseph had tried to ruin it! He'd attempted to embarrass her by inviting some hoochie to her house!

Well, she would deal with him, but later. Forcing a deep breath, she appeared calm. "I want you to get your coat and be out. Take Carissa, too."

"The name's Courtney," Joseph corrected. "Courtney Loché, which you would have known had I introduced—"

"I don'tgivafu— a funky shoe what her name is." Abigail managed not to holler. "I want yu and that woman to go weh. Get out mi house!"

Stunned, Joseph recalled Abigail saying Courtney could stop by. That had not been two hours ago, so why the change? Why the rudeness?

"Hellooo…" The deep throaty voice emanated from Joseph's guest. "Yoo must be Aaabigayal. I'm Courtneee, and yoo have a lovely home."

Abigail didn't touch the sizeable hand as amiably she said, "Hello."

At different stances in the dining room, Sabrina and Patria openly watched as their sister removed herself from the confining circle. Airily she said while doing so, "Charlene, I'll get the door for you, and Joseph."

Patria's laughter bubbled up and out. Covering her mouth with a dimpled hand, the elder sister's whole body shook. That doggone Gaye should have been in movies, deftly flitting in and out of character. Bravo!

Amused too, Sabrina knew their middle sister's offer belied her ire.

Joseph shot Courtney a glance. "You mind waiting a minute?" He knew he'd been barely solicitous, but he didn't care. Striding after Abigail, Joseph gestured at a dining chair. "Courtney, sit—please."

Crossing to the eldest, Sabrina hissed. "So this chick gets to sit and cross her legs. And yu 'n mi get to see that de velveteen coat is too small."

"And we see her crush-up dress."

"She got no iron?" Sabrina sucked her teeth. "She needs a lesson."

Patria nodded. "Sounds like you're thinking what I'm thinking… "

In the kitchen, Abigail tossed food items into a plastic bag. "So you won't be able to say I didn't feed you," she grumbled.

Joseph strained to keep it level. "Abigail, what is the matter with you?"

She threw in a dinner napkin and a plastic fork. "Don't return these."

Joseph was two seconds from strangling her. "Gaye, what's up?"

Though she itched to fight, Abigail forced herself to inquire, "What should be wrong, honey?" She'd nearly choked on the last word.

"I don't know," Joseph breathed, "but it's something because you were fine a while ago." A thought struck, but he dismissed it because Abigail wasn't petty. She would not be upset about that—would she?

At any rate, Joseph called her on it. "Gaye, tell me you're not tripping because of Courtney." Intent to gauge Abigail's reaction, he watched her.

Abigail narrowed her eyes, not about to be baited. Neither would she allow Joseph to make her feel as though she was wrong when he was!

"So you're gonna say nothing," the man half-inquired. "Well, good, because I wasn't about to go through no jealous, little-girl crap, anyway."

"Then go through whatever you want, with your friggin' Corrine!"

There it was, Abigail's JaMerican temper. So she *was* tripping about Courtney. Guess they needed to discuss jealousy. With a finger at his temple, Joseph intended to get a fraction of satisfaction. "Who's Corrine?"

Abigail fumed, "Coreen, Clarise, Cow-hide—whatever she name is!"

Joseph yelled. "What the devil has Courtney got to do with anything?"

"I should snatch you bald!" Abigail spat. Quickly she turned. She breathed deeply so she wouldn't scream. Turning back, levelly, she spoke, and sounded psycho. "I'm not pleased that you invited Carol to my home." Abigail exhaled. "Maybe that's how you roll, entertaining groupies and such, but you won't do it here." Abigail appeared unruffled as she added, "My home is off-limits. Besides, as for some threesome, with Candace, if that's what you had in mind, I decline."

Seething with rage, Abigail shoved the overstuffed food bag at Joseph. She then counted the seconds until he left. Alone, she would remind herself. She could not control the actions of others. However, never again would she tolerate disrespect from one who said he loved her.

"When I told you, Gaye," Joseph began, measured and slow, "because I did not spring this shit on you, you said it was okay."

Abigail pointed, "Out." She felt like Joseph had tried to trick her.

"If that's what you want, kitten." Joseph walked. He then about-faced. "You're sure you don't wanna say bye to Courtney before we go?"

Abigail folded her arms. "I don't care to say goodbye to you."

That did it! Joseph sprinted over. "You care, or you wouldn't be upset."

Abigail shook with rage because Joseph was right. Tightly she clasped her hands; watching, he knew she fought not to throw something or slap him. Ready to catch her arm, he heard her say, "Joe, I do care; but I won't allow you to dog me. You work in a profession full of lost waifs, but I'm not like them. I don't need you, not at the expense of my dignity."

Abigail explained, she was not desperate. She wasn't even dazzled by Joseph's 'Producer' status. Therefore, she wouldn't put up with just anything to feel like, live like, or pretend to be, a star.

Confounded, Joseph asked, "What's my job got to do with anything?"

"If you were listening," Abigail rationalized, "you'd realize that your job with its hype 'n hoopla causes certain types of women to take mess, just to be with someone like you! However, I want exclusivity. I won't knowingly allow you to be with me and others, regardless of your job."

Suddenly Joseph felt utterly worn. Tired of fighting the same battle, he softly said, "Gaye, you, of all people, know better. You know me. You and I have history, babe. You know how I live, how I roll. I've dried your tears, and you cut my hair. You know my social, and I have yours, somewhere. It doesn't get more personal than that. I know every inch of your body. You know mine. We know each other's character...

"It's why you should know, baby, if I said Courtney is a friend, that's it. And think about this; I have never hidden anything from you. Think back to when you came to my house the time I had someone there. I told you. I also said—as you were leaving—that you were more important. Yet you chose to leave anyway. Think Star, about stupid games. Then remember, I don't play them, I take responsibility for my shit. I don't creep, or hide, because I'm a man," unlike that clown she'd been with.

Abigail really didn't hear Joseph, not through the jealousy and hurt cresting through her. She just wanted to be alone, with her tears and her questions. Therefore, she sighed and shrugged. "You still gotta go."

It was apparent he was not getting through, so Joseph guessed it would be best to leave. Hey, wait a sec, he thought and grabbed the insolent woman. Against her will, he held her. He spilled out that he took them seriously. "I'll say it again, Gaye. I do not play—or want—games."

Joseph said he wanted no part of anything that could ruin them. "Understand." He shook Abigail. "I've waited," he whispered with his throat aching, "too long to have you love me, to let anything come between us."

Abigail said nothing. Yet holding her, Joseph wondered how to make her understand. He wanted her, only her—despite her anger—for keeps.

With tears assailing, Abigail said, "Let me go, Joezeff."

He held her tighter, pressing his face to her fragrant neck, "Never."

"Maybe it's what I want."

"Too bad. You're stuck with me." Softly he admitted he didn't want to fight, as soothingly he stroked her back. "I just wanna love you, girl."

Abigail didn't want to fight either. Come to think of it, she knew Joseph had spoken the truth, too, because she knew him. She knew his character, as he'd said. He really did not hide potentially hurtful things from her. They had even discussed that curvy little lying actress with whom he had been photographed. Joseph admitted he'd slept with Actress. However, he'd been unattached then. Therefore, Abigail bit her lip, recalling. Joseph was not a cheat or a liar.

Still, "Why'd you act like this was a brother, a blast from the past?"

It was never supposed to have been a hassle, Joseph thought, wishing Abigail would drop it. "Look, Star, if I'd been thinking, things would have been different. Take my word for it. I know Courtney from way back. I'll tell you about it, but not now." Again, he shook Abigail. "Let – this – go."

Joseph had said it with such finality that Abigail knew not to press. Later she might, but currently, she bumped up against him with her hip.

"Next time you tell me that men aren't stupid," she said and sucked her teeth, "you had betta be able to back up that statement."

Joseph nearly smiled, aware that he would never live this down. Still, he didn't care. He covered Abigail's mouth with his own, and heat flared.

Engaged in kiss, he wished there was no Courtney to take around, no old partners to chat up, no Lyle and Kismet Staar in Astoria, no Fabian, with Valeria, in Lindenhurst Village to see. Were there no others awaiting him and Courtney, Joseph would not have released Gaye. Joseph could have continued to kiss and caress Abigail. He could have taken her on his lap, naked, of course, despite her house full up with guests.

With narrowed eyes, Joseph suddenly wondered how the woman in his arms could get him so riled up and yet keep the conjugal ever before him.

Slightly dazed, Abigail noticed Joseph's telltale vein. It throbbed in time with the pulsing between her thighs.

"Quit looking like that," he growled as her swelling breast tops begged him to bury his face in them. He tapped her booty. "I gotta go."

She put out a hand. "Answer something first."

"One question only, Star."

"You screwing her?"

Joseph palmed his forehead. "What? No!" That was ridiculous! Then because he only wanted simple things, like to be out and hurriedly back, so he could eat Abigail up, Joseph asked, "Where'd that come from?"

"It's just an inquiry," she said and licked her lips.

Joseph caught the gleam in her eye and was barely able to abide the fierce heat they suddenly generated.

Roughly, their bodies met. Their pelvises gyrated. "You wait," he panted, flush against her. His lips roamed her face, her neck, shoulders, and breast tops, while he squeezed and groped. "Wait'll I get back here."

"No." Abigail's breath emitted in spurts, "Mi need you. Now."

"Can't, now." He licked where her breasts met. Man! It wouldn't stave off hunger, the raw need for her, but it would have to do, until he returned.

"I get a no," she shimmied against him. "But what do yu tell Crista?"

Joseph should have released Abigail, but her perfume and her yielding body made it hard. "Yo, I'm trying to leave," he moaned, feeling her tits, not anyone else's. "And you're keeping me here."

Abigail lifted both hands away. "Go. Mi not stopping yu." Nevertheless, in his arms, she twisted, and Joseph knew. If he felt the sweet torture of her hip and her fat ass, one more time, brushing his groin...

"Tell me, Star," Joseph breathed, ardently fondling and kissing her. "Do you want me—as much as you think every other woman wants me?"

Her hands were under his jersey knit shirt, seeking. "I don't want you."

His lips were on hers. "So, you don't want me...to slide - up - in you? You don't want to feel this," his hardness, "in your tight, juicy, hot, spot?"

She pushed at him. "I don't like that term, slide up in." However, utterly frustrated, Abigail's eyes told another story. They said she needed just that. And knowing it, both his and her hands flew to Joseph's zipper, at the very moment that someone called out.

"Let her go, Joe."

"Dag blame it!!" He swore. "Who the devil called Lucy' n Ethel?"

Brushing the snide inquiry aside, Patria entered, followed by Sabrina. The eldest smirked. "Well, now, I don't have to say lower your voices."

Sabrina was jokey. "I don't have to say kiss and make up,"

Yet in Joseph's arms, Abigail chuckled as he asked, why didn't Big and Little disappear? Then he could get back to the matter at hand.

Awkwardly, Abigail twisted as she called, "Peaches, do me a favor."

"Yah?"

"Open de door; Bina, t'row Joezeff girlfriend outta mi house."

"Wow." The youngest grinned. "Cohesive thought, Ma-Ma."

Abigail and Joseph both appeared puzzled. "What?" they chorused.

"Dat chile long gone." Sabrina bowed to Patria. "I thank de queen."

Regally, Patria nodded. "Queen Biggie thanks you too, Bina."

Joseph bellowed. "What are you two thanking each other for?"

"Queen Peaches pulled your 'girlfriend' outta mi sister's cheerr."

"And Bina slammed the door when I pushed your girlfriend's cute but tackay bahind outta our sister's home—that she entered, *uninvited!*"

Raucously then, Abigail and her sisters laughed and laughed. Joseph masked his own smile because, really, the Wallace 3 were too much. Yes, when someone else was being put through the rigors of their antics. Now, though, Joseph soberly thought, he would have to smooth things with Courtney, whom Sabrina speculated had once been a man.

"She beautiful, but with that heavy voice and Adam's apple..."

"Honestly Joe," Patria began, "how could you? Come over here—"

"Mind your business, Peaches."

Patria pointed, "My sister." She reversed the finger, "My business."

"Yo wipe that smirk off your face!" Joseph barked at Thomas.

Sinbad's look-alike had appeared in the doorway behind Patria, his lady. "No smirk, bruh; I'm just assessing the situation." Thomas then spoke to Patria. "That embrace looks mighty cozy, don't it, Queen?"

"Yo, assess this, Thommy-boy," Joseph growled, nodding at Patria while holding Abigail. "That one is always more trying than this one."

Jamaal Sr. also appeared and cautioned his wife. "I heard what you said, Bina, and as Counsel, I advise you. Stay outta peoples' affairs."

Sabrina slyly smiled. "I only stated the obvious, Maal. Joe's pretty friend could have once been a man. If so, then good, big ups to him; and Gaye Denise need not worry. We all know Joe. No ex-man for him."

A few chuckles rose from some gathered. Others appeared under the guise of seeking more to eat.

Jamaal Sr. jumped in on Joseph's behalf. It was unfair, Jamaal said, for three women to gang up on one man, "Even though you, dawg, were colossally stupid. You didn't think, Joe! Bringing a honey up in here?"

Jamaal said, "I'm surprised Sis didn't severe yo' head with one of her flying objects."

Thomas spoke and spooned up cobbler, "Not smart, bruh."

Patria tapped her man's arm. "That's all Bina, and I were saying."

Turning on his sister-in-law, Jamaal Sr. shook his head. "You be quiet, Peaches, because you, my wife, and Sis are trouble." Heady, mouthy, belligerent creatures they were, but the attributes, Jamaal knew, actually covered for three very soft hearts.

"But Joe was wrong," Sabrina mewled.

"Still," Jamaal backed his wife down. "It was three of you against one. That's why I gotta stick up for Joe here because there is a proverb. It says: *He who sleeps while his neighbor's house is afire is a fool.*"

Patria batted her adhered eyelashes. "What?"

"In this situation, the proverb means: Thomas and I can't stand, doing nothing, while Joe goes up in flames, or you three –fire–will burn us, too."

"Jamaal Dudley," Patria called. "Homeboy-turned-law man, that sounds like puffery to me." Magisterially, she waved. "Whatever. The truth is we no longer want you in our family. You're proving disloyal."

People laughed, and the brother-in-law shrugged. "Please, Queen Peaches." Jamaal further scoffed, "You girls need me."

"For what?" The trio of sisters indignantly chorused.

"Control. I keeps Pat and Sis in line. Bina? She needs something else."

Laughter rose, while calmly Jamaal nodded at Joseph and Thomas. "Yo you two need to understand one thing." Especially since Thomas had mentioned the desire to have Patria move into his sprawling colonial. "With these women, you may think you getting one, but trust me, brothas, at points, you will wind up with all three."

Someone guffawed, and Joseph chuckled before he whispered for only Abigail to hear. "I need to go, Star," although he'd have loved to stay.

Abigail watched him make his way to her kitchen door. Then taunting Joseph, she called out, "Give Corina my regards."

Stiffening, Joseph about-faced and worked his way back. Since Gaye wanted to put on a show, he would aid her. Therefore, he dramatically swept Abigail up into a zealous kiss. Palming her head, Joseph devoured her. Startled, Abigail pushed at Joseph, but he refused to release her. Only when she leaned in, wrapped her arms around him, and gave herself over to the pleasure did he step away. To do so took all his strength.

Those congregated cheered.

Falling in step behind Joseph, who again attempted to leave, Jamaal Sr. clapped his back. "Way to go, Joe. Big Maal's proud of you, baby."

With his cobbler bowl in hand, Thomas fell in line behind the men.

Jamaal turned. "See? All you women need is a li-ittle control."

"Uh-huh, and I've got what you need," Sabrina stated, folding her arms beneath her bosom. Imperviously, she pushed her puppies up higher. She watched as Jamaal's eyes rounded. With a gleam in her honey-brown orbs, Sabrina winked and made an announcement. "Oh, but you—husband of mine—won't be getting any of what you need, not tonight, because you crossed me, my Queen, and Mother-Sister."

At Jamaal's surprised look, Sabrina pursed her lips. She also hid a grin as she waggled her fingertips. Waving him off, she sweetly sang out.

"Go on, Counselor, with your big fine chocolate self. You were leaving –with the men. Right?"

# 17

AT nearly 12:45 a.m., Abigail lay in bed mentally replaying the day's events, including the Courtney fiasco. Again, she had dropped the kindness ball, this time with someone other than her ex. For that, Abigail asked forgiveness. Then she recalled kissing Joseph before a crowd. Ugh! How she wanted to forget the scene that Anna called 'the cake's icing.'

Abigail recalled bursting into tears when the crowd disbursed. Offering comfort, both Sabrina and Anna-Maria asked why she cried.

"I don't know," she had said, but Abigail knew. She'd aired dirty laundry before others, as Mama used to say. Abigail had cried for other reasons. Seeing Gram Mary had dredged up old hurts. Knowing Radcliff was getting on with his life hurt more, although his new lady was nice.

Nice new Anna-Maria had even begged Abigail to see that she had pulled off a most successful holiday fete.

Sabrina agreed. "You outdid yourself, Ma-Ma." Then Sabrina puffed herself up like a barnyard rooster. "You did, with a little help, from yours truly." Sabrina curtsied and made Abigail laugh through her tears.

Yet afterward, Abigail cried on, perhaps because she should not have let Gram do all that work. Although Inez had wanted to prepare the lovely breakfast, despite arthritis. It made even simple tasks arduous.

Abigail lay in bed. She recalled Anna-Maria saying the whole 'Joseph thing' had been sweet. Anna-Maria had twittered that anyone could see the love flowing between the beautiful twosome.

Yeah, Abigail thought, anyone but Courtney. Abigail pounded her pillow. Coupled with Abigail's jealousy, Courtney had been the catalyst for the ruckus, while in the other room, the older Wallace family members had remained calm. Gram and her sister Agatha had sewed for their church bazaar, and Radcliff had studied the paper like his daughter and Joseph hadn't raised cane. Forgetting her pillow, Abigail realized she'd done just what Patria had advised her and Sabrina not to do. She'd made a mountain out of a molehill when she should have been courteous. Abigail could have spoken with Joseph later in the evening. Then, she could have told him why his bringing an old friend, a woman, to her home had raised her ire.

*Well, just forgive yourself, and do better next time.*

Abigail wondered if there would be a next time. Sure, she and Joe had 'debated' many times. On a few public occasions, they'd both played the fool. However, he usually shrugged afterward and said their arguments were water under a bridge, forgotten. What if this time was different? What if he wouldn't want to speak with her again? Lord forbid, Abigail ruminated, but what if he was still out with Courtney, snuggled up with her, on her last night in town? While Abigail, Joseph's supposed-to-be woman—or his ex, now—lay in her big bed, worrying. All because she had been distrustful and had driven her man into the arms of another...

*Quit allowing your thoughts to run wild.*

"SHE does need rest," Sabrina agreed. Companionably, she and Inez sat at the table. Beautiful bone china cups and saucers were before them. Sabrina sipped and thought about her father, who, with his lady, now visited friends. Sabrina also thought about Patria and the girlfriend who had come to see her. They had gone clubbing, just like in years past. This time though, they hadn't snuck out of a dormitory window. Thomas and others had gone too, as Patria whooped, "Yes mon, reggae nights!"

Sabrina's thoughts returned to Gram, seated across from her in the now clean, quiet kitchen. Gram was praying, Sabrina knew. It was what Gram did. Sabrina also knew because Gram murmured, "Bread of Heaven." That hymn she often sang when calling on the Lord.

"So, yu, mi, and Agatha de only ones left?" Inez gazed at her granddaughter, seated with her toddler on her lap.

"Jamaal's here," Sabrina said of her husband. In the morning, he would go from the airport to work at the law firm. Rising, Sabrina lowered her son to his great-grandmother's lap. Lifting the coffee pot, she poured the gourmet blend black for her grandmother. "And a splash of Mr. Whiskey for me." When seated, Sabrina watched her son, who profusely sucked on a pudgy thumb. With round eyes, the child absorbed his great-grandmother's every move.

Gingerly, Inez rocked. "Mi pray dem two go on and get married."

"Why Gram?" Sabrina teased. "You want more great-grandchildren?"

"Maybe," the matriarch admitted. She added that the sweetie in her arms could use one his own size to tumble with. "Children need other children;" Inez said it kept them from becoming an adult too soon.

Again, the matriarch mentioned Abigail and Joseph. "Those two seem different, now. You know?"

"I noticed." Sabrina nodded because the couple, always close, currently seemed more consumed with each other than ever before.

Inez seemingly changed the subject. She mentioned a dream she'd had. There had been fish, she said, in murky water.

Sabrina recalled the fish dream and what it meant. The toddler's mother said she wanted nothing to do with another baby any time soon.

"Don't have to be you, chile..." Inez remarked.

"Wait, Gram." Sabrina mentally backtracked, clinking her cup onto its saucer. "You said the water was murky, not clear." That didn't sound right. "You didn't say your dream fish were brightly colored either, as usual."

Inez gazed at her great grandson, whom she continued to rock.

Again, Sabrina sensed that the prayer wheel was turning. She knew for sure when she heard the first strains of 'Rock of Ages...'" Whenever cocoa-colored Inez hummed that hymn, she was definitely praying.

Remaining quiet, Sabrina pondered her grandmother's dream. Sabrina did not like the connotation. Something was amiss. Therefore, the ninety-first Psalm that she'd been taught, the one that she'd recently begun teaching her son, came to mind. [The Person] *that dwells in the secret place of the Most High shall abide under the shadow of the almighty.*

Again, Sabrina pondered the implications of her grandmother's dream. "The last time you told me about fish, Gram, we got him." Sabrina indicated her son. "There was clear water, though. Actually, whenever you had that dream, it meant one soon born; and the fish were beautiful."

Inez closed her eyes, continuing to rock, and pray. Moments later, the matriarch also forced herself to tell her youngest grand the same thing she'd told herself since having the disturbing dream. "Don't fret, baby, because come what may, God will take care."

HER telephone rang, and groggily Abigail peered at her bedside clock. Nearly two a.m.—who would call at such an hour, and for what? Oh Lord, early morning phone calls usually meant trouble... Hurriedly, Abigail reached for the receiver. "Hello?"

"Star. You alright?"

Joseph! Abigail's heart leaped as her eyes opened. "Joezeff, I'm sorry, for today." She sat up, admitting she had no idea what had gotten into her earlier. "I've just been the *strange*st person lately."

Tenderly Joseph replied, "Don't give it another thought." He almost smiled too because he loved the woman, with her impulsive, impossible self. As he had driven Courtney around, Joseph had acknowledged that. He had also realized that Gaye reminded him of his mother.

At one time, Miz Maddie had been recovering from hurt and distrust. As a small boy, he'd watched her push her then-suitor away. Sure, she'd wanted and had even loved Halloway. Still, Joseph's mom hadn't believed the man would stay. Hal persevered and wore down Madeline's defenses. Then together, slowly, they'd deconstructed her wall of containment.

Therefore, as he and Courtney exited his car, the adult Joseph had cogitated, Joseph was like his old man. It was the reason Joseph would keep exercising fortitude. He would tread through Abigail's occasional distrust. However, while chatting up his chums, Joseph had pondered calling Gaye. He'd even fingered his cell phone. Nevertheless, the question of whether she would want to argue rose, so he'd put off calling until he could no longer stand it.

"Look, Sweetness," Joseph said into the phone, immensely relieved that Abigail was calm, "wasn't any harm done today."

Actually, when he'd had gotten alone, Joseph threw his head back and laughed. The precariousness of being crowded in Gaye's kitchen, kissing her, and barking at her family before her guests had been something! In fact, he loved her more, if it was possible. Joseph loved Abigail's kooky clan, too. Sure, the woman caused him angst and stirred emotions in him that he could live without. Her sisters, 'Pam & Gina' were pests. However, they all enriched his life. They were the siblings he'd never had.

Realizing he was still on the phone, Joseph spoke. "Star, I just needed to know you were okay."

"I am," Abigail admitted while wondering *why* Joseph cared when she gave him mostly grief.

"Well. Okay," he said; Abigail knew he would soon hang up. However, she wasn't yet ready to let him go, so lamely she mentioned his food.

"Yeah, I left it," he acknowledged. "I'll get it tomorrow."

Tomorrow was too long away, Abigail thought, suddenly needing to see him and know he hadn't been put off by her earlier actions.

"Gaye?" Joseph called, sensing there was something she hadn't said. "Star, you sure everything's okay?" Joseph felt things were better between them, now that he'd called, but still, there was something more. His sixth sense, which had never failed, indicated it.

Abigail bit her lip. She wanted Joseph to know she needed him, but she had all but handed him to another. So how could she say that she simply wanted to lie in his arms? Or that she needed to know they yet loved.

Unaware of Abigail's thoughts, Joseph felt she still seemed too subdued. "You there, bae?"

"I am," Abigail sniffled, blessed beyond measure to have him care.

"Star, talk to me," Joseph coaxed, knowing she mentally berated herself. "Tell me what's going on."

"I don't know what to say. Maybe I just need a vacation."

Joseph agreed. Abigail really hadn't been herself lately, and he was starting to worry. "Star, I'm gonna look into someplace nice for you." Lounging on the plush sofa in his Tudor home, the producer visualized taking his baby somewhere warm and breezy, a secluded island maybe.

They could lie together beneath swaying palms. He would slowly peel swimwear from her lush oiled-up bod, starting with her top. He would uncover one of her glorious globes, and bending, he would open-mouth kiss and lave it while encircling her nipple with his tongue. Muscular and ready, he would then remove her bikini bottom. With her shapely legs splayed before him, he would use a big hand to open her. He would taste her before she would guide him, enlarged and throbbing, into her heat...

And not one of her friends or family members would be present. His and Abigail's vacation spot would be only balmy breezes and boning.

What did Gaye *mean* she was just asking? 'Where's your friend 'Klondike' did not sound to him like she didn't intend to start shit. Paradise and lovin' disappeared, that fast.

"*Courtney*," Joseph spat, irritated, "is at his—I mean *her*—mother's house. Where she'd have been last night, had her peops been in town." Dadgummit. Joseph felt like Gaye had accused him of something, although she actually hadn't, and Joseph didn't like it.

"Joe, you sound upset."

"I am," he replied and forgot Courtney, whose fault it was that he was in the doghouse, although *Ms. Baby had been right.* How though, Joseph wondered, had Sabrina known?

Courtney had indeed been born with male apparatus.

Upon arriving at Joseph's home, the 'new' Courtney had whinnied that he—she, had always had the heart of a woman. It was why now her outside matched her inside. Joseph had been supportive.

He sighed, knowing he would never hear the end of this Courtney stuff. So he wouldn't mention that the only thing Courtney retained from his days as a natural man was his –or her– name. That and the Adam's apple, the bone of which would soon be shaved down, via surgery.

None of it was confusing to Joseph. He knew Courtney had to live in truth. However, it was confusing for some of their frat brothers. Those men had once looked on Courtney as one of them. Although the fellas wondered, not one had dared ask Courtney what had been done with the male equipment he'd been assigned at birth.

Yet on the phone, and lounging, Joseph sighed. He knew if the truth got out, the Wallace sisters, Jamaal *and* Thomas, would laugh *–not at Courtney, never.* However, they would laugh at *him.* They would say Joseph was blind; he hadn't seen that Courtney wanted him. Someone might even say what Miz Maddie had; that Courtney probably always had, perhaps even since Courtney and Joseph's middle school days.

Joseph sighed because, thankfully, Courtney had been otherwise occupied during his Morehouse College Maroon Tigers football period. Or at Joseph's HBCU, Courtney might have found a way to pat the music major's tight end. The music producer forgot his friend because he only wanted to be near one woman, the one of whom he never stopped thinking. Therefore, Joseph agreed that Abigail was right. His friend could have stayed with someone else. "And just so you know," Joseph sheepishly admitted, "I didn't think about any of that when Courtney called, or when she appeared to show me her new look."

"Typical," Abigail snorted.

"Yo, what's that supposed to mean?" Joseph barked because if Gaye wanted to fight, this time she would do it solo. Shoot. He'd called because he had been worried about her, and this was how she repaid him?

Abigail apologized and promised she wouldn't start again.

Dag-blame-it if she didn't sound sexy, especially when she further humbled herself to say she had embarrassed him and them earlier.

"So for that too, I apologize."

"Who was embarrassed?" Joseph asked, swelling, partially with pride, because his baby had pondered *his* feelings versus her own. "Hey," he suddenly called, riddled with desire. "You feel like some company? I know you've got a house full of people," he told the woman who made him crazy, angry one minute, then slavish and lustful the next. "But suppose I ride out to get you, bring you back here for a while."

"Joe," Abigail breathed, excited. "Just because there are people here doesn't mean you can't come ova."

He wanted no distractions. "I'll pick you up. By the time I take this lil ride, you should be ready. We'll zip back here," and it would be on!

Abigail became philosophical while feeling tingly and naughty. "Joe, Great Neck is too far to travel *from,* then *back to* again, tonight."

"But I wanna make a baby with you, baby." The words were out before he knew it because Abigail was his whole life.

"You didn't let me finish..." Abigail's heart pounded because had Joseph really said that? She'd contemplate later. At present, she had to inform Joe that her father and his lady friend had decided to stay with others. Feeling utterly giddy, Abigail also told her man that Sabrina had remade Radcliff's bed for their grandmother. "So that means—"

"In *your room,* you're alone." Joseph grinned, getting the picture.

Abigail's heart hammered as she whispered, "I'm already wet."

"Well, you know alone, and wet, are the doctor's espesheeali*tay.*"

"So you're coming?" she asked, imagining him there with her.

"Most def." Joseph rose from his sofa, leaving his beautiful den.

"Hurry," Abigail advised. She said they only had a few hours before she would take her sister and brother-in-law, Jamaal, to the airport.

Joseph scoffed. "I'm not interested in airports, Miss Baby or her man."

Abigail's grin was audible. "Then, what *are* you interested in?"

Joseph spoke and pulled on jeans, "What I'll get out of driving so far."

Abigail knew the drive was nothing for him, yet she played along. "You'll get today's mess made up to you..."

"Heckuva lotta making up you're proposing to do," Joseph said and grabbed a jacket. Ah yeah, he would cash in on alleged pain and suffering.

"Well then," Abigail declared, hearing his jangling keys. "Just stay out in Long Island, and we'll continue to *talk* on this phone."

"No way, I'm in the garage, girl. Hear that? House alarm on. Now I'm in the car. Thank you, genie, for raising my garage door. I'm backing out, bae. Driving now, as the garage door closes."

Abigail heard Jasmine Sullivan's *Lions, Tigers & Bears* playing through Joseph's speakers. Abigail just had to say, "I love that song."

Joseph thought the production was great, but he wanted to know what the lyrics meant to his lady.

Softly Abigail replied. "Although there are many scary things in life, like lions, cancer, and other stuff, nothing's as scary to me, as loving you."

Joseph accelerated. "I'm easy to love."

Abigail agreed. "I just don't want to muck this up. You know?"

IN the dimness, she met him at the door, wearing a sheer, peach nightshirt. His soft full lips covered hers, and she tasted the candy that he'd furiously sucked on in anticipation of doing the same to her.

"Mi legs gettin' weak," Abigail said, inhaling Joseph's wonderful scent.

"I got you, Mommy," he murmured with his lips on Abigail's.

She savored his strength, and the feeling of his large hands beneath her nightshirt, roaming her back and exploring her abdomen. When Joseph cupped, fingered, and kneaded her heavy breasts, Abigail moaned. Then with her hands back of his head, she guided his mouth to a needy nipple.

After devouring her through the sheer garment, Joseph dove under it and did the same. Looking up, he frowned. "What's the problem here?"

Abigail cradled his head, desiring more. "You're talking."

"No. You're supposed to make up for today. For what you did to me."

"Oh," Abigail nodded. Okay," she lifted Joseph's pullover. Placing her lips on his inviting brown chest, she sounded muffled, "Mi sorry, lover."

Joseph held his breath while Abigail undid his fly and descended to her knees before him. In lilting patois, she apologized for any and everything. With closed eyes, Joseph murmured he liked when she was apologetic.

"Do you now?" Abigail asked, loving his rod's silken feel, the jump and the seek, each time she moved her hands or her mouth.

"Yes, since I was so hurt." Joseph's mind matriculated. "Actually," he said, needing to extract all from her throaty apology, "I was devastated."

Abigail swirled his tip and looked up. "Were you?"

"I was," he pushed, eager to soak up more of her warm wet penitence. "So...I'm going to need you to be more sorry –so much sorrier, in fact."

Abigail chuckled and took Joseph deeper, as leaning against the door, he bit his lip. He also strained to refrain from taking her then and there.

When he could no longer stand it, he pulled Abigail from her knees. With hands beneath her arms, he slid her scathing hot body upward, over his legs and powerful thighs, so his shaft could meet the nectar in which he longed to baptize himself. Slipping into her humid cavern, Joseph thought, things would only get any better if he glided up inside her.

Wrapping him in her arms, between kisses, Abigail murmured that Joseph should put her down.

"Can't," he breathed. "Want you. Right...now."

Abigail felt Joseph slip and slide. "The chain, on the door," she mentioned. It rattled with their every move. "Joe, we'll wake dem."

She meant her fam. He wanted to forget them, for the time being. "Don't care," Joseph rasped, "Now. Inside." That was all he wanted.

Her lips were on his as her legs encircled him, "Shhh."

Whom was she shushing? He wasn't the one moaning loud enough for a neighbor to hear. This he reminded her while cupping her lush bottom.

"Sweet-sweet," her voice became firm, "put me down."

Reluctantly he slid her, slowly, over his virile body. Ooowh.

"Sit," she whispered as an idea took shape. "No, take off your boots first." Down she tugged his already open jeans. "Now, sit."

He gave her a quizzical look but did as bid.

She watched, noticing the telltale vein. Yesss! That and stand-up-fella said Joseph was more than ready. Abigail eyed beautiful brown skin and rippling muscles, as with a bare foot, she edged his garments aside.

"Mi gonna sit on yu."

Feverishly wanting, Joseph watched as Abigail slowly lowered herself to the lap to which he, with both hands, pinned her. A half-sob escaped her when she found herself impaled and filled, but pleasurably she began to move, on him and around him. Joseph did the same, repeatedly meeting her. Accommodating, her warm body pleasured him. Then he smelled them and heard their coupling. Manically driven, he tore her nightshirt

169

away. Hungrily he fit his mouth over the glorious orbs that he laved, fervently sucked, fondled, and squeezed, ever pushing upward within her.

Abigail shivered, slipping by degrees into waves of ecstasy. While Joseph, holding her hips, purposefully thrust and stirred. Gasping, she felt him, rigid and thick. He felt her, soft and warm, begin to spasm.

"Shhh, Babe," his mouth covered hers as he swallowed her mewls. He also palmed the back of her head. Conscious that her nosey family could come poking about, Joseph forged on, giving Abigail more. "Shhh, my baby." Kissing Abigail and pushing higher, Joseph forgot her peops. Tugging her hair and nibbling her neck, he vowed to leave no place inside her untouched. Repeatedly, he rocked into her. He let her ecstatically ride until...she no longer moved but draped haplessly around him.

Sated, with closed eyes, Abigail pressed her perspiring forehead to Joseph's, and only then did he allow his substance to flower within her.

With their juices pooling warm and satisfying between them, he sighed. Then leaning back, he relaxed against the door.

Placing her palms on Joseph's shoulders, Abigail leaned back in his cradling arms. "What're you grinning about?" she asked.

Joseph shrugged, wanting to say that for some reason, he liked sitting bare behind on the foyer floor with his woman on top of him. However, saying it would have taken strength he no longer had. Therefore, again he shrugged. He asked, hating the very idea, "When do we have to get up?"

Also reluctant to move, Abigail smiled and rested her head on Joseph's shoulder. "Well, we could let Gram catch us... "

"Not a chance." Joseph sighed. He said he'd race Abigail to her room.

Yet on him, she noticed. He didn't move a muscle. While extricating herself from the tangled mass of limbs that they'd become, she said, "Oh, and I'm aware that Coolio is—or was—a man."

"Coolio?" Joseph echoed, then his laughter rumbled out. He knew Gaye meant his onetime fraternity brother, Courtney. So she knew, huh? Yet, she had caused him angst. Well, Joseph surmised, for that, she would pay. Quickly, he devised the impending method of payment. He wanted her again, this time bent over, after midnight in the moonlight.

IN the light of dawn seeping through the filmy ecru panels, Joseph woke beside Abigail in her bedroom. When he offered to drive the Dudley clan to the airport, she groaned. "Mi wish dey leave tomorra."

Thinking Abigail wanted more time with her family, Joseph said, "You're going to miss them, huh?"

"I am," the woman acknowledged, "but if they left tomorrow, I could get some sleep today."

Lying with both sculpted arms behind his head, Joseph heartily laughed because he should have known.

LATER, wearing a roomy, winter-white turtleneck, black leggings, and boots, Abigail crowed when her brother-in-law entered her kitchen. "Look at you, Counselor!" Abigail approved Jamaal Sr.'s tailored, navy, pinstriped suit, feather-print silk tie, and polished leather shoes. "Impeccable," she said of the outfit visible beneath his all-weather trench.

Grasping a napkin, Jamaal selected a Danish. "Got to see a client."

"Oh, okay. Joe went down for those this morning. They're fresh, from the bakeshop up the street. Coffee?" Abigail raised the carafe that she would carry to Joseph's car.

Always subdued in the mornings, Jamaal nodded. He also asked, "Wouldn't it be something, Sis, if we could work in sweats?"

"It would," Abigail nodded. "However, since money haffie mek, ask yourself. Would your clients take you seriously, yu wearing sweats?"

Brother-in-law was pensive, "In my field, most probably wouldn't."

"That's because sometimes the right attire conveys authority and capability. I tell my teenagers," the ones that Abigail mentored, "they should appear to care about details—no scuffed shoes, flyaway hair, body odor, or dirty fingernails. I stress being well-prepared and organized. I tell my girls if we overlook the little things, then our clients will wonder how we can care about the big things. You know?"

Jamaal did know. He also knew that although he considered Sis a true pain in the neck, sometimes, she and the biggest pain—Patria, were both two undeniably smart, formidable businesswomen. It was why they were excelling in their careers; just like his wife.

## 18

ALL was quiet in Joseph's car as the frosty gray morning whizzed by. To Abigail, it seemed that even the nearly naked trees looked forlorn. Beyond her window, they seemed to reach out. To her, they appeared to want to hold her family together, if but for a short while longer.

From the rear of the vehicle, Sabrina spoke. "Mi gon' miss yu…."

Abigail's eyes filled as she turned.

"Don't do that," the younger sister advised. Averting her eyes, she burrowed deeper into the cozy heat of her leather seat.

Aside, Jamaal reached over his son's car seat to take his wife's hand. To the soft-hearted woman, he said, "Don't worry, Sis, as soon as they work my nerves, I'll send both Bina and the baby back."

Abigail smiled and faced forward. Joseph intimately squeezed her knee. She knew he was silently telling her it was okay. He was not leaving.

Because they had time, at the airport, Joseph parked and the four adults tromped inside. Abigail carried her nephew.

When she and Joseph could go no further with the Dudleys, Abigail kissed the baby, who cried. Waking up, he could not understand feeling torn from his 'playmate,' and though she hated to release him, Abigail dutifully opened her arms. Jamaal Sr. gently lifted his toddler away.

"Go with God, Sis," the young father said and kissed her. Facing Joseph, both men clasped hands. "My brother…"

"My brother. Stay strong, Maal."

Ordinarily jovial, Jamaal spoke with his hand in Joseph's. "Got to, bruh; as the keepers and protectors of our women and families."

Joseph nodded. "It's our honor *and* our inherent duty."

Jamaal Sr. squeezed Joseph's hand, and without words, both turned.

Ever fashionable and bundled in 'fur,' Mrs. Dudley lingered. Again she hugged mother-sister. Then teetering on high-heeled boots, Sabrina caught up to her husband. With her brilliant-hued silk scarf billowing, the baby sister turned, mouthing as she walked, 'I love you…'

Then Sabrina, too, was gone, as Abigail prayed, "God keep them." Yet she stood, hoping to glimpse the handsome trio just once more. However, seamlessly, they had become part of the holiday throng.

Standing aside, Joseph imagined the day when he would carry his offspring. And as Sabrina had with Jamaal, Joseph envisioned Abigail walking by his side with her smaller hand in his.

Squeezing her fingertips, he suggested they go. On the ride home, he asked if she wanted to stop, perhaps to eat.

Abigail sighed. Wearily, she said, "I've got so much food at home, still, until I don't want to see any more for a good while."

Joseph understood. At a light, he embraced her. Giving and caring woman that she was, he said she missed her family already, "Right?"

"Gram, Papa, Auntie, and Anna are still here," Abigail replied.

"But you miss those three," Joseph stated because it was okay.

"Sabrina was always my baby," Abigail recalled aloud as he turned onto the Grand Central Parkway. "And though I love her, so much, and my brother too," she voiced, as snow flurried outside, "I think I'll miss the baby most this time." Abigail frowned. "You think that's wrong?"

Joseph reached for her. Keeping his eyes on the blacktop, he inquired. "Now, what could be wrong with loving that little guy?" He also wondered if he should mention that he'd thought about posterity, lately.

"Actually," Joseph began because, indeed, he would share, "I think the baby pinpoints a need we both have right now. For me, the funny thing is I never knew I would feel this way –not before you." He also admitted, "I'm four months from forty. Therefore, I figure, if I don't have a kid soon, Gaye, I probably should forget it. I mean, even if you conceived now, by the time our kid turned eighteen, I'd be about sixty."

Abigail bit her bottom lip and stared. "So your clock ticks too?"

"Shhh." Joseph winked. "It's man's greatest secret."

Abigail smiled as she wondered if Joseph really understood how she longed to nuzzle an infant, her own. As a man, did he too yearn to smell that ever-calling sweet baby scent?

"It'll happen, Star," Joseph assured, as though he'd read her mind.

He was so caring, Abigail thought until she had to love him.

He saw her mouth open and quickly spoke. "I love you too, babe."

"I was going to say that!" She laughed, pressing her lips to his cheek.

173

"I know," Joseph said over Everette Harp's smooth sax. "And if you lean over here again, with them lethal lips, I'll have to pull over."

Eagerly Abigail inquired, "You'll give me more of last night?"

Joseph chuckled. "Star, that happened at three something in the a.m."

"Okay it was this morning. Still, it was good." She licked her lips as she mentally re-lived the steamy shower they'd taken together, in the name of saving time. Her voice became sultry. "You know, being out at the airport –with all that construction— mi feeling kind'a dirty..."

"Oh you're dirty, alright," he laughed. Now she had him wanting to lather her up again and take them both soaring, like he had that morning.

Abigail bit her lip. "I'm imagine myself and yu, in de shower. There'll be bubbles. I'll be slick and slippery, and you'll be hard and—"

"Yo, open your window," Joseph roughly commanded because they had to cool down. Or he'd need her to sit on him, again.

When Abigail finally let her window back up, Joseph recalled the awards presentation to which he had asked her to accompany him. "Remember, it's in Cali, the third week in December. I want you to wear something special. I'll see to it. Call Seraph," the famed New York couturier, "for a showing. I might go with you—check out the goods."

Abigail grinned. "You wanna look at my behind when she fits me."

"That's what I said." Joseph winked. "I'll check out the goods."

Abigail half-listened as Joseph advised her to go all out.

Driving, he felt her going cold, even before she turned to stare out of the window. "Star," Joseph called. "Did you hear me?"

Vaguely his voice penetrated the mental place that lately Abigail found herself escaping to when she felt ill at ease. What was happening? She wondered. Lately, she was often irritable, and why did she feel like she was never well-rested? Then talk about running to the ladies' room!

"Gaye?" Joseph darted her a glance.

Zoning back in, she spoke. "Joe, I don't know that I want to travel." She said she hoped she didn't sound like an ingrate or unwilling to accompany him if he insisted. Abigail looked over at Joseph. Okay, she had indeed made matters worse. Biting her lip, she wondered. How to say, without sounding selfish, that she didn't feel like sitting in a large auditorium with pretentious people? Could she say too that she didn't want to party with them afterward? Moments later, Abigail sighed and covered her face. Perhaps she should have nixed mentioning the hotel and that she liked to sleep in her own bed.

While driving, Joseph shook his head because there was no pleasing the woman lately; although not long ago, she'd moaned about rest and relaxation. "Look, Gaye," he shrugged. "I was looking out for you. You mentioned getting away, so I figured we could make this a mini-vacation."

"Joezeff, I—"

"Nope. Forget it, but remember," Joseph just had to state, "you've never had a problem with hotels in the past." Shoot, he had put her up in places that had cost a ten grand a night, and she hadn't complained. Not even after she had been full-scale shopping, in four-inch heels all day. Actually, she'd returned and put it on him! Suddenly he wondered, what was he going to do with her? What could he do with the woman who worked even his reserved nerve?

"Joe, I didn't say any of that to make you feel bad," Abigail moaned. It was just that she was sick most of the time now, but nobody knew. However, what if she had a terminal disease? She could die, away from home. Then Joseph would feel bad afterward.

Abigail looked at the man who remained silent. She asked if he was upset. "Don't be," she pleaded. "Look, if you want, I'll go."

"No!" He exploded because lately, she was ornery. It seemed the only time she wasn't was when they were screwing, and there were a few more things in life than him pawing her. "Yo, why you a wet blanket?"

"So I'm a drag," Abigail said, with tears forming. She couldn't believe him! Joseph didn't care that she was possibly ill or that he'd touched a nerve— because even she didn't like the new her.

Joseph rode the exit ramp as Abigail fought tears, because, heck if she'd let him see her cry! Instead of with her, he probably wanted to be with Courtney, or with that new girl group. He'd worked an army of late hours with them. And just for that, Abigail told him a few things!

"Okay," Joseph nodded because he'd heard loud and clear. Abigail did not want a vacation in the contiguous United States. "Well, go lounge in the Caribbean, where your precious 'sun and serenity' will do you some good." Joseph spoke loudly, "But know this. I *am going* to my affair and there *will be* a woman on my arm," perhaps even an actress.

"No—I listened to you." He raised a hand, "So let me finish. Since you've got this duality disorder, it's best that you *don't* go."

Oh, he had nerve! Abigail fumed. Joseph probably really thought she wouldn't look right. He was just afraid to say so. That was it. Abigail knew her hips were spreading like wildfire. She'd even mentioned it to Sabrina, but to use the way she looked against her? Ooh, that was mean.

Subsequently, since she could think of nothing scathing to say, Abigail hissed that Joseph should take her home, "Pronto!"

"That's what I'm doing," he growled, rounding a corner. "Can't take you no place else," he mumbled, wanting her for some insane reason.

Abigail's eyes narrowed. "What?"

"I said," he spoke around the cigarette that he hastily lit, "I'ma leave you to your shady self."

"I won't *be* by myself," she retorted. "I've got company, remember?"

"Not for long," Joseph predicted, pulling up before Branford Court. "Holla!" He yelled through the open window, outside of which snow flurried. Abigail pounded up the walk where men decorated for the Advent season. A few of them turned to look as Joseph further yelled, "But don't do it till you can be personable—baybee!"

Abigail whirled, intending to give Joseph a piece of her mind, just as he rolled away. Irritated, she stamped a foot because among other things, she'd left her carafe in his car! As she neared building Alpha, Abigail noticed something. She suddenly hungered for that miserable man.

Driving, Joseph swore. Ding-dang! That woman's perfume clung to him and everything in his car. And darn if he didn't want to get at her!

Abigail chuckled as building Alpha's door attendant greeted her. In the elevator, she laughed outright as she rode upward with blue-eyed hotness. He smiled. "Must have been funny," Blue eyes remarked.

"It was," she said. It was pathetic too. She was crazy in love with a sexy, stubborn, impossible man. He called as she left the elevator.

Crushing out his smoke, Joseph announced he was on his way up. He growled that he just had to see her, get all up in her. Right then.

Rushing to her room, while removing restrictive clothing, Abigail readily agreed. "Joezeff, mi left the door unlocked. Just come. Now."

## 19

MONDAY, noon, Abigail asked Mona Lisa, "What kind of stupidity is a pre-Christmas party? Either it is, or it isn't."

"Who cares, Gaye? You said you would go. Look," Mona Lisa huffed. I laid out my ducats, and I intend to get my money's worth."

"I don't care if you laid out something else." Abigail couldn't see driving out to Wyandanch, Long Island, for some country-behind party. "Anyway, I celebrate Kwanzaa."

"You celebrate Christmas too, G. It's when your Lord was born."

"Christmas is the time that His birth is *celebrated*," Abigail corrected. "Along with the commercialization that causes people to spend goo-gobs of money. However, Mo, it's actually been documented that my savior was most likely born in or near the springtime."

Who cares? Mona Lisa thought. "Enough about Christ the Lord, already! He was born, Gaye. He lives in your heart—and He can live in mine if you say you'll go! Please. This is gonna be the jam of the season. It's the second Saturday in December. You don't want to miss it."

Abigail stressed that she had more pressing issues. "So I need you to understand, Picture Girl." Especially, Abigail thought, since she usually tried to do most of what Mona Lisa asked.

Mona Lisa wasn't trying to hear it, and it hit her. She would drive. "It'll save you the hassle," she said. "Now, can you go?"

In silence, Abigail replaced her printer's ink, as Mona Lisa asked why she felt like she was always begging her friend to do something.

"I can't answer that," Abigail replied, thinking that perhaps she was more settled. She certainly didn't need to rip 'n run in search of 'fun.' She tuned back in just as Mona Lisa launched into her usual. "G, believe me, it's gonna be mad ballers there."

Abigail smiled at Sunny, who appeared. Abigail's assistant pointed at the bracelet watch on her small arm.

"Oh shoot!" Abigail said, noting the time. "Picture Girl, I've got a doctor's appointment. Gotta go. Call you later." Abigail went to hang up.

"Yo G, tell me, yes or no!"

Abigail stared at the receiver before putting it back to her ear. "I will call you. Bye." She grabbed her purse and had to go to the loo, again!

Passing, she called, "Sunshine, I'm spending lunch at Marguerite's."

"Our lovely OB-GYN, how delightful." Sunny sounded preoccupied as she typed. "Well, Dr. Ramirez is the best, so think pleasant thoughts."

"While my bottom's exposed and my feet are in stirrups?" Abigail scoffed. "I'll try. Oh, and Sunshine? I'm glad you're back."

Sunny gazed up. "Me too, friend, and thank you for getting my raise."

"You thanked me already. Actually, you deserve more."

"Go." Sunny pointed and called out afterward, "Kiss-kiss."

Perhaps this visit, Abigail thought, would negate the need for a visit to her general practitioner. Hopefully, her GYN would give her something for the sick stomach with which she had nearly learned to live.

SEATED in a taxi that crept through mid-Manhattan traffic, Abigail pondered what she'd been told. Yesterday, Thursday, her physician had personally called and requested that Abigail revisit the office. Afterward, Abigail had found herself trembling and wondering what turned up during Monday's check-up. Did she have only weeks to live?

Now, staring dazedly from her taxi window, Abigail remembered that Marguerite had delivered the news just half an hour ago. Abigail still felt disbelief and she recalled saying, "You cannot be serious."

The olive-skinned, raven-haired Dr. Ramirez had chuckled, like Abigail had a hangnail, easily remedied. Doc had bobbed her glossy head.

"Gaye, you are *expecting*. Your HCG, Human Chorionic Gonadotropin levels are up, as I explained. And remember, as your trusted practitioner, I ordered urine, and the sophisticated serum," or blood, "pregnancy test."

Abigail said she knew the latter was supposed to be virtually 100% accurate, even as early as the first week after conception. However, what if the technician had erred or mixed up her vial with someone else's?

Dr. Ramirez had rebuffed, saying she'd ordered both tests to be sure. Then she'd followed those up with an examination because she'd wanted to note the physical signs of pregnancy. The doctor confirmed there was a change in the cervix. The uterus was enlarged too. Both were apparent by the six week of pregnancy, and Abigail was farther along. She was going into her second trimester.

Where had she been during the first three months? Abigail wondered. She'd had inquiries too, all of which her physician competently answered.

Then although she didn't want to, Abigail believed the poised woman. The one with whom she had raced around, as an exuberant eight-year-old.

Back at the Private Care Facility holiday parties, both of their mothers, nurses, had calmly socialized. Until the children's noise levels had become unbearable. Then one mother or the other had inevitably hissed, "Calm down." Then the other mom had chimed in, "And stop screaming."

"Don't run either," Eva Rivera had advised. "You might fall." This the mamas had said before transitioning back into party sophisticates.

Marguerite's mother, Eva Rivera, who'd become an administrator, had lost contact with the Wallace family soon after her colleague Glenda passed. Then six years ago, a Women's Health Pavilion opened. Abigail registered to see the recommended doctor. How surprised she'd been when Dr. Ramirez turned out to be her childhood friend!

"Look at you liñda, all grown up and efficient! You look the same, though," Abigail had laughed within a joyful embrace. "You just don't have the curly afro anymore, and you're married, Dr. Rivera-Ramirez."

"*Boricua*," Marguerite smiled. "You haven't changed either, except for your hair, which is quite fabulous. Oh, and I saw you, in The New Yorker, at a charity event. Who was that fine man holding you?"

That easily, physician and patient had once again become friends.

Abigail mentally dragged herself back to the present. She recalled that following her questions, Dr. Ramirez had torn off a sheet of paper. "I want you to have an ultrasound. Not that I'm looking for anything," she soothed. "We just need to be careful, Gaye, because you aren't as young as some first-time mothers, but you should be fine. That is –if you follow your doctor's orders. Don't look scared, *mami*; I'll be with you all the way.

"Remember," Dr. Ramirez had said while appearing almost too calm. "I've been through this, many times –once even my own self. It's what I do, and frankly," her eyes twinkled, "I've become quite good at it."

Admiring the physician's toddler in a photo, Abigail voiced a persistent thought. "Marguerite, I've had my monthly," slight though it had been.

Dr. Ramirez explained that there were cases where menses continued. "No cause for alarm. As long as you keep your doctor visits, take your prenatal vitamins, exercise, eat right, sleep, and follow medical advice. Ah, and this list of books might help. This website can also answer arising questions; call me chica. Now you've got my numbers..."

*Expecting.* The word repeatedly played in Abigail's psyche.

How could it be, she wondered. The birth control stuff—from her contraceptive injection—took three months to vacate a body, right?

"Please, God," she prayed, "let Marguerite be mistaken, this once."

Cryptically, however, Abigail knew the truth and sighed. Well, at least now she wouldn't die, not just yet, she supposed. Now too, she knew why the irritability and why she constantly ran to the loo. Wow, Abigail thought, this was the end of November, so the 'damage' was done in August... *You know the exact date. You can even pinpoint your 'culprit.'*

Buttoning her coat, Abigail recalled summer's unofficial end. It was then that she'd admitted her relationship with Darré was over. She fast-forwarded past him moaning that they should try again.

"No. You killed whatever we could have had," she'd spat. Repeatedly Abigail had also told Darré to unhand her because he'd had nerve. Sleeping with that child, the one who had been about to have a child.

In her creeping taxi, Abigail closed her eyes. She couldn't look at the bike messenger, who nearly got mangled as furiously he pedaled outside the bike lane. She forgot snarled traffic and the massive skyscrapers that were barriers between her and the waning afternoon sun.

It was currently late autumn, but back at the summer's end, she'd wanted to forget that Darré had kept trying her, crawling to her place at night. She'd also wanted to forget all the others he had been with, Pammi included. Abigail did not want to remember the feelings he'd aroused within her. She'd even shook Darré off –after slipping with him that last time. She'd felt guilty and defiled after all the wrestling and pawing.

How had she gotten caught up, to begin with? The Ex wasn't even her type! Why, too, had she lied to herself while they'd been together? She'd told herself that if he hadn't been engrossed in getting his magazine off the ground, they could have been happy. Not so. With him, she'd never have been free from worry. And his search for a gal Friday had proved just that. Abigail recalled Darré and his magazine partner. Both said that the office help they needed had to come cheap –and she had. NaPammitha Rydell had stressed that she could work for little or next to nothing because she was young and getting in on the publication's ground floor.

Darré had eaten that up, repeatedly bragging, "Pammi doesn't complain, and working overtime isn't a problem. She willingly assists me, and Seth," her bosses, "because she knows we 'bout to blow up!'

In her head, Abigail could also hear Darré's silly voice, later, as he spoke of the mess. Pammi was pregnant. She'd told him, her eyes pebble-hard as she rubbed her stomach.

"Awww hell no," he'd yelled, not about to be pinned when he knew the tramp had screwed his partner. Darré had seen them. He'd raced back to the office one evening before meeting an ad agent for drinks. There Seth had been, bent over the folding table that sufficed for Pammi's desk. With pants pooled at an ankle, his pink butt had been visible. Pammi's nude brown legs had been wrapped around Seth's gyrating waist. Therefore, again Darré had yelled. "Hell to the no!"

"Are you saying you didn't sleep with me, over and over again?" Pammi demanded of her boss, Mr. Clankston. Then since he could not classify what they'd done as sleeping, Darré knew he, not Seth, was being set up, and eagerly, he attempted to back out of Pammi's dream.

"Darré," Pammi called, her voice hardening, "you can share all that we're building at the publication, or you can go to jail. It's your choice."

"Jail?" He'd felt sick upon finding out that Pammi was a minor. Then Darré had sort of explained to his fiancé, Abigail.

Peering from her taxi window, Abigail mentally raced past foolhardy Darré's news. It had sent her reeling—and into Joseph's arms. That had led to a six-day hiatus on the isle of Santa Lissa.

She'd intended to use the late August trip to heal from betrayal and hurt. Therefore, with Joseph, Abigail flew to Ventura. There, they partied with friends. Then from that lavish but wild scene, the couple had driven to meet the Esperanza. That gorgeous cruising ketch was owned by Carlo, Joseph's extravagant older acquaintance. Abigail recalled the two-lane highway and the white convertible. The sun had been on her skin, the wind in her hair, and the zippy tune 'It Happened in Monterey' blared.

Zooming down the sun-splashed coast, she and Joseph had been headed for Carlo's floating chateau, replete with its own casino. Seated in the lustrous white roadster, Abigail had taken photos of the cloud-scudded sky and the breathtaking scenery. She'd been grateful that Joseph, bronzed, in shorts and sunglasses, was an adept driver. She was thankful too that he had seen the beauty many times before because had he wrestled with one curve... Abigail recalled the sparkling ocean, miles below the treacherous California curves they'd traversed. She remembered calling out that it was a shame that some children would never see the grandeur of such places.

"Others will," Joseph reminded her. He had known, again at that moment, why he gave to children's charities and fresh air funds. He had also established scholarships for young men who attended his alma mater.

Aboard the Esperanza, Joseph introduced the man who fairly purred his own name. Carlo Angelo waved the help aside to show Abigail his two-hundred-foot yacht. With it yet anchored in a private slip in the Marina Del Rey, he took her on a tour of his three-deck bambino. He said the vessel's name meant promise or hope. Carlo started the tour only after Abigail was served a black pearl, chilled champagne, cognac, and Tia Maria coffee liqueur. Descending a circular staircase, Carlo beamed while showing off the luxurious living space. Abigail glimpsed the master stateroom, and the VIP stateroom, where she and Joseph would stay.

Never would she forget Carlo's hospitality, legend among 'the set,' the nouveau riche, and those of old money, who frequented the little known Santa Lissa isle.

Currently peering from the window of her taxi, Abigail remembered Carlo's Mediterranean tiled villa. With tennis and basketball courts, it had tropical gardens. Carlo's chalet, as he called it, was resplendent with an indoor pool flowing beneath glass into an outdoor infinity pool.

Abigail re-lived the sunshine at the colonnaded poolside—worlds apart from the chill misery just beyond her taxi window. Then she remembered her and Joseph's first night. They'd dined with Carlo and others. All had danced to a live Latin trio. Then Abigail and Joseph had slipped away. Beneath an indigo sky twinkling with stars, their fingers had been intertwined. Sated after making love, she'd murmured. "If we were characters in a book, Joe, you would be Prince Charming."

Staring up, Joseph had chuckled. "No kid's book for us Star; what we just did was X rated—most unsuitable for the young and inquisitive. Yo, where'd you learn that anyway?"

*So you crept, on Darré, huh? And with Joseph! You naughty girl.*

Abigail didn't see it as creeping because she and what's-his-face had been done, thanks to the Pammi debacle. Oh! That was why she hadn't gone again for her scheduled contraceptive injection! Back then, she'd thought, why clog up her system if she wasn't in a relationship?

*But with no birth control you slipped, with Darré.* Abigail sighed because indeed she had, that last time.

*Still, after the slip-up,* her conscience reminded her, *you shared yourself with Joseph too, repeatedly, on the isle of Santa Lissa...*

Now look what all of that had gotten her. Pregnant; expecting; Dr. Ramirez's words floated airborne. Abigail bit her lip, wanting to scream. How would she explain to her fam, and to Joseph?

Well, all she could be was candid. She and Joseph had never lied to one another, so she wouldn't start now. She would simply let Joseph know the possibility. He could be her baby's father, *and...* Abigail hated to think it, but she'd have to tell Joe there was a chance that Darré could be too. Abigail felt sick because she didn't want Darré's baby.

What an effed-up situation!

*Well, the clown crept on you...* Okay, Abigail surmised. In his case, turnabout was fair play, but as for Joseph? There was no way this was fair to him. Gnawing her lip, Abigail wondered how others dealt with this?

*Well, some have* one *peen partner at a time.*

Abigail felt like hurling until she remembered... Gram had told her something. Her colorful fish in clear water dream! Abigail had drifted off while Gram had been talking, but she did remember that Gram's dream always meant new life. So all would be fine.

*And,* Abigail realized, it did not matter who'd fathered her baby. The truth was: the baby was *hers.* She would wholeheartedly love the little person who currently grew inside her, the little one that would be born to *her.* Forget the circumstances of their conception.

*Wow. Someone is really on the road to forgiving The Ex. If you're thinking like that.*

Yep, Abigail mused, and she would soon tell Joseph because he was already suspicious of her mood swings. Also, her spreading hips and bottom would not be camouflaged for much longer.

## 20

**O**H, the circumstances of this unplanned pregnancy.

Abigail bit her lip and, for the fourth day in a row, pondered speaking with Joseph. Although she'd announced that she would accompany him to California, she hadn't mentioned her dilemma.

She would, though, when they were out of town. Right now, she felt slightly fearful—of lots of things. He was sure to have questions. Joseph would want to know how she was feeling and how far along Abigail was.

*Simply put, the man's gonna want to know if the baby is his.*

Abigail sighed because that inquiry gave her the shakes.

All this, she groaned, and just as her and Joseph's lives had come together.

"**I** know we're both busy, Star." Joseph adjusted his cellular earpiece as his sixth sense kicked in. "Still, I feel you're avoiding me."

To steady her nerves, Abigail breathed deeply. Then she mentioned Christmas shopping in December. "You know how it is, Joezeff, especially when I'm usually finished in July..."

Had she sounded normal? Whatever that was these days. She also mentioned the evening prior. "We could've gone out, but I felt—ugh."

"That's why Dr. Feel Good would have made a house call."

*You need to tell him.*

Abigail bit her lip; she would, but not now. She would endure feeling like a deceiver, only for a little while longer. Anyway, it wasn't like she'd lied. She only hoped Joseph wouldn't pop over. If he did, in her home, he'd want a drink, and she wouldn't. Then he'd suspect.

Disengaged, she wondered. Why had her sweetheart needed reassurance that they yet loved? Why had he asked if she was keeping it hot for him? She'd said she was. If heaving over the commode counted.

*Again, you need to TALK to him –didn't he tell you that, at his duplex?* Abigail couldn't say anything yet! Joseph was headed out of town. Therefore, Abigail would stick to her plan. Lord, if only she could speak to her mother. Were Glenda alive, she would have soothing words.

Mama would have –nada. She was gone; that her daughter had to remember. Tearful, Abigail pondered Anna-Maria, who might help.

*Nope.* Abigail shook away thoughts of calling Anna-Maria. Joseph had to be the first to know.

"You alright?"

Abigail raised her head from her arms on her desk.

"You don't look well, friend. You look nice 'n all, but I know something's wrong." Asian-American Sunny frowned. "Um, I meant—"

"I know, Sunshine. I have a dilemma, but I can't talk now, though..."

Sunny watched as Abigail's brown eyes filled. "Well, why not take time off? It's slow around here during the holidays, so go, sort things out." Sunny turned with a handful of overstuffed folders clutched tightly.

"Sunshine?"

The fashionista about-faced, her blunt-cut curtain of hair swinging.

"Sunshine, I—I'll think about what you said, and—"

The Buddhist nodded. "I'll recite *Nam Myoho Renge Kyo* for you."

*You can overcome any problem encountered.* When her door closed, Abigail held her head and quietly, sobbed. Sure, she had a big family, Joseph, and dear friends, but she felt alone. Nagging, too was one fact. She was older than most first-time mothers. What if she started to look like a beat-up old hag? Sweet Jesus! Abigail suddenly thought it because she had to be crazy, attempting a baby at a hop-n-a-skip from forty.

*Yeah, you and ol' man Joe—who is still IN THE DARK*! Abigail rose from her desk. On Wednesday or Thursday of next week, he would know, for better or for worse. Oh, she had nearly forgotten Mona Lisa's party. Since it was lunchtime, perhaps she would go, find something to wear, something that fit. Pushing out of the glass door and into noisy Manhattan, Abigail wondered if Joe would want to kick her from their California hotel suite when she, at last, spilled her beans. Wonder if she'd fit in the outfit on which he'd spent an exorbitant sum. Probably, Seraph had made the bodice invisibly expandable.

With wind whipping her hair and clothing, Abigail vowed to call Sabrina, after she'd had her heart-to-heart with Joseph. Sabrina would be happy to hear that her mother-sister would become a biological momma.

Hey, when thinking about it that way, Abigail realized, she very nearly wished she had no secret.

**21**

"IT'S Thursday!" Mona Lisa whooped. "Two more days until party!"

Oh joy, Abigail wryly thought.

"Why you looking like that, G?"

"Like what?" Abigail wanted to appear interested, but the trendy, too loud restaurant that 'in' crowd frequented hadn't been her idea.

"You look like something's turned your stomach."

Feeling sick, Abigail dismissed all talk of herself. "I want to know," she began, "what you're doing up this way, in all this rain?"

Mona Lisa drank. "Making sure my friend will still attend our party."

Abigail inwardly groaned, but she had agreed to go. "So you drove all the way up here from Queens?"

*When she could have called.*

"No," Mona Lisa replied, eyeing a man obviously engrossed in someone else. "I took the F train. I needed to shop. Gotta get me something to wear."

Abigail cringed when a waiter sent a tray of drinks crashing to the floor.

"Oh, I've got news," Mona Lisa sang out. "My sister's going, too."

Abigail regulated her expression. "So...how will Carla get there?"

"She'll ride with us," Mona Lisa said, as if Abigail should have known.

ABIGAIL could not face that Carla would share the forty-minute ride. The day prior, Mona Lisa had dropped that bomb. Since then, Abigail had pondered what would surely be too long a ride. In her kitchen, wearing a velour bathrobe, Abigail pulled back the curtain. Through sheets of rain she noted oncoming night. She couldn't get Carla Reid off her mind –for many reasons. For one, on the drug crack, Carla continuously lied. Carla claimed she'd gotten it together. Secondly, Abigail couldn't forget what Carla had done, how she'd derailed Abigail's cousin...

Abigail wished she'd mentioned it to Mona Lisa. Back when it happened, Abigail should have said something; even her friend Kismet Staar agreed. Now though, if Abigail spoke, she might appear petty. Still, back in the summer, she should have said, 'Mo, I saw your sister...'

However, that would not have been the whole truth. Abigail had literally run into her cousin Chunky, whom the nickname no longer fit...

"Charles," Abigail had said, colliding with a painfully thin man when she tumbled out of Duane Reade and onto Fifth Avenue.

Chunky displayed missing teeth. "H-h-hey you, re-m-member me?"

Abigail nodded and jostled for position on the crowded sidewalk. In the heat, she knew her younger cousin would follow. She also noticed a woman keeping pace on the opposite side of the street. Feeling a sense of foreboding, Abigail asked, "So, Charles, you taking care of yourself?"

Looking beaten and alley, the younger man hunched a shoulder. "Gue-guess so. Uh G-Gaye Denise, I been m-meaning to talk to you."

"Really?" Abigail knew he would hit her up for money. Still, she gestured, sidetracked. "That woman across the street, you know her?"

Chunky stared straight ahead. "I'on't know nobody out here."

Abigail squinted. That skinny face, nearly hidden beneath a layer of grime, "I've seen her before..." Abigail mumbled.

Chunky wanted his cousin to focus, on him, only. "S-seeing that you c-care 'bout me 'n all, c-could you lend me a ca-couple dollars?"

At Abigail's wry look, Chunky quickly added, "So I can e-eat."

"Look at me, Charles," Abigail ordered, waiting for the light at Forty-Second. "I'm going in there," an eatery a few doors down.

"No. I'on't wanna hold you up," Chunky stammered, the con man in him thinking fast. "Gaye D-Denise, I just need money."

Unwilling to play his game, Abigail said, "Charles, I don't have a lot of time. If you're hungry, come with me. Or I'll see you when I see you."

"N-no." Chunky glanced at the woman who now stood near the New York Public Library. Then for Abigail, cognition dawned. "That's Carla Reid! I knew it," Abigail mumbled, determined to lose Chunky, whom she knew was up to no good. Turning the corner, Abigail called to the younger man who'd once been a lonely overweight mathematical wiz. "Charles, I gotta bounce." Hurrying away, Abigail recalled that her cousin had gone to church and to his job as an actuary at an insurance company. Then he'd met the then-curvaceous Carla. She'd sexed him, for a fee, and introduced him to a proven weight loss system. The drug crack cocaine.

After episodes, including no-call no-shows, and stealing, security officers escorted the drug-addicted Chunky from his employer's premises. That was when Carla taught him to hustle, to feed his fix.

"Look!" Chunky yelled, determined to keep up with Abigail, as something inside growled angrily to life. "C-Carla ain't got money! So help a b-bruva out." He reached for Abigail's arm. "Yo, j-just gimme the m-money, dammit!" Chunky was sick of tap dancing whenever he needed something from somebody that he used to know. All he wanted was the rock, the elusive high that fisted his insides when he couldn't get it. Therefore, the bitch who wanted to get away would not! She was going to stop the twisting fist!

*She that dwells in the secret place...*

Abigail dropped her shopping bag. With honking traffic, and hordes of people passing, but really only engrossed in themselves, she should have felt alone. However, she didn't. Beneath the summer sun, Abigail knew she had a potential fight on her hands. Still, she shook a miniature can quickly pulled from her purse. If Charles forced her to, she would pump out a concoction that included cayenne pepper and bleach. Thus, she said, giving it a spritz, "I will spray your ass black and blue..."

Due to the fumes, Chunky coughed. "Wh-what you saying, Gaye Denise?" His eyes watered, but his mathematician's mind calculated how fast he could snatch her purse and someone else's briefcase as he ran.

"Do it!" Carla screamed, "Now, Chunky!" as she jumped up and down before one of the New York Public Library's marble lions. "Do it!" Carla commanded.

"You'll never see again," Abigail promised, poised to spray.

"Chunky, come on!" Carla frantically called. Clutching a snatched purse, its strap ruined, Carla ran, yelling, "Lea' that ho alone!"

Then Abigail saw, as Chunky did, the quickly pursuing officers weaving through the colorful crowd. Forgetting his cousin, Chunky tore out, running—in the direction opposite Carla.

Remembering that sweltering afternoon and knowing Carla put Chunky up to the deed, Abigail sighed. It was only a matter of time before Carla wound up like her and Mona's mother, or like Chunky had...

Abigail recalled her cousin's funeral. Word was: several times, wild-eyed, he'd raced in to rob convenience stores. He did so one time too many, wielding a broken bottle, and a woman shot him. Blood-spattered, she fell to her knees crying, while on the floor too, Chunky bled away.

At her kitchen window, Abigail tried not to think about sitting with her Aunt afterward. Pumpernickel-colored Mildred had been teary-eyed. Standing, her husband Elroy had spoken of their only son. "Millie, the boy was dead already." Uncle El had sounded distant. "Our son slunk 'round here with that skinny gal, but long ago, them drugs killed him."

In her home, Abigail forgot her mother's brother and his wife. Abigail recalled Chunky's wake and confronting Carla. Vehemently, skinny disheveled had denied involvement in any of Chunky's misdeeds.

"Whatever, Carla. Just know this," Abigail predicted, "you'll wind up just like my cousin because you won't allow anybody to help you."

Turning from her rain-dashed kitchen window, Abigail spooned up hot soup, and her buzzer sounded. She nearly dropped her bowl. Lord, please, she prayed, do not let that be Joezeff, back early from his trip.

"What smells good?" Mona Lisa stepped into her friend's cozy kitchen. "And where's it from?" she asked, washing her freezing hands.

"It's fish chowder. Why yu tink mi not cook it?" Abigail inquired, placing her own steaming bowl and warm coco bread before her friend.

"Well, for one," Mona Lisa pointed out. "No pots on your stove, and that," super-curvy nodded, "looks like a takeout bag."

Chuckling, Abigail reached for another bowl. "You should've been a detective. Coming home, I stopped at Pizzazz." Abigail and Joseph frequented the Caribbean eatery. "Got bread pudding wi' rum sauce too."

Mona Lisa slurped. "Chowder's not like yours, but it's all good."

It was not. Come Saturday, she could not have Carla breathing on her. And such little that it was, she'd looked forward to Mona driving, since Mo had roped her into going. Now, Abigail would have to meet the Reid sisters there. Abigail absently rubbed her belly; she couldn't allow coughing Carla to get germs all over her. Not when Carla often slept on the street, and gave anybody a piece, or head—fellatio—for quick cash.

Handling a hot bowl, Abigail knew a program that had helped others. Oh, forget it. Carla didn't want help. Therefore, Abigail figured she would help herself. She'd drive her own car –if she didn't stay home.

## 22

PARTY night, after wriggling into red worsted wool, Abigail clipped on hanging earrings. She hadn't bought anything to wear, after all. She had a closet brimming with clothes –that no longer fit right now. She stepped into red leather shooties. *Uh-oh.* Her lovely dress super-tightly hugged her enlarging behind and hips. Who cares, Abigail thought. Flippantly, she brushed her hair. She really didn't feel like going out. Neither did she feel like driving in the torrential downpour that had been at it since midweek. Yet, she asked the Heavenly Father to allow her to safely reach her destination. Again, Abigail thought about her annoying friend; Mo was lucky she was even putting forth the effort. This Abigail thought.

*You could always call and beg off*, her conscience advised, again. How Abigail wished, especially now that it had grown so cold that the streets were icing over. *Don't go.* Peering out, Abigail pulled back her cozy bedroom drapes. With a veiled sense of foreboding, she eyed raindrops. They were illuminated by the street lantern's sad yellow light. "From now on," Abigail stated when she got behind her steering wheel, "in my spare time, I will only do things that *I* want. Eff being agreeable." *Do not go.*

On the Southern State Parkway, driving proved horrendous, and Abigail wondered. Why had Mona opted to take it, with all its curves and windings? Frustrated, Abigail could barely see through her rain-dashed windshield. "Why didn't I stay home?" she whined because following Mona Lisa was tedious. Girlfriend drove between two lanes at all times and rarely if ever, used indicators when changing lanes at breakneck speed.

*Hey, you can still surprise her by not showing up.* Halfway to Wyandanch, Abigail pondered doing just that. However, she inched on. She also resumed an audiobook. Ahhh, 'Exodus,' the sensual, mysterious thriller by her favorite author, *April Alisa Marquette.* Listening, Abigail soon forgot killing Mona Lisa if it was the last thing she did. Meekly, she followed girlfriend off the parkway and felt that at last, she could sigh with relief. Until Mona Lisa began making a series of turns. When they left the lighted, commercial district, Abigail became concerned.

Heck, these new darkened streets had better be a shortcut to another lighted area, Abigail ominously mused. Then she braked, just like the car before her. *Ohhh, hell no!* She knew the little voice in her head sounded a lot like Darré, but given the circumstances, hell to the no was right. Look at this place. Abigail peered through the rain. Apparently, Mona Lisa had failed to tell the truth, again! This was no catering hall, as Mona had said. Abigail angrily sputtered because they were at somebody's *house!*

Leaning forward, she watched people plod up a muddy drive. Had she painstakingly driven here, to go…through an in-ground door?!

Exhausted, Abigail felt like crying. That rain-dashed drive had taken the wind from her, and now she wouldn't even get to lounge, for a few calming moments, in a pretty powder room. She had imagined the catering house or the five-star hotel where they should have been. The walls would have had wainscoting. In the ladies' room, there was supposed to be a floral arrangement. It would have been in an expensive vase. Both were supposed to be reflected back from a large, lit mirror. *Careless Hands*, sung by Mel Tormé, or possibly Kirk Whalum's sax, should have streamed through concealed speakers. Abigail would have begun what should have been a festive evening with a raspberry champagne cocktail. Yeah, had she not been expecting, and were she not at this rat-hole!

Well, so much for the fantasy. Abigail sucked her teeth. She peered through the curtain of rain at the rickety-assed house. It looked haunted. She allowed upset to wash over her as she heard the inquiry. *Did you think you'd attend a decent soiree, at MONA's behest—and with Carla tagging along? That should have been the giveaway.* Abigail sucked her teeth and wished she could click her heels and wind up home.

She peered at the cellar door. This was a basement party. Heck, the last time she'd attended one, she'd been in high school, rocking an Afro and bell-bottoms, before Soul Train had become the 'rainbow' coalition. Surveying gnarled trees that swayed and bent in the ferocious wind, Abigail folded her arms. If she got out, she would strangle Mona Lisa.

Having parked, said woman scurried back to Abigail's vehicle. Then beside Abigail's door, Mona Lisa wrestled with her umbrella that had flown up to turn inside out. Crouching, with a fist, Mona Lisa banged on Abigail's window. "What you doing G!"

Warm and dry, Abigail refused to respond.

"What're you waiting for?" Mona Lisa hollered. Chilled, she bounced up and down as her hair blew and plastered itself across her face. "Get out, G! Quit playing games! It's cold and wet out here."

Abigail fumed because who was Mona to talk about playing games?

Again, Mona Lisa banged. "Get out G! I'm serious."

"Quit bashing mi window!" Abigail yelled because she did not need another reason to attack Mona Liar.

Mona Lisa yelled while pulling on Abigail's door. "Get out, get out."

Abigail hollered, "Quit!" She shoved her door open to prevent damage to her handle. "Why'd you lie?" Abigail snarled, grabbing her things.

While quickly tipping to the cellar door, Mona Lisa tossed her ruined umbrella into the lake that had been a lawn, a few days ago. "I'm sick of you, G!" she whined. "And now I'm all wet, friend."

Carla darted over. Rudely, she placed a hand over Abigail's, and pulled.

Jerking her hand and umbrella away, Abigail snarled, "Remove your— paw. And do not try to get under here again."

Inside, Abigail and Mona Lisa both hissed, "I should kill you!"

"For what?" they asked, again in unison.

"I'm all wet," Mona Lisa moaned. "And I paid smelly Kaneesha fithy bucks to pineapple waterfall my hair. Now it's ruined, foolin' with you."

Not capable of caring, Abigail said, "It's fifty. And why'd you lie? Why'd you say we'd be at a hall?" Abigail looked around. She didn't believe 'this' was what she'd reimbursed Mona Lisa for, "Wasted money. I should've known. You never go anywhere worth going," Abigail griped.

Now she wouldn't get a club soda with lime, Abigail realized, nor would she eat from a buffet. And she was hungry, again. Got-durn-it! No black olives, smoked salmon, shrimp, or crab and avocado cocktails. She had so looked forward to even sampling a few hot appetizers.

Mona Lisa tugged on Abigail's sleeve. "Get yo' bougie self in this line."

Why'd she have to be called bougie just because she liked nice things? Abigail wondered as she stepped behind the wet woman who moaned.

"I just wanted you to have some fun, G. That's why I asked you to come."

*No. She wasn't aware that her sister was coming when she asked you. She only wanted company for the drive out here.*

"You weren't thinking of me," Abigail told the woman who moved again. "But that's because you only think about you." Abigail stepped forward. She also felt violently ill because the cellar smelled like mildew.

Near-gagging, she covered her mouth. Abigail also decided she would not hand her coat to the girl who greedily eyed it.

"Hey! If you're gonna have any fun G," Mona Lisa hissed. "Then I suggest you let your 'precious' coat go for a while."

"Yu just worry 'bowt dat hair of yours," Abigail snapped.

Coughing Carla addressed Abigail. "What's ya coat made of, Special?"

"Forget it," Abigail ordered. When a man snatched a Jheri curl bag from his head, she again wondered, what the fu—fig was she doing there?

Entering a room loud with music, Mona Lisa merrily flitted off, with some man, calling out as she went. "Try to have some fun G!"

Abigail decided it would be fun, to count the minutes until she left.

Feeling she should stick it out for at least half an hour, she sat in a tumbledown chair. From her musty corner, she managed to peer through the mass of bodies before her. At the bar—a card table really—littered with bottles in wrinkled brown paper bags stood Carla. No doubt, she ran game on the bewildered-looking man to whose arm she clung.

Abigail forgot skinny. Angling herself just so, she saw people working up a sweat on the broken concrete that sufficed for a floor. When she got tired of trying not to topple over, she stuck out a foot. Sure, then she was balanced, on the sawed-off-leg chair, but she garnered another problem. Her own leg fell asleep. "Dang pins 'n needles feeling," Abigail muttered, waving another man away. As Lizzo loudly played, men really thought Abigail had her shapely leg stuck out as a 'fishing' ploy.

"Not dancing tonight," she informed another admirer as Mona Lisa stepped off that broken concrete. There, to Cardi B, she'd plowed herself into a frenzy with a bald, muscular man in seventies attire. Mona Lisa exclaimed as she dragged a chair over, "Whoooo, honey!" She flopped down and fanned herself. "That was cray."

"I'm leaving," Abigail announced.

Mona Lisa whined. "We came together G, we should leave that way."

"We rode in separate cars—"

"Your choice," Mona Lisa nearly yelled over Grandmaster Flash.

"Whatever. Look, Mo, you asked me to come. I did." *Now, I have a few things I want to do.* This Abigail thought but did not say.

"Yo what is it," Mona Lisa loudly huffed to be heard over the music.

"You think nobody here's good as you? Or as good as Forrester?"

Abigail realized Mona Lisa had been drinking, perhaps from one of those sample bottles, or maybe even on the drive over. Still, none of that gave her the right to become abusive.

Abigail held to her chair's bottom and stood.

Mona Lisa grabbed her arm. "Sometimes you make me sick! You know that G? You think everybody's beneath you."

Abigail stared and shook her arm free. "I should slap you," she hissed, her anger rising. "And lemme tell you something else." Her voice became brittle. "You got me all wrong because if I thought that 'beneath me' shit, yu an' mi would not be friends. Wait—hold up, I am not finished. Another thing, I watched you with that big dancer dude. You're gonna sleep with him—" Abigail raised a hand. "Not finished. It's your business if you gi yourself to him, but I'll ask why? You say you want love, then you waste yourself on men that you know only want one thing—one night, one hit."

"Yo you know nothing, not about anybody here," Mona Lisa scoffed.

"You're right, but I know you. I know you're more than you think."

"I don't need lectures." Mona Lisa waved. "I'm having fun, and I ain't looking for love or any of that other fluff you think everybody needs."

"Well, I'm out." Abigail began to walk, despite her leg being asleep.

"You're wrong, G," Mona Lisa mewled. "You need to sit your behind down. Have a drink, and loosen up; need to stop trying to ruin shit for me!"

Abigail buttoned her coat. She did not need to be spoken to that way, and she was not Mona Lisa's guardian. Ol' girl could do as she wished.

Abigail climbed the raggedy steps, realizing that her sisters may have been right. They'd often said that one day she would see; there was no future in her 'one-sided' relationship with Mona Lisa. Sabrina had also said that Mona Lisa only wanted Abigail around because Abigail caused Mona to look and feel less like a loser.

Back in the cellar…while watching Abigail disappear, Mona Lisa felt anger. Therefore, she yelled, "See ya!" You self-righteous "Bitch!"

Abigail did not glance back. She knew, however, that were she less mature and not expecting, she would have whupped Mona Lisa's lying tail.

Abigail stepped out into blowing icy rain. Gathering her coat and raising her umbrella, she ran, sloshing through mud and *murky water...*

In the cellar, Mona Lisa slumped. She waved away invitations to dance. Why, she wondered, did she suddenly feel bereft of joy? She had been having fun.

The woman with the wet hair and the outlandish outfit didn't care what goody-two-shoes Abigail thought. She, Mona Lisa Reid, was grown. She could do anything she wanted. Right?

Then why did she feel the need to explain? This Mona Lisa wondered as she looked at the man who now sat where Abigail had. "I was only gonna dance with people," Mona Lisa informed him, ignoring his blank stare. "I didn't come looking for anything else..." She pleaded with him –the wrong person– to understand.

"Really," Mona Lisa called as he shook his head and strolled away. "You gotta believe me."

## 23

WHILE waiting for her car to warm, Abigail removed her coat and experienced mixed emotions. Although she loved Mona Lisa, Abigail vowed to limit further interaction with her. If they could get past this. The truth was: Mona had lied, a habit of hers, and this time, she'd gone too far. She'd been snide and rude, without cause, and friends did not treat friends that way.

*Lord help me to forgive.* "Yes, because all I did," Abigail stated aloud, with angry tears assailing her, "was what that child asked. I drove out here, in all this rain, wasting gas, time, and money. Oh, and energy that I do not have." Abigail shook her head and pulled her car into the flooded road. She just wanted to forget the night's debacle. And she would do so, she told herself, as she unbuckled her seatbelt to reach into her dash by restarting 'Exodus.' *Better say a little prayer first.*

Abigail ignored her conscience, thinking the audiobook would take her mind off things. When at a red light, Abigail imagined herself at home. There she would don fuzzy socks and forget this fake night out. By the light of her princess lamp, she would drink ginger tea. It would settle her insides. Better yet, a cup of goldenseal might ward off the chill because she did not need a cold. Abigail further felt if things were truly right, Joseph would not be out of town. He would have already been apprised of her little 'secret' too and he would be amenable.

The light changed, and moving, Abigail wondered why she heard tires on wet pavement. Oh, the light on her dash. It indicated her door was not properly closed. *At the next light, you've got to remedy that.*

Driving along, Abigail felt growing excitement because she would finally get some time to herself. She would get to thumb through her new Essence magazine with no interruptions. She might even take a bath.

Leaving that slap-awful detour, Abigail headed for the parkway. To better hear about the mysterious Miraunga Isle, she upped the volume.

Abigail also muttered, "Will you look at this icy rain?"

Forgetting to pray or re-close her door and re-fasten her seatbelt, she rode the parkway ramp to merge with oncoming traffic.

Leaning forward, she despised black ice. Her foot hovered cautiously over the brake as she guessed it didn't bother other drivers, not with the way some whizzed recklessly around and past her. Flicking on her signal indicator, Abigail intended to get in the slower right lane. She knew she sounded like stocky Gram Mary too when she muttered, "Child, it'll be better for me to get home later than not at all..."

Finally, there was space to ease over, but what was that, a foghorn?

Peripherally, Abigail glimpsed a vehicle, barreling toward her.

Oh! Before she knew it, she felt a ferocious jolt! Her passenger side had been slammed! Going into an unexpected spin due to the impact, her car wildly lurched and sped toward the far left lane. Realizing it, Abigail felt the burning scream as the offending driver riotously bumped up and onto the icy shoulder of the road.

Abigail impulsively stamped her brake, pushing it to the floor. Encountering black ice, she cried out, "Oh, God!" In dizzying open space, her car bucked and swerved as the ninety-first Psalm sprang to mind. *She that dwells in the secret place... She that dwells—*

Abigail thought she heard tires skid as other drivers attempted to avoid her. Also, somewhere, someone besides her yelled.

Through the curtain of driving rain, Abigail glimpsed upstanding concrete. However, it could not be! Moving quickly, it appeared to be headed directly for her, or worse yet, she was headed directly for it!

With all her might, she steered. Furiously, with one hand over the other, she repeatedly turned the wheel and tried to brake, to make a difference. "Oh, God!" Abigail heard herself scream again as her car bucked, this time out of control. She felt it slam into the parkway divide.

She felt her body painfully crash backward as an airbag deployed, destroying her steering wheel. Yet, with no seatbelt for restraint, Abigail bounced like a crash test dummy. Her neck craned as her forehead met something hard. In colliding with another car, her improperly closed door flew open and Abigail was shaken loose.

Thrown from her moving vehicle, on frigid wet pavement, she tumbled, as drivers noisily skidded, their tires screeching. At the same time, other stunned motorists fought to avoid running over the lone person who rolled on the tarmac.

Driverless, Abigail's automobile bounced off the parkway divide. Then on an incline, it careened down the slick asphalt to lodge askew on the frozen shoulder.

Unaware, Abigail ended up yards from where her vehicle had initially hit the concrete wall. On hard, cold asphalt, she lay, face-down in a crumpled heap, as consciousness slowly waned. Amidst, she might have heard voices and sloshing footsteps. But then again, who knew? Perhaps she hadn't heard a thing at all... Abigail did feel shooting pain, however. Coursing through her whole body, the pain rip-roared through her veins as she felt heat too. On her cold face, tears eased beneath her closed eyelids to sting her cheeks. Oh stop, p-pl-pl-eeease, she wailed inside as someone aided her.

"Ma'am, can you hear me? Can you respond?" The man who asked her name and her age must have turned his head.

Was he speaking about—a faint pulse, her own?

Abigail felt released then. Lord be praised! She had been removed. She viscerally transcended serrated pain and cold. Now she could smile again because it was too easy, this effortless glide backward. Into what?

A chasm. It reminded her of her Psalms' secret place.

Ahhh... Steadily, Abigail floated to peace. She felt almost like she swam, but this movement was effortless, a welcome change, unlike swimming. However, amid the blissful removal from the traumatic, Abigail shuddered. She was back! She was conscious and once again aware that her cold, wet body involuntarily jerked. Float me backward! Something within her demanded it as she desperately sought refuge from the pain and cold. Then she heard …a familiar voice, speaking in patois. It reminded her of her little sweetie. Oh Jesus! She'd forgotten. With heinous aches now even seeping through her veins, she'd dismissed the baby that she couldn't leave!

Torn, Abigail could not remain in the cold, wracked with pain and delirium. Therefore, with freezing lips, she whispered, "P-protect," as the fragile slip of flesh cradled within her womb slid from her mind.

Wait. Were those voices? Was that Gram, and Joseph? Sabrina too, and her Conscience? Was that her doctor, sweet Marguerite? All the voices joined to form a loving cacophony. *Dis little sweet one*; 'Call me'

*I love you* 'Take care' *You need to tell him* 'Expecting' *wit' mi bells on* 'I'll be with you;' *mami* 'Always come back to me, Star;' *Rock of Ages* 'Bread of Heaven;' *Comforter* 'Hide myself in thee;' *Old woman's dream* 'Secret place;' *Ma-Ma* 'Murky water;' *Love me a little...*

In a futile grasp at waning consciousness, Abigail coughed up an inquiry. "Joe?" However, she was again claimed by the peace of the chasm. Yet, she felt vaguely plagued by an inquiry. Was that her—the other her, the wet anguished her—profusely weeping? This the cocooned Abigail wondered. Was she crying as she lay out on the ice in the rainy night?

After a time, Abigail Denise Wallace did not know. She no longer cared. Sorrow meant nothing to her. It was not part of the realm to which she now belonged. Where she was, peace reigned. In that place, a voice—the timbre of which was entirely too familiar—edged closer.

That voice. It belonged to...*Glenda.*

'Mama!'

Glenda appeared, so like blinding light, beatific and surrounding.

'Mama!' Joyful tears tripped down Abigail's cheeks; as radioing their ETA, emergency care workers sped toward County Medical.

'Mama, is that you?'

The light warmed, and Abigail sensed there was a smile for the growing girl. The one that the young mother had not wanted to leave so suddenly.

'You're so beeyootiful, child.' The brilliance shimmied with laughter.

'Mama, you're radiant,' even more so than on the day that young Abigail had fallen in love with the one who bore her.

Then the light blinked...*out.*

## 24

ON the plane, she sat, folding and refolding her hands. How could this have happened? Sabrina asked it past the lump in her throat. Thinking about her sister, Dear Lord, please help was all Sabrina could pray.

She could see it again, so vividly. That morning at two a.m., her phone rang. It startled her, although she had already been awake.

Strangely, now, Sabrina felt as though she'd been anticipating that call because moments earlier, she'd risen from a horror-filled dream. In it, Sabrina had attended the funeral of a close relative.

Struggling to wake, frightened and perspiring, she'd sat up. With a trembling hand at her chest, in the dark, Sabrina's eyes had darted about. With moving lips, she'd silently repeated her and Gaye Denise's Psalm.

*She that dwells in the secret place…* Calmer, Sabrina had made the fifth verse personal. *I shall not be afraid of the terrors of the night.* She had also told herself that she'd had a dream. "It wasn't real," Sabrina whispered, although it had seemed so. On her back, the headboard had been cool through the silk of her nightgown, as she recalled. Her dream had been shrouded, unclear. That was good because the part she did remember, Sabrina wished to forget.

Staring from the airplane window, she wondered. How had Jamaal managed to get her a window seat on such short notice? Trying not to think about why she was on the plane, Sabrina gazed at the beautifully tranquil dawn sky. Pavonian blue seeped into lavender which was disappearing into all-encompassing baby blue.

Closing her eyes, Sabrina told herself to forget the jolt that shot through her when her home phone rang. She had known. The caller bore terrible news. Therefore, she'd nudged her sleeping husband, "Maal, phone."

Without protest, he'd reached for it while she turned on the light. She'd noticed that after listening, her husband fully woke. Grabbing a pen, he jotted down what Sabrina knew she would never care to decipher. She turned away, then back again, and Jamaal refused to look at her. Sabrina saw that he'd stopped writing, but his hand shook. Then her heart pounded. Flinging cover, she grabbed her warm robe. On bare feet, she hurried down the carpeted hallway, reminding herself.

*She that dwells in the secret place…* Sabrina had noticed the moon through an unobstructed window. Its milky luminescence seeped eerily through the leafless branches of an oak. Entering her son's room, Sabrina had stood over his crib and prayed. "Lord, please let nothing serious have happened to anyone we know. God, please let Ms. Martha Dora be okay too." Sabrina forgot that mama-bear, mother-in-law, had gotten on her nerves. As usual, Ms. BigStuff, had appeared, attempting to run a household that was not hers. Watching her toddler sleep, Sabrina knew she should brace herself. Still, she wanted to return to her bedroom, to no dilemma. She wanted that call erased, and she wanted her husband asleep.

"Please, God," Sabrina whispered, frightened but unaware why, "let things be like they've been on other nights that I've looked on dis sweet bwoy yu gave us. Please, Father, just let his daddy go back to sleep."

However, Sabrina heard her husband's carpet-muffled footsteps.

Having hurriedly donned jeans and a tee, Jamaal approached his wife. With nimble fingers, she untangled his namesake's sheet. Her body tensed when Jamaal placed an arm around her. "Bina…" With a finger to his lips, she silenced him, so he tried again. "Bina, I've got to tell you."

She shook her head. "I don't want to know."

"You need to," Jamaal said, prying her hands from the crib railing. "B," he whispered, not wanting to wake the child, "don't do this. Come, now."

In their room, Jamaal patted the bed. Pulling a bench over, he faced her. "Babe, I wish this wasn't the case. You've got to pack a few things."

Well, he wasn't sending her away for good, Sabrina thought.

Jamaal held hands with the woman who was obviously in turmoil. "We've gotta get you downstate, right away."

She was going to NYC proper, Sabrina thought, as Jamaal sighed because there was no way to soften what the caller had said. Therefore, with intertwined hands, he told his wife. "Sis needs you. Right now."

Gaye Denise—Oh Jah, Sabrina thought as tears fell. I shall not fear.

With his grip tightening, Jamaal said, "Bina, listen." He heard her wince, but unaware, painfully, he forced her wedding set into the flesh of her finger. "Baby, I want no misconstruing; the situation is severe. Sis was in a car accident…and there's no time." Jamaal hated to say it. "Things look bleak. There are complications." Jamaal felt awful telling her, but he didn't want her hearing it from a stranger. He persevered, knowing they had things to tend. "Wash your face. I'll help you throw some things in—"

Sabrina stood and cried out. She'd tried to muffle the up-surging wail as the ghastly dream recurred, vivid, in the eye of her mind. However, Jamaal yet held her hands. Mist no longer shrouded the latter portion of Sabrina's dream. She'd looked down, into a casket. The woman lying there appeared gray with the pallor of death, like Glenda had in her funeral photographs.

"Not Gaye D," Sabrina moaned as tears streamed from her eyes. Had her hands been free, Sabrina would have clutched her chest. "Not Gaye Deeee," Sabrina moaned, feeling like she would slip to her knees.

Quickly reacting, Jamaal rescued his crumbling wife. He held her. He admitted he was hurt for her and for Sis. God only knew how much Abigail had suffered. "It's why you've got to go.

"Look B," Jamaal became firm, pragmatism kicking in, "Peaches can't be reached, so you're it." He willed Sabrina to grasp the magnitude of what he was saying. "Sis is broken and alone. There's no one but you."

Jamaal rubbed Sabrina's back as she took a deep breath. He wished he could be more to her, somehow. However, there simply was no time.

Sabrina swiped at tears. Although she was afraid of what she might find downstate, she recalled the night that Abigail had cried over Joseph. Sabrina remembered what she had said. If ever Abigail needed her, Abigail should call. Well, the call had been made. Therefore, briskly Sabrina untangled herself. Calmly she spoke, "Mi be ready in ten minutes."

While in the huge master bath, she heard Jamaal mention having to be in court in a few hours. "We'll get you gone, then I'll take J to Mama's."

Sabrina nodded, grabbing her carry-on. She would go to her sister, and her baby would go to his Nana. Sabrina had never minded Martha Dora a.k.a. Ms. BigStuff keeping him. Sure, she and mama-bear often had what Jamaal called querulous dealings. However, Sabrina thought, pulling a sweater over a tee and jeans, sturdy Martha Dora adored her grandson, perhaps as much as she did her own son.

In his car seat, in his father's luxury four-by-four, the toddler slept. Bless his little heart. Forgetting the snow, Sabrina gazed at her baby, still in his PJs beneath his outerwear. She turned from him to embrace his father.

"Go on," she told her bear of a man who appeared as saddened as she felt. "Go," she urged as he stood beside the passenger door. "You needn't get a ticket. Mi call yu."

"Bina," Jamaal stood in the space between his vehicle and its open door. He wanted to delete the mental picture of her crying that morning. "I'll be down as soon as I can." He also offered, "You know I love you, right?"

She nodded and clutched him tightly.

Closing himself around her, the big bear man wished he could shield his girl-woman from paralytic fear. Unable to, he kissed her and told her, as his mother often told him, "Go with God, baby."

When Sabrina walked away, Jamaal wished he could forget the last hour with its hellacious news and tears. It had been one of the worst of his life. Then on the snowy trek to his mom's home, Jamaal prayed one thing; not another call, and not one stating Gaye Denise was deceased...

On the plane, Sabrina replayed those scenes while dabbing her swollen eyes. She missed her husband already. Slightly older, big burly Jamaal was often comforting and strong. Sabrina wondered when she'd become emotionally dependent on him. With Jamaal, it was like it had been with Gaye Denise. Come to think of it, before Jamaal, Abigail had provided solace. She'd had been a cheering section. Therefore, Sabrina knew she could not let Abigail down.

The twenty-something then called on the God of her grandmother. Looking at the sky that was all baby blue now with a cloud covering below the plane, she bit her lip, like her sister often did, and she began to pray.

Sabrina sincerely began, as Gram did every day. "Precious Father, you know me," Sabrina just had to state. She had tried to incorporate The Omnipotent One in every aspect of her life. "I'm the baby sister, the one who didn't wait for trouble to find me before I found you. Father, I don't really know what to say..." It was the truth. Therefore, following a sigh, Sabrina asked for one thing. "It's for me, for my whole family, really." A tear dropped from her eye. "Heaven's Precious," she called, as Gram would have. "Please help Gaye Denise. She is our whole family, and she needs you." Sabrina wiped her nose. "Father, Gaye Denise is the glue that keeps us together, so please let us have more time, productive time, with her."

With her eyes still closed, Sabrina requested courage for what lay ahead. Soon she would be in a taxi, headed for County Medical. She didn't want to clam up, a tendency she had. "Father, please help me think and make clear decisions, for Gaye Denise."

Sabrina sighed and opened her eyes; she took in the majesty of the skies. "I know you'll help me." She added, "So I thank you. Amen."

Leaning back, Sabrina thought about Abigail, who had no children of her own, yet she was the Wallace family mother. Abigail cooked and looked out for everybody. She remembered birthdays and was the person that everyone looked to for advice or a listening ear. In any situation, Abigail never seemed at a loss for what to do. However, she'd admitted that she sometimes felt bewildered and afraid, but she'd also said she prayed and got on with things.

That knowledge gave Sabrina hope. She even attempted a little optimism. Perhaps things weren't as bad as she thought. Gaye Denise might even be out and about by next weekend. At the hospital, mother-sister might even say, "Gurl, dem ah tryin' to keep me here, but mi fine."

Clinging to optimistic visions, Sabrina attempted to ignore pithy fear. "Hang on, Ma-Ma," she breathed, running from the taxi to the hospital door.

Whew! Sabrina was proud of herself because she'd gotten through the rigmarole, the next-of-kin info-giving. She hadn't done too poorly. She'd even remembered Gaye Denise's doctor friend, Marguerite. Therefore, with a grateful heart, Sabrina awaited the on-call doctor.

When he appeared, he affirmed there was a need to worry... Tall, lanky, and appearing to desperately need sleep, Dr. Mortensen stretched his eyes. Running a hand through dark hair, he voiced that Abigail had severe injuries. She was currently comatose due to loss of blood.

Through shock and hurt, Sabrina heard something about a transfusion.

"Although Ms. Wallace suffered respiratory distress," the doctor continued, "We simply have to wait. We'll see how the body responds to medical intervention, which often stabilizes."

"Meaning," Sabrina deduced, "she's been placed on a respirator."

"Yes." The physician added that a neurologist was called in, standard practice for head trauma.

"Head trauma?" Sabrina breathed, her eyes wide.

Abigail's skull was fractured. Quite possibly, the doctor stated, it happened when she was thrown from her vehicle.

Thrown—from her car? Sabrina's eyes further widened. Oh, no!

Dr. Mortensen, looking much like Superman's Clark Kent, said he would be direct. "The first twenty-four hours are most important." He spoke of monitoring due to possible hemorrhaging and the skull fracture.

With a hand at her chest, Sabrina heard that were such the case, holes would have to be bored in the head—Abigail's head—to circumvent the possibility of a hematoma, building blood. It would need to be drained.

Dr. Mortensen saw but professionally distanced himself from the horror in the young woman's eyes. She needed to know there was swelling, fractured ribs and that a plastic surgical consult was advisable, later, for facial injuries. Still, no surgery, other than life-saving attempts, would be performed until the patient was stable.

Sabrina heard that there had been a blow to the forehead. "There are contusions over a third of the body, possibly from the tumble and slide on the pavement..." The doctor took a deep breath to give the attractive but mortified woman, suddenly disoriented, a moment to compose herself.

He said there was more. He hated, as he often did, causing further anguish to a traumatized family member. "Yet it appears," Dr. Mortensen stated, "Ms. Wallace is pregnant, possibly in the second trimester."

"And that could further complicate matters," Sabrina whispered.

Nodding, the doctor pummeled her with additional knowledge. "To put it plainly, the baby is at high risk right now due to trauma." The doctor also explained that one scenario could have the fetus suffering oxygen loss, which would result in fetal brain damage.

"Are you sure," Sabrina slowly inquired, "that my sister is that far along?" Sabrina knew she'd sounded choked, but who cared?

Wearied, Dr. Mortensen said of that one thing they were confident. He did not spare Sabrina the knowledge that sometimes a brace proved necessary instead of a body cast for fractured ribs. "But seeing that Ms. Wallace will naturally enlarge with child, in time—if the fetus is not lost, we'll decide then. Right now, we're monitoring the swelling." The physician said later, bed rest and limited mobility would be called for. "...However, now, again, we are doing all we can."

Thoroughly horrified and overwhelmed, Sabrina lowered her head and willed herself not to cry. The doctor disappeared, and she stumbled to three attached plastic chairs, falling onto one. With streaming tears, she tried to breathe.

At least she's alive, a triumphant little voice reminded Sabrina. Clasping her hands, Sabrina gave thanks. Then she wiped away useless tears.

How, though, she wondered, could her sister be this far along and not say anything? Cautiously, Sabrina wondered if Joe knew.

Squinting, Sabrina calculated backward. If Gaye Denise was into her second trimester, as the doctor suggested, "That would mean: Gaye Denise had still been somewhat with Darré…"

No! Sabrina gasped. But! Gaye D *had* gone to that island with Joseph; wonder what *he'd* say or do—when he found out—assuming he didn't already know. Thinking of that doggone Darré, Sabrina hoped Joe did know—about the baby because that might give him an advantage.

Oh, Ma-Ma, Sabrina thought with a hand at her throat, what a mess.

Sabrina looked around. She needed someone present, but whom? Patria! She was the eldest, so she was supposed to be there. Sabrina wondered where Joseph was. Had he been called? His name was in her sister's wallet, along with her own, under 'in case of emergency.'

Sabrina sighed because her head ached. She despised unanswered questions and all the disastrous new information. *I abide under the shadow of the almighty*. Sabrina inhaled and told herself to think. Okay. She'd been told she could see her sister, soon, but only for a specified amount of time—at, or for, one-hour intervals—she didn't remember which. However, right now, there were things to do, but what? "Think," she said, tapping her forehead. Oh, the frustration! Sabrina inhaled and asked a question. In reversed roles, what would Gaye Denise do? Sabrina did not know and felt on the verge of tears. Everything was complicated. People came and went, but no one could tell her the first thing to do. "Okay," Sabrina said aloud, to steady her frayed nerves. She would—make phone calls! Yes!

Pacing with her cell, she called Jamaal. Then she found out that Patria was out of town, as was Joseph. From her father, she garnered that Gram had taken ill. Yet Radcliff was headed for his girls and the hospital. He also said that Anna-Maria would arrive before he did, from Jamaica.

Sabrina looked at her phone. The woman wasn't even family, not yet, and she was jetting to see about Abigail. It was surprising and comforting.

Sabrina stopped pacing. She needed to keep her mind on Gaye Denise and not on how it would be to have someone present with her. Ashamed of herself, Sabrina bit her lip. How could she think about needing others when her sister needed her? Suddenly, Sabrina realized she needed to locate forty-year-old Patria, get her to the hospital. The eldest Wallace sister needed to be present because, at this, Sabrina was no good. She didn't know Abigail's blood type, and what if she, Sabrina, wasn't it? If needed, she wouldn't even be able to give that necessary but simple offering.

Informing a nurse that she would return in the early afternoon, Sabrina again stated her cell phone number, just in case. She then took a good look at the gray-haired woman. "If my sister weren't going to make it..." Sabrina hated to ask, "Would she wake?"

Seeing the attractive young woman's pain, Nurse Guen truthfully spoke. "Honey, in this case, if she left us, she would not be cognizant."

Sabrina nodded, and surprisingly, the gray-haired nurse squeezed her hand. Feeling somewhat comforted, Sabrina hefted her carry-on.

She had more to be grateful for, Sabrina realized, riding in a cab. After Thanksgiving, she'd not returned Gaye Denise's second set of keys.

In her sister's sumptuous cream-colored abode, Sabrina checked Abigail's voicemail. The hospital, calling for next of kin, then Kismet Staar, Gaye's longtime friend, and Mona Lisa

The woman babbled, "I know you're mad at me, G, but call me anyway. After you left, it was epic. You don't believe it, but lemme know you got home okay. Then you can be upset with me again when we hang up."

Sabrina turned in a semi-circle. Unable to breathe, she bent, attempting to inhale. She murmured, feeling faint. "Lord, don't let this be! Do not let my sister have been out with that—thing, and that's why she wound up...like this." Sabrina pressed a fist to her lips, wondering.

Was the accident, the hospital, and all of it Mona's fault?

"Do not jump to conclusions," Sabrina told herself, but how many times had she and Patria admonished Gaye Denise to stay away from that so-called 'friend' of hers. Sabrina remembered arguing that Mona wasn't friend material. Abigail had asked why not. Sabrina had huffed that Mona was ghetto. Sabrina had further said, "Gaye Denise, garbage, dem hang out wit' yu for what dem cyan get from you –not because they care a thing about you!" The sisters had argued, but it hadn't made an iota of difference, and look! Now Abigail was in the hospital. Fighting heartache, Sabrina swore. If this was that woman's fault...

Wait. Sabrina remembered. Her energy was needed for aiding her sister. When Sabrina breathed near-normal, she vowed not to mention the grievous message or its connotation to anyone, not even to Jamaal. But if it proved true, that harlot would need divine intervention to save her.

Sabrina ran a hot shower. Who knew, she wondered while peeling off clothing, that talking to people about a tragedy could be so exhausting? Standing beneath pelting water, she recalled dialing Gaye's assistant. Sunshine had immediately burst into tears. Both hurt, Gram Mary and Aunt Mildred had asked what was needed. They said Glenda's brother El would drive them to the hospital to pray.

Out of the shower, Sabrina felt calmer. Dressed and picking at a bran muffin, she reached for the phone. She left another message for Patria. Nervously, Sabrina paced Abigail's apartment. Without Gaye D, the place felt empty and wrong. Steeping ginger tea, Sabrina remembered. She'd picked up Abigail's phone to call Peaches and the dial tone had been staggered. Someone had left voicemail. Joseph! Sabrina's heart pounded. Joseph had called while she'd showered. He said most likely, he'd be home tomorrow. He was still in Canada; unexpected turns. Anyway, he hoped Abigail was ready for Cali on Wednesday. "I love you, girl—oh, and I'ma need to do the hallway floor again. Even though on Halloween, you said you'd had enough of the on-the-floor stuff."

What did that mean? Sabrina wondered, furiously scribbling. When she called, an answering service intercepted. Leaving a short message, Sabrina felt maybe this way was better. Since Joseph didn't seem to know anything, she could sort out how best to tell him.

Sabrina picked up Abigail's ringing phone. "Hello? Thomas."

"Hey B." Thomas said he'd been walking that horse he called a dog. "Got your message and wanted to get back to you before the game." On this Sunday, Thomas sounded like he hadn't a care in the world, with his jolly looking-like-Sinbad-self. "So Bina, what's up?"

Horrified after he learned of Abigail's accident, Thomas sounded shaken. "I hate to tell you, B, but Peaches left Philly for Atlantic City."

Quickly, however, he offered hotel information. Again, Thomas said, "I'm sorry about Gaye Denise." Somberly stroking his dog, he said she was so real. "She's fire, but down to earth, and such a good cook. Actually," the man murmured, "she's like somebody's really cool mom. You know?"

Sabrina's eyes filled as she admitted she did know. Abigail was all of that and more. "Thomas, thanks, I've got to go, gotta reach Peaches."

Sabrina dialed and prayed. "Lord, please do not let this be the one day that my late-sleeping sister is out gallivanting, early."

Patria's phone rang...and rang. Sabrina wanted to scream.

Finally, a sleep-laden voice breathed, "Hullo?"

"Peaches!" Sabrina tumbled headlong into telling nearly everything.

Bolting awake, the oldest Wallace sister felt the scream. Inside, it bubbled up. Noooo! She inwardly wailed, as she managed to promise, she'd be at the hospital in a few hours.

Yet Sabrina babbled.

"Binky!" Patria yelled. "Bina, get—off—dis phone, now!" Super-sized sexy's voice gentled. "Please, baby gurl, so mi cyan shower and get dere."

"Oh." Sabrina blinked. "Sorry, Queen."

Patria swiped at falling tears, barely able not to sob. "Mi too, hon."

Sabrina also fought not to weep as her voice broke, "Peaches?"

"Yah."

"Hurry, okay?"

"Yah baby, soon come." Patria dropped the phone. Leaning over, she pressed fingers to her eyes. Not realizing she hadn't rung off, she sounded strangled; thus, Sabrina heard, "Whyyy?" Aloud Patria sobbed, "Lord, why Gaye Denise? Why not take heathen me?"

Disconnecting, Sabrina dabbed tears and grabbed her coat. The cab would arrive at any moment. Oh-oh. Sabrina turned. Perhaps that was the doorman alerting her. Into the phone, she breathed, "Yes?"

"Ms. Baby."

"Joe! Oh, God, Gaye Denise is in the hospital—"

Joseph sounded sunk. "I got your message. I'm on my way. Well, whenever I get a flight. The weather's bad, I'm on standby, but I made calls..." Someone would see that he got where he needed to go. Money and status had benefits, for which he was grateful right about now.

Suddenly Joseph became a blizzard of inquiries, and Sabrina wound up feeling frustrated because she had few answers. She said so, and Joseph became reassuring. He claimed it was okay. Then in take-charge mode, he said they would know all they need to in a little while.

Disengaged, Sabrina saw why her sister loved Joseph. He had tried to sound confident, but Sabrina knew the news had taken a bite out of him. Still, the man loved Abigail so much, he'd pretended optimism for her baby sister. "Father God, those two need more time," Sabrina prayed. Actually, she thought, they'd seemed to be working things out before all of this.

In the cab, Sabrina again prayed and swiped at falling tears. Honestly, she couldn't remember crying so –well, not since the birth of her son.

SABRINA was told she could look in on Abigail. Thus, Sabrina hurried to Intensive Care. At the designated unit, she stopped short, with heartache blitzing her. Unshed tears burned Sabrina's throat as she thought, Oh Jah because she hadn't braced herself for the first lay-eyes.

Sure, Sabrina had subconsciously been aware of the ravages of such an accident; however, the initial look proved heart-wrenching.

Lying in a railed bed that loomed large and foreboding, Abigail's head was wrapped sweatband-style in sterile gauze. She appeared mummified, frail, and small. Tubes, it seemed, were everywhere; and suddenly, Sabrina wanted to back away. Yet she prevailed, placing one foot before the other until she was entirely in the room.

Abide in the secret place, she told herself. God is our refuge.

What was that smell? It sickened Sabrina. Was it antiseptic she wondered, or blood, or fear? As she forced herself forward, Sabrina recalled the old folk. They said when death came a'calling, one could smell it.

Sabrina could hardly abide the barely discernable stench. Therefore, using a sleeve, she covered her nose because she had to see her sister.

Despite the gauze wrapping, Sabrina saw that Abigail's forehead was swollen and bruised. Her closed eyes appeared sunken and dark. Her cheek! Sabrina nearly gasped. It was raw and crudely stitched.

To keep from retching, Sabrina pinched her sensitive nose. Moving forward, she noted her sister's bandaged arm. There were open-wound bruises on the brown side of Abigail's hand. It rested on the flat sheet.

What had those women said, as they'd stood in Aunt Mildred's little sanctified church, testifying? Oh, often they'd praised God for life and for not allowing them to die while they'd slumbered. Wearing white, those women had been grateful that their beds had not become their cooling boards, nor their sheets their shrouds...

Mentally, Sabrina hissed because she had to get hold of herself! She had to stop thinking about death. She also had to stop questioning why Gaye Denise? She simply swallowed the scream that nearly strangled her.

Yes, her sister's lips were cracked and swollen. There were tubes, wires, and adhesives, just stuff attached to needles pricking Gaye Denise's flesh everywhere. Still, Sabrina had to believe that all those contraptions were to monitor, keep blood flowing, and dehydration at bay. Although Gaye Denise's lips, powdery and white, suggested she was indeed parched.

Agonizing, Sabrina couldn't keep her heart from going out to the young woman who meant more to her than she had ever said. Sabrina realized that never before had she thought of her sister as young. However, Sabrina wanted it to be so; Gaye Denise had to be too young to die.

Sabrina swiped tears, not wanting Gaye Denise to wake at that moment, a miracle that it would be, to find her crying, although the elder appeared different and not like herself at all. In truth, she looked like...a corpse.

Shaking with fear, Sabrina lifted a hand. She wanted to touch Abigail, but where? Nearly every place was swollen, black, purple, and blue.

Then Sabrina saw the sheet. Somewhat tucked around the bruised body, displayed was the obvious, a protrusion, Abigail Denise Wallace's baby.

Sabrina berated herself for not knowing. She was a mother, for crying out loud! How had she not known? Had she not cared enough to notice? Had she been that self-centered that she'd missed all the telltale signs?

Sabrina nearly despised herself for having failed the woman who had loved and sacrificed for her, although a small voice prevailed. Gently it asked if she had known would that have changed fate.

Swiping tears, Sabrina swallowed hurt to notice Abigail's hand. It resembled a fist. Then despite the anguish, Sabrina smiled because it was a sign. Gaye Denise had always been a fighter. Her loosely clenched fingers gave the semblance, such little that it was, that she'd not given up. She was willing to fight her way back. Was she not?

Feeling buoyed, Sabrina vowed not to give up either, and she inched closer to the imposing bed and bent over the side. She pressed her lips to the only patch of un-bruised skin. Then she whispered, "I'm here, Gaye D. It's me—Binky."

Suddenly Sabrina remembered. If only she could retrieve some things! "Ma-Ma," Sabrina whispered, "I know I told you not to call me Binky." A tear escaped and fell onto Abigail's dehydrated mouth, "But you can call me anything you want." Sabrina hiccupped, "If you just come back, to me."

Sabrina turned, drawing breath. She tried to contain her sorrow because if Gaye Denise heard anything, Sabrina wanted it to be positive.

Softly Sabrina said, "Ma-Ma, you're going to pull through this."

From her peripheral, Sabrina glimpsed a nurse. Sabrina would soon have to leave. Good, because she felt defeated, but Sabrina felt something else. Inside, newness rose. Strong and loving, it made her speak.

"Heaven's precious, please breathe life into my sister, once again." Suddenly Sabrina knew that she, like Gram, had a prayer wheel. In Gram's absence, Sabrina's wheel had begun to turn. It called on God to deliver.

Sabrina heard herself say to her sister, "You are so loved, Ma-Ma." In a soothing voice, Sabrina said, "Gaye Denise, you're going to have all the help you'll need to get well, because…" Sabrina forced her voice to sound fanciful, "Who would take care of all of us if you didn't?"

Sabrina bit her lip and mentally pled with Abigail to hold on. You hang in there, Ma-Ma, for me, she wanted to say. However, Sabrina said, "You keep providing strength for our new baby."

Sabrina remembered Gram saying that little rambunctious Jamaal needed one his own size to tumble with. Therefore, Sabrina told her sister, "Mi chile needs 'im first cousin." Rising, Sabrina also said that Peaches, Anna-Maria, Radcliff, and hordes of others would soon arrive.

"Oh, and Joe, your sweet man, is on his way. He said he loves you 'Star' more than any ting between earth and sky…"

Sabrina stopped speaking then because the words 'Gaye, you're my mother,' lodged in her throat and built to a desperate scream. "You're the only mother I've ever known." Gaye Denise had taught her how to mother. This Sabrina wanted to blurt over hurt. "Don't slip away," Sabrina managed. "Don't let me wind up orphaned, again. Please."

Sabrina bit the back of a fist because if Gaye Denise slipped away, she'd have lost two mothers, due to two intoxicated drivers. Stumbling from the room, Sabrina sobbed. Her chest heaved and her nose ran. Leaning against the wall outside ICU, she gave vent to the outpouring that had waited, ever since she'd left home, to claim her. Why? *Why*? She railed, both afraid and angry.

After she pulled herself together, Sabrina went to sit in the small waiting area not far from the nurses' station. She wiped her nose with rough tissue graciously offered by Nurse Guen. Then for the longest time, Sabrina closed her eyes. Placing elbows on denim-clad knees, she wondered. Why not give in to total despair? She was no good at being strong. That was Gaye Denise's job. Abigail was the family's rock, their centerpiece.

Finally, tired of sitting, Sabrina stood, intending to walk a bit. She made it to the end of the hallway, where a hand shot out, grabbing her arm.

Startled, Sabrina turned. Involuntarily, she fell on the other woman, hugging her hard and tight. "Oh, Peaches," Sabrina breathed, in her sister's arms, "This isn't good. Gaye Denise may lose the baby, if not her own life."

"She told me she wants children." Yet within Patria's fragrant embrace Sabrina revealed, "But now she's suffering, and the doctor said—"

"B," Patria bent her knees and held her sister's head in two dimpled hands. "Gurl, we must abide in the secret place, remember?"

The younger sister nodded, and the heavier sister spoke, more to herself. "Gaye Denise wouldn't want me 'n yu out here crying, like two babies."

She would not, Sabrina agreed. She let her oldest sister go.

Patria removed her coat. When ready, she went to Abigail.

She soon came away with the wind knocked out of her. Plopping solidly onto the chair beside her sister, Patria reached for Sabrina's hand.

Clutching tightly, they silently sat to wait, and pray.

## 25

**W**HEN Anna-Maria came through the swinging doors of the Intensive Care Unit, both sisters rushed toward their father's fiancé. Although neither could have explained why, they stood for the longest time, six arms locked together. Taking a backward step, Patria said, "Anna-Maria, thank you for coming. You didn't have to, but your support is greatly appreciated."

The older woman folded her coat onto a chair. Adjusting her beautiful gold bangles, she asked what was there to do, "Anything?"

"Only wait," Sabrina replied, her eyes averted.

Anna-Maria turned to Patria, who explained what she had been told. Patria concluded, "I hope Gaye Denise is aware we're here because studies show that people in her condition need to know loved ones are near."

Sabrina rolled her eyes. Peaches needed to forget what she'd read. The bookworm needed to face the truth. Nothing could prepare anyone for what they were experiencing. Sabrina angrily thought everybody needed to keep shit real. There was a chance they could lose Gaye Denise.

For a while, all was quiet. Noticing the oppressive silence, Sabrina and Patria spoke simultaneously. They sounded optimistic. However, Anna-Maria knew better. She, too, had used ruses when her first husband had lain dying. So she felt for the sisters as she saw the agony in the eyes they averted. She knew despair consumed them. Anna-Maria also knew they attempted to present a united front, for her sake, and the notion touched her. In that regard, they were like their father. Crossing her ankles, Anna-Maria recalled that Radcliff had tried to soften the telling of 'the accident.' He'd called her home and downplayed the severity, aware that she'd grown fond of Abigail. Poor man, Anna-Maria sighed, how he feared losing his daughter. More frightening was the prospect of him seeing her helpless.

"She couldn't live like that," he'd said, ready to drive to the airport.

Turning from zippering a bag, Anna-Maria touched Radcliff's cheek. Then he startled her by swiftly encircling her. He'd buried his face in her neck. Not a man given to shows of emotion, his breathing had become labored. He'd held on tightly. Rubbing Radcliff's back, Anna-Maria had said spirited Abigail would return fully to him and the Wallace family.

"You must believe." When Radcliff released her, Anna-Maria pulled a rattan chair from her lovely walnut dining table. With a breeze sighing through her wooden blinds, she could have dashed off to the big city. Like now, though, she would not have been helpful. But Radcliff had needed her, so she'd remained, to offer—if nothing else—the comfort of her presence. Beneath the whirring ceiling fan, Radcliff had sorrowfully knelt. With hands on his shoulders, Anna-Maria's eyes had filled, for Radcliff and for Abigail. Upon reaching Kennedy airport, Anna-Maria had telephoned back, only to hear that her staying had meant the entire world to Radcliff.

Inconspicuously, Anna-Maria glanced at the sisters. Her heart seemingly enlarged with a newfound love for them. Tragic though it was, she realized, the accident had now bound her, irrevocably, to both Patria and Sabrina.

Anna-Maria only hoped one day they would know and feel similar. Seated between them, their intermittent conversation lulled Anna-Maria, who prayed that the tragedy would soon become triumph.

Sabrina mentioned Abigail's unborn baby, and Anna-Maria sighed. She'd had no children of her own, yet she would love to hear a baby's gurgle. She also wanted to watch Abigail—who had so much to live for—when she'd be up and tending her new baby. Anna-Maria just hoped Abigail would allow her, the 'old outsider,' a small role in the child's life.

Oh, I'm thinking too far ahead, Anna-Maria scolded. Abigail was not her daughter. It didn't matter that the younger woman had called, quite a few times. Abigail had told her father that she hadn't wanted to speak with him but with his fiancé. It didn't matter that Abigail had requested advice the way a daughter would have asked it of a mother. Anna-Maria told herself not to make more of things because she could wind up hurt. However, Abigail was warm, caring, and she and Anna-Maria shared a beautiful bond.

"You know Anna," Abigail had said the week prior. "I feel like I've known yu longer than mi cyan remember, and mi love yu."

Anna-Maria's eyes filled, like when Abigail said it. Again, Anna thought what she had said; she felt the same, and wasn't love grand?

Yet, Anna-Maria reminded herself, none of it meant she should assume. Adjusting her gold bangles, she cogitated for the thousandth time. She should have taken Gil's advice all those years ago. They should have adopted a little girl when they'd been young, healthy, happy, and in love, instead of simmering in salty tears because she'd been unable to conceive.

With a sigh, Anna-Maria reminded herself that she hadn't done what she could have. Therefore, now, she could not grasp straws.

Oh-oh. Anna-Maria's hand fluttered to her chest.

Noticing, Sabrina wanted to ask if the woman was okay; but she didn't. When Anna-Maria relaxed, Sabrina realized if she'd inquired, she might have appeared nosey. Then again, Gaye Denise always asked if people were okay. Like at the market, a woman had been bent over her grocery buggy, her face perspiring. Gaye Denise had walked over and asked if anything was needed. Wanly, the woman had smiled and said thank you, but no. She said she was nine months pregnant, "Overdue, and exhausted." The woman revealed, "Me shopping on swollen feet doesn't help, either."

Still, Sabrina told herself, she was not Mother-Sister. Anyway, now Anna-Maria appeared okay, with that little smirk on her face.

Unaware that Sabrina was watching, Anna-Maria felt like Abigail could recover in record time. Anna-Maria recalled other times that her heart had sped and slowed. Those occasions, like now, had been indications that things would get better. Although, after sweet Gilchrist had seemingly recovered, he'd died...

TOO many days later, Sabrina sat holding her head. Why did it take Anna-Maria and Radcliff so long to speak with the doctor? Sabrina looked up; that was probably them now. Nope. With narrowed eyes, Sabrina fumed because Mona Lisa approached, with Darré in tow.

Patria groaned and stood. Unaware, Darré kissed her cheek and leaned to kiss Sabrina. She outmaneuvered him. Who knew where his lips had been? Better that he kept them off her, Sabrina thought.

Nonplussed, Darré asked about Abigail, but before either Wallace sister could reply, he explained. He'd come, upon finding out, from Mona Lisa.

Now, how had she known? Patria wondered. Previously, she'd asked if Gaye's 'friend' was informed, and curtly she'd been told no.

Eyeing the woman whom she despised, Sabrina pondered saying 'Mona, you look guilty, so perhaps you're the reason we're all here.' Sabrina nodded because she could also say, 'How dare you, Mona Fake Lisa, come flouncing up to this hospital—with my sister's re-tread."

Cutting her eyes, Sabrina vowed to dismiss the two, or she would jump up and hurt that skank. Wait, Sabrina reflected. Mona Lisa had informed

Darré of Abigail's hospitalization. How had she known? And that 'through the grapevine' shit wouldn't work. Loudly, Sabrina sucked her teeth. Yeah, that got Mona Lisa looking.

Fixed with the evil eye, Mona Lisa turned uneasily away.

Watching the severely rumpled woman, Patria had her own doubts. Who wouldn't have, seeing the flyaway hair and unmade face? Heck, if ol' girl looked busted on Tuesday, a workday, had she been fired, again?

Patria pinched Sabrina and whispered with barely moving lips. "Gurl, slap de crap outta me if ever mi leave de house without mi face on."

Sabrina wanted to laugh, but she couldn't. If she opened her mouth, everything she knew might tumble out. Therefore, she clamped her lips and realized. She was in Mona Lisa's face! Roughly, Sabrina knocked the taller woman to the wall. Sabrina kneed and hissed. "You did this!"

"Wh—what're you talking about?!" Mona Lisa stammered, her nose and shin shooting pain. Her yaki was also coming unglued. She knew it as she bent, holding to the store-bought hair while her scalp felt aflame.

Whipping her arm out of reach, Sabrina warned her sister as she pulled on and swung Mona Lisa about. "Don't fuckin' hold me, Peaches!"

"I will pull you if I have to," the elder announced as the younger slammed her prey into the wall. "Bina, come over here a minute."

Sabrina leaned down. Lethally, she promised, "I'm gonna pick your eyes out, you counterfeit ho." Giving Mona Lisa's weave one last malicious jerk, Sabrina told the whimpering woman, "When mi finish workin' mi root on yu, no one will recognize yu!" Shoving the taller, larger Mona Lisa once more, for good measure, Sabrina made herself walk away. She watched, however, over a shoulder. "Peaches, why cyan't we talk back dere? I got questions for that whore."

"B, turn around." Patria spoke calmly, "Walk this way. Look at me."

Sabrina sighed and did as bid. She also whined, "Your hand is hot."

"Maybe it's you that's heated," Patria offered, no longer touching her sister. "Now tell me, Bina," Patria folded her arms. "What got into you? Hey!" Patria snapped her fingers. "Here. Look here."

Sabrina cut her eyes. She didn't like Mona acting as though she was okay, for Abigail's ex.

"Baby girl, what's up?" Patria placed a finger beneath her sister's chin.

Sabrina could have cried; she was so frustrated. No, she could have raced back and slammed Mona to the floor, WWF style. With crossed arms,

Sabrina didn't know how much longer she could keep her secret, not with that tramp standing around like she'd done nothing, while Abigail lay bruised and broken on a borrowed bed!

Patria pulled a tissue. "Take this. You're omitting something. I know it."

Blowing her nose, Sabrina sounded muffled, "Maybe mi just upset."

"Cut it out," Patria advised, exasperated. "I'm way too old for game. You can't stand what's-her-face, but there's more. You want to kill her. Your eyes are red, blazin' and yu breathin' too hard. Gurl, talk to me."

She would stop being so transparent. This Sabrina told herself since she needed to stake Mona Lisa out. She also told a partial truth. "Peaches I'm riled up from being here night and day, you know?"

Patria eyed Darré and Mona Lisa, whispering.

She knew her sister was evasive, yet she rubbed Sabrina's arm. "Bina, we don't want you to wind up in one of these beds, too, so calm down."

Sabrina nearly growled, "What's between de two'a dem?"

Patria sighed and said she did not know, but she had known, the moment that Mona Lisa appeared, that something would jump off. It seemed everywhere that woman went, confusion and drama followed.

Sabrina became belligerent. "So you don't want to know?"

"I want you to calm down."

"Well, I want to kick her stank behind."

Anna-Maria appeared, seemingly from nowhere. "Maybe," she stated, looking from one sister to the other. "It would be best if I asked 'the others' to leave..." Her eyes rested on Patria.

"They're Gaye Denise's friends. Well, the woman's supposed to be," Patria replied, realizing she didn't care one way or another. Perhaps Mona did deserve a beat-down because she had nerve, strutting up with Gaye's ex. He was nervy too, appearing, after all he'd put Abigail through.

Sabrina's voice was soft yet mean-spirited as she thumbed a finger at Darré. "He's probably boinking that beeyotch, and she's liking it."

Patria laughed, and Anna-Maria's eyes widened when Sabrina further said, "That heifer probably bends over every night, telling him to call her Gaye, because Gaye Denise is who she really wants to be."

"Okay," the older sister admonished, chuckling, "forget them." Unaware that Darré approached, Patria noticed Anna-Maria's flaring eyes.

Turning slowly, Patria acknowledged Darré, who ignored his vibrating phone. He claimed he and Mona Lisa didn't want to cause trouble.

Puh-lease, Sabrina thought as Darré said he and Mona only wanted to lend support. He clicked his cellular off because when would his wife stop calling? The little pest, she'd called twenty times in one hour.

Patria, who wasn't feeling Darré, or Mona Lisa, simply said, "Suit yourselves." Then she wearily turned and walked toward a seat.

Sabrina followed, eyeing 'that woman' as she did.

Seated, Patria asked a question. "Bina, did Gaye Denise ever tell you that Mona spoke badly 'bowt him?" Patria nodded at Darré.

"She did."

"I see." Patria eyed the woman who yet stood in the corner into which she'd been backed. So Mona had talked Darré down while he and Abigail had been together. Some friend; and Patria would bet that just as Sabrina said, that tramp was screwing Darré; she might have been, all along...

Appearing defeated, Mona Lisa eyed Abigail's sisters. They had always despised her. They didn't want her present, but so what? Abigail was her friend. Mona Lisa wanted her friend, her best friend, to be okay, but the wicked sisters' eyes glinted as they somehow felt everything was her fault.

Patria Wallace forgot Mona Lisa, who appeared on the verge of tears. Patria pondered Darré, the trifling dog who would trail any bitch in heat. Well, it was good Gaye Denise hadn't jumped the broom with him –even if Bina was correct in surmising that he could be Gaye's baby daddy.

Forgetting Darré, Patria noticed Radcliff, returned from the gift shop.

A few floors down, the attendant had slyly suggested that Abigail's father buy the day's paper, "So you won't have to settle for reading only portions of it." Ignoring the leather-faced man, Radcliff had left. Now, aware of the tension, he offered a brief nod to Mona Lisa and Darré.

Anna-Maria gazed over her half spectacles. Closing her worn book of prayers, she told her beloved that there was no news yet.

Seemingly unaware of the discomfit that he and Mona Lisa caused, Darré announced that he would hang out a while. He then seated himself on the floor. Sabrina felt he was too close to the attached chairs on which she, Patria, and Anna-Maria sat. After texting his pesky wife, Darré said he just wanted to be near, although he knew he couldn't do anything for Abbie.

An uneasy silence followed, and Patria sighed with relief when sagely Anna-Maria said, "Thank you, son, for the gesture."

Abbie, Sabrina knew her sister despised being called that.

In the ensuing silence, Mona Lisa remained in her corner, aloof. She wanted no part of the family that wanted no part of her.

Radcliff, who refused the notion of a seat, went to stare out of a far window. Sometime later, Anna-Maria suggested going home, "One or all of you really should." Radcliff heard his fiancé state, "So you can rest."

Although exhausted, each person strove to appear reluctant to leave. Anna-Maria tried again, this time looking to Radcliff for reinforcement. She suggested that he and she take the remainder of the night's watch.

Radcliff agreed and said he would go for coffee. Still, no one moved. When he returned, Sabrina discouraged the paper cup held out to her. Again Anna-Maria almost begged someone to leave. She said that person could come back to cover the morning shift if they chose.

Looking sullen, Mona Lisa mumbled she had to go. Feigning smoothness, Darré struggled up from the floor saying Mona was his ride.

"Yeah, I'll bet," Sabrina mumbled, "in more ways than one."

Patria yawned as the pair walked away. "Come to think of it," she said and stretched, "I could shower, and I'm hungry. Still, I'll wait," Patria said to no one in particular, "until Heckle' n Jeckle are gone." She grasped her coat as Sabrina opted to remain, wanting to hear the morning report.

"Well ring me, Bina," Patria called as she and her father—who could no longer sit, due to feeling idle—walked toward the elevator. "Where yu going, Papa, with no coat?" Patria asked as they descended.

Shrugging, with hands deep in his cords pockets, Radcliff admitted he didn't know. He would walk, maybe to the deli. He'd get a paper or gum.

Aware of the similarities between this accident and the one two decades prior, Patria sympathized. Her father had aged a few years in just a few days. Knowing the anguish of losing her mother again hung heavy, Patria looked up at Radcliff. Poor man, he'd been left with teenagers and a toddler. "I guess you've got to get out, Papa—go somewhere, right, in search of something that'll shave off some time, correct?"

Radcliff nodded, and Patria thought it was too bad there wasn't a nearby bar. Oops, that would be for her. Her father would need to sit in a church.

UPSTAIRS, Sabrina and Anna-Maria sat. They spoke of how nice it was that people like Sunshine, Abigail's assistant, had visited. "She was so hurt," Sabrina remarked. "Good thing her husband drove her."

Anna-Maria agreed. "The music engineer with the measurement name came too. And good Lord, all those girls! Some were crying so hard."

Sabrina smiled because, although busy, Kilo had made time to see Abigail, so had the girls she mentored. Getting up, as they had since the ordeal began, Sabrina peeked at their beloved. When she sat, she heard Anna-Maria humming. Mellifluous, the little tune suffused Sabrina with peace, a feeling she had all but forgotten amid the reigning confusion.

Sabrina raised tear-filled eyes. "Anna, what if Jah takes Gaye Denise?"

Anna-Maria quit knitting to ask, "May I share something with you?"

The younger woman nodded.

"Sabrina," Anna-Maria began, facing her. "I believe our Heavenly Father doesn't take our loved ones. Death does. It is a spirit, which entered the world through sin. Sure, some don't believe it. However, if you do, maybe you know that for Death, the Bible offers comfort. It says *to be absent from the body is to be present with the Lord.*

"So Sabrina, should your sister leave us, we will know that she is with the Father. Although if that happens, we will be hurt and miss her dearly. Still, we will know that she will then be better off than we."

Sabrina swallowed heartache. "We can ask the Father to allow her to stay, though. I've learned He desires to give, and have relationships with us. I read too," Sabrina said, and knew she sounded like her bookworm sister, "that we can ask whatever we will, and the Father will hear us."

"That is true, and often, the Father permits and grants our desires."

"You alluded to *sometimes*," Sabrina said as her eyes shimmered with tears. "That's because our Heavenly Father is sovereign."

Anna-Maria nodded. "That's the part humans have trouble with."

"I'm okay with that," Sabrina stated, "because, like the Heavenly Father, I'm a parent. I have rules, I don't grant all my son's wishes."

"Just like the Heavenly Father doesn't grant all of ours."

Sabrina nodded, "Because He is not a genie, Anna."

"Right. Therefore, we must pray." Anna-Maria bowed her head.

"Let's ask for recovery," Sabrina breathed, both afraid and hopeful.

"We shall." Then sensing palpable fear and grief, Anna-Maria forgot possible rejection. She simply opened her arms. "Sabrina dear, let us also *believe* that our Father will allow what is best."

Without hesitation, Sabrina tucked herself into the offered embrace. "Anna?" she called, needing to apologize. "Anna, I—"

"Do not think of it, dear."

Yet Sabrina needed to ask forgiveness, so she raised herself to peer into the older woman's eyes. "I wasn't nice when you visited for Thanksgiving. I was mean," and churlish, and did not want to accept that Radcliff had someone new. "I was wrong." Sabrina realized she sounded a lot like Gaye Denise, who could entreat anyone. "Forgive me, please. Will you?"

Anna-Maria's smile was dazzling. It eased the strain between Sabrina's brows. "Done. Now," briskly, the older woman spoke, "we shall pray to get your sister through this."

EXITING the elevator, Patria walked alongside her father. Ignoring the hustle and bustle of the hospital's first floor, she thought of the chapel. There, Radcliff could pray for Gaye Denise and for the family. Knowing her father, Patria mused, undoubtedly, he'd already been, numerous times.

Pushing outside through revolving doors, coatless, Radcliff could nearly feel his eldest daughter's despair. Therefore, despite cutting wind, he stopped. Radcliff hugged Patria and initially startled her with the gesture.

Afterward, she and he moseyed along in the brisk morning cold. While under the sullen sky, with traffic passing, Patria felt hurt and disillusioned.

"Well, thanks Papa," she said past pain as Radcliff chivalrously opened her car door. Easing in, Patria looked up. She wanted to say, 'Papa, go back inside; you need not stand around and catch a cold.' Instead, her face crinkled, and her eyes watered and stung. Utterly worn, Patria gave in to hurt. She lay her head on her steering wheel. Uncontrollably she sobbed.

In the cold Radcliff stood, with his peachy-skinned firstborn, the one who had been the most regal round girl. Just inside her driver's door, Radcliff remained. He simply wanted to be there, for her—like Anna-Maria had been for him. The girl-dad did so, knowing there were times when a grieving person really could not say that they needed another, desperately.

SABRINA rested her head on Anna-Maria's shoulder.

Feeling supremely warmed, Radcliff's fiancé smiled as Sabrina drifted.

Sabrina dreamed of sitting beside Abigail's bed. Gram was present. Softly Gram hummed. Then Gram was gone, yet her voice remained. It emanated from Sabrina's mouth. Through Sabrina, Gram said The Comforter cradled all His children in His loving arms.

Again, Gram spoke through Sabrina; Gram said The Comforter was also a rainmaker. He knew when a woman went through a drought, a time of seemingly no life, and no verdant green. Then the rainmaker would step forth, parting the curtain of time and space. Striding from mystifying eternity into time, He would call forth precipitation, dewdrops from Heaven. These would saturate the place where there had only been desiccated despair.

Then…in her dream, Sabrina found herself alone. Barefoot and out of doors, she stood on a carpet of luxurious green grass. With an upturned face, Sabrina reveled in the warm rain that gently began to fall. As she stood there, the rain started to fall faster and harder. It washed away all her anxiety and every one of her fears.

When it ceased, leaving a deafening hush, Sabrina knew. She stood in the sanctuary of the breath of Heaven –where there was life and joy.

Waking and stretching, Sabrina looked around. She had never left the hospital. Neither had Anna-Maria, and Gram was not physically present. Yet back in Jamaica, doubtless, the old woman prayed. It was why in New York, in the trauma center, with death and disease all around, for Sabrina, the serenity of the breath of Heaven remained.

## 26

IT was morning, yet the lanky doctor looked tired. Sabrina forgot that, though, to tune back in. Abigail, who had been weaned off the respirator, would undergo a battery of tests. Some, the physician alluded, would monitor fetal vital signs. If there wasn't internal bleeding, and should neurological tests go well, Abigail would be moved to a step-down unit.

Anna-Maria squeezed Radcliff, her man's hand, as well as Sabrina's. Watching, the physician appeared puzzled. "I thought I'd mention this. When Ms. Wallace murmurs, it's about...a *forest*?"

Sabrina grinned because *Forrester* was ever on her sister's mind. That, Sabrina could not wait to tell Jamaal, who had come and gone.

Disengaged from family, Sabrina walked. With folded arms, she knew she should have been happy. Abigail had not wound up in a coma that lasted for more than three days. In her case, that would have been harmful, so said the doctor. The family had prayed for that. Still, Sabrina wanted Gaye Denise well, *now*. Sabrina also wanted to go home. She wanted to cook in her custom-designed kitchen. She wanted to scold her busy boy, and haggle with his nosey Nana, a.k.a. mama-bear.

Sabrina also longed for *Joseph*. He was Gaye Denise's man. Therefore, it was his *duty* to shoulder some of the burden, wasn't it? Sabrina walked the hall that she now abhorred, with its bland tile floor. She was sick of Joseph's questions. She was not his assistant. If he was so concerned, he needed to get himself to the hospital. Putz.

Sabrina scolded herself because Joseph even loved the ground her sister walked on, unlike that other character, who only loved himself.

Pacing, Sabrina knew Joseph wasn't present because Radcliff had told him to go on to California. Joseph had sincerely protested because some wealthy friend—a Carlos maybe—stood by with a private jet.

However, Radcliff told the truth. Joseph had been with Abigail for everyone in the family, so the family would be with her, for him.

Sabrina hated keeping secrets, but she hadn't told Joseph that she'd recently seen Abigail. Bruised and swollen, mother-sister had appeared distant. She'd lain in the hospital bed, staring away from her baby sister.

Sabrina wondered, what was going on in Gaye Denise's shell? Nurse Guen had said that trauma patients sometimes suffered slight amnesia. "In time, the nurse had helpfully offered, "that should dissipate."

With a sigh, Sabrina wondered if *she* should go to Papa's chapel. There, she could ask for patience and forgiveness. She needed to become a more compassionate sister, because, Lord knew when *she* had been at the birthing center, near 'bout to die, Gaye Denise had been there for her. Joseph had been too...

Abigail had fed her baby sister ice chips. Then in the birthing tub, with Sabrina, Abigail kneaded hard labor pains from Sabrina's back.

Later, without the exhausted Sabrina's knowledge, Abigail slipped from the private suite with its pretty wallpaper to walk with Jamaal. Softly she encouraged and kept him from falling apart. Abigail acknowledged that yes, the long hours of labor had taken a toll; "But your wife wants to be conscious, not dazed and drugged." Of that, Abigail had reminded Jamaal and that Sabrina had moaned, just moments prior, that she *still* wanted to be cognizant of everything.

"Binky wants it this way, Maal." Then Abigail coaxed the big man back into the suite, telling him he couldn't quit on his wife. "If she can't quit, how can you? She needs *you*—your strength—daddy..."

Yet walking the hospital hall, Sabrina recalled Jamaal saying, days after their son's birth, that her sister was extra! He'd explained and added with a smirk, "But Sis, *and* Peaches, Thelma and Louise, will always be colossal pains in my neck."

Sabrina smiled as peace from her beautiful dream again settled on her. She also wondered, how did Gaye Denise do it? She always put others first.

## 27

"Huh? Wh-what time is it?" Radcliff looked at his intended.

"It's late afternoon," Sabrina chimed and set a box on her father's knees. "We brought food. Look Peaches, bread pudding, brown stewed chicken, rice and peas, cabbage, and plantain."

Patria peeked inside. "Smells delicious—a home-cooked meal, Papa."

"Who?" Radcliff asked because it had only been a few hours.

"I slept," Sabrina admitted.

"Sweet Anna," Radcliff sounded gruff. "Yu didn't have—"

"But we're glad you did," Patria interrupted, "if there's some for me…"

"There is." Anna-Maria smiled, "And it was no trouble at all."

"Any word?" Sabrina asked, hoping to stave off melancholia.

"Not yet," Patria replied as baby sister closed her eyes. Patria knew how Sabrina felt. Patria stood. Pulling her oversized black turtleneck sweater down in the back, she remarked, "B, Anna, I'm going to walk. Then…"

Sensing Patria's need to be alone, Anna-Maria nodded. "Take time."

Patria stared out of 'her father's window, telling herself that she would eat in a minute, even as the day, gray and bleak, peered back. It forced her to recall her own stay in a hospital –for her eating disorder…

Patria did not know when she'd started poking fingers down her throat to bring back the high caloric meals she loved. She only knew that afterward, she felt better. Until she started suffering what she believed was never-ending heartburn. Then Patria had become deathly ill.

Yet Gaye Denise loved her and visited often throughout treatment. Joe appeared too. Gaye Denise had not judged Patria. She'd simply sat in weekend sessions, and sometimes she'd spoken for her sister. Gaye Denise had washed and flat-ironed Patria's hair. Abigail spoon-fed and shush-shushed the elder sister who'd cried and sputtered that eating would make her fat again. "No, Queen," Abigail had whispered, "you are beautiful."

Now, Patria sadly thought, she couldn't even sit with or feed Gaye Denise, her sister, her precious friend. Sadly, Patria couldn't return the favor because all she could do was stand around and look big, and stupid.

Through the window, Patria observed people huddled against the wind. They climbed from cars and got off buses. When a woman with a bundled baby stepped into view, Patria wondered. Would Gaye Denise ever blanket her baby and carry him or her out of doors?

Patria turned because why had she been gawking out anyway? Pulling her sweater sleeves down over her cold hands, she realized. She had been staring from 'Papa's window' for over an hour. It was how she spent the majority of her time 'imprisoned' at the hospital –this time, and last time.

Patria's voice rang out then, loud and shrill, saying she couldn't take it anymore! The waiting! At the eating disorder facility she'd hated it too. Facing her sister and Anna-Maria, who rushed over, Patria asked what were they were supposed to do. Neither startled-looking woman knew.

Just what she'd thought; Patria heard herself continue, in a voice so unlike her own. She asked who could wait, gracefully, praying day after day? They groveled to Jah, who didn't seem to hear. Who wouldn't panic or feel headache-y? Also, who could take the never knowing?

Then with Sabrina and Anna-Maria staring blankly, their minds visibly matriculating, each searching for the right words, Patria bit the back of a dimpled hand. She really didn't want to act out. "I know 'they' expect us to act like fools," she said and blinked at the pale man, with his tuft of red hair, peeking from his end of the hallway. "They call us muddies 'n jungle bunnies. They say we cut the fool, but how can *anyone* stand this?"

Tossing her head, Patria turned in a semi-circle. She mirrored a disoriented child, as her sister and Anna-Maria, who had become family under adverse conditions, attempted to console.

Amid sweet shushing, Anna-Maria gingerly suggested that the sisters go to the gift shop or even to the cafeteria. There, Patria might eat at a table. Maybe, Anna-Maria offered, there would be news when they returned.

Tears plagued Patria, but she swallowed them because here was Anna, trying to be strong, for everybody. Poor thing wasn't even married into the family yet; but they had no levelheaded Gaye Denise to tell them what to do. Therefore, Radcliff's fiancé had stepped up. Surely, the woman was now wondering, what in blazes had she gotten herself into –with Radcliff's family. This Patria thought, shamefaced at having been a huge baby. She pulled herself together. Again regal, she flounced toward the elevator. Unable to look at anyone, she tossed out, "I am going to the café."

Alone, in the elevator, she promised to do better, to minimize stupid outbursts. Then before the doors closed, Patria heard Sabrina speak.

Baby sis sounded near defiant. "Well, *I'm* staying."

Anna-Maria smiled. Radcliff's daughters were each so spirited. In that way, they were not at all like their father. Therefore, Anna-Maria concluded, their mother must have been something.

A while later, Anna-Maria jumped. Startled from her reverie, she noticed handsome Joseph! The man sprinted and stopped.

Radcliff, who never visibly rattled, raised his eyes, "Hey, mon."

"Where is she," Joseph asked, half out of his mind with worry.

"They're running tests in another part of the hospital," Sabrina chimed.

"So we wait?" Joseph queried.

"We wait," Sabrina looked away when Joseph began with the questions.

Forgetting his vow to appear calm 'n collected, Joseph was a fount of inquiries. "Well does she," he finally inquired, "respond if you speak?"

Anna-Maria stood. Calmly she apprised Joseph of all that Dr. Mortensen had said earlier.

Afterward, Joseph apologized for rushing up to be a pain, but he was worried, and he just could not lose Gaye, he thought but did not say.

Sabrina remembered then that no one but Papa had greeted the man who should have been her brother-in-law. Shame on them. Joseph had not been present all along. Opening her arms, Sabrina apologized because she never wanted her husband Jamaal's people to disregard her or her concerns.

"Joe, I should have kissed you hello."

He knew Sabrina had to be traumatized, with all the days and nights spent hoping and praying for a sister who was more her mother. "Don't sweat it, Ms. Baby," he said, hugging her. Then he sat, pondering all.

"So you say this doctor looks like Superman, huh?"

"No, like Clark Kent," Sabrina corrected. "Superman's alter ego,"

"That's a little better," Joseph stated, "because his name…"

"It's bad," Sabrina agreed. It reminded her of Latin for death, Mort – in – sin. Sabrina recalled that Joseph had always been easy to talk to, even though she probably couldn't tell him about Abigail's 'friend.' Then again, perhaps Sabrina could because Joe didn't like Mona, either.

"Papa," Joseph turned. "Sir, any ideas where Gaye was going when this happened?" Joseph hadn't wanted to ask, but he had to, especially since he couldn't question the pregnancy, which had been hard to hear about.

Radcliff solemnly admitted, "Son, I wish we knew."

Anna-Maria confessed that she'd never thought to ask. "Sabrina," Anna-Maria called, appearing pensive. "Wasn't it said that Gaye was on the Southern parkway? Going west, I believe."

"If you're right," Joseph jumped in, "my baby was on her way home." From where though, on the Southern State parkway? Joseph wanted to know. Moreover, why hadn't he known that Gaye was this pregnant?

Joseph wondered for the umpteenth time before he realized he had known—something. His sixth sense had alerted him. Ever since Thanksgiving, he'd felt it, just beyond reach. He had even asked if Gaye needed to tell him anything. Joseph scrubbed a hand over stubble. He only hoped she'd said nothing because she had known nothing.

Sabrina looked at the man, who appeared to need a good stiff drink. It really must have been hell to have such misery sprung on him, and all while he'd been away, especially the bit about the baby. Was it his, or the clown's? Both Joseph and Sabrina wondered. "Something's not right," Joseph mumbled, plunking down on Radcliff's vacated seat. The producer jumped back up. "I need Mona's number." Grimly he, mirroring a warrior god, swung to face Sabrina. "I'll bet she knows something."

"Good luck getting it. I tried to beat it out of her, with no luck."

Joseph grinned down for a split second. "Really?"

Sabrina pecked at her cell phone contacts. "I'd do it again, too. Okay, this is Colonial Carpet Outlet. Gaye D gave this to me a while back."

"That where Mona works now?"

Sabrina shrugged. "She could've gotten the shaft, but try it." Sabrina also told Joseph that when the other woman had been present, she hadn't said word-one to anybody. "She just meowed a bit when I jumped her ass."

A chuckle escaped Joseph. "You really did it. I'd have paid to see that."

"I did, and after, she stood in a corner—looking stupid till she left." Sabrina then clamped it because she would wind up telling. Oh heck, Joseph was bound to hear it anyway. "*He* came with her."

The clown. In Joseph's jaw, a muscle worked. "Yo, what was he doing with—" Joseph shook his head. He did not care, "Forget them."

Anna-Maria piped up, her perspective different. "I suppose Mona Lisa could be pretty shaken up, with her and Abigail being friends and all."

Joseph glanced over. "You got a home number, in case this job is bogus?" He didn't care a thing about marauding Mona being 'shaken.' He simply needed answers. Anna-Maria didn't yet understand; she was new.

"Try information," Sabrina suggested. "Ask for…Brooklyn—or hell."

Working his phone, Joseph laughed. He walked away. He didn't want Gaye's older family members to hear, should he lose it.

In disgust, he recalled the way Mona Lisa had actively pushed up on him. He stepped out into the frigid early evening. Noticing that it was nearly dark, Joseph wondered. Was it nearing five already? Beyond upset, he lit a cigarette. Forgetting the time, he hoped Gaye's 'friend' wouldn't try his patience. Not this evening.

Returned and smelling of smoke, Joseph mumbled. "No luck. You know, Ms. Baby," he voiced, feeling miserably akin to her, "I've always thought Mona was flaky."

It was the first laugh she'd had since... Sabrina could not remember when. "Now your suspicions are confirmed?"

"Yeah, but at what cost?" Joseph rhetorically inquired.

"I feel you, babe." Sabrina was glad she wasn't the only one still able to speak the truth. She couldn't clam up or pretend that everything was okay.

Appearing before anyone noticed, Dr. Mortensen began speaking.

Patria, returning with a yellow bear, saw the physician and rushed over.

The prognosis was good, the doctor said. "There has been—"

"What does that—the prognosis statement—mean?"

Patria impatiently waved. "Listen, Joe. Inquire later."

He sounded sarcastic. "Well, hello to you too, Queen Big Sis."

The doctor spoke as Patria sheepishly hugged Joseph. "It's Queen *Biggie*, to you," she corrected.

There was no injury to the brain and no hemorrhaging. However, for Abigail's fractured ribs, movement would be restricted since she, with child, would not be placed in a body cast. In time, bruising and scrapes would heal.

Anna-Maria interrupted. "What about the baby?"

"There'll be monitoring, but as far as we can tell—"

Sabrina rolled her eyes, understanding doctor speak, at last. To escape malpractice, she thought, just never commit to anything.

Dr. Mortensen pushed at his glasses. "Fetal vitals are stable."

Sabrina cut to the chase. "When can we see her?"

"Possibly," the physician said, "tomorrow—afternoon, the earliest."

Whoops, and hallelujahs soared as unanimous chatter followed.

Dr. Mortensen raised a hand. "Ms. Wallace is still ve-er-ry disoriented, at times." They needed to understand, "But that's to be expected." The physician eyed the rugged male, who reminded him of a sleek, predatory jungle cat. "You're Mr. Wallace," I assume...

The family chuckled as Patria nodded. "Yep, he's the man."

Standing beside 'Mr. Wallace,' Sabrina smiled up. She caused Joseph's heart to race upon mentioning that Abigail had repeatedly called for him.

Then it was decided. The family would leave until one, possibly two people, might spend a few moments with her the next day.

The doctor chuckled. He also said, "Now that's a first," because never before had he been invited out to share a family's celebratory meal.

"No more hospital food!" Someone yipped.

Amid the plans and the joy, Joseph opted to remain. He actually didn't feel much like making merry, although he gave thanks. Solemnly, he affirmed that, indeed, he would stay the night. Then the others could return at the designated time.

"Call us, big Joe," Patria magisterially ordered, "for any reason."

"I got this, Peaches," Joseph stated as she stepped on the elevator.

When the doors reopened, Sabrina peered out. "Got my number, right, Joe?"

The man nearly laughed. "Stop it."

"He's been blowing up your cell," Patria guffawed. "Course he's got your number. Get in here. Give us free!"

Moments later, in the quiet, Joseph did not know whether to sit or pace. So many things plagued him. Some loomed larger than others.

What was he going to do? Really, what could he do, now that his woman was with child?

However, whose child? Joseph wondered. Inwardly, he asked for the thousandth time, what exactly did that mean –for him?

## 28

**T**HE following afternoon the Wallace family, including Grandma Mary, Aunt Mildred, Uncle El, twins Jenna & Deidre, and Abigail's friend Kismet Staar, all crowded into the hallway. All knew that only two could enter. After consternation, it was finally decided. Radcliff and Patria would see Abigail. Again, the nurse reiterated, neither could remain long; but seeing the joy, the nurse remembered why she'd chosen her profession.

Separately, on tiptoe, Radcliff and Patria entered. Both found Abigail disoriented and able to speak only a few unintelligible words. She drifted off to sleep. However, they and those waiting were overjoyed.

"I'm so thankful," Radcliff gruffly stated and squeezed Anna-Maria.

Sabrina watched her father kiss his fiancé. Tearfully, Sabrina smiled when Anna-Maria gushed that Abigail's recovery was miraculous.

"Bina, don't," Patria ordered, snatching tissues from her purse.

Accepting one, Sabrina sniffled, "I can't help it. I prayed every day."

Patria grasped and held her sister tight. "I did too, heathen ol' me."

"You never know when you'll lose a person," Sabrina hiccupped, a fistful of sister's tunic-back in her hand. "So you just... "

"Come on, you two," Joseph groaned because now *his* throat ached. "Ladies," a muscle in his jaw worked. "We're supposed to be happy."

The sisters burst out laughing, despite tears. They also reached for Joseph. "You're too cute, you know that?" Patria winked up at the man, who was already their brother.

"Ain't he, though?" Sabrina pulled Joseph closer.

Chuckling, Anna-Maria twittered, "Awww, he's in love."

The women cooed, forming a bosomy embrace about Joseph.

Patria pointed, "View Papa,"

Appearing sheepish, Radcliff gruffly spoke. "Let de man go."

From the perfumed circle, Anna-Maria beckoned, "Come, my sweet."

Attempting to untangle himself, Joseph said, "I'm gonna tell Gaye."

"Do that," Patria advised the man who had been family for seven years. "Tell her that in her absence, her sisters luuuved her dude a little."

"Peaches stop," Sabrina giggled. "You're embarrassing him."

Radcliff smirked. He said he believed that was their queen's intention. More jovial than they'd been in days, the Wallace family left.

At the hospital, Joseph kept the night vigil. Abigail mostly slept, even when she was moved to the med-surg floor. Still, Joseph was grateful for the time with her. He held her hand and spoke soothingly to her. He nodded at the nurses, who regarded him as the sexy husband.

Long into the night, Joseph sat, watching over Abigail. In silence, he tamped down the battle raging inside him. Joseph prayed that Abigail would fully recover. He also tried to forget the times when he had to be away from her. Then, he was at work, or at home, alone. When at either place, Joseph wanted to be at the hospital, although nowhere could he forget what ailed. Half the time, at work, he couldn't concentrate. At home, he couldn't sleep or eat. Joseph walked the floors, or he just sat, before the Dark Lady. He tried to tickle her ivories. Listlessly he plunked out melancholy melodies and hummed sad tunes.

Since this ordeal, the gift of song really would not come to him. Not anymore, and not even when Joseph sat with gray dawn light washing over him. Previously, that had been his most productive time. His piano, his music, had always given him such pleasure. Lately, however, the music, such little that came, was only a source for releasing angst.

In addition, Joseph's house in Great Neck, the one he'd once loved, now provided no solace. Instead, it seemed there were only ghosts. Conjured by loneliness, they meandered the sumptuous rooms. The grounds seemingly also echoed with their whispers.

*Gaye, where are you, love? Return, return to me...*

Joseph had heard the chant one time too many. Then he did what he had not, in all the time that he and the Dark Lady had been involved. He pulled her dress down, so to speak. He closed her lid, thus hiding her gleaming onyx and white keys. Then wearily, he laid his head on his muse while his soul shrieked. Gaye *had* to get better, to come back to him. But what if she didn't? Joseph felt powerless because what if his baby slipped away. *Or* what if she got well and didn't know him, or what if she said something he couldn't bear to hear.

Joseph sighed because he didn't *want* there to be another man's child within Abigail's womb, not when he'd dreamed, steadily, of her having his baby. But if that was the case, would she leave him for the other man? Joseph knew *his* leaving wasn't a question. He'd loved Gaye far too long. Joseph knew, walking away would never remove this particular woman from his heart. Therefore, he would stay, if she let him.

Subsequently, that would present another problem. If *the clown* was the baby's father. Joseph would then never be free of bozo. This Joseph knew, and not because Darré would care for Abigail or baby, but because that mama's boy was truculent, just a skinny bad-tempered fool.

Then again, Joseph mused, that joker did not necessarily have to be *it* because there *had* been that time... In Santa Lissa, under the stars, Joseph had given Abigail all. Afterward, she'd mentioned them and a fairytale. She said something about him being Prince Charming. Joseph almost smiled because how he loved that woman.

Hey, maybe *he* was the baby daddy. Perhaps his daughter, Summer or Stormy, would soon be born. Or maybe Joe Jr., his *son*, grew daily. If so, wouldn't Halloway be overjoyed? Old Dude would be the best Pop-Pop.

That reminded Joseph. Early one cold morning, in the older man's cozy breakfast spot, silver-haired Hal had said things would assemble themselves. "My boy, stuff has a way of working out." Hal noticed condensation on the diner window. Seeing his grieved son slouched and half-hidden in a hoodie, Hal had continued. "It's not always like we hope, Joey, but whatever happens, you'll pray and make the best of it."

With the scent of coffee in the air, the sound of dishes clanging, and other patrons murmuring, Joseph thought aloud. "Things would be so much easier, Dad, if Gaye and I could have a normal life. I'm tired of stuff always cropping up –to spoil shit!"

"Ay! Watch ya mouth." Hal bit into the marmalade toast that his Madeline would have burned at home. "Sometimes, life ain't easy." Hal, a semi-retired dry cleaner, looked up at the woman in the rubber-soled shoes and uniform. "Hey, Grace. I got Kerrie today. Yes, my son, you met him. Alright, cookie, see you tomorra." Silver-haired Hal picked up where he'd left off, "Other times, life can be easy. Just roll with it, Joey. And quit fingering them cigarettes. Need to forget about all that smoking. How many times I gotta say it? It's not good for ya."

Remembering Hal's seemingly innocuous words of sagacity, Joseph sighed. He vowed to simply be there for Gaye and to roll with things.

In Abigail's hospital room, shifting slightly, Joseph looked over her array of mementos. Noticing his restaurateur friend's card, he recalled sitting forlorn and heartsick in his favorite haunt. Sure, Raul had refused to pour him any more alcohol, but Joseph hadn't cared. He had only needed to say, while smoking, that his woman was laid up. "We met here."

"Many times I've heard," Raul solemnly stated, with pity in his eyes.

Raul asked about sending a card to Joseph's beautiful flower. Raul had also mentioned his wife. He said now Nuria loved a dress that she'd previously abhorred, "Before your lady said it was Caribbean colored." Raul smiled. "*Mujeres* like fashion, my friend. Therefore, never again does my Nuria say that I try to make her look like *anciana*. Like—how you say? *Froompy* grandmother."

Seated beside the sleeping Abigail, Joseph smiled, despite ever-raging fears. Replacing Raul and Nuria's card, Joseph realized. He and Abigail had so many people pulling for them.

That had to mean *something*. Didn't it?

## 29

SOON after the possibility of physical therapy was broached, Abigail began to stay awake longer. She even smiled when Sabrina and Anna-Maria visited, but Radcliff elicited tears. With his arms around Abigail, Radcliff's voice became emotion-filled. Aloud, he thanked God that his big girl was back.

Clutching her father, Abigail tearfully remembered how much she loved him. From where, though, had all the white in his hair come? Why, she also wondered, did he look older than she remembered?

PATRIA headed back to Philadelphia with a promise to return. "I'll be bearing gifts, baby!" she announced, with shimmering eyes.

As she crossed the GW Bridge, Patria promised herself one thing. She would become her old self again, sister fabulous, who didn't cry every day.

YET present, Sabrina winked at Joseph one evening as they stood beside Abigail's bed. "Joe, Nurse Guen teased that you and I are here so much until now we're considered hospital staff."

Abigail wanted to chuckle too, but it would have been hard. However, she hoped she was smiling, at least a little.

Joseph, she thought, sneaking a peek at him. Did he still love her as she loved him? Was she on his mind as often as he was on hers?

ONE evening, during visiting hours, Darré Clankston appeared, toting a wildflower bouquet. He made small talk until Abigail drifted off. Then seated bedside, he wondered, just how had he let this woman get away?

He sucked his teeth. His vibrating phone, again. He would have to go, but he wondered. Had he seen a man lurking outside Abbie's room? Darré felt a brotha couldn't be too careful, not when he had a woman laid up. Nowadays, psychos frequented hospitals, preying on the incapacitated.

Hearing Abigail's room door open, Darré jerked around.

Walking toward Abigail's bed, 'the lurker' authoritatively barked. "Visiting hours are over."

"Yo, who're you," to be giving orders? Darré asked and stood.

"I'm the law," Joseph sarcastically quipped. Annoyed at the clown's very presence, Joseph thumbed toward the door. "You gotta go."

"I know you ain't talkin' to me," Darré scoffed, not about to be ordered around by some big goon trying out for the Sunday Pageant.

Joseph kept his voice level. "Look, I said be out. Now." Then vowing to remain calm, Joseph stepped back. He gave Darré room to exit.

When Darré didn't move, Joseph's tolerance level plummeted.

Hey, Darré recalled having seen Abigail with big dude a few times. Therefore, Darré deduced he could leave because it really was time. If he didn't get home, Pammi would jump him, yowling about where he'd been. Therefore, donning his jacket, Darré said he was leaving, not being run off.

With his eyes, Joseph gave the man a scathing once-over.

Darré too eyed Joseph who wore heavy denim and boots. "Seems I've seen you before," Darré theorized. "Who are you?"

Step 'n Fetchit had smirked as he'd said it, Joseph thought, as ominously he replied. "You know who I am."

"Hey, I just asked a question, playa. What you got to hide?"

Joseph had had it! Because there would be snowballs in hell before he would answer to the likes of clown-assed Clankston.

Joseph icily eyed the joker and gestured. "Keep it moving because I ask the questions around here, although I'm not interested in yo' story."

Darré laughed, and Joseph felt an inner growl. He really did not need games right now, and especially not from this dude.

Darré neared the door. "Tell my boo her baby daddy'll call her later."

This dude right here! Joseph's eyes narrowed because he just knew he had not heard right! Before he was cognizant of doing so, Joseph dashed and grabbed. He startled Darré who struggled against the unexpected force.

Aware that he could break something or wake Abigail, Darré quickly pondered his options. One: continue to struggle, or two: stiffen, and sell a woof ticket. Stiffening, with hands atop Joseph's, Darré said, "Let go."

In defiance, Joseph tightened his grip.

Darré spoke, attempting to exude the confidence he no longer felt.

Joseph laughed. "Get my hands off you? That what you said?"

"Yo, you heard me!" Darré squalled. He recalled having read that people, like animals, could sense fear. Therefore, he reiterated while telling himself that he was not afraid, "Get off me, man."

Joseph fought the urge that suggested he snap the court jester's neck as softly he spoke. "You're gonna make me beat you down, aren't you?"

Darré felt fear but was unaware of what to do. "Get off me, I said."

Joseph's eyes darted about. He could not possibly handle his business where he stood, so he dragged the yokel with him out into the hallway.

With his smooth-bottom dress shoes sliding against his will, Darré realized he had been snatched up in a madman's plan, just before he was slammed into a shiny tiled wall!

"Step to me," Joseph angrily ordered, tapping his chest. "Come on."

To Darré, the bigger man sounded out of control. Darré also realized, with his vertebrae in screaming pain, that he would meet an unwanted fate. Yet Darré attempted to appear fearless, as crazily his eyes skittered about.

The hallway was empty! No! Where was security? Who would rescue him? Darré attempted to stall by dropping his jacket. "Yo, bruh, let's—"

"Save it, clown." Joseph's fist connected with Darré's jaw. Feeling like a prizefighter, Joseph flexed and punched again, while calling Darré a liar.

Angered, Darré jumped bad because no one called him out of his name! But oww-ow! His face hurt horribly.

"You're a liar," Joseph reiterated, as Darré stumbled back into the wall, after seeing only the blur that was the big fist that again sailed into his face.

Aware that Joseph danced, Darré managed to stagger just enough to keep himself upright, and his seeking fingertips found blood. His own.

Reeling with pain and anger, Darré had no idea what to do, but he had to do something. Therefore, appearing bewildered, he got a running start—his dress shoes slipping on the polished tiles. Wildly propelling himself forward, he launched, head-first, into the other man. Feeling like he'd been shot out of a cannon…he did not connect.

Instead, he was pulled backward, by hospital security.

At last! With them surrounding him, he could finally jump at Joseph.

"Yo, you aww whu-whucky man," Darré slurred through swelling lips. He'd meant to say lucky, as his ears rang. Darré also thought big dude had better recognize he'd lucked out; "Because," Darré woofed, "if theesch people weren't holdin' me…ooh-wrooh!"

"Settle down," one of the uniforms advised, as nauseous, Darré wondered if he'd slip to the floor. "You, sir;" the uniformed officer turned to the bigger man, the alleged assailant, "accompany us as well."

As the one who'd physically attacked another, Joseph nodded.

Reaching for his jacket, Darré's stomach roiled. Fighting to keep his lunch down, he hoped he wouldn't ruin his shoes. Last year Abbie had bought them for him.

Following the unsteady, unsavory character, Joseph's irascibility decreased a bit because he fully intended to cooperate. He would give security a statement, or he'd file a report, whatever. Joseph would answer any and all inquiries because he wanted there to be no mistaking. He'd whupped Darré's punk ass. Joseph had done so for many reasons –among them the fact that during Darré and Abigail's relationship, the clown had not only broken Abigail's heart, but Darré had put his hands on her. For that, and other things, Joseph could beat Darré down again and again, because *he* was Abigail's man. *He*, Joseph D. Forrester, was her protector. He was many things to and for that woman, until *she* said differently.

JOSEPH left security, dismissing Darré's threats, all that ol' yang-yang about watching his back. Popinjay was nothing; he'd crumpled like paper.

Back on Abigail's floor, a concerned nurse rushed over. Politely, Joseph assured her he was fine. He also accepted a cold compress. Thanking the woman, he shouldered into Abigail's room.

Propped up in bed, she mentioned having heard quite a commotion.

"A little while ago?"

"Uh-huh." Abigail nearly nodded, despite the pain.

Joseph waved. Forgetting Darré, he said, "That was nothing." However, Abigail appeared skeptical, so Joseph leveled with her. "I took care of a lil something, but enough of that."

He kissed the tip of her nose. "You're certainly looking better, lady."

Some of her swelling had gone down, and her eyes were no longer sunken and purple-ringed. Her lips appeared normal. Yet she was scraped and bruised, but she was on the mend, for which he was most grateful.

To the man who smelled great, despite the smoke clinging to his clothing, Abigail replied. "I feel okay." She knew she looked a fright, but thanks to Gram Mary, she wore a lovely gown, and Aunt Mildred had beauty-fully braided her hair. Wishing she were altogether better, Abigail turned away and raised a hand to her head. At Joseph's alarm, she explained. "It hurts, but I deal with it."

"Should I ring for painkiller?" he asked, concerned.

"Um, no." Abigail blinked. "Trying not to—the baby. You know?"

So…now we get to the truth, Joseph miserably thought.

239

With averted eyes, Abigail spoke. "I can't believe my ribs are fractured, and I wonder how bad I'll feel later since breathing is painful now. You know Joe," she truthfully continued, "when I found out—about my—baby, I never dreamed I'd wind up in a near-fatal accident, too."

He remained silent, watching the woman who had yet to look at him. Not a good sign, especially since she worried her lip with her teeth.

Finally glancing his way while absently stroking her stomach, Abigail asked, "How long have I been in here?"

"Couple of weeks," Joseph stated, refusing to give vent to nagging thoughts and inquiries. "So, I suppose you're ready to go home."

She was, but before then, a few things needed settling.

Thinking the same thing, Joseph took Abigail's hand. Seated aside, he gazed at her. Although she looked away, all he could think was how he wanted only her. Sure, other women presented themselves daily, they always had. Yet, he had pursued this one woman for years. Given half the chance, he would do so for many more. Actually, Joseph realized, despite Abigail appearing nothing like she had when he'd fallen in love with her, he still wanted her *that* way. He scolded himself for thinking such things because she had been hurt. She was in the hospital, *and* she was carrying a baby whose parentage was questionable. However, none of that mattered, Joseph realized, because the depth of emotion he felt for her, he always would. *Moreover,* because of her, he would most likely always feel like he was losing his mind. The proof? The Darré-pounding episode, earlier.

*What* had he been thinking? Joseph was no longer young or a brawler. He was supposed to be wiser, especially since he made his living with his hands. Besides, his profession had taught him that people were litigious. When they thought one had money they loved to sue. So again, he wondered, what had he done? Joseph sighed and guessed that if it involved Gaye, in any way, he was doomed to play the fool. However, forgetting all that, he voraciously devoured her with his eyes. Loving her, Joseph said he was happy, that she'd been given back, "To me, Star."

When she did not reply, Joseph's throat burned because what if she hadn't been given back *to him*?

Abigail inched her hand out of Joseph's and asked him not to stare. It made her uncomfortable, she said. Oh, what the heck. Since she felt that way, she might as well roll on, get things out in the open.

"Joe," she called. "Why yu not ask about mi baby?"

He swallowed, looking elsewhere because now came the verdict.

"Joe?" Abigail called, and the man felt baited. He hated it. "Joezeff, I need to know," Abigail quietly stated, "how you feel. What you think."

He sounded weary. "You don't want to know what all I feel."

"I do."

"Okay." He wouldn't beat around the bush. "Lemme ask you this." Joseph jumped right in. "Were you gonna say anything?"

Abigail kept her eyes averted.

"It's not like you could have hidden it forever. Yo, you know what?" Joseph lashed out. "You want me to be the bad guy. You want questions too—shitty questions like: is it mine, and are you going to keep it?"

Acrid tears stung Abigail's eyes because Joseph was vexed, and he was hurt. She felt it was her fault. Perhaps too, Joseph was even in the kind of turmoil she'd been in before the accident. Maybe he felt betrayed, more than anything, and if he did, Abigail could sympathize. *She'd* had time to bat things about, but Joseph had not. It was why she called him.

He didn't acknowledge her. Sitting bedside, Joseph seemed miles away.

Watching him, Abigail really could not remember *why* she hadn't told Joseph right away. Had she, she would not be on the verge of losing him. Again. She thought of all they had been through to become a couple. It caused her to mentally claw around for what to do.

*Talk to him. Be honest.* Words tumbled from her lips; she hadn't wanted to hide the truth. She had only delayed the telling. She had been afraid of losing Joseph, but she had planned to tell him in California, and now she'd missed it. Nervously, Abigail twisted her fingers. "Whether or not you believe me, Joe, I want *us*. I'm not saying that because I need a father for my baby." She stroked her stomach, "This baby that I'd never give up."

Joseph remained quiet, and around them the air seemed electrically charged. Then he exploded. "You messed me up, Abigail! You put me in a position where I had to question you and us—our validity. I didn't like it—Shit! I *don't* like it! If I need to know something, you need to speak up. I told you before, and for the record, I still feel like I felt before all this."

241

Joseph swallowed. His throat was on furious fire as he whispered. "You're my music, Star, my existence. I *breathe* you." His agony was palpable as he also revealed, *"All I have ever cared about...is you."*

Joseph did not speak for a while. He simply stared, his eyes anguished and red. "Gaye," he whispered, "you couldn't tell me. That lets me know, you're still unaware, baby... for me, it has always been *you*."

Tears fell from Abigail's eyes because Joseph actually loved her, still.

He eyed his bruised knuckles, unable to look at the woman when he spoke. "Star, when I got Ms. Baby's call, I wondered if you'd make it. I prayed and blamed myself. I felt like I should've *insisted* on you going with me to my Canadian conference—the one Carlo rescued me from. I felt you'd have been safe with me. We'd have gone to Cali, and on to our lives, no hitch." Joseph flexed his hand. "Then I found out, and what hurt most was that I didn't—" His Adam's apple bobbed, "I didn't *kiss you* goodbye."

Abigail noticed that stubbly-faced Joseph appeared as wrecked as she.

"Star, I never want to forget to love you all I can, while I can."

Abigail reached for Joseph through her tears.

"I was worried," he continued, "that you'd lose organs or limbs. I worried that you would lose...your precious baby. I didn't want that because I know one thing. *I laid it down*, Star. Maybe somebody else was there, but *I* loved you too. You know I did."

Joseph's eyes held Abigail's that shimmered. "I calculated, girl, and I was there. We sinned together, as Gram would say. You were coming out of the clown phase, but on Carlo's island *I* gave you my seed. That baby *could be* mine," Summer, Stormy, or Joe, Jr. "You think about that?"

Abigail's heart raced because Joseph was defending his right to be with her and her child. *How*, she wondered, had she ever doubted him?

He broke into her thoughts. He said that on Thanksgiving, he'd believed they were *finally* beginning to build the life he had always wanted, with the *only woman* he had ever wanted. "Then came all this.

"Look, Gaye, I need to know," he said harshly. "Am I still your man?"

"Joezeff, you have always–"

"Hey," he nearly yelled over her. "Maybe this'll make up your mind. It doesn't matter if that baby," he pointed, "belongs to *Dracula*; you belong to *me*! So what's it gonna be?"

Although she was overwhelmed, in the best way, and despite searing pain, Abigail managed to whisper. "It's you and me."

Joseph suddenly looked uneasy. "Me? For real, tho?"

Abigail nodded and nearly laughed because her man sat so still.

He appeared drained, and his reddened eyes watered as all that he and she had been through fell heavily on him. He whispered that he did not know how he would have gone on had she slipped away. He then became so emotional it precluded speech.

Holding her arms open, Abigail whispered, "Don't think about it, honey. I'm *here*, with you." Thanks be to God. Holding Joseph, Abigail felt supremely warmed and nearly shocked. One, because this was the turnabout of which she and Sabrina had spoken. And two, because her man had never before uttered so many words at one time.

Abigail smiled. "Maybe you could write me two songs, Joe." The words he had spoken earlier rang in her head. "One should say, *I Breathe You*. The other could be about *never forgetting to love all we can,* while we can."

Joseph's voice reverberated through the breast upon which he rested because, wow, he could actually feel the spark. Inside, his music magic slowly ignited. "Star, I just may be able to oblige you..."

Holding Abigail gingerly, Joseph also spoke of Hal. "You know silver loves me, right? I know smoov dude could have loved only Mama, but he chose me, too, and he was good to me. Actually, I feel like I'm his seed. So you know what? I'll do a Hal." Joseph's large palm gently rested on Abigail's. "I choose Baby Bump, like my ol' man chose me, years ago.

"And when baby gets here, we ain't gotta go checking because I told you Star, I just want you—and whatever comes with you."

Prince Charming moved then so that Abigail could see his face. "Like Maal says," Joseph grinned, remembering the man who would be his brother-in-law; "to have *you*, I'll put up with the clown—if I have to; I'll even take Shanaynay 'n Keylolo, them trouble-making sisters of yours."

Following a resigned sigh, Joseph mumbled. "I *guess* I can deal with Will 'n Carlton, *occasionally*."

Recalling TV's 'Fresh Prince,' Abigail burst out laughing, despite her fractured ribs. In pain, she moaned. "I'm gonna tell my Queen and Bina that you keep calling them out of their names."

Joseph smirked. Then as though to ward off evil, he made the sign of the cross. "Please don't."

## 30

MONA Lisa showed up at visiting hour and Abigail thought, more flowers? Her office, her church, Dr. Marguerite, Abigail's longtime friend Kismet Staar, the girls she mentored, and her Branford Court neighbors had all sent flowers.

Mona Lisa forced a smile as she handed over her bouquet. "Guess you're glad you're going home tomorrow, right?"

Abigail made the requisite sniff and recalled that only four people had not presented flowers. Aunt Mildred had brought incidentals, body wash, moisturizer, and dry shampoo for fresh hair. Gram Mary had personally delivered a bevy of beautiful gowns and matching robes. Hal, Joseph's dad, the third non-flower person, had sent two audiobooks and a hand-held video game...

"Hey, lil cookie," the older man had sung out when Abigail called to thank him. "I know my Madeline took you flowers and sweets, but I sent that other stuff for the times when my Joey ain't up there –Hahaha." Hal had heartily laughed. Sounding pleased with himself, the semi-retired dry cleaner had also said, "That game will help right your sight and hand coordination." Bless Hal's heart.

As Mona Lisa took a seat, Abigail recalled Darré's aunt Rubie. Ever practical, she'd sent a large sum gift certificate. She was the fourth non-flower person. Aunt Rubie had enclosed a watercolor note, apologizing for Pammi's crass behavior at Dottie-Mae's funeral. Rubie also apologized for her sister's boy, Darré –who will never get sense and quit running idly around. She'd written, He keeps showing us who he really is.

Laughter bubbled up, as Abigail realized, Rubie was much like Darre's mother, her sister. Rubie had signed her note, Get well honey, love always, your A'nt Rue. She'd added P.S. Gaye, go on. You're beautiful 'n special-- WAY better than my simple nephew. Rubie had scrawled her number. She'd penned, Let's not be strangers. I will babysit. Dot would have, had my sweet sister lived. Remember, even if that baby is not kin, you and yours will always be mine.

That had been touching. *Why* did Aunt Rubie, or anybody—for that matter—care? Abigail wondered. Why, too, she wondered, did *she* care for Mona Lisa?

Seated aside and staring from the hospital window, Mona Lisa felt Abigail's eyes on her. Turning, she announced, "Joseph called me."

"I told him to," Abigail stated. That suggestion had sparked a *debate*.

"I haven't seen Mo," Abigail mewled, "since we went..." Abigail stopped speaking, and immediately Joseph became livid.

"Wait." He looked hard at Abigail. "You don't want me to know. You were out with *her*." Joseph cussed a blue streak. Knowing he created undue stress, he whirled. "So where was *she*? Why she ain't laid up, too?"

"*I* drove," Abigail retorted and was glad she hadn't mentioned Carla.

Joseph walked a few paces. Hell! He had always known Mona was bad news –even before she'd begun pushing up on him every chance she got.

Abigail understood. Joseph hadn't wanted to call 'the piranha.' Yet she'd begged and recited a number. "Ask my friend to come see me."

"If she *was* your friend," Joseph snapped, "she'd have been here!"

"She was. Bina told me; and I had a feeling I should've stayed home."

"So it was another of her parties, huh?" Joseph huffed, "I gotta go."

Though her head hurt, Abigail raised her weak voice. "Call her, Joe." The man had stormed out, as Abigail called, "Don't be mean; I didn't close my door, fix my seat belt –or pray."

Now Mona Lisa was present, and Abigail asked, "Why, Mo?"

Mona Lisa understood and mumbled about having come, "With Darré."

"I heard." Abigail revealed that even *he* had visited thrice since, to Mona Lisa's surprise. "But Mo, *you* had to be specially invited. Why?"

The heavier woman shrugged. "Darré's taking Forrester to court."

"You two must speak a lot, for Mr. Proud to have mentioned that. Look, forget Darré," with his black eye and split lip. "What's up with *you*?"

Mona Lisa eyed her lap. "Well... Darré told me—"

*Him again?*

"—That if I kept coming, I'd get blamed for what happened." Mona Lisa recalled watching Mr. Smooth Chocolate. Seated on the edge of her worn futon, he'd exhaled smoke as she'd touched his bare back. "What'd I do?" she asked when Darré jerked away and blew more smoke.

"D, I thought," Mona Lisa mewled, "you liked being with me."

*Moaning Lisa*, he thought. She disgusted him with her whining. Tapping out another cigarette, Darré forgot that he'd made her legs shake, although she'd had the hardest time letting herself go. Still, she was like all the rest. He'd put it on her too, The Black Mojo. Then she'd screamed his name. Now she dreamed of him. Man! Darré bitterly thought, this easy squeezie blew up his cell nearly as much as his pesky wife. And he'd given this one only a touch of the mojo, just enough so that he could control her.

He growled, "Stop it with them fake nails, will you?" Shit. She couldn't keep her hands off him, an irritating by-product of his all-powerful loving.

Trying not to cry, Mona Lisa asked, "What'd I do, boo?"

Please. He was not her boo, but since she was asking, he would explain. "I don't want you at that hospital." Darré glared at Mona Lisa, lying there like she was a real sex kitten. What a joke.

Mona Lisa's voice became brittle. "You still want *her*—don't you?"

Aware that she spoke of his true love, Darré stubbed out his cigarette. "Naw boo," he sounded sweeter, "I'm just looking out for *you*. Abbie's fam wants to place blame. You know how they are." Darré winked,"So my advice? Stay away a while, or the little sister's husband, that hot-shit lawyer'll find a way to pin *you* with charges. His wife will talk him into it. Remember how she got all up in your grill the night we went up there." Yeah, she waxed that *ass*! "Hey," he shrugged, "folk get *framed*, daily..."

Wrapping herself in her nearly threadbare sheet, Mona Lisa's mind whirred as Darré wondered, why did she fake modesty? He'd already had his fill of sucking on her stretch-marked tits. "I know you miss your girl." He sounded caring versus calculating, "But see her later. Okay?"

Darré smirked because by that time, he would be so permanently installed in Abbie's life that nothing could move him, especially if her brat turned out to be his. He would then milk mama for all she was worth. Yeah, he internally admitted, he *needed* Abbie because, unlike his pregnant again *wife* and all them other hos, Abbie had loot—that wasn't his. Yeah, some of her money he would use to make sure the big goon who'd botched up his face, split his lip, and hurt his back, went to jail. The rest he'd party with. Oh, and pour into his failing publication. However, to execute his great plan, Darré thought and ran a hand over Moaning Lisa's hip; he couldn't let this chicken-head ruin things.

"So, Darré said we'd blame you," Abigail repeated, burning with anger. "You can't even *say* it, can you, Mo?"

Mona Lisa knew that tone. She wondered what G was mad about, now.

"I was in an *acc-i-dent*, Mona. You're tipping around that fact." Abigail blinked as something occurred to her. "You feel this was *your* fault..."

Mona Lisa got loud. "Yo, you left! I told you to stay but—"

"Mo-na" Abigail called. "An *accident* is something that isn't *supposed* to happen, but—"

"Oh, you're saying," Mona Lisa interrupted, "that you're a *victim* because of me! See? I didn't have to come up here for this mess."

Though it took great composure, Abigail calmly responded. "I was saying: I was almost killed. I was about to say I'd thought we were friends, that we had each other's backs, but I see differently. You allowed somebody—*Darré*—to cause you to abandon me."

"No." That wasn't the case! But Mona Lisa didn't want to shoulder the blame either. "G, you left. You drove when I said I would."

Abigail shook her head. "Mi not talkin' 'bowt dat. How about after I got here? You could have come, like I would have, for you, every day."

So now, Abigail was throwing in her face that in the past she had done things? "I'm not you, G." Mona Lisa would not give Gaye accolades for bringing homemade soup when her friend was sick. Nor because Abigail had stayed up nights when Mona Lisa couldn't sleep. Abigail hadn't been forced to do those things! Just like she wasn't forced to leave the party.

Watching Mona Lisa, whose arms were folded, Abigail felt fury, which mightily hurt her head. Even as a little voice said, *forgiveness, remember?*

Looking into the seemingly nonchalant face of the woman she'd tried to befriend, Abigail heard herself say, "Mo, tell me something. Was it worth it, with *Darré*, this loss of our friendship?"

Mona Lisa blinked. "Wh-what are you talking about?"

"No more games. I know he's your jump-off. I know when it started. I'm aware that you've always wanted whatever you thought was mine. You crept with him, even before he and I fully broke up."

Mona Lisa was stunned. Abigail knew?

"Don't look shocked, just answer; was the sex worth losing 'us' over?"

Mona Lisa pondered it in those terms. Unwittingly, she had assumed she could have Abigail *and* Darré, and possibly even Joseph, too, because something inside her was twisted. She realized it for the first time.

"So you don't want to be friends?" Mona Lisa finally inquired.

"*Friends* don't do the things to friends that you and Darré do. Y'all only think of yourselves and what you want, although you'll have to be lightning fast to keep up with that man's lies and schemes."

"What do you mean?"

"He's been here, trying to get back with *me*," Abigail softly announced. "He probably thinks I'll become his sugar mama. He needs a sponsor."

The little *prick*! Mona Lisa's eyes smarted because she had known! Darré had just never seemed that into her, not like he'd been with Gaye.

Abigail laid back, her eyes wandering to the window. Watching her, Mona Lisa felt exhausted and like she couldn't do anything right.

Indeed, she had tried to be strong and brave, for Gaye, albeit away from the hospital. She had even *prayed* to Gaye's Jesus, Jah, Allah, Yahweh, or whoever He was. It seemed He hadn't heard. The truth was Mona Lisa hadn't wanted to do as Darré said. She'd *wanted* to be at the hospital. She had even tumbled off her ratty futon when sleep wouldn't come. Down on her knees, she'd bitterly wept. She knew she was stupid, *and* Gaye was fool enough to be her friend. Therefore, Gaye had seemed doomed to die.

Crawling in the dark, on the cold floor, Mona Lisa had acknowledged that *she* was the dirty unfit one. She'd been born into a family of zeros. Her life had been all cheap tricks, and every chance she got, she dragged Gaye into her dim world. Since Gaye had been stupid enough to care, she'd wound up hurt, and wrongfully so. Mona Lisa knew *she* was the one who deserved to be bruised or dead, like her mama and her brother Montego.

Feeling like Gaye now hated her, Mona Lisa recognized. She wanted the pain to end. It was exhausting being the stupid, loud, fast outsider. She no longer wanted to be a doormat for men. She was sick of playing hooker, too, for her boss, but she wanted companionship, so she accepted the married-man-'n-side-chick crap. However, she would do everyone a favor. Mona Lisa would end it all, but she wanted Gaye to know. Indeed, Mona Lisa had loved Abigail.

Mona Lisa stood up to leave, never to be seen again. "G, I know I'm nothing." She swiped at tears, "But you need to know. *I'm sorry*. Really. I thought I was doing right, *for once*." Sadly, Mona Lisa shook her head. "I hope you have a good life too, when you leave here. I hope you have a sweet baby, maybe a girl, because you're a good mom." Mona Lisa's eyes filled because to her, Gaye had been a mother, a loving good one. Much better than that druggie she'd had, the one who'd been killed years ago.

Mona Lisa turned, blinded by tears. "Just know," she eked, unable to bear Gaye's stunned look. "I loved you the best I could."

Abigail felt sorrow and was momentarily unaware of what to say or do. At the same time, she realized. Overwhelming despair had always resided with Mona Lisa. It remained just beneath her façade of fun and cheer. Suddenly Abigail *knew*. She had to call the picture girl back, or Lord only knew what would happen. "Mona... "

Hearing her name, the rounder woman stopped but did not turn. Mona Lisa did not want to go back, to Gaye or to her lonely life.

Okay, she could return to Gaye, but she wanted to end the despair, the never-ending hurt that had become too much.

"Mona..." Abigail called, despite massive aches. While waiting, Abigail heard a sweet song from her past. '*Come to Jesus, Come to Jesus...just now. He will save you, He will save you, just now...*' Abigail stretched forth a bruised hand. "Come..." Softly, she bid Mona Lisa. "Come, baby..."

Mona Lisa did not know how she got there, on Abigail's bed, with her face pressed to Abigail's shoulder. She didn't know when she'd begun to profusely sob, to cough up all the anguish that she hadn't known resided within her. All Mona Lisa knew was that sweet Abigail held her like she had always wanted to be held, with no dirty stuff, and vaguely, Mona Lisa heard Abigail say she would pray, for them both.

"Mi been stupid," Abigail whispered, running her hands soothingly over and over Mona Lisa's back. "Here I was, thinking 'bowt *me* when I should've been worried about *yu*, little gurl." Abigail knew it was unlike Mona Lisa to leave her alone, even for a day. Thus, Abigail should have known that Mona's absence had meant something was wrong.

"Father, forgive me, please," Abigail whispered in prayer as her own tears fell. "Mi dropped de ball, *again*!" She sounded anguished. "I really don't want to do that anymore. I ask you to forgive mi friend, too, for whatever. She knows, and you know." Abigail sniffled, yet holding Mona Lisa, despite her aching body. "But most of all, give mi chile peace. She's been hurt, so she hurts others. She needs you, Father. *We* need you. Please give us both comfort. Wisdom, too." Abigail raised her eyes. "This we ask, not just for now, not just for today, but for always. Amen."

## 31

HE walked up while Abigail prayed. Then Joseph and his snazzy Miz Maddie stood just beyond the hospital room doorway. Elegant Madeline bowed her head. With one hand at her chest, the older woman used her other to take her big fine son's hand. "Precious, *precious* Lord," she breathed aloud. Then quietly she prayed, right along with Abigail.

Moments later, with his throat all-out aching, Joseph peered into Abigail's room. He heard her say, "Picture Girl, if you invite Him to, the Lord will enter your heart and help, despite all you've been through."

Then Joseph knew.

When Abigail kissed Mona Lisa's forehead, Joseph was done. There was no going back. He would never, ever, love his sweet baby more... than he did at that moment.

LATER in the week, Joseph entered Abigail's hospital room. He bent to kiss her nose.

Bright-eyed and childlike, she held his large hand. "Guess what?"

"Chicken butt," he said and sought her suitcase.

"You are so corny." Forging on, Abigail announced, "You and I have been invited to a wedding, with a big cake, music, and family 'n friends."

"Who's getting married?"

Abigail beamed, "Anna and Papa."

"No second-time generic blues for them, huh?" Joseph pretended to be impressed, although never would he understand why weddings excited women. Eyeing Abigail, he gently reminded her that sort of 'on the bench' she would probably miss the festivities.

Yet she beamed and said she wouldn't miss a thing.

"How you gonna go anywhere in your condition?"

She could have taken offense, but Abigail did not. "Yu wanna know why mi going? In my condition—as you put it."

Joseph had to hear this, "Why?"

"Because dem ah having it t'ree months after mi baby come!"

Okay, now he was impressed, a little.

"My little man and I will have it together by then." Abigail gushed that her baby would be all rosy and round, and she would have her sexy back.

Joseph's voice grew husky, as ferociously wanting her, he attempted not to growl. "You're sexy now, bae." Curiously then, he eyed her.

Still a bit self-conscious due to her injuries, she asked, "What is it?"

"You said something. I just caught it. Now I have to ask, why do you think our baby will be a boy?"

Abigail appeared smug. "I know."

Joseph persisted. "Did you take some test that I don't know about?"

"Nope," Abigail truthfully stated, "but some things a Mama knows."

Joseph nodded, realizing that in him, his shining star would always have someone who loved her. Feeling it was time, at long last, Joseph patted around until he got the right pocket. He presented a small, felt-covered jewelry box, as he said, "Seven years, beautiful."

Abigail took the box with trembling fingers. She lifted the little lid, then missed the something that fell to the floor. Joseph retrieved it and touched the brown side of Abigail's hand.

"Oh," she gasped, staring at itty-bitty, matte gold baby booties strung on a delicately linked chain. "Put them on me," she breathed, "please."

Joseph did and leaned around to see his love stroke the gift with her fingertips. Satisfied, he asked if she was ready to go home, to Long Island.

She asked, as though she hadn't heard, "You really want my baby, Joe?"

He swallowed against the ache in his throat, as gently he took her in his arms, because when would she get it? "Star...my baby's baby *is* my baby."

Appearing with a wheelchair, a hospital attendant cleared his throat.

"Maybe you'll finally believe," Joseph stated, as he helped ease Abigail onto the padded seat, "after we're married."

As she was wheeled down the hallway, Abigail looked up and smiled at the man who strode along, carrying her belongings. It appeared that had been their way, for seven years.

Out of doors, it was cold, and gingerly, Joseph helped Abigail into an SUV. "Joe, whose vehicle is this?" she asked, noting the new-leather scent.

With one key fob on his palm, he pressed another to hers. "I don't want you bending a lot, Star. You know, entering and exiting..."

Abigail stared, "So you rented this?"

"You've got a key fob," Joseph stated, pulling into traffic. "I do too. Go figure."

"I hate riddles," Abigail grumbled, about to fold her arms. Thinking better, she stopped.

"Me too." Joseph grinned and glanced at her hands in her lap. "It's yours."

"Mine?" Abigail felt dazed and excited. "This is mine? Why? When did you—?"

The hand he didn't steer with, Joseph raised. His jaw was tight as he fumbled for a smoke. "Your car is totaled," he bit out, hating to recall it. "It would be hard, too," he opined, "if you struggled to get on and off buses and trains with my kid. I say that because I know. Momz did it for years. I also don't want you fighting revolving doors or elevators when you're home, not when I can help. I can make things easier. So, as I said, your new address will be in Great Neck. And Harlem," and everywhere else that Joseph had property. He glanced at her. "Don't you think it's time?"

Abigail's heart crazily bumped about as she touched the gleaming navigation system. When older, her little one could even watch movies as he or she rode. "This must have cost a fortune."

At a light, Joseph shrugged and smiled because look who was talking about cost. She was so free-hearted, she gave to colleges and charities. She bought extravagant gifts for people, even the girls that she mentored, and most times on a whim. "Money is simply a means of exchange." He leaned close, unbuckling Abigail's seatbelt. She felt his warmth, smelled his intoxicating cologne, despite smoke. He pointed to the rear. "Take a look."

When she managed to turn, wincing through stabbing pain, Abigail saw the baby seat. Then she could not help it, she dissolved in tears.

Buckling her back up, Joseph swallowed emotion as he drove. "Well, since you're crying," tears of joy, he hoped, "you might as well cry about this too. I contacted Seraph," since Abigail had at last admitted her love for him. "The couturier knows your taste, and she's got your measurements. So, I told her what I'm telling you. You *will* be Mrs. Forrester before my son is born."

"Ah, but my Joezeff," Abigail saucily replied, "what if he's a she?"

Joseph sighed, tapping his fingers to Frank Sinatra accompanied by Count Basie and his orchestra. "I'll love her just the same, Big Mama."

Joseph sang along with Sinatra on 'I've Got You Under My Skin,' and Abigail's eyes narrowed. "Big Mama." Wrinkling her nose, she said she didn't like that name. "Yuck, that is so not for me."

Laughing, Joseph brightly predicted, "You'll get used to it." He winked. "Actually, I thought about how many more times we could do the hallway floor..." He could see nudging his hardened member into Abigail as she lowered herself, tight, slick, and heated, onto him. His fingers would sink into the lush ripe flesh of her ample hips and bottom as they bumped about, in her new home, his home –that would be *their* home. While driving, Joseph 'saw' Abigail's beautiful enlarging breasts, the ones he longed to get his mouth on. He envisioned her rounded belly, her curvaceous legs too. The scenario he found greatly arousing. "Got a few other things I wanna try—in time, of course."

Abigail stared, and Joseph grinned. "Believe me, girl; I'm gonna have you this way at least two more times. So the name will fit."

On the gearshift, Abigail's hand covered his, "Sounds chauvinistic."

"Not to you," Joseph proclaimed, "because you want the same thing."

Suddenly Joseph Desmond Forrester knew something else as he glanced down at the protrusion in his lap. "You want *this*." His voice lowered as his telltale vein became visible. "You want what I want."

"What's that?" Abigail asked as her heart began to excitedly pound.

"You want my mouth, on you, and my tongue in your—"

"Shhhh," Abigail cautioned. She didn't say it but Joseph was getting her so excited until her head painfully throbbed. "Maybe I want those things." Her voice became sand-papery and sultry. "Joe, maybe mi want u right now. Then again," she said, losing the accent, "Maybe I'm going to need a ring. Oh, and I might like Usher to sing 'Here I Stand' at our wedding..."

Throwing his head back, Joseph guffawed. He was thrilled. They'd grow old together. He spoke while crushing out his cigarette. "My baby, a ring you shall have, and we'll see about your song. All I ask is that you take pity on a brotha."

Abigail appeared curious. "How and why would I do that?"

"Well," Joseph sighed. "I've been 'without' for so long—since before I went to Canada. So as soon as you can, I'm gonna to need you to t'row dat ting 'pon me, gurl."

Laughing at his Jafake-an accent, despite pain, Abigail realized. Each of her prayers were truly being answered, one – by – one.

Photo: Tina Dennis©

As an author, editor, and motivational speaker,
***April Alisa Marquette***
pens fiction as well as non-fiction.
A lover of art and literature, she is committed to creating beautifully
detailed works about people of color and others.
Ever working on something,
she is currently tweaking one of the exciting novels in her
*Sea Isles Series*.
Visit her at www.aprilalisamarquette.net